iBT 托福分類字彙

TOEFL®

MUST WORDS 5600

作者：林功　譯者：林錦慧

[增訂版]

眾文圖書股份有限公司

作者序

暢銷 NO. 1、備受台灣考生推薦的《TOEFL 托福分類字彙》改版了。這次的改版，除了維持「藉由聽．讀訓練聽力、閱讀並學習字彙」的概念，更針對 TOEFL®iBT 的測驗方式，提供對應的學習法。

TOEFL®iBT 已實施多年，出題形式跟出題方向差不多都固定了。對考生來說，最難的就是摸不著出題方向，一旦清楚了出題的原則，就可以依循一套方式去解套，所以考生現在應該抱持著「雖然難，但一定有方法」的態度來正面迎戰 TOEFL®iBT。

TOEFL®iBT 測驗考生的英語「聽．說．讀．寫」能力，測驗的原則在於要判定考生在英語系國家求學時，是否有能力流暢地運用英語。筆者認爲，從某個層面來說，iBT 是追求理想的測驗，也可以說是「不會出簡單題目」的測驗。對於考生來說，面對這個測驗，首先要面對的就是字彙的挑戰。

TOEFL®iBT 的字彙難度都相當高，如果不能掌握這些高難度的字彙，就很難跨越 iBT 100 分這座高牆。因此，爲了實際幫助考生，本書以最有效的方式，教導考生如何運用技巧記下這些高難度字彙的字義、拼法和發音。

我們從這幾年來讀者的回應，並參照 TOEFL®iBT 的出題方向及形式，修訂完成《TOEFL iBT 托福分類字彙》。本書整理出 iBT 測驗出題率最高的單字，搭配相關領域的英文文章，並仿 TOEFL®iBT 聽力測驗的速度朗讀錄音，希望透過訓練聽力及閱讀的方式，有效提升考生的字彙能力。考生只要持之以恆，利用本書不間斷地學習，必能成功攀登 TOEFL®iBT 這座高峰。

林功

TOEFL®iBT 簡介

TOEFL®iBT 爲一種英文能力檢定測驗，測驗成績主要作爲考生申請國外大學或研究所時的英文能力證明。TOEFL®iBT 最主要的特色是使用電腦在網路上進行答題，分爲「聽．說．讀．寫」四項測驗。

TOEFL®iBT 的測驗內容

測驗項目	測驗時間	測驗題數	測驗內容
閱讀測驗（滿分 30 分）	60-80 分	36-56 題	3-4 篇 700 字左右的長篇文章。內容皆爲與學術領域相關的文章，包括社會學、自然科學、生命科學、人文科學、藝術等。
聽力測驗（滿分 30 分）	60-90 分	34-51 題	分爲對話題及授課題兩種。對話內容可能包括選課、授課內容、報告、工讀等。授課內容全是通識程度的學術相關內容，考生不必具備相關專業知識，也能夠作答。
休息 10 分鐘			
口說測驗（滿分 30 分）	20 分	6 題	分爲獨立題與整合測驗題兩種。獨立題內容跟考生的生活經驗有關。整合測驗題則需要先看一篇文章跟聽一段對話後，再回答問題。
寫作測驗（滿分 30 分）	50 分	2 題	分爲整合測驗題與申論題兩種。整合測驗題需要先看一篇文章跟聽一段對話，再寫一篇相關的文章。申論題則是根據題目發表意見。

本書使用說明

TOEFL®iBT 最大的特色，是以「聽．說．讀．寫」四項測驗來評斷考生的英語聽說讀寫能力，雖然看似四個獨立的測驗，其實閱讀與聽力測驗是在測驗考生的英語理解能力，而口說及寫作部分則是在測驗考生的表達能力。因此，我們可以說 TOEFL®iBT 是要考生追求高標準的英語能力，取得高分的考生也就等於是英語高手了。

不過，不管讀者目前的英語能力如何，只要下定決心，都可以成功挑戰這個測驗。以下介紹如何透過本書，提高在 TOEFL®iBT 中取得高分的勝算。

Part 1 的文章訓練法

提升聽力能力

對 TOEFL®iBT 的考生來說，學會單字，不只是要懂得單字的意思，更要知道單字的正確發音。不會發音，單字只能說只背了一半。

TOEFL®iBT 的聽力測驗，內容有相當大的比例跟課堂討論有關，所以考生在背關於語言學、地質學、天文學、歷史等領域的單字時，一定也要同時學會單字的正確發音。我曾經在班上實際測驗過一次，結果發現認得 pharaoh（法老王）這個單字的學生，竟有七成聽不出這個單字。

以下針對不同程度的讀者，介紹如何利用本書提升英文聽力！

基礎級（TOEIC 650/TOEFL iBT 61）

1. 先聽三次 Key Sentences（不看句子），並試著理解聽到的內容。
2. 再聽三次 Key Sentences，這次搭配閱讀英文句子和翻釋。
3. 唸出 Key Sentences 的藍色字部分，並記住這部分的意思。
4. 再聽三次 Key Sentences。

5. 接著聽文章朗讀（不看內容），重複聽兩次，並試著理解聽到的內容。
6. 看翻譯，確認意思。然後再聽一次。
7. 最後，在 Double-Check 的部分，把不理解的詞彙標上記號，以方便再次複習。
8. 如果想要做進一步練習，可以進行聽寫練習。

中級（TOEIC 650-790/TOEFL iBT 61-80）

1. 先聽三次 Key Sentences（不看句子），並同時記下重點。
2. 再聽三次 Key Sentences，這次搭配閱讀英文句子和翻釋。
3. 唸出 Key Sentences 的藍色字部分，並記住這部分的意思。
4. 再聽三次 Key Sentences，並做跟讀練習。
5. 接著聽文章朗讀（不看內容），重複聽兩次，並跟讀。第一次，要試著發出正確的音，第二次，要試著理解聽到的內容。
6. 看著文章，進行兩次跟讀練習（注意每個字都要唸清楚，不能含糊帶過）。
7. 看翻譯，確認意思。然後再聽一次。
8. 最後，在 Double-Check 的部分，把不理解的詞彙標上記號，以方便再次複習。

＊上面這些步驟都能很順利進行的考生，可以試試進行高級部分的練習。

高級（TOEIC 800 以上 /TOEFL iBT 80 以上 /IELTS 6.0 以上）

1. 直接聽文章，並試著記下重點（並非聽寫，而是要試著摘錄出文章重點）。
2. 再聽一次文章，修正筆記內容，並且確認第一次漏聽或聽錯的單字。
3. 閱讀文章，確認漏聽或聽錯的單字。之後再聽一次。
4. 看翻譯，修正聽解時的錯誤理解。

5. 不看句子，進行三次 Key Sentences 跟讀，要留意語調的部分。
6. 接著聽文章朗讀（不看內容），重複聽兩次，並跟讀。第一次，要試著發出正確的音，第二次，要試著理解聽到的內容。
7. 看著文章，進行兩次跟讀練習（注意每個字都要唸清楚，不能含糊帶過）。可以錄下自己的聲音。
8. 看翻譯，確認意思。然後再聽一次。
9. 最後，在 Double-Check 的部分，把不理解的詞彙標上記號，以方便再次複習。

提升閱讀能力

TOEFL®iBT 的閱讀測驗，長篇文章每篇約有 700 字（作答時間爲 20 分鐘）。本書的各篇文章約 200-300 字，不到 TOEFL®iBT 的一半，因此，閱讀時間可以設定在 3-5 分鐘。

1. 選定文章，並且在時間限制內閱讀文章，舉例來說，如果是第 46 篇的 Ocean Water（272 字），那麼時間限制可定爲 4 分鐘。
2. 接著，試著將文章摘要用條列的方式寫在紙上，同樣時間限制 4 分鐘。用英文或是中文寫都可以。不過，記住不要在文章上畫線或是做記號，因爲TOEFL®iBT 是在電腦上進行，可以用紙寫下筆記，但是無法在螢幕上做記號。
3. 當文章下方出現 Q 的時候，請務必作答。
4. 閱讀 Key Sentences 和文章的翻譯，確認自己所寫下的摘要有沒有錯誤。
5. 將摘要裡頭弄錯或不清楚的單字記在自己的單字本中。
6. 最後，聽 MP3，並同時在腦中進行翻譯。

Part 2 的分類字彙活用法

這些字是在 TOEFL®iBT 中經常出現的字彙，讀者可依照以下三個 Tip 好好學習。

Tip 1

對地質學、天文學或歷史等常出題的領域，或是比較不熟悉的領域，考生首先要將這些領域的單字大致看過，並記下標上星號的「重點單字」。然後挑戰 Part 1 同領域的文章。

Tip 2

做過 Part 1 的文章練習後，若覺得還是很難，除了可反覆背誦 Part 2 的重點單字之外，也可以將 Part 1 的 Key Sentences 讀熟，然後再挑戰一次文章。

Tip 3

程度較佳的考生，可以將單字從頭到尾看過一次，將不熟的單字做上記號，反覆背誦，直到記起來。

如何有效征服托福字彙

1. 將單字視為英文句子的點

我的學生中有不少人在 TOEFL®iBT 的閱讀與聽力測驗取得 30 分滿分，不過這並不代表他們完全了解測驗裡的每個單字。他們的確具備相當程度的字彙能力，不過能取得高分，更是因爲他們知道把英文句子視爲一個一個的「點」，透過這些「點」，就可以串連成一條「線」。做測驗時，考生不必認得這條線上的所有點，只要能透過關鍵的幾個點，將它們組合起來，就可以推敲出整個句子的意思。

但是，如果「點」太少就無法成功串連成一條「線」，也就無法確實掌握整個句子的意思。我想這也是大部分考生的難處，所以該怎麼有效記憶單字，增加字彙量呢？

2. 運用字彙書與自製單字本

常有學生問我要如何有效記憶單字，以我多年的教學經驗，覺得最有效的辦法，就是利用市售的托福字彙書，搭配自製的單字本。我的學生中，有很多都是運用這樣的方法而取得托福高分。其中一個學生透過這樣的方法，他在一月時 iBT 考了 68 分，到了九月時已經達到 108 分。

3. 標注單字字義時不可以太貪心

在做托福測驗練習題時，遇到不懂但明顯是重要單字時，就要把單字加進自製單字本裡，不過單字的意思只要寫出練習題上的那個就好（頂多再加另一個重要字義），千萬不能貪心。在練習題中碰到的單字，會比較容易記住，所以要先確實把這個意思記下來。另外，已經知道的字義沒有必要寫下來，寫下來反而增添麻煩。

4. 製作有效的單字本

我覺得一本有效的單字本，不應該只是單字的彙整，它更要能刺激大腦的運作，有效幫助記憶。舉例來說，afford 這個單字，可能有以下幾種筆記方式：

afford (v.) 足夠…；提供	(△)
afford 提供	(○)
afford = (g______)	(◎)
afford = (g______) / Reading affords us pleasure.	(◎)

右邊的△、○、◎，是我針對這四種單字筆記，基於實用性跟有效性所做的評價。afford 這個單字，當「足夠…」這個意思幾乎是所有托福考生都曉得的字義，因此沒有必要特別記錄下來。第三、第四種筆記方式，提供了同義字的聯想與例句，可以刺激大腦的運作，更能有效地記下單字。

5. 要連同義字、衍生字一起記下來

要應付 TOEFL®iBT 的聽說讀寫四項測驗，考生必須加強同義字的字庫。在閱讀與聽力測驗中，常會出現某一件事用不同方式表達，或文章中某個字在題目中以同義字出現的情形。而在口說與寫作測驗中，考生也要避免一直使用相同的表達方式，如果出現 repetitive（不斷重複）的狀況，分數可能會因此受到影響。因此，平時就要加強同義字與衍生字的訓練。例如，看到 give 這個字時，就應該同時想起它的同義字 afford, confer, grant, endow, bestow, accord 等。如此，iBT 100 這個高分點，就不再是遙不可及的夢了。

6. 要記在腦中，就不要限定方式

要提升「聽．說．讀．寫」的英語能力，記單字時，除了字義，也要連同用法、發音、拼法一起記下來，這樣才是有效率的學習方法。另外，記單字時要模仿 MP3 的發音。此外，也可以將單字寫在紙上，運用聯想法整理出相關字彙，協助自己記憶。總而言之，記單字的方法有許多種，不用侷限背單字的方法。

7. 持之以恆，每天記 30-50 個單字

記單字是件無聊的事，但要增進英文能力，這是絕對必須做的一件事。不要逃避，用「拚了！」的態度，每天撥出時間記 30-50 個單字，運用各種可以幫助記憶的方式，持之以恆，一定就會看到成效。

Contents

Contents

Contents

Appendix 附錄

Part 1

Articles for Reading & Listening

閱讀・聽力精選短文

abolitionist dinosaur cubic vulgar well-heeled union deal angular statistical appetite string bankrupt monopoly persistent withdraw calculate muscle champion possessive ordinary community turbulent tariff simultaneous legislate spew notorious resultant kernel punish seize mortgage reliable quality biotechnology blacken chivalry circumvent refugee commodity obedience secretary quench potential jolt margin luxurious hypothesis permission revive keen optimism meadow landslide radioactive institute refuge irrigate impenetrable lining habitat procession memento dutifully violation stereotype merger intoxicate omnivorous enormous traverse subsidiary hall timber fabulous impact fringe manifesto expectation haunting negotiate thread enterprise hatred gestation machine gravel hypocrisy enactment erosive contemptible scavenge reluctantly prudently timber solar witness visage talkative revive proximate abolitionist dinosaur cubic union deal angular statistical appetite string bankrupt monopoly persistent withdraw calculate muscle champion possessive community turbulent tariff simultaneous legislate spew notorious resultant kernel punish seize mortgage reliable quality biotechnology blacken chivalry vulgar well-heeled

Anthropology

01 Modern Physical Anthropology

現代體質人類學

Key Sentences

MP3 002

1 A major shift in the approach to physical anthropology occurred with the discovery of genetic principles.

因為發現了**基因遺傳原理**，**體質人類學**的研究產生了重大轉變。

2 Gregor J. Mendel had formulated the first laws of heredity.

葛瑞格．J．孟德爾**提出最早的遺傳定律**。

3 He had laid the foundation of the science of genetics.

他**為遺傳學這門科學奠定了基礎**。

4 Genes are the units within sex cells.

基因是生殖細胞中一組一組的單位。

5 Genes transmit specific hereditary traits from one generation to the next.

基因**將特定的遺傳特徵**從一代**傳**到下一代。

6 Characteristics are thought to be discarded in the hereditary process.

一般認為特徵**在遺傳過程中被摒棄**。

7 Blood types are genetically determined.

血型是**由遺傳決定的**。

8 We can trace early migration patterns.

我們可以**追溯早期的移民模式**。

Reading Focus 250字

MP3 003

A major shift in the approach to physical anthropology occurred at the beginning of the 20th century with the discovery of genetic principles and of the ABO blood groups. Genetics was actually rediscovered. In 1865 an Austrian monk, Gregor J. Mendel, had formulated the first laws of heredity and laid the foundation of the science of genetics. His findings were almost entirely ignored at the time. In 1900 three other European botanists arrived at the same conclusions that Mendel had published 35 years earlier, and in researching the literature on the subject they found his work.

Genes are the units within sex cells such as the sperm and egg that transmit specific hereditary traits from one generation to the next. The study of inherited traits has become essential to anthropologists in seeking to understand human variations and differences between races. Genetics has modified the theory of progressive evolution somewhat, because it has been shown by experiment that there may be genetic reversals—that is, reversions back to traits and characteristics thought to be discarded in the hereditary process.

Early in the 20th century another Austrian, a physician named Karl Landsteiner, discovered the blood groups, or types, known as O, A, B, and AB. This led anthropologists to investigate blood differences among the races. They have noted that certain races and subraces have particular distributions of one or another blood type. This has enabled scientists to categorize the races and, since blood types are genetically determined, to trace early migration patterns.

文章中譯

20 世紀初，因爲發現了**基因遺傳原理**以及 A、B、O 等不同血型，**體質人類學**的研究產生了重大轉變。事實上，遺傳學根本是全盤改寫。1865 年，奧地利修士葛瑞格．J．孟德爾**提出最早的遺傳定律，為遺傳學這門科學奠定了基礎**。他的發現在當時幾乎完全被忽視；到了 1900 年，有另外三位歐洲的植物學家得出孟德爾早在 35 年前就已經公開發表的相同結論，他們在研究這個領域的文獻時，發現了孟德爾的研究成果。

基因是生殖細胞（例如精子和卵子）**中一組一組的單位，負責將特定的遺傳特徵**從一代**傳**到下一代。遺傳特徵的研究已經成爲人類學家重要的課題，以求了解人類的變異與不同種族間的差異。遺傳學在某個程度上已經改變了進化的理論，因爲實驗顯示遺傳是有可能逆轉的，亦即，會退回到原本被認爲**在遺傳過程中被摒棄**的特徵或特質。

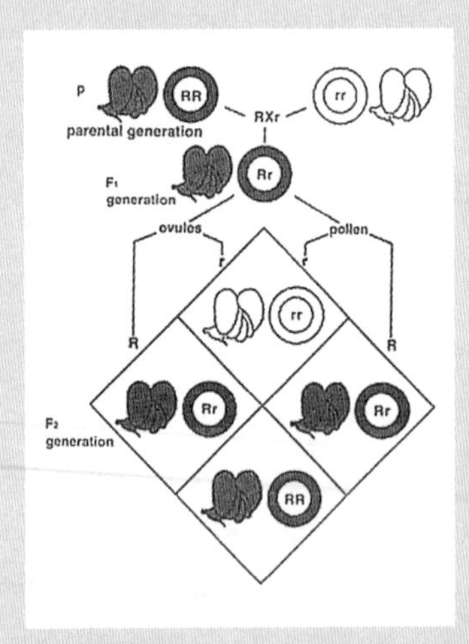

基因遺傳圖解

20 世紀初期，另一位奧地利人，卡爾．蘭德施泰納醫師發現了血型，也就是大家熟知的 O 型、A 型、B 型和 AB 型。這個發現促使人類學家研究不同種族之間的血型差異，他們發現某些族群或亞族群會出現某種血型人口特別多的情形。這個發現使得科學家能夠將種族分類，而由於血型是**由遺傳決定的**，因此可以透過血型的分布**追溯早期的移民模式**。

Double-Check

- physical anthropology [ˌænθrəˋpɑlədʒɪ] — 體質人類學
- genetic principles [dʒəˋnɛtɪk] — 基因遺傳原理
- the ABO blood groups [blʌd] — A、B、O 等血型
- formulate the first laws of heredity [ˋfɔrmjəˌlet] [həˋrɛdətɪ] — 提出最早的遺傳定律
- lay the foundation of the science of genetics [faʊnˋdeʃən] — 爲遺傳學這門科學奠定了基礎
- Genes are the units within sex cells. [dʒinz] — 基因是生殖細胞中一組一組的單位。
- the sperm and egg [spɝm] — 精子和卵子
- transmit specific hereditary traits [həˋrɛdəˌtɛrɪ] [trets] — 傳遞特定的遺傳特徵
- genetic reversals [rɪˋvɝsl̩z] — 遺傳逆轉
- be discarded in the hereditary process [dɪsˋkardɪd] — 在遺傳過程中被摒棄
- be genetically determined [dʒəˋnɛtɪklɪ] — 由遺傳決定
- trace early migration patterns [maɪˋgreʃən] — 追溯早期的移民模式

Anthropology

02 Human Migration
人類的遷徙

Key Sentences

MP3 004

1 Although we don't think of ourselves as migratory in the way we do of other animal species, people have always been on the move.

儘管我們並不**認為自己**像其他動物一樣**常常遷徙**，但人類確實一直**在移動**。

2 This migration coincided with successive cycles of glacial periods known as the "Ice Age."

這場遷徙**與**冰期**循環**（也就是「冰河時期」）**同時發生**。

3 Humans survived the bitterly cold weather that prevailed in these regions due to their ability to make things.

人類之所以能**在**這些地區的**酷寒氣候中生存下來**，歸因於他們有能力製作物品。

4 Human migration has not just involved taking over unused land.

人類的遷徙也不光只是**接收無人使用之地**。

5 People have also invaded land occupied by other peoples through killing, displacing, or genetically mixing with the land's existing inhabitants.

人類也會透過殺戮、逼人離開或與當地原住民混種等方式，**入侵其他民族原本生存的土地**。

6 To sum up, migration seems to be a fundamental human instinct.

總而言之，遷徙似乎是**人類基本的本能**。

Reading Focus 212字

MP3 005

Although we don't think of ourselves as migratory in the way we do of other animal species, people have always been on the move. A few hundred thousand years ago, humans migrated from the savannahs of Africa and spread rapidly into present-day Europe and Asia. This migration coincided with successive cycles of glacial periods known as the "Ice Age," and it probably occurred as humans followed the advance and retreat of plants and animals. Humans survived the bitterly cold weather that prevailed in these regions due to their ability to make things such as shelter and clothing, and more importantly, due to their ability to control fire.

Later migrations took humans to Japan, on to Indonesia, and finally to Australia. They also migrated across the Bering land bridge into North America and spread quickly down to the southern tip of South America. Later movements brought people to the eastern part of the Canadian Arctic and to northern Greenland.

Human migration has not just involved taking over unused land. People have also invaded land occupied by other peoples through killing, displacing, or genetically mixing with the land's existing inhabitants. Looking at today's world, it is clear that we continue to do this. To sum up, migration seems to be a fundamental human instinct.

文章中譯

儘管我們並不**認為自己**像其他動物一樣**常常遷徙**，但人類確實一直**在移動**。數十萬年前，人類從非洲大草原向外遷移，快速擴散到現在的歐洲和亞洲。這場遷徙**與**冰期**循環**（也就是「冰河時期」）**同時發生**，大概也是因爲人類隨著動植物的進退而跟著移動。人類之所以能**在**這些地區的**酷寒氣候中生存下來**，歸因於他們有能力製作遮蔽物和衣服等物品，更重要的是，因爲他們知道如何使用火。

日後的遷徙將人類帶到日本，接著到印尼，最後來到澳洲。人類也越過白令海陸橋，進入北美，並快速擴散到南美洲的南端。日後的移動則把人類帶到加拿大北極圈的東部，以及格陵蘭島的北部。

人類的遷徙也不光只是**接收無人使用之地**，人類也會透過殺戮、逼人離開或與當地原住民混種等方式，**入侵其他民族原本生存的土地**。看看現在的世界，很顯然我們仍然繼續這麼做。**總而言之**，遷徙似乎是**人類基本的本能**。

Double-Check

- think of ourselves as migratory [`maɪgrə,torɪ] 認爲自己有遷徙特性
  - 參 migrate [`maɪ,gret] (v.) 遷移，遷徙，移居
- on the move 移動中，遷移不定
- coincide with successive cycles 與循環同時發生
  - 參 coincide [,koɪn`saɪd] (v.) 同時發生
- survive the bitterly cold weather [sə`vaɪv] 在酷寒的氣候中生存下來
- involve taking over unused land 與接收無人使用之地有關
  - 參 involve [ɪn`vɑlv] (v.) 涉及，與…有關
  - take over... 接收…
- invade land occupied by other peoples 入侵其他民族原本生存的土地
  - 參 invade [ɪn`ved] (v.) 入侵，侵略
  - occupy [`ɑkjə,paɪ] (v.) 占領，占據
- to sum up [sʌm] 總而言之
- a fundamental human instinct [`ɪnstɪŋkt] 人類基本的本能

Archaeology

03 Archaeological Research
考古學研究

Key Sentences

1 The exact methods of finding archaeological sites vary.

發掘**考古遺跡**的確切方法千變萬化。

2 In sampling, a limited number of strategic spots in the region are checked for signs of an underlying archaeological site.

採樣的時候，會在**整個區域**設定一定數量**的重要探勘點**，探查地底下是否有考古遺跡的跡象。

3 This act, designed to protect the archaeological heritage of an area, has encouraged archaeological sampling of areas.

這個爲了**保護**區域內**考古學遺產**而制定的法案，鼓勵了地區的考古採樣。

4 To find sites that have no surface traces, archaeologists may use aerial photographs.

爲了找出**地表上沒有跡象**的遺跡，考古學家可能會利用**空中俯瞰照片**。

5 Archaeologists may simply probe the ground with sound.

考古學家可能直接**用聲波探查地面**。

6 A probe, or periscope, may be inserted into the ground to locate walls and ditches.

所使用的探針或潛望鏡，可以插入地面，**確定牆壁和水道的位置**。

Reading Focus 269字

MP3 007

The exact methods of finding archaeological sites vary, primarily because there are so many different types of sites. Some sites—such as mounds, temples, forts, roads, and ancient cities—may be easily visible on the surface of the ground. Such sites may be located by simple exploration: by an individual or group going over the ground on foot, in a jeep or car, or on a horse, mule, or camel. This kind of survey can be comprehensive—that is, the entire area may be covered—or it can involve the technique of sampling. In sampling, a limited number of strategic spots in the region are checked for signs of an underlying archaeological site. Sampling was not widely used in the United States until the passage of the Archaeological Resources Protection Act of 1979. This act, designed to protect the archaeological heritage of an area, has encouraged archaeological sampling of areas in which archaeological remains might exist that are in danger of being destroyed by construction or by the growth of cities.

To find sites that have no surface traces, archaeologists may use aerial photographs taken from balloons, airplanes, or satellites by cameras with remote sensors, infrared film, or other devices. The archaeologist checks these photographs for clues such as variations in soil color, ground contour, or crop density that may indicate the existence of a site.

Archaeologists may simply probe the ground with sound to check for variations in reflection of sound that would indicate the presence of structures or hollows in the ground. A probe, or periscope, may be inserted into the ground to locate walls and ditches.

文章中譯

發掘**考古遺跡**的確切方法千變萬化，主要是因為有太多種不同的遺跡。有些遺跡（例如墳塚、寺廟、堡壘、道路、古城）可以很容易在地表上看出來。這一類遺跡只要經過簡單的勘查就可以找出它們的位置：一個人或一群人只要經過地表，不論是步行、開吉普車或普通汽車，或者騎馬、騎驢、騎駱駝就可以找到。這種勘查方式可以是很廣泛的（也就是可能包含整個區域），或者也可以納入採樣技術。採樣的時候，會在**整個區域**設定一定數量**的重要探勘點**，探查地底下是否有考古遺跡的跡象。在美國，一直要到 1979 年通過考古資源保護法案後才廣泛使用採樣。這個為了**保護**區域內**考古學遺產**而制定的法案，鼓勵了地區的考古採樣。這些地區可能有考古遺跡，而且正因為都市建設或發展而面臨遭受破壞的威脅。

為了找出**地表上沒有跡象**的遺跡，考古學家可能會利用氣球、飛機、人造衛星，透過配備有遙控感應器、紅外線底片或其他設備的相機拍攝**空中俯瞰照片**。考古學家檢查這些照片以搜尋線索，例如土壤顏色的變化、地形輪廓、種植穀物的密度等都可能顯示有遺跡存在。

考古學家可能直接**用聲波探查地面**，從聲波反射的變化探查地底是否有建築物或洞穴；所使用的探針或潛望鏡，可以插入地面，**確定牆壁和水道的位置**。

Double-Check

- archaeological sites　考古遺跡
  [ˌarkɪəˋladʒɪkḷ]

- strategic spots in the region　該區域的重要探勘點
  [ˋridʒən]

- protect the archaeological heritage　保護考古學遺產
  [ˋhɛrətɪdʒ]

- surface traces　地表的跡象
  [ˋsɜfɪs]

- aerial photographs　空中俯瞰照片
  [ˋɛrɪəl]

- ground contour　地形輪廓
  [ˋkantʊr]

- probe the ground with sound　用聲波探查地面

  參 probe [prob] (v.)（用探針）探查；（詳細）調查 (= investigate/examine/inspect)
  ! 經常出現在太空、政治類文章中。

- periscope　(n.) 潛望鏡
  [ˋpɛrəˌskop]

- locate walls and ditches　確定牆壁或水道的位置
  [ˋdɪtʃɪz]

  參 locate [loˋket] (v.) 找出…的位置 (= find out/rummage)

Archaeology

Mummy
木乃伊

Key Sentences

MP3 008

1 The Egyptians had an elaborate notion of the afterlife.

埃及人對來生有**一套詳盡的想法**。

2 They took great precautions in the treatment of corpses.

他們**小心翼翼地處理屍體**。

3 The internal organs were removed and stored separately in stone jars.

臟器取出來後，分別儲存在不同的石罐裡。

4 The body was steeped in chemicals.

屍體會**被浸泡在化學藥劑中**。

5 The body was wrapped in bandages which were smeared with pitch to make them waterproof.

屍體**用繃帶纏繞**，**用樹脂黏合**以防水。

6 They were most conscious of the waxy pitch with which the bandaged corpse was coated.

他們特別注意到**纏滿繃帶的屍體上塗滿**一層**像蠟的樹脂**。

7 The conditions keep the flesh reasonably intact.

這些狀態下**使肉體保持得還算完整無缺**。

Reading Focus 262字

MP3 009

It was important in the ancient Egyptian way of life to preserve the body physically after death. The Egyptians had an elaborate notion of the afterlife and felt that to take full advantage of it, the physical body must remain in existence.

They took great precautions, therefore, in the treatment of corpses, especially of high-placed individuals and most particularly of pharaohs. The internal organs (which decayed most easily) were removed and stored separately in stone jars, although the heart, as the very core of life, was replaced in the body.

The body was then steeped in chemicals. No secret, forgotten preservatives were involved. Common substances such as beeswax, oil, and salt were used, though the procedure could be very complicated and took up to seventy days. The body was then wrapped in bandages which were smeared with pitch to make them waterproof.

Foreigners who came to Egypt were always amazed at this care for corpses, for in all other lands, bodies were buried or burnt or otherwise quickly disposed of. The Persians, who conquered Egypt in 525 B.C., were among those amazed at the preserved corpses. They were most conscious of the waxy pitch with which the bandaged corpse was coated, and their word for this was "mum." To the Arabs this became "mumia" and to us it is mummy. The word has acquired broader meaning. Any body, animal as well as human, which has accidentally been preserved under conditions which keep the flesh reasonably intact is said to be "mummified." Mummified mammoths have been discovered under the Siberian ice, for instance.

文章中譯

在古埃及人的生活中，人死後保存屍體的完整是非常重要的一件事。埃及人對來生有**一套詳盡的想法**，認爲如果要充分享受來世，就必須保存肉體。

因此，他們**小心翼翼地處理屍體**，尤其是位高權重者的屍體，特別是法老王。**臟器**（因爲最容易腐壞）取出來後，分別儲存在不同的石罐裡；不過心臟被認爲是代表生命的核心，所以會再放回身體裡。

接著屍體會**被浸泡在化學藥劑中**，其中使用的防腐材質並無祕方，至今仍流傳下來，用的都是些普通的材料，像是蜜蠟、油膏、鹽巴，不過過程非常複雜，處理時間長達 70 天。然後屍體**用繃帶纏繞，用樹脂黏合**以防水。

來到埃及的外國人總是對這種費心處理屍體的方式感到驚嘆，因爲在其他所有地方，屍體都是用埋葬、火化或其他方式快速處理掉。西元前 525 年征服埃及的波斯人就對這種保存良好的屍體大感驚嘆。他們特別注意到**纏滿繃帶的屍體上塗滿一層像蠟的樹脂**，波斯話稱爲「瑪姆」(mum)，阿拉伯人則稱之爲「瑪米亞」(mumia)，到了英文就變成「瑪咪」（mummy，中文翻成木乃伊）。這個字的涵義後來變得更加廣泛，任何屍體，不論是動物或人類，只要是**肉體部分**偶然被**還算完整地保存下來**，都可以稱作「木乃伊」。例如，在西伯利亞的冰層下就曾發現長毛象的木乃伊。

木乃伊

Double-Check

an elaborate notion [ɪˋlæbərɪt]	一套詳盡的想法
take great precautions [prɪˋkɔʃənz]	小心翼翼地
the treatment of corpses [ˋtritmənt] [ˋkɔrpsɪz]	處理屍體
pharaoh [ˋfɛro]	(n.) 法老王
the internal organs [ɪnˋtɜnl̩] [ˋɔrgənz]	臟器
be steeped in chemicals [stipt] [ˋkɛmɪkl̩z]	被浸泡在化學藥劑中
be wrapped in bandages [ˋbændɪdʒɪz]	用繃帶纏繞
be smeared with pitch [smɪrd] [pɪtʃ]	用樹脂黏合
be buried or burnt or otherwise quickly [ˋbɛrɪd] disposed of	用埋葬、火化或其他方式快速處理掉
the waxy pitch [ˋwæksɪ]	像蠟的樹脂
the bandaged corpse was coated with... [ˋkotɪd]	纏滿繃帶的屍體上塗滿…
keep the flesh reasonably intact 參 intact [ɪnˋtækt] (adj.) 完整無缺的	使肉體保持得還算完整無缺

Art History

05 Introduction

概論

Key Sentences

MP3 010

1 Art historical research has two primary concerns.

美術史研究**主要關切的議題**有兩個。

2 The first is to authenticate an art object.

第一個議題是**鑑定藝術作品的真偽**。

3 This chiefly involves the enumeration and analysis of the various artistic styles, periods, movements, and schools of the past.

這主要**包括列舉**和分析**過去**各種不同的藝術風格、時期、運動和**流派**。

4 Art historical scholarship depends greatly on the intuitive judgment and critical sensitivity of the scholar in making correct attributions.

在美術史的研究中，判斷作品出處時需要仰賴學者的**直覺判斷以及敏銳的鑑別力**。

Reading Focus 228字

MP3 011

Art historical research has two primary concerns. The first is (1) to discover who made a particular art object (attribution), (2) to authenticate an art object, determining whether it was indeed made by the artist to whom it is traditionally attributed, (3) to determine at what stage in a culture's development or in an artist's career the object in question was made, (4) to assay the influence of one artist on succeeding ones in the historical past, and (5) to gather biographical data on artists and documentation (provenance) on the previous whereabouts and ownership of particular works of art.

The second primary concern of art historical research is to understand the stylistic and formal development of artistic traditions on a large scale and within a broad historical perspective; this chiefly involves the enumeration and analysis of the various artistic styles, periods, movements, and schools of the past. Art history also involves iconography, which is the analysis of symbols, themes, and subject matter in the visual arts, particularly the meaning of religious symbolism in Christian art.

Art historical scholarship depends greatly on the broad experience, intuitive judgment, and critical sensitivity of the scholar in making correct attributions. An extensive knowledge of the historical context in which the artist lived and worked is also necessary, as well as empathy with and understanding of a particular artist's ideas, experiences, and insights.

！注意 assay 的發音！另外，to gather 很容易誤聽成 together，請小心。

文章中譯

美術史研究**主要關切的議題**有兩個。第一個議題包括：(1) 找出某特定藝術作品的創作者（也就是鑑定作者）；(2) **鑑定藝術作品的真偽**，確定該藝術作品是否出自一直以來大家所認定的藝術家之手；(3) 決定研究中的藝術作品是在文化發展的哪一個階段、或是藝術家創作生涯中哪一個時期所創作的；(4) 分析過往歷史中，一藝術家對後繼藝術家的影響力；(5) 收集藝術家的傳記資料以及特定藝術作品流傳和易主過程的相關文件與出處證明。

美術史研究關切的第二個議題是：從整體的角度、廣泛的歷史觀出發，去了解藝術傳統在風格和形式上的發展過程，這主要**包括列舉**和分析**過去**各種不同的藝術風格、時期、運動和**流派**。美術史同時也包括了圖像學研究，也就是分析視覺藝術中的符號、主旨、題材，尤其是基督教藝術中宗教符號的意旨。

在美術史的研究中，判斷作品出處時需要仰賴學者的豐富經驗及**直覺判斷，還有敏銳的鑑別力**。另外，還必須對藝術家的生活和創作當時的歷史背景有廣泛的了解，然後還要能夠心領神會，了解個別藝術家的理念、經驗和洞察力。

Double-Check

- primary concerns 主要關切的議題
  [`praɪ,mɛrɪ][kən`sɜnz]

- authenticate an art object 鑑定藝術作品的真偽
  [ɔ`θɛntɪ,ket]

- assay the influence 分析影響力
  參 assay [ə`se] (v.) 分析，檢驗

- gather biographical data 收集藝術家的傳記資料
  [,baɪə`græfɪkḷ]

- provenance (n.) 出處
  [`prɑvənəns]

- involve the enumeration of the schools of the past 包括列舉過去的流派
  [ɪ,njumə`reʃən]

- art historical scholarship 美術史研究
  [`skɑlɚ,ʃɪp]

- intuitive judgment 直覺判斷
  [ɪn`tjuɪtɪv]

- critical sensitivity 敏銳的鑑別力
  [,sɛnsə`tɪvətɪ]

- correct attributions 作品正確出處
  [,ætrə`bjuʃənz]

American History

The Changing Style of the Plains Indians 平原印地安人生活方式的轉變

Key Sentences

MP3 012

1 They found aboriginal cultures that were agriculturally oriented.

他們發現了**農業導向的原住民文化**。

2 The daily routine of the Indians centered on the subsistence cultivation of corn, beans and squash.

印地安人**每天的例行工作**主要忙於**自給式的農業耕作**，作物包括玉米、豆子、南瓜。

3 About once a year, the tribes went on a major bison hunt to supplement their vegetable diet and to obtain hides, sinew, bone and other raw materials.

大約一年一次，部落**大舉出動獵捕北美野牛**，以**補充蔬菜為主的飲食**，同時**取得牛皮**、牛筋、牛骨以及其他原料。

4 The mobility offered by the horse resulted in the convergence of diverse aboriginal groups onto the Plains.

馬匹帶來了機動性，使得**不同的原住民族群全都聚集到平原上**。

5 The Indian population of the Plains had tripled to an estimated 150,000.

平原上的印地安人口**增加為三倍，估計有 15 萬人**。

6 The aboriginals of the Plains became nomadic hunters.

平原上的原住民變成了**遊牧獵人**。

Reading Focus 189字

MP3 013

When the first Europeans arrived in the Great Plains of North America, they found aboriginal cultures that were agriculturally oriented. The daily routine of the Indians centered on the subsistence cultivation of corn, beans and squash. About once a year, the tribes went on a major bison hunt to supplement their vegetable diet and to obtain hides, sinew, bone and other raw materials. (A) Hunting did not occupy much of their time. (B)

The Indians obtained the first horses after the Spaniards settled New Mexico in 1598. (C) By 1800, the use of the horse had spread throughout the tribes of the Great Plains. (D) The mobility offered by the horse resulted in the convergence of diverse aboriginal groups onto the Plains to take advantage of the material wealth afforded by hunting the great bison herds. Within 100 years of the introduction of the horse, the Indian population of the Plains had tripled to an estimated 150,000. A new way of life was established, one dependent upon following bison herds. Thus, subsistence agriculture was largely abandoned and the aboriginals of the Plains became nomadic hunters; gardening simply was not as profitable as hunting.

Q The following sentence can be added to the passage.

This way of life, however, was drastically changed by the introduction of the horse.

Where would it best fit in the passage? Choose the one best answer, (A), (B), (C) or (D).

A (B)

文章中譯

第一批歐洲人抵達北美大平原時，發現了**農業導向的原住民文化**。印地安人**每天的例行工作**主要忙於**自給式的農業耕作**，作物包括玉米、豆子、南瓜。大約一年一次，部落**大舉出動獵捕北美野牛**，**以補充蔬菜為主的飲食**，同時**取得牛皮**、牛筋、牛骨以及其他原料。打獵並沒有占去他們太多時間。（然而，這樣的生活方式卻因爲引進馬匹而大大改變了。）

西班牙人於 1598 年在新墨西哥開始殖民以後，印地安人才首度得到馬匹。到了 1800 年，大平原上所有的印地安部落都已經在使用馬匹。**馬匹帶來了機動性**，使得**不同的原住民族群全都聚集到平原上**，以獲得獵捕大群野牛帶來的物質財富。引進馬匹之後 100 年內，平原上的印地安人口**增加為三倍**，**估計有 15 萬人**。他們建立了新的生活方式，靠著追逐野牛群爲生。因此，原有的自給式農業幾乎遭到遺棄，**平原上的原住民**變成了**遊牧獵人**；種植的獲利就是比不上打獵。

印地安遊牧獵人

Double-Check

- aboriginal cultures 原住民文化
  [ˌæbəˋrɪdʒənl̩]
- agriculturally oriented 農業導向的
  [ˌægrɪˋkʌltʃərəlɪ] [ˋorɪˌɛntɪd]
- the daily routine 每天的例行工作
  [ˋdelɪ] [ruˋtin]
- the subsistence cultivation 自給式的農業耕作
  [səbˋsɪstəns] [ˌkʌltəˋveʃən]
- a major bison hunt 大舉出動獵捕北美野牛
  [ˋbaɪsn̩]
- supplement their vegetable diet 補充蔬菜為主的飲食
  [ˋsʌpləˌmɛnt] [ˋdaɪət]
- obtain hides 取得牛皮
  [əbˋten] [haɪdz]
- the mobility offered by the horse 馬匹帶來的機動性
  [moˋbɪlətɪ] [ˋɔfɚd]
- the convergence of diverse aboriginal groups onto the Plains 不同的原住民族群全都聚集到平原上
  [kənˋvɝdʒəns] [dəˋvɝs]
- triple to an estimated 150,000 增加為三倍，估計有 15 萬人
  [ˋtrɪpl̩] [ˋɛstəˌmetɪd]
- the aboriginals of the Plains 平原上的原住民
- nomadic hunters 遊牧獵人
  參 nomadic [noˋmædɪk] (adj.) 遊牧的

American History

The Third President

美國第三任總統

Key Sentences

MP3 014

1 In an effort to restore a balance of Republicans in government office, Jefferson started what came to be known as the "spoils system."

爲了**讓共和黨在政府機關中的權力恢復平衡**，傑佛遜發起了後來稱爲「政黨分贓制」的制度。

2 He tried in vain to control the Supreme Court in the interests of the will of the people.

為了維護人民的利益，他試圖控制**最高法院**，不過並沒有成功。

3 Jefferson also launched the Lewis and Clark Expedition.

傑佛遜也**發起了路易斯與克拉克遠征**。

4 Aaron Burr was accused of making a treasonable effort.

亞倫・伯爾因爲**意圖叛國**而遭到起訴。

5 In the trial that followed the suppression of this Burr conspiracy, Jefferson's personal animosity toward Burr and toward Chief Justice John Marshall did him little credit.

在**鎮壓伯爾陰謀叛國行為**之後的審判中，傑佛遜**個人**對伯爾及首席大法官約翰・馬歇爾**的敵意**卻**為他自己帶來不好的評價**。

6 His Embargo Act was a daring and original means of keeping the peace.

他頒布**禁運法案**，意圖藉此維持和平，這個**做法大膽且創新**。

Reading Focus 262字

MP3 015

In an effort to restore a balance of Republicans in government office, Jefferson started what came to be known as the "spoils system." He tried in vain to control the Supreme Court in the interests of the will of the people. He negotiated the purchase of the vast Louisiana territory on doubtful constitutional grounds.

Jefferson also launched the Lewis and Clark Expedition. He was responsible for the fighting of our first war as a nation, on the shores of Tripoli against the Barbary pirates. His efforts to prevent a second war with England only postponed it until 1812.

Jefferson was slow but successful in meeting the first real threat to the new American union. Aaron Burr was accused of making a treasonable effort to set up an independent government in the Southwest. This was halted when it had scarcely begun. However, in the trial that followed the suppression of this Burr conspiracy, Jefferson's personal animosity toward Burr and toward Chief Justice John Marshall did him little credit.

His Embargo Act was a daring and original, but eventually unsuccessful, means of keeping the peace. However, it may have been one of the most successful and inspired diplomatic moves of the young republic. In effect it applied economic pressures against Britain and France, who were at war with each other. It was Jefferson's answer to the British Orders in Council and the Impressment Acts, directed against neutral (in this case, mainly American) shipping. The Embargo Act stopped American shipping, thus in intent depriving European nations of some of the raw materials needed for war.

文章中譯

爲了**讓共和黨在政府機關中的權力恢復平衡**，傑佛遜發起了後來稱爲「政黨分贓制[1]」的制度。**為了維護人民的利益**，他試圖控制**最高法院**，不過並沒有成功。他在缺乏明確的憲法根據下，協商購得了路易斯安那廣大的土地。

傑佛遜也**發起了路易斯與克拉克遠征**[2]。美國獨立建國後第一場戰事同樣也是由傑佛遜發起的，在的黎波里海岸抵抗巴巴里[3] 海盜。雖然他極力避免第二場戰爭，但最後也只是把美國與英國的戰爭延後至 1812 年。

傑佛遜慢慢地成功克服了美國成立聯邦後首次面臨的嚴重威脅。亞倫．伯爾[4]因爲**意圖**在美國西南部成立獨立政府的**叛國行為**而遭到起訴。伯爾的行動還沒開始，就已經畫下句點；但是，在**鎮壓伯爾陰謀叛國行為**之後的審判中，傑佛遜**個人**對伯爾及首席大法官約翰．馬歇爾**的敵意**卻**為他自己帶來不好的評價**。

傑佛遜頒布**禁運法案**，意圖藉此維持和平，這個**做法大膽且創新**，但是最後卻以失敗告終。然而，這卻可能是美國這個年輕的共和國最成功、最具有啓發性的外交行動之一，對當時正在交戰的英國和法國造成經濟壓力。禁運法案是傑佛遜對英國樞密院令及徵召令的回應，對中立地區（在此主要是指美國地區）船運規定的反動。禁運法案禁止美國輸出貨品，有意阻止歐洲國家獲得戰爭所需的部分原料。

---

1 指競選獲勝的政黨將公職委派給獲勝政黨支持者的制度。

2 從現今的美國東岸往西橫越大陸抵太平洋沿岸的往返遠征考察活動，領隊爲路易斯和克拉克。

3 巴巴里指北非沿海回教地域。

4 當時的副總統。1800 年的總統大選，傑佛遜與伯爾代表當時的民主共和黨參選，兩人獲得相同票數的選舉人票，後由眾議院表決選擇傑佛遜爲總統，伯爾爲副總統。

Double-Check

- restore a balance of Republicans [rɪˋpʌblɪkənz] 讓共和黨的權力恢復平衡
- government office [ˋgʌvənmənt] 政府機關
- the Supreme Court [səˋprim] 最高法院
- in the interests of the will of the people [ˋɪntrɪsts] 為了維護人民的利益
- negotiate the purchase [ˋpɜtʃəs] 協商購買
- constitutional grounds [ˌkanstəˋtjuʃənl̩] 憲法根據
- launch the Lewis and Clark Expedition [lɔntʃ] [ˌɛkspɪˋdɪʃən] 發起路易斯與克拉克遠征
- make a treasonable effort [ˋtrizənəbl̩] 意圖叛國
- the suppression of this Burr conspiracy [səˋprɛʃən] [kənˋspɪrəsɪ] 鎮壓伯爾陰謀叛國行為
- personal animosity [ˌænəˋmasətɪ] 個人的敵意
- do him little credit [ˋkrɛdɪt] 為他帶來不好的評價
- Embargo Act [ɪmˋbargo] 禁運法案
- a daring and original means [ˋdɛrɪŋ] 大膽且創新的做法

American History

08 Confederate States of America
美利堅邦聯

Key Sentences

1 Six southern states declared their withdrawal (secession) from the United States.

美國南部有六州**宣布退出**美國聯邦。

2 They organized a separate and independent government called the Confederate States of America.

他們組成獨立自主的政府，稱爲**美利堅邦聯**。

3 The preamble of the new Confederate constitution declared that each state was "acting in its sovereign and independent character."

邦聯政府的新憲法在前言中載明，各州「**主權獨立自主**」。

4 Never before had the issue been charged with the emotional factor of the abolition of black slavery.

以前這個議題從來沒有和**廢除黑奴制度**這項情感因素牽扯在一起。

5 The president was given the right to veto separate items of appropriation bills.

總統**有權否決預算案**中的**各項支出**。

Reading Focus 236字

MP3 017

Between Dec. 20, 1860, and Feb. 1, 1861, six southern states declared their withdrawal (secession) from the United States. On February 4, at Montgomery, Ala., they organized a separate and independent government called the Confederate States of America. The states that set up this government were South Carolina, Mississippi, Florida, Alabama, Georgia, and Louisiana. A seventh state, Texas, was admitted to the confederation on March 2. Jefferson Davis of Mississippi was elected president and Alexander H. Stephens of Georgia, vice-president.

The preamble of the new Confederate constitution declared that each state was "acting in its sovereign and independent character." This right had been asserted at earlier periods in American history. Never before, however, had the issue been charged with the emotional factor of the abolition of black slavery.

The constitution of the Confederate States reflected the then prevailing belief in the South that slavery was the only practicable status for the large black population of that section. It forbade any legislation impairing the institution of slavery though it did prohibit foreign slave trade.

The remainder of the constitution was largely based on that of the Union from which the states of the lower South were withdrawing. Among the modifications was a six-year term for the president, who could not succeed himself. The president was, in addition, given the right to veto separate items of appropriation bills. Congress was prohibited from adopting a protective tariff on imports.

Q Look at the word "It" in paragraph 3. Find out the word or phrase in paragraph 3 that "It" refers to.

A The constitution (of the Confederate States)

文章中譯

在 1860 年 12 月 20 日到 1861 年 2 月 1 日這段期間，美國南部有六州**宣布退出**美國聯邦。他們於 2 月 4 日在阿拉巴馬州的蒙哥馬利市組成獨立自主的政府，稱爲**美利堅邦聯**。參與組成新政府的有南卡羅萊納、密西西比、佛羅里達、阿拉巴馬、喬治亞、路易斯安那等六州。德州在 3 月 2 日獲准加入邦聯，成爲第七個州。密西西比州的傑佛遜．戴維斯被推選爲總統，喬治亞州的亞歷山大．H．史蒂芬斯爲副總統。

邦聯政府的新憲法在前言中載明，各州「**主權獨立自主**」。這項權力在美國早期歷史中已經聲明過，但是以前這個議題從來沒有和**廢除黑奴制度**這項情感因素牽扯在一起。

南方邦聯政府的憲法反映出當時盛行於南方的看法：南方人口衆多的黑人唯一能夠得到的地位就是奴隸。這部憲法禁止制訂任何損及奴隸制度的法律，不過它同時也禁止從國外進口奴隸買賣。

南方憲法的其他部分大多是根據這些南方州政府退出的美國聯邦憲法而制定。修改部分包括將總統任期改爲六年，不得連任。除此之外，總統**有權否決預算案**中的**各項支出**。國會則被禁止對進口採取保護關稅措施。

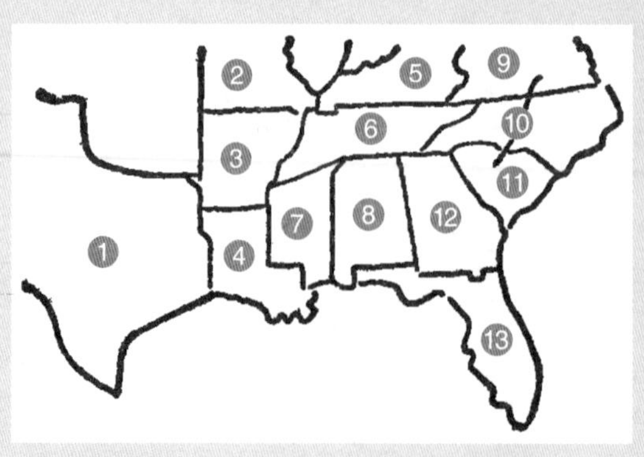

❶ 德克薩斯州
❷ 密蘇里州
❸ 阿肯色州
❹ 路易斯安那州
❺ 肯塔基州
❻ 田納西州
❼ 密西西比州
❽ 阿拉巴馬州
❾ 維吉尼亞州
❿ 北卡羅萊納州
⓫ 南卡羅萊納州
⓬ 喬治亞州
⓭ 佛羅里達州

美國西南部各州

Double-Check

- declare their withdrawal (secession) 宣布退出
  [dɪˋklɛr] [wɪðˋdrɔəl]
  參 secession [sɪˋsɛʃən] (n.) 脫離聯邦

- the Confederate States of America 美利堅邦聯
  [kənˋfɛdərɪt]

- the preamble of the new Confederate constitution 邦聯政府的新憲法前言
  [ˋpriæmbl̩] [ˏkɑnstəˋtjuʃən]

- sovereign and independent character 主權獨立自主
  [ˋsɑvrɪn] [ˏɪndɪˋpɛndənt]

- the abolition of black slavery 廢除黑奴制度
  [ˏæbəˋlɪʃən] [ˋslevərɪ]

- prevailing belief 盛行的看法
  [prɪˋvelɪŋ]

- the only practicable status 唯一能夠得到的地位
  [ˋpræktɪkəbl̩] [ˋstetəs]

- legislation impairing the institution of slavery 制訂損及奴隸制度的法律
  [ˏlɛdʒɪsˋleʃən] [ɪmˋpɛrɪŋ]

- prohibit foreign slave trade 禁止從國外進口奴隸買賣
  [proˋhɪbɪt]

- the right to veto separate items 否決各項支出的權力
  [ˋvito][ˋsɛpərɪt]

- appropriation bills 預算案
  [əˏproprɪˋeʃən]

- a protective tariff 保護關稅措施
  [prəˋtɛktɪv] [ˋtærɪf]

American History

09 The Civil War Era

南北戰爭時期

Key Sentences

1. White Southerners had been embittered by Northern defiance of the 1850 Federal Fugitive Slave Act.

   1850 年聯邦政府通過逃亡奴隸法案，南方白人對北方人的挑釁態度懷恨在心。

2. The Southern states seceded from the Union and formed the Confederacy.

   南方各州退出聯邦政府，自組美利堅邦聯。

3. Preservation of the Union, not the abolition of slavery, was the initial objective of President Lincoln.

   林肯總統最初的目標並非爲了廢除奴隸制度，而是爲了維護聯邦的完整。

4. Lincoln believed in gradual emancipation.

   林肯認爲解放奴隸要一步步來。

5. Black leaders vigorously recruited blacks into the Union armed forces.

   黑人領袖積極招募黑人加入聯邦政府軍。

6. They performed heroically despite discrimination in pay, rations, equipment, and assignments and the unrelenting hostility of the Confederate troops.

   儘管在待遇、配給、裝備、任務分配等方面受到不公平的對待，又面對南方軍隊毫不退讓的敵意，他們仍然表現得非常英勇。

Reading Focus 261字

MP3 019

By the end of the 1850s, the North feared complete control of the nation by slaveholding interests and the white South believed that the North was determined to destroy its way of life. White Southerners had been embittered by Northern defiance of the 1850 Federal Fugitive Slave Act and had been alarmed in 1859 by the raid at Harpers Ferry, W. Va., led by the white abolitionist John Brown. After Abraham Lincoln was elected president in 1860 on the antislavery platform of the new Republican Party, the Southern states seceded from the Union and formed the Confederacy.

The Civil War, which liberated the nation's slaves, began in 1861. But preservation of the Union, not the abolition of slavery, was the initial objective of President Lincoln. Lincoln believed in gradual emancipation, with the federal government compensating the slaveholders for the loss of their "property." But in September 1862 he issued the Emancipation Proclamation, declaring that all slaves residing in states in rebellion against the United States as of Jan. 1, 1863, were to be free. Thus the Civil War became, in effect, a war to end slavery.

Black leaders such as the author William Wells Brown, the physician Martin R. Delany, and Douglass vigorously recruited blacks into the Union armed forces. Douglass declared in the *North Star*, "Who would be free themselves must strike the blow." By the end of the Civil War more than 186,000 black men were in the Union army. They performed heroically despite discrimination in pay, rations, equipment, and assignments and the unrelenting hostility of the Confederate troops.

文章中譯

1850 年代末期，北方害怕整個國家受到支持蓄奴制度者的操控，而南方白人則認爲北方人決意破壞他們的生活方式。1850 年**聯邦政府通過逃亡奴隸法案**，南方白人**對北方人的挑釁態度懷恨在心**；而 1859 年廢奴主義者白人約翰．布朗帶領支持者突擊西維吉尼亞州的哈伯渡口，更震驚了南方白人世界。1860 年重新改組的共和黨候選人林肯提出反對奴隸制度的宣言，並當選爲總統，南方各州隨即**退出聯邦政府，自組美利堅邦聯**。

使得美國奴隸重獲自由的南北戰爭於 1861 年爆發。但是林肯總統**最初的目標**並非爲了**廢除奴隸制度**，而是爲了**維護聯邦的完整**。林肯認爲**解放奴隸要一步步來**，由聯邦政府補償奴主的「財產」損失。但是在 1862 年 9 月，林肯發表了《解放宣言》，宣布南方叛亂各州境內所有奴隸將在 1863 年 1 月 1 日當天獲得自由。由此，南北戰爭變成了終結奴隸制度的戰爭。

黑人領袖如作家威廉．威爾斯．布朗、馬丁．R．迪勒尼醫師、道格拉斯等**積極招募**黑人加入**聯邦政府軍**。道格拉斯在《北方之星》上寫道：「想要獲得自由的人，一定要起而奮戰。」南北戰爭結束前，已經有超過 18 萬 6 千名黑人加入聯邦軍隊。儘管**在待遇、配給、裝備、任務分配等方面受到不公平的對待**，又面對**南方軍隊毫不退讓的敵意**，這些黑人仍然表現得非常英勇。

南北戰爭時的林肯總統（圖中戴高帽者）與麥克雷倫將軍

Double-Check

- be embittered by Northern defiance 對北方人的挑釁態度懷恨在心
  [ɪm`bɪtəd] [dɪ`faɪəns]
- Federal Fugitive Slave Act 聯邦政府的逃亡奴隸法案
  [`fɛdərəl] [`fjudʒətɪv]
- secede from the Union 退出聯邦政府
  [sɪ`sid]
- form the Confederacy 組成美利堅邦聯
  [kən`fɛdərəsɪ]
- preservation of the Union 維護聯邦的完整
  [ˌprɛzɚ`veʃən]
- the abolition of slavery 廢除奴隸制度
  [ˌæbə`lɪʃən] [`slevərɪ]
- the initial objective 最初的目標
  [ɪ`nɪʃəl] [əb`dʒɛktɪv]
- gradual emancipation 一步步的解放
  [`grædʒuəl] [ɪˌmænsə`peʃən]
- vigorously recruit 積極招募
  [`vɪgərəslɪ] [rɪ`krut]
- the Union armed forces 聯邦政府軍
- discrimination in pay, rations, equipment, and assignments 在待遇、配給、裝備、任務分配等方面受到不公平的對待
  [dɪˌskrɪmə`neʃən] [`reʃənz] [ɪ`kwɪpmənt] [ə`saɪnmənts]
- the unrelenting hostility 毫不退讓的敵意
  [ˌʌnrɪ`lɛntɪŋ] [has`tɪlətɪ]
- the Confederate troops 南方軍隊
  [kən`fɛdərɪt] [trups]

Business Administration & Economics

10 The Great Depression
大蕭條

Key Sentences

1 On Oct. 24, 1929, the collapse of the stock market began; about 13 million shares of stock were sold.

1929 年 10 月 24 日**股市全面崩盤**，有大約 1 千 3 百萬股的股票遭到拋售。

2 The value of most shares fell sharply, leaving financial ruin and panic in its wake.

大多數股票的價格暴跌，**造成金融崩潰與恐慌**。

3 There had been financial panics before, and there have been some since, but never did a collapse in the market have such a devastating and long-term effect.

過去也曾發生過金融恐慌，後來也陸續發生過幾次，但從未有股市崩盤**造成這麼大的災難和長期效應**。

4 Wages for those still fortunate enough to have work fell precipitously.

有幸仍保有工作的人，薪資也**大幅減少**。

5 The government itself was sorely pressed for income at all levels as tax revenues fell.

政府本身則因為稅收減少，**各層級部門的經費嚴重短缺**。

6 The international structure of world trade collapsed, and each nation sought to protect its own industrial base by imposing high tariffs on imported goods.

全球貿易的國際架構崩解，每個國家為了保護自己的產業基礎，**對進口貨物課以高額的關稅**。

Reading Focus 237字

MP3 021

On Oct. 24, 1929, the collapse of the stock market began; about 13 million shares of stock were sold. Tuesday, October 29—known ever since as Black Tuesday—extended the damage; more than 16 million shares were sold. The value of most shares fell sharply, leaving financial ruin and panic in its wake.

There had been financial panics before, and there have been some since, but never did a collapse in the market have such a devastating and long-term effect. Like a snowball rolling downhill, it gathered momentum and swept away the whole economy before it. Businesses closed, putting millions out of work. Banks failed by the hundreds. Wages for those still fortunate enough to have work fell precipitously. The value of money decreased as the demand for goods declined.

Most of the agricultural segment of the economy had been in serious trouble for years. With the arrival of the depression it was nearly eliminated altogether, and the drought that created the 1930s Great Plains Dust Bowl compounded the damage.

The government itself was sorely pressed for income at all levels as tax revenues fell, and the government at that time was much more limited in its ability to respond to economic crises than it is today.

The international structure of world trade collapsed, and each nation sought to protect its own industrial base by imposing high tariffs on imported goods. However, this only made matters worse.

文章中譯

1929 年 10 月 24 日**股市全面崩盤**，有大約 1 千 3 百萬股的股票遭到拋售，到了 10 月 29 日星期二——後來被稱爲「黑色星期二」——情況更加惡化，超過 1 千 6 百萬股遭到拋售。大多數股票的價格暴跌，**造成金融崩潰與恐慌**。

過去也曾發生過金融恐慌，後來也陸續發生過幾次，但從未有股市崩盤**造成這麼大的災難和長期效應**。就像滾下山的雪球一樣，動能不斷累積，橫掃整個經濟體系。公司倒閉，造成數百萬人失業；破產的銀行數以百計；有幸仍保有工作的人，薪資也**大幅減少**；隨著商品的需求下滑，幣值也跟著下跌。

大部分的農業原本就已陷入嚴重困境多年，隨著經濟衰退的到來幾乎完全被摧毀，而 1930 年代造成大平原沙塵暴的乾旱更使得損害加劇。

政府本身則因爲稅收減少，**各層級部門的經費嚴重短缺**，且當時的政府與今日的政府相較，比較沒有能力處理經濟危機。

全球貿易的國際架構崩解，每個國家爲了保護自己的產業基礎，**對進口貨物課以高額的關稅**，而這只是讓問題雪上加霜。

Double-Check

- the collapse of the stock market　股市全面崩盤
  [kə`læps]

- leave financial ruin and panic in its wake　造成金融崩潰與恐慌
  [`ruɪn]

  參 wake [wek] (n.) 餘波

- have such a devastating and long-term effect　造成這麼大的災難和長期效應
  [`dɛvəs,tetɪŋ]

  參 devastate [`dɛvəs,tet] (v.) 使荒蕪，破壞，蹂躪

- fall precipitously　大幅減少
  [prɪ`sɪpətəslɪ]

- be sorely pressed for income at all levels　各層級部門的經費短缺

  參 be pressed for... …吃緊

- by imposing high tariffs on imported goods　對進口貨物課以高額的關稅
  [`tærɪfs]

  參 impose [ɪm`poz] (v.) 課徵（稅），強加

Business Administration & Economics

Managerial Decision Making

經營決策

Key Sentences

1 The guidelines governing management decisions cannot be reduced to a simple formula.

左右經營決策的準則無法簡化成一個簡單的公式。

2 The goal of a business enterprise is to maximize its profits.

企業的目標是追求最大利潤。

3 Today's profits can be increased at the expense of profits years away by cutting maintenance, deferring investment, and exploiting staff.

今天的獲利有可能是以刪減維護費用、拖延投資、剝削員工換來的，也就是以往後數年的獲利為代價。

4 These are part of the necessary performance incentives for executives.

這些是激勵高階主管表現的必要支出。

5 Some proponents of such expenditure believe that they serve to enhance contacts, breed confidence, improve the flow of information, and stimulate business.

贊成這類支出的人認爲，這些支出可以強化人脈、培養信心、增進資訊流通、刺激業務。

6 Management asserts primacy of profits.

管理高層主張獲利至上。

Reading Focus 249字

MP3 023

The guidelines governing management decisions cannot be reduced to a simple formula. Traditionally, economists have assumed that the goal of a business enterprise is to maximize its profits. There are, however, problems of interpretation with this simple assertion. First, the notion of "profit" is itself unclear in operational terms. Today's profits can be increased at the expense of profits years away by cutting maintenance, deferring investment, and exploiting staff. Second, there are questions over whether expenditure on offices, cars, staff expenses, and other trappings of status reduces shareholders' wealth or whether these are part of the necessary performance incentives for executives. Some proponents of such expenditure believe that they serve to enhance contacts, breed confidence, improve the flow of information, and stimulate business. Third, if management asserts primacy of profits, this may in itself send negative signals to employees about the systems of corporate values. Where long-term success requires goodwill, commitment, and cooperation, a focus on short-term profit may alienate or drive away those very employees upon whom long-term success depends.

Generally speaking, most companies turn over only about half of their earnings to stockholders as dividends. They plow the rest of their profits back into the business. A major motivation of executives is to expand their operations faster than those of their competitors. The important point, however, is that without profit over the long term no firm can survive. For growing firms in competitive markets a major indicator of executive competence is the ability to augment company earnings.

文章中譯

左右經營決策的準則無法簡化成**一個簡單的公式**。傳統上，經濟學家都主張**企業**的目標是**追求最大利潤**。可是，這個簡單的主張本身有幾點疑慮。首先，就運作面而言，「利潤」這個概念本身是不清楚的，今天的獲利有可能是以刪減維護費用、**拖延投資**、**剝削員工**換來的，也就是**以往後數年的獲利為代價**。其次，花在辦公室、汽車、員工支出以及其他彰顯地位外表的費用，會不會縮減了股東的財富或者說這些是不是**激勵高階主管表現**的必要支出，這些問題仍有待商榷。**贊成這類支出的人**認爲，這些支出可以**強化人脈**、**培養信心**、增進資訊流通、刺激業務。第三，如果管理高層**主張獲利至上**，可能會在企業價值方面對員工傳遞出負面訊息。長期的成功必須仰賴商譽、承諾、合作，著眼於短期獲利可能會把那些能造就長期獲利的員工給疏遠、趕走。

一般來說，大多數公司只會交出半數左右的盈餘給股東當股利，其餘的獲利再投入公司營運。高階主管的主要動機是比競爭對手更快速拓展營運，不過重點是，如果沒有長期獲利，沒有任何一家公司可以存活。對處於競爭激烈的市場、正在成長的公司而言，高階主管是否適任的一大指標是：是否有能力提高公司盈餘。

Double-Check

- the guidelines governing management decisions [`gaɪd,laɪnz] 左右經營決策的準則
- a simple formula [`fɔrmjələ] 一個簡單的公式
- a business enterprise [`ɛntɚ,praɪz] 企業
- maximize its profits [`mæksə,maɪz] 追求最大利潤
- at the expense of profits years away [ɪk`spɛns] 以往後數年的獲利爲代價
- defer investment [dɪ`fɝ] [ɪn`vɛstmənt] 拖延投資
- exploit staff [ɪk`splɔɪt] 剝削員工
- performance incentives for executives [ɪn`sɛntɪvz] [ɪg`zɛkjʊtɪvz] 激勵高階主管表現的誘因
- some proponents of such expenditure [prə`ponənts] [ɪk`spɛndɪtʃɚ] 贊成這類支出的人
- enhance contacts [ɪn`hæns] 強化人脈
- breed confidence [brid] 培養信心
- assert primacy of profits [ə`sɝt] [`praɪməsɪ] 主張獲利至上

Business Administration & Economics

12 Government and Private Enterprise

政府與民營企業

Key Sentences

1 A principal effort of the government traditionally has been the fostering of competition through enforcement of antitrust laws.

傳統上，政府主要致力於透過**反托拉斯法的實施**來**打造一個競爭環境**。

2 These are designed to combat collusion among companies and, where feasible, to prevent mergers that significantly reduce competition.

這樣的設計，是為了**打擊企業互相勾結**，並試圖**避免企業合併**，導致競爭力大幅降低。

3 The major area of government regulation of economic activity is through fiscal and monetary policy.

政府主要透過**財政與貨幣政策**來**規範經濟活動**。

4 The government exerts considerable leverage on certain sectors of the economy.

政府在某些經濟產業**發揮龐大的影響力**。

5 The government endeavors to support farm incomes through payments to farmers, controls on output, price supports, and the provision of storage and marketing facilities.

政府**努力**透過給付農人、控制產量、支撐價格、**提供儲存設備與行銷工具**等方式來**維持農家收入**。

Reading Focus 245字

MP3 025

The U.S. government plays only a small direct part in economic activity, being largely restricted to such agencies as the U.S. Postal Service and the Nuclear Regulatory Commission. Enterprises that are often in public hands in other countries, such as airlines and telephone systems, are run privately in the United States.

A principal effort of the government traditionally has been the fostering of competition through enforcement of antitrust laws. These are designed to combat collusion among companies with respect to prices, output levels, or market shares and, where feasible, to prevent mergers that significantly reduce competition. The vigor with which antitrust laws and regulations are to be enforced is a matter of perennial political debate.

The major area of government regulation of economic activity is through fiscal and monetary policy. The government also exerts considerable leverage on certain sectors of the economy as a purchaser of goods, notably in the aircraft and aerospace industries. Proposals for governmental controls of prices and incomes have been a frequent source of much controversy.

Farming is a field in which the government strongly influences private economic activity. It endeavors to support farm incomes through payments to farmers, controls on output, price supports, and the provision of storage and marketing facilities. One disadvantage of the system is that payments are related to farm output, so the benefits often go to the larger commercial farms rather than to the so-called family farms that were originally the main object of governmental concern.

文章中譯

美國政府只直接涉入經濟活動的一小部分，大致僅限於美國郵局和核子管理委員會這類機構。在其他國家通常屬於公共部門的事業，例如航空、電信，在美國都是私人經營。

傳統上，政府主要致力於透過**反托拉斯法的實施**來**打造一個競爭環境**。這樣的設計，是爲了**打擊企業**在價格、產量、市占率等方面**互相勾結**，並試圖**避免企業合併**，導致競爭力大幅降低。反托拉斯法與規範的執行效力是長年的政治爭議。

政府主要透過**財政與貨幣政策**來**規範經濟活動**，也會以商品採購者之姿，在某些經濟產業**發揮龐大的影響力**，特別是在航空與太空產業。提議由政府掌控價格和收入，一直是爭議的來源。

與農業相關的民間經濟活動則是政府極力干涉的領域。政府**努力**透過給付農人、控制產量、支撐價格、**提供儲存設備與行銷工具**等方式來**維持農家收入**。這套制度有一個缺點，因爲給付金額與農產量有關，所以好處通常都落到大型商業農場的手中，而不是所謂的農家，而他們才是政府原本主要關心的對象。

Double-Check

- be run privately 私人經營
  [ˋpraɪvɪtlɪ]
  參 run [rʌn] (v.) 經營，營運；運轉

- the fostering of competition 打造競爭環境
  [ˋfɔstərɪŋ] [ˌkɑmpəˋtɪʃən]

- enforcement of antitrust laws 反托拉斯法的實施
  [ɪnˋfɔrsmənt] [ˌæntɪˋtrʌst]

- combat collusion among companies 打擊企業互相勾結
  [kəˋluʒən]

- prevent mergers 避免企業合併
  [ˋmɝdʒɚz]

- government regulation of economic activity 政府規範經濟活動
  [ˌrɛgjəˋleʃən]

- fiscal and monetary policy 財政與貨幣政策
  [ˋfɪskḷ] [ˋmʌnəˌtɛrɪ]

- exert considerable leverage 發揮龐大的影響力
  [ɪgˋzɝt] [ˋlɛvərɪdʒ]

- endeavor to support farm incomes 努力維持農家收入
  [ɪnˋdɛvɚ]

- the provision of storage and marketing facilities 提供儲存設備與行銷工具
  [prəˋvɪʒən] [ˋstorɪdʒ] [fəˋsɪlətɪz]

Education

Educational Theory and Practice

教育理論與實踐

Key Sentences

MP3 026

1 In formulating educational criteria and aims, he drew heavily on the insights into learning offered by contemporary psychology.

他在**制定教育準則**與目標時，大量運用了**當代心理學**在**學習方面的洞見**。

2 He viewed thought and learning as a process of inquiry starting from doubt or uncertainty and spurred by the desire to resolve practical frictions or relieve strain and tension.

他把思考和學習視爲**一種探究的過程**，從懷疑或不確定開始，並因爲**渴望解決實際摩擦**或**紓解壓力緊張而受到激勵**。

3 Among the results of Dewey's administrative efforts were the establishment of an independent department of pedagogy and the University of Chicago's Laboratory Schools.

杜威在**行政方面的努力**所獲得的成果包括：把**教育獨立**出來成爲**一個部門**，成立芝加哥大學實驗學校。

4 The Laboratory Schools attracted wide attention and enhanced the reputation of the University of Chicago as a foremost center of progressive educational thought.

芝加哥大學實驗學校**獲得廣大注意**，也**強化**了芝加哥大學身爲**進步教育理念重鎮**的**聲望**。

Reading Focus 261字

MP3 027

Dewey's work in philosophy and psychology was largely centered on his major interest, educational reform. In formulating educational criteria and aims, he drew heavily on the insights into learning offered by contemporary psychology as applied to children. He viewed thought and learning as a process of inquiry starting from doubt or uncertainty and spurred by the desire to resolve practical frictions or relieve strain and tension. Education must therefore begin with experience, which has as its aim growth and the achievement of maturity.

Dewey's writings on education, notably his *The School and Society* (1899) and *The Child and the Curriculum* (1902), presented and defended what were to remain the chief underlying tenets of the philosophy of education he originated. These tenets were that the educational process must begin with and build upon the interests of the child; that it must provide opportunity for the interplay of thinking and doing in the child's classroom experience; that the teacher should be a guide and coworker with the pupils, rather than a taskmaster assigning a fixed set of lessons and recitations; and that the school's goal is the growth of the child in all aspects of their being. Among the results of Dewey's administrative efforts were the establishment of an independent department of pedagogy and the University of Chicago's Laboratory Schools, in which the educational theories and practices suggested by psychology and philosophy could be tested. The Laboratory Schools, which began operation in 1896, attracted wide attention and enhanced the reputation of the University of Chicago as a foremost center of progressive educational thought.

文章中譯

杜威在哲學與心理學方面的成果，主要是以他首要的興趣為重心：教育改革。他在**制定教育準則**與目標時，大量運用了**當代**兒童**心理學**在**學習方面的洞見**。他把思考和學習視為**一種探究的過程**，從懷疑或不確定開始，並因為**渴望解決實際摩擦**或**紓解壓力緊張而受到激勵**。因此，教育必須從體驗開始，目標是成長與成熟。

杜威在其教育方面的著作中，特別是《學校與社會》(1899) 以及《孩子與課程》(1902)，針對他所創的教育理念，提出並捍衛其背後的主要原則（這些原則至今仍是其教育理念的核心）。這些原則包括：教育過程必須以孩子的興趣為基礎並作為出發點；教育必須提供機會，讓孩子在課堂上有思考與動手做交互並行的體驗；老師應該是學生的引導者和合作者，而不是制式授課、要學生背誦的監督者；學校的目標是孩子在各方面的成長。杜威在**行政方面的努力**所獲得的成果包括：把**教育獨立**出來成為**一個部門**，成立芝加哥大學實驗學校，在此實驗心理學和哲學領域所提出的教育理論和作法。芝加哥大學實驗學校從 1896 年開始運作，**獲得廣大注意**，也**強化**了芝加哥大學身為**進步教育理念重鎮**的**聲望**。

Double-Check

- formulate educational criteria 制定教育準則
  [ˋfɔrmjəˏlet] [kraɪˋtɪrɪə]
- the insights into learning 在學習方面的洞見
  [ˋɪnˏsaɪts]
- contemporary psychology 當代心理學
  [kənˋtɛmpəˏrɛrɪ] [saɪˋkɑlədʒɪ]
- a process of inquiry 一種探究的過程
  [ɪnˋkwaɪrɪ]
- be spurred by the desire 被渴望所激勵
  [spɝd]
- resolve practical frictions 解決實際摩擦
  [ˋfrɪkʃənz]
- relieve strain and tension 紓解壓力和緊張
  [rɪˋliv] [stren]
- the chief underlying tenets 背後的主要原則
  [ˋtɛnɪts]
- assign a fixed set of lessons and recitations 制式授課、要學生背誦
  [əˋsaɪn] [ˏrɛsəˋteʃənz]
- administrative efforts 行政方面的努力
  [ədˋmɪnəˏstretɪv]
- an independent department of pedagogy 一個獨立的教育部門
  [ˋpɛdəˏgodʒɪ]
- attract wide attention 獲得廣大注意
  [əˋtɛnʃən]
- enhance the reputation 強化聲望
  [ˏrɛpjəˋteʃən]
- a foremost center of progressive educational thought 進步教育理念的重鎮
  [ˋforˏmost] [prəˋgrɛsɪv]

Ethnology

14 The Ethnics
族裔

Key Sentences

1 Current usage confines the term "ethnic" to the descendants of the newest immigrants.

「族裔」一詞**現在的用法**侷限於「**最新移民的後裔**」。

2 Its proper, more comprehensive meaning applies to all groups unified by their cultural heritage.

比較合適及**廣泛的定義**是泛指可與他們的**文化傳統**融合的任何族群。

3 Tightly knit communities, firm religious values, and a belief in the value of education earned them prominent positions in business, in literature and law, and in cultural and philanthropic institutions.

組織緊密的社群、**堅定的宗教價值觀**、對教育價值的信仰，**替他們**在商業界、文學與法律界、文化界與**慈善機構之間掙得顯赫的地位**。

4 These people preserved affiliations with the Democratic Party until the 1960s.

這些人一直到 1960 年代之前都與民主黨**保持友好關係**。

Reading Focus 246字

MP3 029

Although current usage confines the term "ethnic" to the descendants of the newest immigrants, its proper, more comprehensive meaning applies to all groups unified by their cultural heritage and by their experience in the New World.

In the 19th century, Yankees formed one such group, marked by common religion and by habits shaped by the original Puritan settlers. From New England, the Yankees spread westward through New York, northern Ohio, Indiana, and Illinois and on to Iowa and Kansas. Tightly knit communities, firm religious values, and a belief in the value of education earned them prominent positions in business, in literature and law, and in cultural and philanthropic institutions. They long identified with the Republican Party.

Southern whites and their descendants, by contrast, generation after generation remained preponderantly rural as migration took them westward across Tennessee and Kentucky to Arkansas, Missouri, Oklahoma, and Texas. These people remained primarily rural until the industrialization of the South in the 20th century, and they preserved affiliations with the Democratic Party until the 1960s.

The colonial population also contained other elements that long sustained their identities as groups. The Pennsylvania Germans, held together by religion and language, still pursue their own way of life after three centuries, as exemplified by the Amish. The great 19th-century German migrations, however, contained a variety of elements that dispersed in the cities as well as in the agricultural areas of the West; to the extent that ethnic ties have survived, they are largely sentimental.

! philanthropic [ˌfɪlənˋθrɑpɪk] 的發音比較困難，請特別注意。

文章中譯

雖然「族裔」一詞**現在的用法**侷限於「**最新移民的後裔**」，但比較合適及**廣泛的定義**，泛指可與他們的**文化傳統**融合或與他們在新世界中有同樣經歷的任何族群。

在 19 世紀，美國北方人形成了這樣一個族群，他們有共同的宗教，也有最初清教徒移民流傳下來的共同習慣。北方人從新英格蘭向西擴散，來到紐約、俄亥俄州北部、印地安納州、伊利諾州，再繼續到愛荷華州和堪薩斯州。**組織緊密的社群、堅定的宗教價值觀**、對教育價值的信仰，**替他們**在商業界、文學與法律界、文化界與**慈善機構之間掙得顯赫的地位**。他們長久以來認同的是共和黨。

對照之下，南方白人和其後裔代代大多還是以務農爲主，他們往西遷徙橫越田納西州和肯塔基州，到達阿肯色州、密蘇里州、奧克拉荷馬州和德州。這些人一直到南方在 20 世紀工業化以前都是以務農爲主，而且在 1960 年代之前都與民主黨**保持友好關係**。

殖民地時期的人口還包括了其他一些組成分子，這些人長期以來維持著他們族群的特質。靠著宗教與語言凝聚在一起的賓州德國人在過了三個世紀之後，仍然在追尋他們自己的生活方式，例如亞米緒人。不過，19 世紀的大批德國移民發展則很多元，四散到城市與西部農村，以至於族裔的連結雖然保留了下來，但大多是情感上的連結。

Double-Check

- current usage 現在的用法
  [`kɜənt] [`jusɪdʒ]

- the descendants of the newest immigrants 最新移民的後裔
  [dɪ`sɛndənts] [`ɪməgrənts]

- comprehensive meaning 廣泛的定義
  [ˌkamprɪ`hɛnsɪv]

- cultural heritage 文化傳統
  [`hɛrətɪdʒ]

- tightly knit communities 組織緊密的社群
  [nɪt]

  參 tight [taɪt] (adj.) 緊密的

- firm religious values 堅定的宗教價值觀
  [rɪ`lɪdʒəs]

- earn them prominent positions 替他們掙得顯赫的地位
  [`pramənənt]

- philanthropic institutions 慈善機構
  [ˌfɪlən`θrapɪk] [ˌɪnstə`tjuʃənz]

- preserve affiliations 保持友好關係
  [əˌfɪlɪ`eʃənz]

Film

15 Tools of Filmmaking

電影製片使用的方法

Key Sentences

MP3 030

1 All motion pictures are based on an illusion of motion made possible by a characteristic of visual perception called persistence of vision.

所有的電影都是利用**移動幻覺**製作而成的，而這是因爲人類有種叫做**視覺暫留**的**視覺認知**特性。

2 The brain retains an impression for 1/16 to 1/10 of a second after the eye has stopped looking at an illuminated image.

眼睛停止注視**發光的影像**後，腦部還能**保留**影像的**印象** 1/16 到 1/10 秒左右。

3 The pages are riffled at a rather fast pace.

快速翻閱這一疊紙。

4 In motion pictures, persistence of vision is used to create the illusion of motion from still photographs.

電影就是利用視覺暫留的原理，透過**靜止的照片**創造出移動幻覺。

5 The time lapse between images is normally 1/24 of a second in most cameras.

大部分攝影機所拍攝到的影像的**時間間隔**通常是 1/24 秒。

6 Persistence of vision causes the separate images to be projected as a continuously moving scene.

視覺暫留使得一張張分離的圖片**投影成連續移動的場景**。

Reading Focus 266字

MP3 031

All motion pictures are based on an illusion of motion made possible by a characteristic of visual perception called persistence of vision. The brain retains an impression for 1/16 to 1/10 of a second after the eye has stopped looking at an illuminated image. When a series of pictures of an object is presented in steady, rapid succession, with the position of the object slightly altered in each picture to represent successive stages of movement, the brain blends the different pictures into one another, creating the illusion of motion.

A simple way to demonstrate the illusion of motion is to draw a line in the lower right-hand corner of each page of a pad of paper, altering the angle of each line very slightly in a single direction. If the pages are then riffled at a rather fast pace, the eye will perceive the illusion of a moving line.

In motion pictures, persistence of vision is used to create the illusion of motion from still photographs. By means of a shutter that opens and closes at high speed, the motion-picture camera photographs a series of still images. Because the time lapse between images is normally 1/24 of a second in most cameras, the differences between images are small. The illusion of motion is provided by the projector, in which the film is moved past a light source at the same speed at which the images were photographed. Persistence of vision causes the separate images to be projected as a continuously moving scene. If there were no separations between images, the pictures would appear as a blur.

Q The word "still" in paragraph 3 is closest in meaning to:

(A) persistent (B) faster (C) silent (D) motionless

A (D)

文章中譯

所有的電影都是利用**移動幻覺**製作而成的，而這是因為人類有種叫做**視覺暫留**的**視覺認知**特性。眼睛停止注視**發光的影像**後，腦部還能**保留**影像的**印象** 1/16 到 1/10 秒左右；如果有某個物品的一系列圖片，以穩定的速度一張張迅速通過眼前，每一張圖片中物品的位置略微移動，代表連續動作中的各個階段，大腦就會將這些不同的圖片連在一起，創造出物體正在移動的幻覺。

有個簡單的方法可以證明移動幻覺，就是拿一疊紙，在每一張紙的右下角畫一條線，每一條線都往同一個方向略微傾斜一點點，然後**快速翻閱**這一疊紙，眼睛就會看到有一條線正在移動的幻覺。

電影就是利用視覺暫留的原理，透過**靜止的照片**創造出移動幻覺。藉由高速開關的遮光器，電影攝影機拍攝到一系列靜止的影像。大部分攝影機所拍攝到的影像的**時間間隔**通常是 1/24 秒，因此每一個影像的差異非常微小。然後由投影機製造出移動的幻覺，在投影機中，影片以和拍攝時同樣的速度通過光源。視覺暫留使得一張張分離的圖片**投影成連續移動的場景**。如果兩個影像之間沒有間隔，整部影片看起來會是一片模糊。

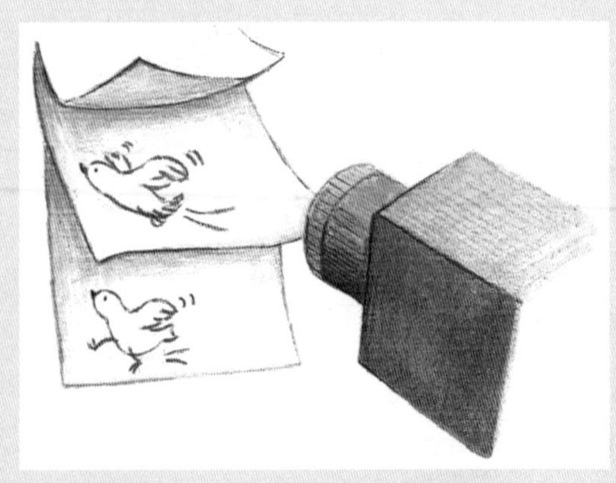

利用視覺暫留創造出移動的幻覺

Double-Check

- an illusion of motion — 移動幻覺
  [ɪ`luʒən]
- visual perception — 視覺認知
  [pə`sɛpʃən]
- persistence of vision — 視覺暫留
  [pə`sɪstəns]
- retain an impression — 保留印象
  [rɪ`ten]
- an illuminated image — 發光的影像
  [ɪ`luməˌnetɪd] [`ɪmɪdʒ]
- be riffled at a rather fast pace — 快速翻閱
  [`rɪfl̩d]
- still photographs — 靜止的照片
  [`fotəˌgræfs]
- the time lapse — 時間間隔
  參 lapse [læps] (n.)（時間的）流逝，間隔
- be projected as a continuously moving scene — 投影成連續移動的場景
  [kən`tɪnjuəslɪ]

Music

16 Origins of Jazz

爵士樂的起源

Key Sentences

1 Because of its spontaneous, emotional, and improvisational character, and because it is basically of black origin and association, jazz has to some extent not been accorded the degree of recognition it deserves.

因爲爵士樂具有**自發的**、**訴諸情感的**、**即興的特色**，再加上基本上是來自黑人，所以某種程度來說，爵士樂並沒有**獲得應有的認可**。

2 European audiences have often been more receptive to jazz, and thus many American jazz musicians have become expatriates.

歐洲聽眾通常**比較容易接受爵士樂**，因此許多美國爵士樂手就**成了旅居國外者**。

3 Jazz tended to suggest loose morals and low social status.

爵士樂往往暗示著**不講究道德**、**社會地位低下**。

4 Show tunes became common vehicles for performance, and, while the results were exquisite, rhythmic and harmonic developments were impeded until the mid-1940s.

百老匯歌曲變成**表演的固定曲目**，雖然演出成果很精緻，但直到 1940 年代中期之前，**節奏及和聲的發展**卻也因此**受到阻礙**。

5 The vocal and instrumental aspects of the blues were and are a vital component of jazz.

藍調音樂中的人聲和樂器等元素不論在過去或現在都是**爵士樂不可或缺的成分**。

Reading Focus 242字

MP3 033

Jazz developed in the latter part of the 19th century from black work songs, field hollers, hymns, and spirituals whose harmonic, rhythmic, and melodic elements were predominantly African. Because of its spontaneous, emotional, and improvisational character, and because it is basically of black origin and association, jazz has to some extent not been accorded the degree of recognition it deserves. European audiences have often been more receptive to jazz, and thus many American jazz musicians have become expatriates.

At the outset, jazz was slow to win acceptance by the general public, not only because of its cultural origin, but also because it tended to suggest loose morals and low social status. However, jazz gained wide acceptance when white orchestras adapted or imitated it, and it became legitimate entertainment in the late 1930s when Benny Goodman led racially mixed groups in concerts at Carnegie Hall. Show tunes became common vehicles for performance, and, while the results were exquisite, rhythmic and harmonic developments were impeded until the mid-1940s.

Jazz is generally thought to have begun in New Orleans, and then spread to Chicago, Kansas City, New York City, and the West Coast. The vocal and instrumental aspects of the blues were and are a vital component of jazz, which includes, roughly in order of appearance: ragtime; New Orleans or Dixieland jazz; swing; bop or bebop; progressive or cool jazz; neo-bop or hard-bop; third stream; mainstream modern; Latin-jazz; jazz-rock; and avant-garde or free jazz.

（來源：Infoplease.com）

文章中譯

爵士樂起源於 19 世紀下半葉，源自黑人的工作歌、田野上的吶喊、聖歌和靈歌，其和聲、節奏、旋律主要都是非洲風格。因爲爵士樂具有**自發的**、**訴諸情感的**、**即興的特色**，再加上基本上是來自黑人，所以某種程度來說，爵士樂並沒有**獲得應有的認可**。歐洲聽眾通常**比較容易接受爵士樂**，因此許多美國爵士樂手就**成了旅居國外者**。

一開始，爵士樂很慢才獲得一般民眾的接受，不只因爲其文化起源，也因爲它往往暗示著**不講究道德**、**社會地位低下**。不過，等到有白人樂團改編或模仿爵士樂後，爵士樂便廣爲大眾接受。而在 1930 年代後期，班尼．古德曼帶領了一支融合不同種族成員的樂團在卡內基廳登場表演後，爵士樂從此成爲正當娛樂。百老匯歌曲變成**表演的固定曲目**，雖然演出成果很精緻，但直到 1940 年代中期之前，**節奏及和聲的發展**卻也因此**受到阻礙**。

一般認爲爵士樂是從紐奧良開始，然後傳到芝加哥、堪薩斯市、紐約市以及西岸。藍調音樂中的人聲和樂器等元素不論在過去或現在都是**爵士樂不可或缺的成分**，爵士樂的流派依出現的順序大致分爲：散拍爵士、紐奧良爵士樂或狄西蘭爵士樂、搖擺、咆勃、激進爵士或酷派爵士、新咆勃或硬式咆勃、第三流派爵士、主流現代爵士、拉丁爵士、爵士搖滾、前衛或自由爵士。

Double-Check

- spontaneous, emotional, and improvisational character 自發的、訴諸情感的、即興的特色
  [spɑn`tenɪəs] [ˌɪmprəvaɪ`zeʃənl]
  參 improvisation [ˌɪmprəvaɪ`zeʃən] (n.) 即興演出
  improvise [`ɪmprəˌvaɪz] (v.) 即興創作、表演

- be accorded the degree of recognition it deserves 獲得應有的認可
  參 accord [ə`kɔrd] (v.) 給予，贈予

- more receptive to jazz 比較容易接受爵士樂
  [rɪ`sɛptɪv]

- become expatriates 變成旅居國外者
  [ɛks`petrɪˌets]

- loose morals and low social status 不講究道德、社會地位低下
  [`stetəs]
  參 loose [lus] (adj.) 鬆散的；放蕩的

- common vehicles for performance 表演的固定曲目
  參 vehicle [`viɪkl] (n.) 曲目

- rhythmic and harmonic developments were impeded 節奏及和聲的發展受到阻礙
  [`rɪðmɪk] [hɑr`mɑnɪk]
  參 impede [ɪm`pid] (v.) 阻礙，妨礙

- a vital component of jazz 爵士樂不可或缺的成分
  [`vaɪtl] [kəm`ponənt]

Journalism

17 Newspapers
報紙

Key Sentences

MP3 034

1 With the advent of radio and television in the 20th century, the use of the term has broadened.

隨著廣播與電視在 20 世紀**問世**，這個詞彙的涵義也隨之擴大。

2 In China during the Tang dynasty a court circular called a bao, or "report," was issued to government officials.

在中國的唐代，有一份**發給朝廷官員**傳閱的刊物叫做《報》(也就是「報導」)。

3 At first hindered by government-imposed censorship, restrictions, and taxes, newspapers in the 18th century came to enjoy the reportorial freedom and indispensable function.

報業一開始**受到政府強加的審查**、限制、稅賦等等**阻礙**，到了 18 世紀開始享有報導自由，也才成爲**不可或缺的角色**。

4 The growing demand for newspapers owing to the spread of literacy and the introduction of steam-driven and then electric-driven presses caused the daily circulation of newspapers to rise from the thousands to the hundreds of thousands and eventually to millions.

由於**識字率普及**，再加上蒸氣印刷機和**電動印刷機**先後問世，報紙需求日益增加，使得每日發行量從數千份成長到數十萬份，最後高達數百萬份。

Reading Focus 231字

MP3 035

The word journalism was originally applied to the reportage of current events in printed form, specifically newspapers, but with the advent of radio and television in the 20th century, the use of the term has broadened to include all printed and electronic communication dealing with current affairs.

The earliest known journalistic product was a newssheet circulated in ancient Rome called the *Acta Diurna*. Published daily from 59 BC, it was hung in prominent places and recorded important social and political events. In China during the Tang dynasty a court circular called a bao, or "report," was issued to government officials. This gazette appeared in various forms and under various names more or less continually until the end of the Ching dynasty in 1911. The first regularly published newspapers appeared in German cities and in Antwerp around 1609. The first English newspaper, *the Weekly News*, was published in 1622. One of the first daily newspapers, *The Daily Courant*, appeared in 1702.

At first hindered by government-imposed censorship, restrictions, and taxes, newspapers in the 18th century came to enjoy the reportorial freedom and indispensable function that they have retained to the present day. The growing demand for newspapers owing to the spread of literacy and the introduction of steam-driven and then electric-driven presses caused the daily circulation of newspapers to rise from the thousands to the hundreds of thousands and eventually to millions.

! current的發音有時候不容易辨識，要特別注意。

文章中譯

「新聞」一詞最初是指平面印刷的時事報導，特別是報紙，不過**隨著廣播與電視**在 20 世紀**問世**，這個詞彙的涵義也隨之擴大，所有報導時事的印刷與電子傳播都涵蓋在內。

目前所知最早的新聞產品是古羅馬時代發行的單張消息紙，名為《每日紀聞》，從西元前 59 年開始每日出刊，貼在醒目的地方，記錄重要的社會與政治事件。在中國的唐代，有一份**發給朝廷官員**傳閱的刊物叫做《報》（也就是「報導」）。這份公報出現過多種不同格式，也換過幾個名稱，斷斷續續出刊直到 1911 年清朝結束為止。定期出刊的報紙大約在 1609 年最先出現於德國各城市和（比利時）安特衛普市。第一份英文報紙《每週新聞》於 1622 年出刊。首創日報先河之一的《每日新聞》則是於 1702 年問世。

報業一開始**受到政府強加的審查**、限制、稅賦等等**阻礙**，到了 18 世紀開始享有報導自由，也才成為**不可或缺的角色**，一直到今日。由於**識字率普及**，再加上蒸氣印刷機和**電動印刷機**先後問世，報紙需求日益增加，使得每日發行量從數千份成長到數十萬份，最後高達數百萬份。

Double-Check

- with the advent of radio and television　　隨著廣播與電視問世

  參 advent [ˋædvɛnt] (n.) 出現

- a court circular [ˋsɝkjələ]　　在朝廷內傳閱的刊物

- be issued to government officials [ˋɪʃʊd]　　發給朝廷官員

- be hindered by government-imposed censorship [ɪmˋpozd] [ˋsɛnsəˏʃɪp]　　受到政府強加的審查阻礙

  參 hinder [ˋhɪndə] (v.) 阻撓，阻礙 (= prevent/keep)

- indispensable function [ˏɪndɪsˋpɛnsəbl̩]　　不可或缺的角色

- the spread of literacy [sprɛd]　　識字率普及

  參 literacy [ˋlɪtərəsɪ] (n.) 識字，讀寫能力

- electric-driven presses [ˋdrɪvən]　　電動印刷機

Law

18 Changing a Constitution
修憲

Key Sentences

MP3 036

1 Processes of amending a constitution are normally provided for in the document itself.

憲法本身通常有涵蓋**修憲的程序**。

2 The amendment process is time-consuming and cumbersome.

修憲過程**耗時又繁瑣**。

3 The fundamental law of the land is not easily subject to the whims of special-interest groups.

這部國家基本大法並不會輕易隨著**特殊利益團體一時興起的某些念頭**而改動。

4 Those constitutions having lengthy sections of what amounts to statute law are subject to frequent amendment.

那些有著長篇**成文法**的憲法就容易遭到修改。

5 The statute represented the desires of a substantial faction of the American population at the time.

這條法令反映了當時**相當多數**美國人民**的期望**。

6 Prohibition was repealed, or withdrawn, by the 21st Amendment in 1933.

到了 1933 年，根據憲法第 21 條修正案將禁酒法令加以**廢除**（或說**撤銷**）。

! prohibition 的 h 不發音，唸成 [ˌproəˋbɪʃən]，要特別注意。

Reading Focus 244字

MP3 037

Processes of amending or changing a constitution are normally provided for in the document itself. The United States Constitution has only been amended 26 times since it went into effect in 1789, and ten of those amendments consist of the Bill of Rights that was added in 1791. Because the amendment process is time-consuming and cumbersome, the fundamental law of the land is not easily subject to the whims of special-interest groups, factions, or even the majority of the population at any given time.

The shorter and more basic a constitution is, the less likely it is to be changed. The most successful constitutions confine themselves primarily to the procedures of government. By contrast, those constitutions having lengthy sections of what amounts to statute law are subject to frequent amendment. If a constitution embodies, for example, provisions that guarantee full employment, housing, or college education, it may fail if the government is unable to live up to these promises.

It was just this type of situation that led to the one failed experiment in the United States Constitution. The 18th, or Prohibition Amendment was added in 1919. It was a law prohibiting the manufacture and sale of alcoholic beverages. The statute represented the desires of a substantial faction of the American population at the time. But it proved unenforceable and failed miserably because too many people disliked it and refused to obey it. It was repealed, or withdrawn, by the 21st Amendment in 1933.

文章中譯

憲法本身通常有涵蓋**修憲**（或更改憲法）**的程序**。美國憲法自從 1789 年實施以來只修改過 26 次，而且其中 10 次是跟 1791 年增加的《人權法案》有關。因爲修憲過程**耗時又繁瑣**，這部國家基本大法並不會輕易隨時隨著**特殊利益團體**、黨派甚至絕大多數人民**一時興起的某些念頭**而改動。

憲法愈是簡短、基本，就愈不可能修改。最成功的憲法主要侷限於政府相關法規，對照之下，那些有著長篇**成文法**的憲法就容易遭到修改。舉例來說，如果有一部憲法明文規定要保障充分就業、有房子可住、接受大學教育，要是政府無力達成這些承諾，這部憲法就失敗了。

美國憲法過去就曾出現這種失敗的例子。1919 年增加了第 18 條修正案（或稱禁酒法令），禁止酒精類飲料的製造與販售。**這條法令反映了**當時**相當多數**美國人民**的期望**，但最後卻無法執行，以慘敗收場，因爲有太多人不喜歡而不願遵守。到了 1933 年，根據憲法第 21 條修正案將這條法令加以**廢除**（或說**撤銷**）。

Double-Check

■ processes of amending a constitution [͵kanstə`tjuʃən] 參 amend [ə`mɛnd] (v.) 修改，修正	修憲的程序
■ time-consuming and cumbersome [kən`sumɪŋ] 參 cumbersome [`kʌmbəsəm] (adj.) 麻煩的，繁瑣的	耗時又繁瑣
■ the whims of special-interest groups [hwɪmz]	特殊利益團體一時興起的某些念頭
■ statute law [`stætʃut]	成文法
■ The statute represented the desires.	這條法令反映了期望。
■ substantial [səb`stænʃəl]	(adj.) 多的，大量的
■ faction [`fækʃən]	(n.) 小集團
■ repeal [rɪ`pil]	(v.) 廢除（法令）
■ withdraw [wɪð`drɔ]	(v.) 撤銷，撤回

Criminology

19 Correction
犯罪懲治

Key Sentences

MP3 038

1 A major interest of criminologists is correction.

犯罪學者主要關心的一個議題就是懲治。

2 Until well into the 19th century, penalties consisted primarily of public humiliation, beatings or torture, banishment or exile, death, fines, or confiscation of property.

直到 19 世紀中，刑罰主要包括**當衆羞辱**、鞭打、拷問、流放邊疆或是驅逐出境、死刑、罰款或是**沒收財產**。

3 Imprisonment as a penalty became common after the 16th century but only for lesser offenses.

16 世紀之後，**監禁**成爲**一種**普遍的**刑罰**，但是只適用於**比較輕微的犯罪**。

4 Probably the most significant correctional developments of the late 19th century were probation and parole.

19 世紀後期懲治制度上最重要的發展，或許可以說是**緩刑和假釋**。

5 Under probation the sentence of a selected convicted criminal is suspended.

根據緩刑規定，**特定的犯人**可以延緩**執行刑罰**。

6 Parole involves conditional release from confinement after part of a sentence has already been served.

假釋是在受刑人已經服滿部分刑期後，**有條件釋放**受刑人。

Reading Focus 224字

MP3 039

A major interest of criminologists is correction: what should be done with the criminal once he has been caught, tried, and convicted. Until well into the 19th century, penalties consisted primarily of public humiliation, beatings or torture, banishment or exile, death, fines, or confiscation of property. Imprisonment as a penalty became common after the 16th century but only for lesser offenses.

Not until the late 19th century did imprisonment become the most common penalty for most crimes. This resulted in great part from the work of criminologists who persuaded society against the uselessness of other punishments. Gradually the purpose of imprisonment began to shift from confinement to attempts to turn prisoners away from the life of crime when they were released. Prisons for young offenders, the first of which was established at Elmira, N.Y. in 1876, were called reformatories. They gave greater emphasis to education for their inmates.

Probably the most significant correctional developments of the late 19th century were probation and parole. Under probation the sentence of a selected convicted criminal is suspended if the criminal promises to behave well, accept some supervision of his life, and meet certain specific requirements. Parole involves conditional release from confinement after part of a sentence has already been served. It is granted only if the prisoner seems to have changed into an honest and trustworthy person.

Q The word "criminal" in paragraph 1 is closest in meaning to:
(A) reformatory (B) offender (C) inmate (D) probation

A (B)

文章中譯

犯罪學者主要關心的一個議題就是懲治：也就是罪犯被逮捕、審判和定罪後，我們應該對他做些什麼。直到 19 世紀中，刑罰主要包括**當衆羞辱**、鞭打、拷問、流放邊疆或是驅逐出境、死刑、罰款或是**沒收財產**。16 世紀之後，**監禁**成爲**一種**普遍的**刑罰**，但是只適用於**比較輕微的犯罪**。

一直要到 19 世紀末，監禁才變成大部分犯罪最普遍的刑罰方式。這項轉變主要歸因於犯罪學者的努力，他們說服社會大衆反對其他無用的懲罰。漸漸地，監禁的目的從限制罪犯行動轉變成希望受刑人釋放後可以遠離犯罪的生活。爲年少的犯罪者所設立的監獄稱爲少年感化院，最早設立於 1876 年，地點在紐約州的艾米拉。少年感化院非常強調對少年犯的教育。

19 世紀後期懲治制度上最重要的發展，或許可以說是**緩刑和假釋**。根據緩刑規定，**特定的犯人**如果承諾表現良好，同意接受一些生活上的監管，並且符合某些特定要求，即可以延緩**執行刑罰**。假釋則是在受刑人已經服滿部分刑期後，**有條件釋放**受刑人。但唯有在受刑人看似已變得誠實並且值得信賴才得給予假釋。

Double-Check

- a major interest of criminologists [ˌkrɪməˋnɑlədʒɪsts] — 犯罪學者主要關心的一個議題
- correction [kəˋrɛkʃən] — (n.) 懲治
- public humiliation [hjuˌmɪlɪˋeʃən] — 當衆羞辱
- confiscation of property [ˌkɑnfɪsˋkeʃən] [ˋprɑpətɪ] — 沒收財產
- imprisonment as a penalty [ɪmˋprɪzn̩mənt] [ˋpɛnl̩tɪ] — 以監禁爲刑罰
- lesser offenses [ˋlɛsɚ] [əˋfɛnsɪz] — 比較輕微的犯罪
- prisons for young offenders [əˋfɛndɚz] — 爲年少的犯罪者所設立的監獄
- reformatory [rɪˋfɔrməˌtorɪ] — (n.) 少年感化院
- education for their inmates [ˋɪnmets] — 對囚犯的教育
- probation and parole [proˋbeʃən] [pəˋrol] — 緩刑和假釋
- the sentence of a selected convicted criminal [kənˋvɪktɪd] — 對特定犯人的刑罰
- conditional release from confinement [kənˋfaɪnmənt] — 有條件釋放

Linguistics

20 Animal Communication and Human Language 動物的溝通方式與人類語言

Key Sentences

MP3 040

1. Animals cannot communicate about abstract concepts.

動物無法傳遞**抽象的概念**。

2. Animals cannot "talk" about objects that are not in their immediate environment.

動物不能「談論」不在**當下環境**中的東西。

3. Their communication apparatus is limited to simple gestures.

牠們的**溝通機制**限於簡單的姿勢。

4. Animal communication systems are genetically inherited.

動物的溝通系統**由基因遺傳而來**。

5. Social interaction is fundamental to human language.

社會互動是人類語言的基礎。

6. Our language is defined and controlled by the community.

我們的語言是**由社群所界定與掌控**。

Reading Focus 208字

MP3 041

Apes, chimpanzees, and dolphins seem capable of communicating with one another; however, their communication systems are very simple. They cannot communicate about abstract concepts and ideas or "talk" about objects that are not in their immediate environment. Their communication apparatus is limited to simple gestures and a very limited range of vocal utterances that vary primarily in pitch and volume. On the other hand, human speech is built up from a variety of units which, loosely speaking, correspond to vowel and consonant sounds. While animal communication systems are genetically inherited, this is not true of human language. At birth, humans are programmed to learn language: the ability to learn is genetically inherited. However, language itself is learned from interaction with individuals in society. If a child were raised in an environment where language was never used, that child would never learn a language. Fortunately children are brought up in a language-rich environment, and they quickly acquire language skills.

Social interaction is fundamental to human language. More precisely, our language is socially dependent and conventional. This means that our language is defined and controlled by the community in which we live; speakers within our language community accept a system of rules, called grammar, which governs our language.

Q Look at the word "this" in paragraph 1. Find out the word or phrase in paragraph 1 that "this" refers to.

A communication systems are genetically inherited

文章中譯

人猿、黑猩猩、海豚似乎能夠和同類溝通；但是牠們的溝通系統非常簡單。牠們無法傳遞**抽象的概念**、想法，也不能「談論」不在**當下環境**中的東西。牠們的**溝通機制**限於簡單的姿勢以及非常有限的發音，主要是靠改變音調和音量來表示。另一方面，人類的話語是由許多不同的組合成分建構而成，以鬆散的標準來看，這些成分可分爲母音和子音。雖然動物的溝通系統**由基因遺傳而來**，人類語言卻不是這樣。人類在出生時，就已經設定好要學習語言：這種學習能力是基因遺傳而來的。然而，語言本身卻是透過與社會中的個體互動而習得。如果有個小孩生長在完全不使用語言的環境，這個小孩就永遠無法習得語言。幸運的是，孩子都在語言豐富的環境中成長，很快就習得了語言技巧。

社會互動是人類語言的基礎。更準確地說，我們的語言取決於社會環境，是約定俗成的。這表示我們的語言是**由**我們所生存的**社群所界定與掌控**，同一個語言社群中的說話者接受同一套規則系統，也就是主宰語言的文法。

Double-Check

- abstract concepts 抽象的概念
  [ˋæbstrækt]
- immediate environment 當下環境
  參 immediate [ɪˋmidɪɪt] (adj.) 當前的，當下的
- communication apparatus 溝通機制
  [ˌæpəˋretəs]
- a very limited range of vocal utterances 非常有限的發音
  [ˋʌtərənsɪz]
  參 utter [ˋʌtɚ] (v.) 發出聲音，說
- loosely speaking 以鬆散的標準來看
  [ˋluslɪ]
  參 loose [lus] (adj.) 鬆散的
- be genetically inherited 由基因遺傳而來
  [ɪnˋhɛrɪtɪd]
- true of human language 人類語言是這樣
- raise (v.) 養育 (= bring up/rear)
  [rez]
- acquire language skills 習得語言技巧
  [əˋkwaɪr]
  參 acquired [əˋkwaɪrd] (adj.) 習得的，後天的
- social interaction 社會互動
  [ˌɪntɚˋækʃən]
- conventional (adj.) 按習俗的，傳統的
  [kənˋvɛnʃənl̩]
  參 convention [kənˋvɛnʃən] (n.) 習俗，協定
- define (v.) 界定，下定義
  [dɪˋfaɪn]
  參 definition [ˌdɛfəˋnɪʃən] (n.) 定義

Linguistics

21 Language Acquisition by Children

兒童語言習得

Key Sentences

MP3 042

1 No psychological theory of learning, as currently formulated, is capable of accounting for the process.

在**現今有系統的**心理學理論中，沒有任何學習理論能解釋這個過程。

2 Research on language acquisition has been strongly influenced by Chomsky's theory of generative grammar.

語言習得的研究深受喬姆斯基的**生成語法**理論所影響。

3 It is possible for young children to infer the grammatical rules underlying the speech.

幼兒能夠從話語中**推論出**潛藏的**文法規則**。

4 It is this innate knowledge that explains the success and speed of language acquisition.

正是因爲擁有這種**與生俱來的知識**，才能成功且迅速地習得語言。

5 It is not grammatical competence as such that is innate but more general cognitive principles.

與其說人類天生具有文法能力，不如說是具有一般性的**認知原則**。

6 The basic semantic categories and grammatical functions can be found in the earliest speech of children.

在兒童早期所說的話裡可以發現基本**語意類型**與文法**功能**。

Reading Focus 269字

MP3 043

One of the topics most central to psycholinguistic research is the acquisition of language by children. The term acquisition is preferred to "learning," because many psycholinguists believe that no psychological theory of learning, as currently formulated, is capable of accounting for the process whereby children, in a relatively short time, come to achieve a fluent control of their native language.

Since the beginning of the 1960s, research on language acquisition has been strongly influenced by Chomsky's theory of generative grammar, and the main problem to which it has addressed itself has been how it is possible for young children to infer the grammatical rules underlying the speech they hear and then to use these rules for the construction of utterances that they have never heard before. It is Chomsky's conviction, shared by a number of psycholinguists, that children are born with a knowledge of the formal principles that determine the grammatical structure of all languages, and that it is this innate knowledge that explains the success and speed of language acquisition. Others have argued that it is not grammatical competence as such that is innate but more general cognitive principles and that the application of these to language utterances in particular situations ultimately yields grammatical competence.

Many recent works have stressed that all children go through the same stages of language development regardless of the language they are acquiring. It has also been asserted that the same basic semantic categories and grammatical functions can be found in the earliest speech of children in a number of different languages operating in quite different cultures in various parts of the world.

文章中譯

心理語言學研究最重要的課題之一就是兒童語言習得。習得這個詞彙比「學習」好，因爲許多心理語言學家相信，在**現今有系統的**心理學理論中，沒有任何學習理論能解釋爲何兒童能夠在相當短的時間內流利掌控母語的過程。

從 1960 年代初期起，**語言習得**的研究就深受喬姆斯基的**生成語法**理論所影響。生成語法理論所探討的主要問題，是幼兒如何從聽見的話語中**推論出**潛藏的**文法規則**，然後用這些文法規則建構出他們以前從沒聽過的發音。喬姆斯基和許多心理語言學家確信，兒童生來就具有語言形式原則的相關知識，這些原則決定了所有語言的文法結構。正是因爲擁有這種**與生俱來的知識**，兒童才能成功且迅速地習得語言。有些人卻認爲，與其說人類天生具有文法能力，不如說是具有一般性的**認知原則**，因爲在特定的情境下將這些原則運用於語言表達上，最後才產生了文法能力。

近來許多研究強調，不管習得的是何種語言，所有的兒童都經歷同樣的語言發展階段。也有一種說法是，世界各地不同文化所使用的各種語言中，在兒童早期所說的話裡可以發現同樣的基本**語意類型**與文法**功能**。

Double-Check

- currently formulated 現今有系統的
  [ˋkɜəntlɪ]
  參 formulate [ˋfɔrmjəˌlet] (v.) 有系統地說明、闡述

- language acquisition 語言習得
  參 acquisition [ˌækwəˋzɪʃən] (n.) 習得 (= acquirement)，獲得

- generative grammar 生成語法
  [ˋdʒɛnərətɪv]

- infer the grammatical rules 推論出文法規則
  [ɪnˋfɜ]

- the construction of utterances 建構出發音
  [kənˋstrʌkʃən]
  參 utter [ˋʌtɚ] (v.) 發出聲音，說

- Chomsky's conviction 喬姆斯基確信
  [kənˋvɪkʃən]

- innate knowledge 與生俱來的知識
  [ɪˋnet]

- cognitive principles 認知原則
  [ˋkɑgnətɪv]

- semantic categories 語意類型
  [səˋmæntɪk]

- function (n.) 功能
  [ˋfʌŋkʃən]

Architecture

22 Roman Arch

羅馬拱橋

Key Sentences

MP3 044

1 One architectural feature Rome perfected is the arch.

羅馬人擅長的一項建築特色是拱橋。

2 Roman arches are comprised of several parts such as a keystone, a voussoir, and a pier.

羅馬拱橋**包含好幾個部分**，例如基石、拱石、橋墩。

3 Its name "keystone" comes from its importance: without it, the arch would collapse.

「基石」這個名稱取自其重要性：要是少了它，**拱橋就會垮下來**。

4 The keystone is surrounded on each side by voussoirs, or wedge-shaped bricks or stones.

基石的**兩側皆有拱石**，又稱楔形磚或楔形石。

5 The thrust of the voussoirs pushes outward and downward in a Roman arch.

羅馬式的拱橋中，**拱石的推力**會向外、向下擠壓。

6 The use of voussoirs creates arches, which can be used to span large distances and bear heavy loads.

使用拱石可以打造出能**橫跨長距離**並可承受極大重量的拱橋。

7 A Roman arch's pier is the wall or stone on which the arch rests.

羅馬拱橋的橋墩是支撐拱橋的那面牆或那塊石頭。

Reading Focus 259字

MP3 045

Ancient Rome greatly influenced architecture, and continues as a major influence even today. One architectural feature Rome perfected is the arch. Romans did not invent the arch, but they greatly expanded its use and designed arches that could support massive amounts of weight. Roman arches are comprised of several parts such as a keystone, a voussoir, and a pier.

The keystone, or capstone, is the center stone found at the top of the arch. In this position it supports the surrounding bricks or stones and helps distribute the weight of the remainder of the arch. Its name "keystone" comes from its importance: without it, the arch would collapse. Romans were the first to use keystones in their arches.

The keystone is surrounded on each side by voussoirs, or wedge-shaped bricks or stones. The term voussoir comes from French and Latin roots meaning "to turn." The thrust of the voussoirs pushes outward and downward in a Roman arch. Roman arches are noted for their semi-circular, non-pointed curves. The use of voussoirs creates arches, which can be used to span large distances and bear heavy loads. An example of this can be seen in the arches used in construction of ancient Roman aqueducts, many of which still stand today.

The keystone and voussoirs of an arch need a base on which to rest. These bases are called piers. A Roman arch's pier is the wall or stone on which the arch rests. Concrete and stones were often used in the construction of piers, which are usually square or rectangular in shape.

（來源：ehow.com）

文章中譯

古羅馬對建築的影響很大，影響的深遠程度甚至持續至今日。**羅馬人擅長的一項建築特色**是拱橋。拱橋並不是羅馬人發明的，但羅馬人大大拓展了它的用途，並將拱橋設計成可以支撐極大重量。羅馬拱橋**包含好幾個部分**，例如基石、拱石、橋墩。

基石（或稱頂石）是拱橋頂端中央的那塊石頭。在這個位置上，它可以支撐旁邊的磚塊或石頭，並將拱橋其他部分的重量分散出去。「基石」這個名稱取自其重要性：要是少了它，**拱橋就會垮下來**。最早將基石用於拱橋的就是羅馬人。

基石的**兩側皆有拱石**，又稱楔形磚或楔形石。拱石一詞源自法文和拉丁文的字根，意指「轉彎」。羅馬式的拱橋中，**拱石的推力**會向外、向下擠壓。羅馬拱橋以沒有尖頂的半圓弧形聞名，使用拱石可以打造出能**橫跨長距離**並可承受極大重量的拱橋，古羅馬水道橋的拱橋就是一例，許多水道橋至今仍屹立不搖。

拱橋的基石和拱石需要有個基座來支撐，這些基座稱為橋墩。**羅馬拱橋的橋墩**是支撐拱橋的那面牆或那塊石頭。橋墩通常是用混凝土或石頭建造而成，而且通常是正方形或長方形的。

Double-Check

- one architectural feature Rome perfected 羅馬人擅長的一項建築特色
  [ˌarkəˋtɛktʃərəl]

- be comprised of several parts 包含好幾個部分
  參 comprise [kəmˋpraɪz] (v.) 包含，包括

- the arch would collapse 拱橋會垮下來
  [artʃ] [kəˋlæps]

- be surrounded on each side by voussoirs 兩側有拱石
  [vuˋswarz]

- the thrust of the voussoirs 拱石的推力
  [θrʌst]

- span large distances 橫跨長距離
  參 span [spæn] (v.) 橫跨，跨越

- a Roman arch's pier 羅馬拱橋的橋墩
  [pɪr]

Art

23 Romanticism
浪漫主義

Key Sentences

MP3 046

1 Romanticism started as a reaction against the perceived strictures of the preceding age.

浪漫主義運動的開始，是對前一個世代所約束的部分進行反動。

2 In this case, early romantic writers wished to move away from the philosophical formalism of the neoclassical age.

就浪漫主義運動而言，早期浪漫主義的作家希望能夠遠離新古典主義時代的形式主義。

3 Theology reestablished the place of humans within a completely untamed natural world.

神學重建了人類在完全未開化的自然世界中的地位。

4 Transcendentalism was taking its place as a serious philosophical stance.

超越主義身爲正統哲學的地位正在逐漸確立。

5 The basic premise resides in the realization that neither theism nor deism can adequately answer the burning question of man's relationship with God.

基本前提在於體認到，不論是一神論或自然神論都無法充分解釋人神關係這個熱門的問題。

6 Transcendentalists chose a form of pantheism to articulate their view of the universe.

超越主義者選擇以一種泛神論的形式表達他們對宇宙的觀感。

Reading Focus 256字

MP3 047

Like many literary and artistic movements, Romanticism started as a reaction against the perceived strictures of the preceding age. In this case, early romantic writers wished to move away from the philosophical formalism of the neoclassical age. Man's relation to the natural world was reestablished while the basis of philosophy began to shift toward what would later be called Transcendentalism, the belief system that places God back in nature.

Landscape art, gardening, music, even theology reestablished the place of humans within a completely untamed natural world. The emphasis in all areas of creative endeavor was in the reliance upon emotions and the natural senses while placing humans in a new Eden.

Critics and historians now look back upon the years between 1850 and 1855 as the American Renaissance, primarily due to the fact that so many writers of pivotal importance were busily recording their world at the time: Emerson, Thoreau, Melville, Hawthorne, and others. Moreover, Transcendentalism was taking its place as a serious philosophical stance. Beginning in the Far East and traveling through Europe, Transcendentalism finally found its way to America through the writings of Ralph Waldo Emerson and Henry David Thoreau. The basic premise resides in the realization that neither theism nor deism can adequately answer the burning question of man's relationship with God. Instead, Transcendentalists chose a form of pantheism to articulate their view of the universe. The major group of Transcendentalists comprised young intellectuals in the Boston area who were, for the most part, concerned with the theology of the liberal Unitarian church.

文章中譯

如同許多文學與藝術運動，**浪漫主義運動**的開始，是**對前一個世代所約束的部分進行反動**。就浪漫主義運動而言，早期浪漫主義的作家希望能夠遠離**新古典主義時代的形式主義**。人與自然世界的關係重新建構，同時哲學的基礎開始轉向後來大家所稱的超越主義，也就是將上帝置於自然之中的信仰系統。

風景畫、園藝、音樂，甚至**神學**，重建了人類在**完全未開化的自然世界**中的地位。所有創造領域所強調的重點，就是追隨情感與自然的感官知覺，把人類置於新的伊甸園中。

現在批評家與歷史學家回顧過去，把 1850 到 1855 年這段時間稱爲美國文藝復興時期，主要是因爲有太多重量級作家在這段期間忙著記錄自己的世界：包括愛默生、梭羅、梅爾維爾、霍桑以及其他人。此外，**超越主義**身爲**正統哲學的地位**正在逐漸確立。從遠東開始，穿越歐洲，超越主義透過愛默生與梭羅之筆，終於打進了美國世界。超越主義的**基本前提，在於體認到不論是一神論或自然神論都無法**充分解釋人神關係這個熱門的問題。超越主義者選擇以**一種泛神論的形式表達他們對宇宙的觀感**。超越主義最重要的學派由波士頓地區的年輕知識分子構成，他們主要關切的還是神體一位論自由主義教派的神學思想。

Double-Check

- Romanticism [ro`mæntə͵sɪzm̩] — (n.) 浪漫主義，浪漫主義運動
- a reaction against the perceived strictures [pɚ`sivd] [`strɪktʃɚz] — 對被約束的部分進行反動
- the preceding age [pri`sidɪŋ] — 前一個世代
- the philosophical formalism of the neoclassical age [͵fɪlə`sɑfɪkl̩] [`fɔrml̩͵ɪzm̩] [͵nio`klæsɪkl̩] — 新古典主義時代的形式主義
- theology [θɪ`ɑlədʒɪ] — (n.) 神學
- a completely untamed natural world [ʌn`temd] — 完全未開化的自然世界
- Transcendentalism [͵trænsɛn`dɛntə͵lɪzm̩] — (n.) 超越主義
- a serious philosophical stance [stæns] — 正統哲學的地位
- The basic premise resides in the realization... [`prɛmɪs] [rɪ`zaɪdz] [͵riələ`zeʃən] — 基本前提在於體認……
- neither theism nor deism [`θiɪzm̩] [`diɪzm̩] — 不論是一神論或自然神論都無法
- pantheism [`pænθi͵ɪzm̩] — (n.) 泛神論
- articulate their view of the universe [ɑr`tɪkjə͵let] — 表達他們對宇宙的觀感

Art

24 Imitation and Expression

模仿與表現

Key Sentences

MP3 048

1 The movement away from art as imitation, or representation, probably started in France with the work of the impressionists in the 19th century.

脫離**模仿藝術（或稱為「再現」）**的運動大概從 19 世紀法國印象派的作品開始。

2 Such art can be said to express the inner life, imagination, or emotions of the artist. Or it may be art that refers to nothing at all—just pure abstraction for its own sake.

這種藝術可以說是表達了藝術家的內在生命、想像力或情感，或者也可以什麼都不是，只是**純粹為了抽象而抽象**。

3 Critics have contended, for instance, that all representational art is to some degree abstract.

舉例來說，**批評者強烈主張**所有的再現藝術某種程度也是抽象的。

4 While some features of its subject are emphasized, others are ignored or downplayed.

雖然畫作中強調了主繪物的部分特徵，但**其他部分被忽略或輕描淡寫了**。

5 The Gothic art of the Middle Ages was abstract to some degree in that it did not pretend to depict literal reality.

中世紀的歌德派藝術某種程度也是抽象的，它並沒有要**描繪現實**。

Reading Focus 248字

MP3 049

The movement away from art as imitation, or representation, probably started in France with the work of the impressionists in the 19th century. The word impressionist is itself suggestive. The artist is not just painting a representation, because the artwork is giving a personal impression of what is seen. The artist is not trying to be a photographic realist.

The late 19th and early 20th centuries, therefore, created a sharp break with all past understandings of art. A painting or a piece of sculpture no longer had to refer to something familiar. It could instead consist of only abstract lines, shapes, and colors. Such art can be said to express the inner life, imagination, or emotions of the artist. Or it may be art that refers to nothing at all—just pure abstraction for its own sake.

The theory of art as expression has generally replaced the belief of art as imitation. Critics have contended, for instance, that all representational art is to some degree abstract. While some features of its subject are emphasized, others are ignored or downplayed. The Gothic art of the Middle Ages was abstract to some degree in that it did not pretend to depict literal reality. It was intent on portraying religious symbolism, but the abstractions were not so removed from normal experience that they were not easily recognizable by the viewers. Abstract portraits of saints and depictions of events in the life of Jesus had become familiar to viewers through long-term association.

文章中譯

脫離**模仿藝術（或稱為「再現」）**的運動大概從 19 世紀法國印象派的作品開始。從印象主義一詞本身就看得出來，印象派藝術家並不只是模擬再現，因爲他們的藝術作品反映了藝術家眼中的個人印象。他們並不是要成爲逼眞的現實主義藝術家。

因此，19 世紀末到 20 世紀初跟過去所理解的藝術分道揚鑣。一幅畫作或一件雕塑不再非得指涉某個熟悉的事物，而是可以只由抽象的線條、形狀和顏色構成。這種藝術可以說是表達了藝術家的內在生命、想像力或情感，或者也可以什麼都不是，只是**純粹為了抽象而抽象**。

這種表現藝術的理論廣泛取代了把藝術視爲模仿的看法。舉例來說，**批評者強烈主張**所有的再現藝術某種程度也是抽象的。雖然畫作中強調了主繪物的部分特徵，但**其他部分被忽略或輕描淡寫了**。中世紀的歌德派藝術某種程度也是抽象的，它並沒有要**描繪現實**，而是要描繪宗教的象徵符號，不過這種抽象仍然不脫一般體驗，不至於令觀賞者看不懂。長期下來，聖人的抽象畫像以及耶穌生平事蹟的描繪，對觀賞者來說已經很熟悉。

Double-Check

- art as imitation, or representation　　模仿藝術，或稱爲「再現」
  參 representation [ˌrɛprɪzɛnˋteʃən] (n.) 再現

- pure abstraction for its own sake　　純粹爲了抽象而抽象
  [æbˋstrækʃən]

- critics have contended　　批評者強烈主張
  參 contend [kənˋtɛnd] (v.) 強烈主張

- representational art　　再現藝術
  [ˌrɛprɪzɛnˋteʃənl̩]

- others are ignored or downplayed　　其他部分被忽略或輕描淡寫
  [ˋdaʊnˌpled]

- depict literal reality　　描繪現實
  [dɪˋpɪkt][ˋlɪtərəl]

Literature

25 Emily Dickinson
艾蜜莉・狄金生

Key Sentences

MP3 050

1 Such compression makes her work aphoristic like Emerson's but also results in occasional obscurity.

這種壓縮使得她的作品像愛默生一樣具有警句的風格，但是偶爾也會變得晦澀難懂。

2 The language of the poems is precise, instantly expressive, and richly connotative.

詩作所使用的語言很精確，可立即傳達並具有豐富的義涵。

3 She delighted in such indirections as ambiguities, incongruities, paradoxes, and puns.

她喜歡間接迂迴的表達方式，例如模稜兩可、前後不一致、自相矛盾的陳述以及雙關語。

4 Her prosody, at first sight, seems the most derivative of her techniques, for her meters are essentially those of English hymns.

她寫詩的韻律，第一眼看來似乎是她的技巧中最缺乏獨創性的部分，因爲她所使用的格律本質上和英國讚美聖詩的格律相同。

5 She frequently abandoned exact for approximate rhymes.

她常常放棄完全相同的韻腳，改用近似的韻腳。

Reading Focus 259字

MP3 051

In that totality we call style, Emily Dickinson's poems were unique. No doubt influenced by her Yankee heritage, she squeezed worlds of meaning into the smallest space. Her longest poem extends to only fifty lines. Such compression makes her work aphoristic like Emerson's but also results in occasional obscurity. The language of the poems is precise, instantly expressive, and richly connotative. Like the Elizabethans, Dickinson not only exhibited a lust for all kinds of words but also took noticeable liberties with grammar. She delighted in such indirections as ambiguities, incongruities, paradoxes, and puns—a method well described in her poem "Tell All the Truth but Tell It Slant." Capitalization served her as a sort of underlining to emphasize any word she wished. For punctuation she used dashes with such abandon that her manuscripts have constantly frustrated their editors. Thomas H. Johnson and others even attribute a musical function to these dashes.

Her prosody, at first sight, seems the most derivative of her techniques, for her meters are essentially those of English hymns. In fact, most of her poems employ probably the best-known of all meters, the so-called common meter, used traditionally in ballads as well as hymns. Yet Dickinson never felt bound to these forms but experimented with them, sometimes mixing several meters in a single poem. Rhyme in her hands proved equally flexible and functional. She frequently abandoned exact for approximate rhymes. Although this freedom with rhyme invites comparison with such poets as Vaughan and Emerson, it is safe to say that Dickinson went the furthest in it.

文章中譯

從我們稱之爲風格的整體來看，艾蜜莉．狄金生的詩是獨一無二的。狄金生毫無疑問受到美國北方傳統的影響，把意義世界擠壓成最小的空間。她最長的詩作也僅僅延續了 50 行而已。**這種壓縮使得她的作品**像愛默生一樣**具有警句的風格**，但是**偶爾**也會變得**晦澀難懂**。詩作所使用的語言很精確，可立即傳達並具有**豐富的義涵**。和伊利莎白時代的英國人一樣，狄金生不僅展現了對各種字彙的強烈渴求，同時在文法上明顯表現得相當自由。她喜歡間接迂迴的表達方式，例如**模稜兩可**、**前後不一致**、**自相矛盾的陳述以及雙關語**——這種方法在她的詩作《只說眞話但別直說》中，發揮得最爲淋漓盡致。對她來說，大寫字母就像畫底線的作用一樣，可以用來強調任何她想強調的字。在標點符號上，她任意使用破折號，使得編輯總是對她的手稿感到相當頭痛。湯瑪斯．約翰森及其他人甚至認爲這些破折號具有音樂性的功能。

狄金生**寫詩的韻律**，第一眼看來似乎是**她的技巧中最缺乏獨創性的部分**，因爲她所使用的**格律**本質上和**英國讚美聖詩**的格律相同。事實上，她大部分的詩作採用的可能是所有格律中最爲人所知的所謂「普通調」，這是民謠和聖歌中習慣使用的格律。然而，狄金生從來不受這些形式的束縛，而是在形式上做實驗，有時會在一首詩中混合數種格律。韻腳在她的筆下顯得既有彈性又具有功能性。她常常放棄完全相同的韻腳，改用**近似的韻腳**。這種押韻上的自由使得狄金生常被拿來與別的詩人如沃恩、愛默生做比較，但是狄金生的韻律最爲自由這一點，卻是無庸置疑的。

Double-Check

- compression
  [kəm`prɛʃən] — (n.) 壓縮
- aphoristic
  [ˌæfə`rɪstɪk] — (adj.) 警句的
- occasional obscurity
  [ə`keʒənl] [əb`skjurətɪ] — 偶爾晦澀難懂
- connotative
  [`kɑnəˌtetɪv] — (adj.) 隱含意義的
- ambiguity
  [ˌæmbɪ`gjuətɪ] — (n.) 模稜兩可
- incongruity
  [ˌɪnkɑŋ`gruətɪ] — (n.) 前後不一致
- paradox
  [`pærəˌdɑks] — (n.) 自相矛盾
- pun
  [pʌn] — (n.) 雙關語
- with abandon
  [ə`bændən] — 任意，盡情
- prosody
  [`prɑsədɪ] — (n.) 韻律
- derivative
  [də`rɪvətɪv] — (adj.) 衍生的，無獨創性的
- meter
  [`mitɚ] — (n.)（詩的）格律
- English hymns
  [hɪmz] — 英國讚美聖詩
- approximate rhymes
  [ə`prɑksəmɪt] [raɪmz] — 近似的韻腳

Theater

26 Theatrical Music

戲劇音樂

Key Sentences

1 The secular theater in the Middle Ages established itself as deliberate parodies tolerated by the church as a safety valve to consistent piety.

中世紀的通俗劇成為教會容許的諷刺模仿劇，以作為維持虔誠於不墜的保障。

2 The annual Feast of Fools in 15th-century Paris incorporated an obscene parody of the mass.

15 世紀在巴黎登場的年度「愚人節」納入了猥褻的仿作彌撒曲。

3 Surviving texts suggest that there was little choral music as such.

現存的資料顯示，當時的合唱音樂並不多。

4 The constituent parts of the entertainment varied widely from place to place.

這種娛樂的組成要素隨著地方不同，差異也很大。

5 Musicians probably had little or no acquaintance with musical notation.

音樂家大概也不太了解樂譜。

6 Musicians played pieces from their regular repertory.

音樂家把他們固定的曲目拿出來演奏。

Reading Focus 260字

MP3 053

In a pattern that was to repeat itself after the birth of opera 200 years later, the secular theater in the Middle Ages established itself either as lighthearted interludes in serious moralities or as deliberate parodies tolerated by the church as a safety valve to consistent piety. The annual Feast of Fools in 15th-century Paris, for instance, incorporated an obscene parody of the mass performed in song and dance within the church. By the year 1400 numerous comedies and farces had appeared, usually performed on festive occasions in aristocratic houses or on open stages in municipal squares.

These plays often employed musical forces comparable to those of the religious plays and used them for similar purposes. Choirboys from the church sometimes took part, but surviving texts suggest that there was little choral music as such. The individual actors incorporated parts of songs chanted monophonically to embellish or heighten the dramatic effect, and dancing to specific instrumental music also had a regular place in the entertainment. Professional musicians might be hired and they might also be required to act; the constituent parts of the entertainment varied widely from place to place.

The fact that, except for songs, documents of the period contain almost no music directly linked with the theater is thought to indicate that very little original instrumental music was written for theatrical purposes at this time. Whatever was suitable for weddings, banquets, and other feasts perhaps served a theatrical purpose as well. Musicians probably had little or no acquaintance with musical notation and played pieces from their regular repertory.

文章中譯

在歌劇誕生 200 年之後，中世紀的**通俗劇**透過一種一再重複的形式，不是作爲穿插於嚴肅的道德劇之間的輕鬆幕間劇，就是**教會容許的諷刺模仿劇**，以作爲**維持虔誠於不墜的保障**。舉例來說，15 世紀在巴黎登場的年度「愚人節」**納入了猥褻的仿作彌撒曲**，在教堂裡以歌舞的形式演出。到 1400 年已經出現了衆多的喜劇和鬧劇，通常是節慶時在貴族大宅裡或市政廣場的開放舞台上演出。

這些戲劇通常會採用宗教劇所用的音樂規格，用意也差不多。教堂的唱詩班少年有時會參加，但現存的資料顯示，當時的**合唱音樂**並不多。個別的演員將單聲部詠唱的部分歌曲融入戲劇中，以美化或加強戲劇效果，此外，隨著特定器樂起舞也是這種娛樂形式的常態。可能會雇用職業音樂家，甚至要求他們在劇中演出，**這種娛樂的組成要素**隨著地方不同，差異也很大。

除了歌曲以外，這段時期的文件紀錄幾乎沒有記載任何直接與這種戲劇相關的音樂，因此一般認爲當時爲戲劇而創作的器樂非常少。只要是適合用在婚禮、宴會和其他盛宴上的音樂，或許也可以用於戲劇。音樂家大概也**不太了解樂譜**，只是把**他們固定的曲目**拿出來演奏。

Double-Check

- the secular theater 通俗劇
  [ˋθiətɚ]

  參 secular [ˋsɛkjəlɚ] (adj.) 通俗的，世俗的 (= worldly)

- deliberate parodies tolerated by the church 教會容許的諷刺模仿劇
  [dɪˋlɪbərɪt] [ˋpærədɪz] [ˋtɑlə͵retɪd]

- a safety valve 安全閥
  [vælv]

- consistent piety 不墜的虔誠
  [kənˋsɪstənt] [ˋpaɪətɪ]

- incorporate an obscene parody of the mass 納入了猥褻的仿作彌撒曲
  [ɪnˋkɔrpə͵ret] [əbˋsin] [mæs]

- choral music 合唱音樂
  [ˋkorəl]

- the constituent parts of the entertainment 這種娛樂的組成要素
  [kənˋstɪtʃʊənt] [͵ɛntɚˋtenmənt]

- have no acquaintance with musical notation 不了解樂譜
  [əˋkwentəns] [noˋteʃən]

- pieces from their regular repertory 他們固定的曲目
  [ˋpisɪz] [ˋrɛgjəlɚ] [ˋrɛpɚ͵torɪ]

Philosophy

Atomism

原子論

Key Sentences

1 Atomism explains complex phenomena in terms of aggregates of fixed particles or units.

原子論以固定粒子或單位的聚合來解釋複雜的萬物現象。

2 The material universe is composed of minute particles.

物質世界是由微小的粒子組成的。

3 Atomism is in essence an analytical doctrine.

基本上，原子論是分析式的學說。

4 In contrast to holistic theories, atomism explains the observable properties of the whole by those of its components and of their configurations.

不同於整體論，原子論是以某個整體的組成成分和其排列組合來解釋該整體看得到的特性。

5 The atoms are absolutely indivisible, qualitatively identical, and combinable with each other only by juxtaposition.

原子是絕對不可分割的、在性質上是完全一樣的、彼此只能靠並列的方式來結合。

Reading Focus 216字

MP3 055

Atomism is a doctrine that explains complex phenomena in terms of aggregates of fixed particles or units. This philosophy has found its most successful application in natural science: according to the atomistic view, the material universe is composed of minute particles, which are considered to be relatively simple and immutable and too small to be visible. The multiplicity of visible forms in nature is based upon differences in these particles and in their configurations; hence any observable changes must be reduced to changes in these configurations.

Atomism is in essence an analytical doctrine. It regards observable forms in nature not as intrinsic wholes but as aggregates. In contrast to holistic theories, which explain the parts in terms of qualities displayed by the whole, atomism explains the observable properties of the whole by those of its components and of their configurations.

In order to understand the historical development of atomism and, especially, its relation to modern atomic theory, it is necessary to distinguish between atomism in the strict sense and other forms of atomism. Atomism in the strict sense is characterized by three points: the atoms are absolutely indivisible, qualitatively identical (i.e., distinct only in shape, size, and motion), and combinable with each other only by juxtaposition. Other forms of atomism are less strict on these points.

! aggregate 作名詞與形容詞時，發音爲 [ˋægrɪgɪt]；作動詞時，發音爲 [ˋægrɪˏget]。另外，要特別注意 minute 在此的發音。

文章中譯

原子論是個學說，以**固定粒子或單位的聚合**來**解釋複雜的萬物現象**。這套原理最成功的應用是在自然科學方面：根據原子論的看法，物質世界**是由微小的粒子組成的**，粒子被認為是相對簡單且不可改變的，甚至小到看不見。自然界各種可見形體的多樣性是基於這些粒子本身以及相互間排列上的差異，因此，任何看得到的變化最後一定可以歸結到這些粒子排列的變化。

基本上，原子論是**分析式的學說**，不把自然界看得到的形體視為固有的整體，而是視為聚合的結果。不同於**整體論**（整體論是以整體所呈現的特性來解釋組成成分），原子論是以某個整體的組成成分和其**排列組合**來解釋該整體**看得到的特性**。

要了解原子論的歷史發展，特別是它與現代原子理論的關聯，就一定得先對嚴格定義的原子論和其他形式的原子論做個區隔。嚴格定義的原子論有三個特點：原子是**絕對不可分割的**、**在性質上是完全一樣的**（只有形狀、大小、運動會有所不同）、**彼此只能靠並列的方式來結合**。其他形式的原子論在這三方面的定義比較不嚴格。

Double-Check

- atomism (n.) 原子論
  [`ætəmɪzm̩]
- complex phenomena 複雜的萬物現象
  [fə`nɑmənə]
- aggregates of fixed particles or units 固定粒子或單位的聚合
  [`ægrɪgɪts]
- be composed of minute particles 由微小的粒子組成
  參 minute [maɪ`njut] (adj.) 微小的，細微的 ！要特別注意發音。
- an analytical doctrine 分析式的學說
  [ˏænə`lɪtɪkl̩] [`dɑktrɪn]
- holistic theories 整體論
  參 holistic [ho`lɪstɪk] (adj.) 整體論的
- the observable properties 看得到的特性
  [əb`zɝvəbl̩]
- configuration (n.) 排列組合
  [kənˏfɪgjə`reʃən]
- absolutely indivisible 絕對不可分割的
  [`æbsəˏlutlɪ] [ˏɪndə`vɪzəbl̩]
- qualitatively identical 在性質上完全一樣
  [`kwɑləˏtetɪvlɪ] [aɪ`dɛntɪkl̩]
- juxtaposition (n.) 並列
  [ˏdʒʌkstəpə`zɪʃən]

Psychology

28 Behaviorism
行為主義

Key Sentences

1 Behaviorism became a major thrust of American psychology during the first half of the 20th century.

行為主義是 20 世紀上半葉**美國心理學一股主要的推動力**。

2 Human thought is an inference from behavior and that all psychology could be, or should be, concerned only with behavior.

人類的想法都是**從行為推斷而來**，所有心理學都可以（或者都應該）只考慮行為層面。

3 Pavlov observed that when he paired a neutral (conditioned) stimulus, such as a buzzer, with a natural (unconditioned) stimulus, such as food, the reflex response to the food—salivation—eventually came to be elicited by the buzzer.

巴夫洛夫觀察到，如果他把**一個中性刺激（制約刺激）**，例如鈴聲，搭配上一個自然刺激（未制約刺激），例如食物，**看到食物會產生的反射反應**——**分泌唾液**——到最後會**被**鈴聲給**誘發出來**。

4 Pavlov called the response to the conditioned stimulus a conditioned reflex.

巴夫洛夫把這種對制約刺激所產生的反應稱為**制約反應**。

5 This model was extended to all subdisciplines within psychology.

這個模範**擴展到**心理學旗下**所有分支學科**。

6 Early studies in child psychology were modeled after studies of animal learning and had children learning in mazes not unlike those used in animal investigations.

早期的兒童心理學研究是**仿效動物學習的研究**，讓兒童在類似於研究動物時所用的迷宮中學習。

Reading Focus 236字

MP3 057

Behaviorism became a major thrust of American psychology during the first half of the 20th century when psychologists such as Clark L. Hull at Yale University and B.F. Skinner at Harvard argued that human thought is an inference from behavior and that all psychology could be, or should be, concerned only with behavior. It was not until about 1960 that American psychologists returned to the definition of psychology as the investigation of human thought as well as behavior.

A major influence in turning American psychology to behaviorism came from the work of the Russian physiologist Ivan Pavlov. Pavlov discovered what he called the conditioned reflex. Pavlov observed that when he paired a neutral (conditioned) stimulus, such as a buzzer, with a natural (unconditioned) stimulus, such as food, the reflex response to the food—salivation—eventually came to be elicited by the buzzer. Pavlov called the response to the conditioned stimulus a conditioned reflex.

Pavlov's research on the conditioned reflex became the model for a great deal of research in American psychology, which regarded learning and conditioning as the major concerns. This model was extended to all subdisciplines within psychology. Early studies in child psychology, for example, were modeled after studies of animal learning and had children learning in mazes not unlike those used in animal investigations. Although psychologists are still concerned with learning, it no longer holds the central place in psychology that it once did.

文章中譯

行爲主義是 20 世紀上半葉**美國心理學一股主要的推動力**，當時耶魯大學的克拉克．L．赫爾和哈佛大學的 B．F．斯金納主張：人類的想法都是**從行為推斷而來**，所有心理學都可以（或者都應該）只考慮行爲層面。一直到 1960 年左右，美國心理學家才回歸「心理學是研究人類想法與行爲」的定義。

促使美國心理學轉向行爲主義的一大推力是俄羅斯的生理學家伊凡．巴夫洛夫的研究結果。巴夫洛夫發現了他所謂的制約反應。巴夫洛夫觀察到，如果他把**一個中性刺激（制約刺激）**，例如鈴聲，搭配上一個自然刺激（未制約刺激），例如食物，**看到食物會產生的反射反應——分泌唾液**——到最後會**被**鈴聲給**誘發出來**。巴夫洛夫把這種對制約刺激所產生的反應稱爲**制約反應**。

巴夫洛夫的制約反應研究成爲美國很多心理學研究的模範，也就是將學習與制約視爲其中最主要的關鍵，這個模範**擴展到**心理學旗下**所有分支學科**。舉例來說，早期的兒童心理學研究是**仿效動物學習的研究**，讓兒童在類似於研究動物時所用的迷宮中學習。雖然心理學家仍然在研究學習，但學習已經不像以前那樣被置於心理學的主要位置了。

Double-Check

- behaviorism [bɪ`hevjə͵rɪzm̩] — (n.) 行為主義
- a major thrust of American psychology [θrʌst] — 美國心理學一股主要的推動力
- an inference from behavior [`ɪnfərəns] [bɪ`hevjɚ] — 從行為推斷而來

  參 infer [ɪn`fɝ] (v.) 推論
- a neutral stimulus [`njutrəl] [`stɪmjələs] — 中性刺激
- the reflex response to the food—salivation [`riflɛks] [͵sælə`veʃən] — 看到食物會產生的反射反應——分泌唾液
- come to be elicited [ɪ`lɪsɪtɪd] — 被誘發出來
- a conditioned reflex — 制約反應
- major concerns — 最主要的關鍵
- be extended to all subdisciplines [sʌb`dɪsəplɪnz] — 擴展到所有分支學科
- be modeled after studies of animal learning — 仿效動物學習的研究

Psychology

29 Memory and Motivation

記憶與動機

Key Sentences

1 The ability of the brain to register the notion of heat, remember it, and later recall it means that a specific piece of information has been learned.

大腦能夠**收錄熱的概念**，記住這個概念，之後回想起這個概念，這表示**一則特定的資訊**已經被學起來了。

2 The mind would be a storehouse of miscellaneous, unassorted data.

心智就會像**一座倉庫，堆滿了五花八門、未經分類的資料**。

3 Immediate memory lasts no more than a couple of seconds, the time it takes for a sensory impression to register.

立即記憶延續不超過二、三秒，也就是**感官收錄印象**所需要的時間。

4 Information may be lost through disuse or may become flawed through reinterpretation.

如果**不加以使用**，資訊可能會**流失**，也可能會**因為重新詮釋而有誤**。

5 One way this is done is by repetition and rehearsal.

有種方式是**藉由不斷的重複、練習**。

6 An actor might memorize his or her lines from a script.

演員**背誦腳本中的台詞**。

Reading Focus 252字

MP3 059

One learns that a burning candle is hot by feeling the heat. The ability of the brain to register the notion of heat, remember it, and later recall it means that a specific piece of information has been learned. Memory, therefore, is essential to learning.

Learning is a selective process. Far more is perceived than remembered; otherwise the mind would be a storehouse of miscellaneous, unassorted data.

There appear to be three levels of memory: immediate, short-term, and long-term. Immediate memory lasts no more than a couple of seconds, the time it takes for a sensory impression to register. Short-term memory is a matter of seconds or minutes: One looks up a phone number in the directory and makes a call; by the time the call is completed, the number has normally been forgotten. Long-term memory can last a lifetime, but some experts believe that information may be lost through disuse or may become flawed through reinterpretation.

Information often is transferred from short-term to long-term memory. One way this is done is by repetition and rehearsal, much the way an actor might memorize his or her lines from a script. Novel or vivid experiences seem to be more readily shifted to long-term memory. Other means of transfer are by the association of an unfamiliar name or fact with something that is already known, or grouping things together so that fewer facts at a time need to be absorbed. Many strategies are taught for improving memory, and most people develop their own devices.

文章中譯

因爲感受到熱度，人學到燃燒中的蠟燭是熱的。大腦能夠**收錄熱的概念**，記住這個概念，之後回想起這個概念，這表示**一則特定的資訊**已經被學起來了。因此，記憶對學習而言是非常重要的。

學習是一種選擇性的過程。我們感知到的遠遠超過所記憶的，否則心智就會像**一座倉庫，堆滿了五花八門、未經分類的資料**。

記憶似乎可以分爲三個層次：立即記憶、短期記憶、長期記憶。立即記憶延續不超過二、三秒，也就是**感官收錄印象**所需要的時間。短期記憶可以延續幾秒至幾分鐘：一個人翻閱電話簿查到一個號碼然後打電話，講完電話後，通常就已經忘記這個號碼了。長期記憶可以延續一輩子，但是有些專家認爲，長期記憶的資訊如果**不加以使用**，可能會**流失**，也可能會**因為重新詮釋而有誤**。

資訊往往從短期記憶轉換成長期記憶，有種方式是**藉由不斷的重複**、**練習**，就像演員**背誦腳本中的台詞**一樣。新奇或鮮明的經驗似乎更容易轉換成長期記憶。其他轉換方式還包括把不熟悉的名字或事實和已知事物做連結，或是把一群東西歸類爲一組，這樣一次要吸收的事實就會比較少。有很多策略被用來教導如何增進記憶，大部分人會發展出自己的方法。

Double-Check

- register the notion of heat 收錄熱的概念
  [ˋnoʃən]
- a specific piece of information 一則特定的資訊
  [spɪˋsɪfɪk]
- a storehouse of miscellaneous, unassorted data 一座堆滿了五花八門、未經分類的資料的倉庫
  [ˏmɪslˋenjəs] [ˏʌnəˋsɔrtɪd]
- for a sensory impression to register 感官收錄印象
  [ˋsɛnsərɪ]
- be lost through disuse 因為不使用而流失
  [dɪsˋjus]
- become flawed through reinterpretation 因為重新詮釋而有誤
  [flɔd] [ˏriɪnˏtɝprɪˋteʃən]
- by repetition and rehearsal 藉由不斷的重複、練習
  [rɪˋhɝsl̩]
- memorize lines from a script 背誦腳本中的台詞
  [ˋmɛməˏraɪz] [skrɪpt]
- novel or vivid experiences 新奇或鮮明的經驗
  [ˋnɑvl̩] [ˋvɪvɪd]
- be more readily shifted to long-term memory 更容易轉換成長期記憶
  [ˋʃɪftɪd]
- many strategies 很多策略
  [ˋstrætədʒɪz]
- develop their own devices 發展出他們自己的方法
  [dɪˋvaɪsɪz]

Political Science

30 Political Science in the U.S.

美國的政治學

Key Sentences

MP3 060

1 The debates about ratification of the Constitution led to the writing of the federalist papers by John Jay, James Madison, and Alexander Hamilton in 1787.

美國憲法批准與否的辯論，造就出約翰・傑伊、詹姆斯・麥迪森、亞歷山大・漢彌爾頓於 1787 年寫就的**聯邦主義論文**。

2 "*Democracy in America*" is probably the best analysis of United States political institutions ever written.

《民主在美國》大概是有史以來對美國**政治制度**最精闢的分析。

3 Politics has played a significant role in the American consciousness ever since the colonial era.

自**殖民地時期**以來，政治在**美國人的意識**中一直扮演著重要角色。

4 The term political science was coined after the president of Harvard College added to the curriculum a course in ethics and politics.

哈佛學院的校長在課程表上增加了一堂倫理與政治的課程，**政治學一詞**在那之後**被創造出來**。

5 The first permanent professorship in political science was created at Columbia University in 1857.

1857 年哥倫比亞大學首開先河，設立了政治學的**第一個常任教授職**。

Reading Focus 244字

MP3 061

Political science was taken up enthusiastically in the United States, a nation with a history of political experimentation. Some of the most notable works on government were written about the American system. The debates about ratification of the Constitution led to the writing of the federalist papers by John Jay, James Madison, and Alexander Hamilton in 1787. In the 1830s Alexis de Tocqueville published his "*Democracy in America*," which is probably the best analysis of United States political institutions ever written. Two generations later the British writer James Bryce published "*The American Commonwealth*."

Politics has played a significant role in the American consciousness ever since the colonial era. As early as 1642, before the term political science was coined, Henry Dunster, president of Harvard College, added to the curriculum a course in ethics and politics. In the mid-19th century the president of Yale College, Theodore Dwight Woolsey, introduced a course on political philosophy into the school.

The first permanent professorship in political science was created at Columbia University in 1857. The first man to teach the course was Francis Lieber, a German immigrant and author of "*On Civil Liberty and Self-Government*" (1853). In 1880 a whole school of political science was established at Columbia by John W. Burgess. In the same year the Academy of Political Science was founded. Another professional organization, the American Political Science Association, was founded in 1903. From 1880, faculties of political science began appearing at more colleges and universities.

文章中譯

在美國這個有政治實驗歷史的國家，對政治學充滿了熱情。有一些探討政府制度的名著就是描寫美國的制度。**美國憲法批准與否**的辯論，造就出約翰．傑伊、詹姆斯．麥迪森、亞歷山大．漢彌爾頓於 1787 年寫就的**聯邦主義論文**；1830 年代，亞歷希斯．托克維爾出版《民主在美國》，這大概是有史以來對美國**政治制度**最精闢的分析；兩個世代後，英國作家詹姆斯．布萊斯出版《美利堅聯邦》。

自**殖民地時期**以來，政治在**美國人的意識**中一直扮演著重要角色。早在 1642 年，**政治學一詞被創造出來**之前，哈佛學院的校長亨利．鄧斯特就在課程表上增加了一堂倫理與政治的課程。19 世紀中葉，耶魯學院校長希爾多．度埃特．伍爾希將一門政治哲學的課程引進學校。

1857 年哥倫比亞大學首開先河，設立了政治學的**第一個常任教授職**。第一位教授這門課的人是法蘭西斯．李伯，他是德國移民，也是《論公民自由與自治》(1853) 一書的作者。1880 年，哥倫比亞大學的約翰．W．柏吉斯成立政治系，同年，政治學院成立。另一個專業組織──美國政治學會，在 1903 年成立。從 1880 年開始，有愈來愈多的學院和大學開始出現政治學系所。

Double-Check

- ratification of the Constitution [ˌkɑnstəˋtjuʃən] — 憲法的批准
  - 參 ratification [ˌrætəfəˋkeʃən] (n.) 承認，批准，認可
- the federalist papers [ˋfɛdərəlɪst] — 聯邦主義論文
- political institutions — 政治制度
  - 參 institution [ˌɪnstəˋtjuʃən] (n.) 制度；機關
- the American consciousness [ˋkɑnʃəsnɪs] — 美國人的意識
- the colonial era [kəˋlonjəl] [ˋɪrə] — 殖民地時期
- The term political science was coined. — 政治學一詞被創造出來。
  - 參 coin [kɔɪn] (v.) 創造（詞彙）
- the first permanent professorship [ˋpɝmənənt] [prəˋfɛsɚˌʃɪp] — 第一個常任教授職

Women's Study

31 Women's Movement
女權運動

Key Sentences

1 During the 1960s and 1970s, the women's movement made considerable progress in elevating public awareness of inequalities between the sexes.

1960 至 1970 年代間，女權運動在**提升大眾對兩性不平等的認知上**有相當大的進展。

2 The National Organization for Women (NOW) was formed in 1966 by Betty Friedan and other like-minded activists to promote women's rights through legislation.

「美國全國婦女組織」（簡稱 NOW）於 1966 年由貝蒂．傅瑞丹和其他**有志一同的社運人士**發起，旨在**透過立法提高婦女的權利**。

3 NOW lobbied for the end of job discrimination.

全國婦女組織**遊說國會議員，要求立法禁止工作歧視**。

4 The Equal Rights Amendment was passed by Congress.

平等權利修正案獲得國會通過。

5 The organization also sought the legalization of abortion.

該組織也尋求**墮胎合法化**。

6 The women's movement also helped to forge a new sense of identity and shared experiences among women.

女權運動也幫助女性**建立嶄新的身分認同感**，分享彼此的經驗。

Reading Focus 245字

MP3 063

During the 1960s and 1970s, the women's movement made considerable progress in elevating public awareness of inequalities between the sexes. A central player in the movement was the National Organization for Women (NOW), which was formed in 1966 by Betty Friedan and other like-minded activists to promote women's rights through legislation. In the late 1960s NOW lobbied for the end of job discrimination and for government-supported child-care services for professional mothers. In 1972 NOW helped to secure support for Title IX of the Education Amendments Act, which required colleges to guarantee equal opportunities for women, and the Equal Rights Amendment, which was passed by Congress but subsequently failed in the ratification process. The organization also sought the legalization of abortion, a goal achieved with the Supreme Court's decision in the Roe vs. Wade case of 1973.

In addition to its political achievements, the women's movement also helped to forge a new sense of identity and shared experiences among women. An important part of this process was the creation of publications specifically for women, such as *Ms.*, a feminist magazine founded in 1970 that provided a forum for women's issues. Other publications, such as the influential book *Our Bodies, Ourselves*, helped many women to feel more comfortable about their bodies and encouraged them to discuss formerly taboo topics such as birth control, lesbianism, and rape. In addition, schools and universities began to offer courses in women's issues; by 1974 nearly 80 institutions offered women's studies programs.

文章中譯

1960 至 1970 年代間，女權運動在**提升大衆對兩性不平等的認知上**有相當大的進展。這場運動中的一個主要推手是「美國全國婦女組織」(簡稱 NOW)，於 1966 年由貝蒂．傅瑞丹和其他**有志一同的社運人士**發起，旨在**透過立法提高婦女的權利**。1960 年代晚期，全國婦女組織**遊說國會議員，要求立法禁止工作歧視**，以及由政府補助職業婦女的托兒服務。1972 年，全國婦女組織大力支持教育修正案第九條與**平等權利修正案**，前者規定大專院校必須提供女性平等的入學機會，後者原已獲得國會通過，但卻在後來的批准過程中以失敗告終。全國婦女組織也尋求**墮胎合法化**，這個目標在 1973 年的「羅伊與韋德判例」中獲得最高法院判決通過。

除了政治上的成就，女權運動也幫助女性**建立嶄新的身分認同感**，分享彼此的經驗。在這個過程中很重要的一個部分是發行女性專屬的出版品，例如 1970 年創刊的女性雜誌《仕女》就提供了討論女性議題的論壇。其他的出版品，例如影響深遠的著作《我們的身體，我們自己》，幫助許多女性對自己的身體感到更加自在，並鼓勵女性討論以往視爲禁忌的話題如節育、女同性戀、強暴等。除此之外，一般學校和大學也開始開設女性議題的相關課程；到了 1974 年，有將近 80 所學校機構開設女性研究課程。

Double-Check

- elevate public awareness 提升大眾的認知
  [`ɛlə,vet] [ə`wɛrnɪs]
- inequalities between the sexes 兩性不平等
  [,ɪnɪ`kwɑlətɪz]
- like-minded activists 有志一同的社運人士
  [`æktəvɪsts]
- promote women's rights through legislation 透過立法提高婦女的權利
  [,lɛdʒɪs`leʃən]
- lobby for the end of job discrimination 遊說國會議員，要求立法禁止工作歧視
  [`lɑbɪ] [dɪ,skrɪmə`neʃən]
- the Equal Rights Amendment 平等權利修正案
  [ə`mɛndmənt]
- the ratification process 批准過程
  [,rætəfə`keʃən]
- the legalization of abortion 墮胎合法化
  [,ligəlaɪ`zeʃən] [ə`bɔrʃən]
- forge a new sense of identity 建立嶄新的身分認同感
  參 forge [fɔrdʒ] (v.)（鐵的）打造；促成
- a forum for women's issues 討論女性議題的論壇
  [`forəm]

Sociology

Railroad
鐵路

Key Sentences

1 The public was seized by what was called "railroad mania."

大家陷入所謂的「鐵路狂熱」之中。

2 The new steam machine was mechanically and visually arresting.

嶄新的蒸汽火車不論在機械設計上或視覺上都很引人注意。

3 The railroad evoked a widely shared sense that an almost magical enhancement of human power was about to take place.

鐵路喚起了一種廣泛的認同感，認為人類的力量即將神奇地增強。

4 The steam-powered locomotive was the first important innovation in overland transportation.

蒸汽動力火車頭是陸上運輸首次的重大創新。

5 It was the railroad that made it feasible to ship goods long distance over land.

鐵路使經由陸路長程運送貨物成為可能。

Reading Focus 224字

MP3 065

社會學

Of all the great modern innovations, the railroad may well be the one to which historians have allowed the most dramatic and far-reaching influence. No sooner had the first passenger railroads begun operations in England and the United States, around 1830, than the public was seized by what was called, even then, "railroad mania." The new steam machine was as great a source of astonishment then as the computer is today. It could pull more weight faster than people had thought possible; it was mechanically and visually arresting; and it almost immediately began to change common ideas of time, space, and history. The railroad evoked a widely shared sense that an almost magical enhancement of human power was about to take place.

The more historians have learned about the changes caused by the railroad, the less maniac, the more reasonable or at least understandable, that initial mania has come to seem. They remind us that the steam-powered locomotive was the first important innovation in overland transportation since before the time of Julius Caesar, and many economic historians have described the railroad as one of the chief pivots on which the industrial revolution turned. Before large-scale production could be profitable, farmers and manufacturers had to gain access to larger markets. It was the railroad that made it feasible to ship goods long distance over land.

Q The word "innovations" in paragraph 1 is closest in meaning to:

(A) operations (B) new inventions
(C) magical enchantment (D) common ideas

A (B)

文章中譯

近代所有偉大的創新發明中，鐵路很可能是歷史學家認可爲最戲劇性、影響最爲深遠的一項發明。大約在 1830 年時，第一個載運乘客的鐵路系統開始在英國和美國營運，**大衆**隨即**陷入**所謂的「鐵路狂熱」（當時就有這種說法了）之中。當時嶄新的蒸汽火車就像現在的電腦一樣，是衆人注目驚嘆的焦點。蒸汽火車拉動的重量與速度，都超乎人們的想像，不論在機械設計上或**視覺上**都**很引人注意**，而且幾乎馬上開始改變了大家的時間感、空間感和歷史觀。鐵路**喚起了一種廣泛的認同感**，認爲**人類的力量**即將**神奇地增強**。

歷史學家對鐵路造成的改變了解愈深入，就愈覺得一開始的狂熱似乎也沒那麼狂熱，或者說看來較爲合理，或至少較可以理解。歷史學家提醒了我們，**蒸汽動力火車頭**是從凱撒以前的時代以來，**陸上運輸**首次的重大**創新**；許多經濟歷史學家更形容鐵路是工業革命的關鍵轉捩點之一。在大規模生產能夠獲利之前，農人或製造商必須設法打入更大的市場，而**使**經由陸路長程**運送貨物成為可能的**，正是鐵路。

Double-Check

- The public was seized by... [sizd] — 大衆陷入……
- visually arresting [ˋvɪʒuəlɪ] [əˋrɛstɪŋ] — 視覺上很引人注意
- evoke a widely shared sense [ɪˋvok] — 喚起了一種廣泛的認同感
- magical enhancement of human power [ˋmædʒɪkl̩][ɪnˋhænsmənt] — 人類的力量神奇地增強
- the steam-powered locomotive [ˌlokəˋmotɪv] — 蒸汽動力火車頭
- innovation in overland transportation [ˌɪnəˋveʃən] [ˌtrænspɚˋteʃən] — 陸上運輸的創新
- the chief pivots [ˋpɪvəts] — 關鍵轉捩點
- gain access to larger markets — 打入更大的市場
  - 參 access [ˋæksɛs] (n.) 接近的方法
- make it feasible to ship goods [ˋfizəbl̩] — 使運送貨物成爲可能

Astronomy

33 The Galaxies
星系

Key Sentences

MP3 066

1 The larger galaxies may contain as many as a trillion stars.

較大的星系中可能有多達上兆的星星。

2 Galaxies can be up to 100,000 light-years in diameter.

星系的直徑可達 10 萬光年。

3 Galaxies were long thought to be more or less passive objects, containing stars and interstellar gas and dust and shining by the radiation that their stars give off.

一直以來星系被認爲或多或少算是被動的物體，內含恆星、星際氣體、塵埃，並因爲其中的星體發出光和熱而閃耀。

4 A number of galaxies emit large amounts of energy in the radio region.

不少星系以無線電波的形式發射大量的能量。

5 This radiation had been given off by charged particles of extremely high energy moving in magnetic fields.

這種輻射是由帶電粒子所放射出來，這些粒子帶有極高的能量，在磁場中活動。

Reading Focus 239字

MP3 067

Stars are found in huge groups called galaxies. Scientists estimate that the larger galaxies may contain as many as a trillion stars, while the smallest may have fewer than a million. Galaxies can be up to 100,000 light-years in diameter.

Galaxies may have any of four general shapes. Elliptical galaxies show little or no structure and vary from moderately flat to spherical in general shape. Spiral galaxies have a small, bright central region, or nucleus, and arms that come out of the nucleus and wind around, trailing off like a giant pinwheel. In barred spiral galaxies, the arms extend sideways in a short straight line before turning off into the spiral shape. Both kinds of spiral systems are flat. Irregular galaxies are usually rather small and have no particular shape or form.

Galaxies were long thought to be more or less passive objects, containing stars and interstellar gas and dust and shining by the radiation that their stars give off. When astronomers became able to make accurate observations of radio frequencies coming from space, they were surprised to find that a number of galaxies emit large amounts of energy in the radio region. Ordinary stars are so hot that most of their energy is emitted in invisible light, with little energy emitted at radio frequencies. Furthermore, astronomers were able to deduce that this radiation had been given off by charged particles of extremely high energy moving in magnetic fields.

Q Look at the word "emit" in paragraph 3. Find out the word or phrase in paragraph 3 that "emit" refers to.

A give off

文章中譯

大群星星聚集在一起，稱爲星系。科學家推算，**較大的星系**中可能有多達**上兆的星星**，最小的星系則可能只有不到百萬的星星。星系的**直徑可達 10 萬光年**。

星系通常可分爲四種形狀：橢圓星系幾乎看不出或根本沒有組織結構可言，形狀變化從中等扁平到呈球狀都有；螺旋星系中央有塊小小的發光區，稱爲星系核，還有從星系核向外伸展的旋臂，如同一個巨大的紙風車。在棒旋星系中，棒狀的臂向兩旁直線延伸出一小段之後，才變成螺旋形狀。這兩種螺旋星系都是扁平狀。不規則星系的規模通常小很多，沒有特定的形狀或結構。

一直以來星系被認爲或多或少算是被動的物體，內含恆星、**星際氣體**、塵埃，並因爲**其中的星體發出光和熱**而閃耀。等到天文學家能夠準確觀察太空傳來的無線電波頻率時，才驚訝地發現有不少星系**以無線電波的形式發射大量的能量**。普通的星體熱度甚高，大部分的能量以不可見光的形式發散出去，另有小部分的能量以無線電波頻率的形式發散。此外，天文學家得以推論這種輻射是由**帶電粒子**所放射出來，這些粒子帶有極高的能量，在**磁場**中活動。

螺旋星系

Double-Check

- the larger galaxies [`gæləksɪz] 較大的星系
- a trillion stars [`trɪljən] 上兆的星星
- up to 100,000 light-years in diameter [daɪ`æmətɚ] 直徑達 10 萬光年
- elliptical galaxies [ɪ`lɪptɪkl̩] 橢圓星系
- from moderately flat to spherical in general shape [`mɑdərɪtlɪ] [`sfɛrɪkl̩] 形狀變化從中等扁平到呈球狀都有
- spiral galaxies [`spaɪrəl] 螺旋星系
- interstellar gas [ˏɪntɚ`stɛlɚ] 星際氣體
- the radiation that their stars give off [ˏredɪ`eʃən] 星體發出的光和熱
- emit large amounts of energy [ɪ`mɪt] 發射大量的能量
- the radio region [`riʤən] 無線電波的領域
- deduce [dɪ`djus] (v.) 推論
- charged particles [tʃarʤd] [`partɪkl̩z] 帶電粒子
- magnetic fields [mæg`nɛtɪk] 磁場

Astronomy

34 The Planets
行星

Key Sentences

MP3 068

1 All the planets travel around the sun in elliptical orbits that are close to being circles. Mercury and Pluto have the most eccentric orbits.

所有繞著太陽運轉的行星都在近乎圓形的**橢圓形軌道**上運行。水星和冥王星有最大的**離心軌道**。

2 Mercury's orbit is tilted 7 degrees to the plane of Earth's orbit.

水星的軌道**比**地球的軌道**平面傾斜七度**。

3 Most of the planets rotate on their axes in the same west-to-east motion. Most of the axes are nearly at right angles to the plane of the planets' orbits.

大多數行星都是**以自己的軸為中心**、由西向東**自轉**。大部分的軸幾乎都**跟**該行星的軌道**平面成直角**。

4 It is rolling on its side as it orbits the Sun.

它繞著太陽轉時，同時一面**以側面滾動**。

5 The inner planets lie within the asteroid belt.

內行星位於**小行星帶**之內。

6 They are dense, rocky, and small. Since Earth is a typical inner planet, this group is sometimes called the terrestrial planets.

這些行星密度高、多岩石、體積小。由於地球是典型的內行星，所以這一類行星有時又稱爲**類地行星**。

7 Since Jupiter is the main representative of the outer planets, they are sometimes called the Jovian, or giant, planets.

由於木星是外行星**的主要代表**，所以這一類行星有時又稱爲類木行星或巨行星。

Reading Focus 271字

MP3 069

All the planets travel around the sun in elliptical orbits that are close to being circles. Mercury and Pluto have the most eccentric orbits. All the planets travel in one direction around the sun, the same direction in which the sun rotates. Furthermore, all the planetary orbits lie in very nearly the same plane. Again, Mercury and Pluto have the most tilted orbits: Mercury's is tilted 7 degrees to the plane of Earth's orbit (the ecliptic plane); Pluto's is tilted by about 17 degrees.

Most of the planets rotate on their axes in the same west-to-east motion (the exceptions are Venus, Uranus, and Pluto). Most of the axes are nearly at right angles to the plane of the planets' orbits. In other words, those axes of rotation are basically perpendicular to their orbital planes. Uranus, however, is tilted so that its axis lies almost in the plane of its orbit, which basically means that it is rolling on its side as it orbits the Sun.

The planets can be divided into two groups. The inner planets—Mercury, Venus, Earth, and Mars—lie within the asteroid belt. They are dense, rocky, and small. Since Earth is a typical inner planet, this group is sometimes called the terrestrial planets.

The outer planets lie beyond the asteroid belt. With the exception of Pluto, they are much larger and more massive than the inner planets, and they are much less dense. Since Jupiter is the main representative of the outer planets, they are sometimes called the Jovian, or giant, planets. Pluto is an outer planet, but it is not usually regarded as a Jovian planet.

文章中譯

所有繞著太陽運轉的行星都在近乎圓形的**橢圓形軌道**上運行。水星和冥王星有最大的**離心軌道**。所有行星都朝著太陽自轉的方向繞著太陽運轉。此外，所有行星軌道都幾乎在相同的平面上，而又是水星和冥王星的軌道最傾斜：水星的軌道**比**地球的軌道**平面**（黃道面）**傾斜七度**，冥王星則傾斜 17 度左右。

大多數行星都是**以自己的軸為中心**、由西向東**自轉**（金星、天王星、冥王星除外）。大部分的軸幾乎都**跟**該行星的軌道**平面成直角**，換句話說，那些自轉軸基本上跟它們的軌道平面互相垂直。不過，天王星是傾斜的，所以它的軸幾乎與軌道平面平行，基本上就是說，它繞著太陽轉時，同時一面**以側面滾動**。

行星可以分成兩類。內行星——水星、金星、地球、火星——位於**小行星帶**之內。這些行星密度高、多岩石、體積小。由於地球是典型的內行星，所以這一類行星有時又稱爲**類地行星**。

外行星位於小行星帶之外，除了冥王星之外，體積和質量都比內行星大得多，密度也比較低。由於木星是外行星**的主要代表**，所以這一類行星有時又稱爲類木行星或巨行星。冥王星是外行星，但通常不被歸類爲類木行星。

Double-Check

- elliptical orbits 橢圓形軌道
  [ɪ`lɪptɪkl] [`ɔrbɪts]

- eccentric orbits 離心軌道
  [ɪk`sɛntrɪk]

- be tilted 7 degrees to the plane 比平面傾斜七度
  [`tɪltɪd]

- rotate on their axes 以自己的軸爲中心自轉
  [`rotet] [`æksiz]

- at right angles to the plane 跟平面成直角

- perpendicular (adj.) 垂直的，成直角的
  [ˏpɝpən`dɪkjələ˞]

- roll on its side 以側面滾動

- the asteroid belt 小行星帶
  [`æstəˏrɔɪd]

- the terrestrial planets 類地行星
  參 terrestrial [tə`rɛstrɪəl] (adj.) 地球的，陸地的

- the main representative of… …的主要代表
  [ˏrɛprɪ`zɛntətɪv]

Health Science

35 Pesticides and Cancer

殺蟲劑與癌症

Key Sentences

1 While pesticides have gotten a lot of negative publicity, some of it may not be justified.

一直以來大眾對殺蟲劑的觀感不佳，但其中有些或許不盡公平。

2 These chemicals were found to be risky in tests in which rats consumed doses thousands of times greater than humans typically consume.

實驗發現這些化學藥劑有（致癌）風險，而實驗中老鼠吃進的劑量是人類一般吃進劑量的數千倍。

3 There are natural chemicals in our foods that are much more toxic than pesticide residues.

我們的食物裡也有天然化學藥劑，毒性遠比殺蟲劑殘留還要強。

4 The best way to fight these toxins is to destroy the fungi that are responsible for producing them.

對抗這些毒素的最佳方法，就是摧毀製造這些毒素的菌類。

5 Eating more fruit and vegetables can reduce the risk of cancer by a significant amount.

食用愈多水果和蔬菜可以顯著降低罹癌風險。

6 Because pesticide use leads to an increase in fresh food consumption, it indirectly saves lives by cutting the incidence of cancer.

由於使用殺蟲劑可以提高新鮮食物的消耗量，等於減低癌症的發生率而間接拯救了生命。

Reading Focus 239字

MP3 071

While pesticides have gotten a lot of negative publicity, some of it may not be justified. Contrary to popular belief, there are no pesticides approved for use in the U.S. that are known to cause cancer in humans. It's unlikely that pesticide residues have caused cancer in any individual, but there are approved chemicals that are listed as suspected of causing cancer. However, these chemicals are listed because they were found to be risky in tests in which rats consumed doses thousands of times greater than humans typically consume. I would like to suggest that this is not a realistic method of testing pesticide risks, particularly for humans.

Furthermore, there are natural chemicals in our foods that are much more toxic than pesticide residues. These natural toxins are associated with several kinds of cancer. The best way to fight these toxins is to destroy the fungi that are responsible for producing them. This can be achieved by pesticide treatment. In this way, pesticides may actually reduce the incidence of cancer.

A final, important point is that the use of pesticides has allowed us to dramatically increase the supply of cheap, attractive fruit and vegetables throughout the year. We are now discovering that eating more fruit and vegetables can reduce the risk of cancer by a significant amount. Thus, because pesticide use leads to an increase in fresh food consumption, it indirectly saves lives by cutting the incidence of cancer.

文章中譯

一直以來大眾對殺蟲劑**的觀感不佳**，但其中有些或許不盡公平。跟普遍認知相反，美國核准使用的殺蟲劑當中，目前所知並沒有任何一種對人體有致癌風險。殺蟲劑殘留不太可能導致任何個人罹癌，不過確實有核准使用的化學藥劑被列爲疑似會致癌。可是，這些化學藥劑之所以榜上有名，是因爲實驗發現它們有致癌風險，而實驗中老鼠**吃進的劑量是**人類一般吃進劑量的**數千倍**。我想說的是，這並不是測試殺蟲劑是否有風險的實際可行方法，特別是對人類而言。

再說，我們的食物裡也有天然化學藥劑，**毒性遠比殺蟲劑殘留還要強**。這些天然毒素跟好幾種癌症有關。**對抗這些毒素**的最佳方法，就是摧毀**製造這些毒素**的菌類，而使用殺蟲劑可以達到這個目的。這樣一來，殺蟲劑其實反倒會降低癌症發生率。

最後也很重要的一點是，殺蟲劑的使用讓我們得以大幅提高一整年便宜、賣相又佳的蔬果的供應量。現在我們已經發現，食用愈多水果和蔬菜可以**顯著**降低罹癌風險，因此，由於使用殺蟲劑可以提高新鮮食物的消耗量，等於**減低癌症的發生率**而間接拯救了生命。

Double-Check

- have gotten a lot of negative publicity 一直以來得到的觀感不佳

  參 publicity [pʌb`lɪsətɪ] (n.) 名聲；宣傳

- consume doses thousands of times greater 吃進數千倍的劑量

  參 consume [kən`sum] (v.) 吃完；消耗

- much more toxic than pesticide residues 毒性遠比殺蟲劑殘留還要強

  toxic [`tɑksɪk] pesticide [`pɛstɪˌsaɪd]

  參 residue [`rɛzəˌdju] (n.) 殘餘，剩餘

- fight these toxins 對抗這些毒素

  toxins [`tɑksɪnz]

- be responsible for... 負責…；成為…的原因，引起…

  responsible [rɪ`spɑnsəbḷ]

- by a significant amount 顯著地

  significant [sɪg`nɪfəkənt]

- by cutting the incidence of cancer 減低癌症的發生率

  incidence [`ɪnsədəns]

Veterinary Study

36 Cat Disease

貓的疾病

Key Sentences

MP3 072

1 Upper respiratory infections are exceedingly common.

上**呼吸道感染**是極為常見的疾病。

2 Rabies is an invariably fatal viral disease.

狂犬病是**一種絕對致命的病毒感染疾病**。

3 It is therefore advisable that all cats in such areas be given preventive vaccinations.

因此建議應該讓這些地區的所有貓隻都接受**預防疫苗接種**。

4 These may cause ulcers or completely obstruct the digestive tract.

這些（毛球）可能**引起潰瘍**，或完全**阻塞消化道**。

5 Bite wounds may become infected.

咬傷的傷口可能會**感染**。

6 The cat cannot heal the wound by licking it.

貓**舔舐傷口**並沒有**治療傷口**的功效。

7 Many apparently normal cats have tiny mineral crystals in their urine.

很多外表看來正常的貓，**尿液中卻有微小的礦物結晶**。

8 A urinary obstruction is a grave emergency.

泌尿道阻塞是**很嚴重的緊急狀況**。

Reading Focus 268字

MP3 073

Upper respiratory infections are exceedingly common, and the best-known are pneumonitis and rhinotracheitis. Symptoms resemble those of the common cold in humans and distemper in dogs. The cat's "colds," however, cannot be passed on to humans or dogs although they are highly infectious for other cats.

Rabies is an invariably fatal viral disease. It is transmitted by the bite of a rabid animal. Rabies has become established among the wild animals in many parts of the world. A cat that roams outdoors in an area where rabies occurs may be bitten by a rabid animal. It is therefore advisable that all cats in such areas be given preventive vaccinations.

A cat that swallows large amounts of fur while grooming may develop fur balls or hair balls. Occasionally these may cause ulcers or completely obstruct the digestive tract. Prevention, in the form of frequent combing and brushing, is best. If fur balls occur in spite of grooming, the animal may be given a teaspoonful of mineral oil in its food or a dab of petroleum jelly on its paws twice a week.

Bite wounds may become infected and cause serious problems. Contrary to popular belief, the cat cannot heal the wound by licking it. It is better to seek veterinary attention as soon as possible.

Many apparently normal cats have tiny mineral crystals in their urine. For reasons not yet fully understood, these crystals often clump together to form sandlike particles or small stones which may cause irritation or obstruction of the urinary passages. A urinary obstruction is a grave emergency and must be treated immediately by a veterinarian.

文章中譯

上**呼吸道感染**是極爲常見的疾病，其中最爲人所熟知的就是肺炎和鼻氣管炎，症狀類似人類一般的感冒以及犬瘟熱。不過，儘管貓的「感冒」在貓跟貓之間具有高度傳染力，卻不會傳染給人類或狗。

狂犬病是**一種絕對致命的病毒感染疾病**，經由患有狂犬病的動物咬齧而傳染。世界上有許多地方的野生動物都已經確定帶有狂犬病；在狂犬病流傳的地區，貓如果在戶外遊蕩，很可能被患有狂犬病的動物咬到。因此建議應該讓這些地區的所有貓隻都接受**預防疫苗接種**。

貓在清潔身體時，如果呑下了大量的毛髮，可能會形成毛球。有時候這些毛球可能**引起潰瘍**，或完全**阻塞消化道**。預防是最好的方法，例如時常爲貓梳理毛髮或刷毛。如果幫貓梳理之後還是有毛球，可以在貓食中添加一茶匙的礦物油，或是在貓的腳掌上塗一點凡士林，一週塗兩次。

咬傷的傷口可能會**感染**，造成嚴重的後果。和一般人的觀念相反，貓**舔舐傷口**並沒有**治療傷口**的功效，最好盡快請獸醫診療。

很多外表看來正常的貓，**尿液中卻有微小的礦物結晶**。目前尙未完全了解成因，但這些結晶常常凝結在一起，形成像沙子的微粒或是小型結石，可能導致疼痛發炎或阻塞泌尿道。**泌尿道阻塞**是**很嚴重的緊急狀況**，必須立刻由獸醫治療。

Double-Check

- respiratory infections　　呼吸道感染
  [rɪˋspaɪrə͵torɪ] [ɪnˋfɛkʃənz]

- pneumonitis and rhinotracheitis　　肺炎和鼻氣管炎
  [͵njuməˋnaɪtɪs] [͵raɪno͵trekɪˋaɪtɪs]

- rabies　　(n.) 狂犬病
  [ˋrebiz]

- an invariably fatal viral disease　　一種絕對致命的病毒感染疾病
  [ɪnˋvɛrɪəbl̩ɪ] [ˋfetl̩] [dɪˋziz]

- a rabid animal　　患有狂犬病的動物
  [ˋræbɪd]

- preventive vaccinations　　預防疫苗接種
  [prɪˋvɛntɪv] [͵væksn̩ˋeʃənz]

- cause ulcers　　引起潰瘍
  [ˋʌlsɚz]

- obstruct the digestive tract　　阻塞消化道
  [əbˋstrʌkt] [dəˋdʒɛstɪv] [trækt]

- become infected　　感染
  [ɪnˋfɛktɪd]

- heal the wound by licking it　　藉由舔舐來治療傷口
  [wund] [ˋlɪkɪŋ]

- seek veterinary attention　　請獸醫診療
  [ˋvɛtərə͵nɛrɪ]

- tiny mineral crystals in their urine　　尿液中有微小的礦物結晶
  [ˋmɪnərəl] [ˋkrɪstl̩z] [ˋjurɪn]

- a urinary obstruction　　泌尿道阻塞
  [ˋjurə͵nɛrɪ] [əbˋstrʌkʃən]

- a grave emergency　　很嚴重的緊急狀況
  [grev]

Biology

37 Evolution

進化論

Key Sentences

MP3 074

1 Charles Darwin published his theory of evolution in a book entitled *On the Origin of Species by Means of Natural Selection*.

查爾斯·達爾文將他的**進化理論**寫成專書出版，書名爲《論**物種起源**——**天擇說**》。

2 His thoughtful presentation provided a sound biological explanation for the existence of multitudes of different organisms in the world.

他經過深思熟慮，在**生物學上**提出**一套完整的解釋**，說明世界上爲何有**這麼多不同的生物體**存在。

3 Genetics and the mechanisms of inheritance were unknown during Darwin's time.

在達爾文的時代還沒有**遺傳學和遺傳機制**的概念。

4 New species can be formed—and others become extinct.

新物種形成——以及其他物種**滅絕**。

Reading Focus 207字

MP3 075

New biological concepts and theories developed rapidly during the 18th and 19th centuries and challenged many old ideas. In 1859 Charles Darwin published his theory of evolution in a book entitled *On the Origin of Species by Means of Natural Selection*. The concept of natural selection and evolution revolutionized 19th-century thinking about the relationships between groups of plants and animals. His thoughtful presentation provided a sound biological explanation for the existence of multitudes of different organisms in the world and suggested that they might be related to one another. To support his ideas Darwin used examples from geology, domestic animals, cultivated plants, and from his personal observations of the wealth of biological variability and similarity that can be found among living creatures. Although genetics and the mechanisms of inheritance were unknown during Darwin's time, he noted that certain life forms are more likely to survive than others. This concept of natural selection provided, for the first time, a universal explanation for the variations observed in nature. He made a powerful case that new species can be formed—and others become extinct—by a gradual process of change and adaptation made possible by this natural variability. Darwin's ideas influenced the field of biology more than any other concept.

Q The word "challenged" in the paragraph is closest in meaning to:

(A) questioned (B) projected (C) survived (D) revolutionized

A (A)

文章中譯

18、19 世紀間，新的生物學概念與理論快速發展，挑戰了許多舊有的想法。1859 年，查爾斯・達爾文將他的**進化理論**寫成專書出版，書名爲《論**物種起源——天擇**說》。天擇和進化的概念，革新了 19 世紀對動植物族群之間關係的想法。他經過深思熟慮，在**生物學上**提出**一套完整的解釋**，說明世界上爲何有**這麼多不同的生物體**存在，暗示所有生物彼此可能互有關聯。爲了支持自己的論點，達爾文從地質學、家畜、栽培植物之中援引例證，並於現存的生物中觀察到大量生物學上變異與相似之處，從中找到支持其論點的例證。雖然在達爾文的時代還沒有**遺傳學和遺傳機制**的概念，他卻注意到某些生命形式比其他形式更能存活下來。這種物競天擇的觀念，首度提出了一個放諸四海皆準的說法，解釋了在自然界中觀察到的物種變異現象。達爾文提出了一個強有力的理由，說明新物種之形成——以及其他物種之**滅絕**——乃是一個漸進的改變與適應過程，因爲自然的變異性而得以達成。達爾文的想法對生物學領域造成深遠的影響，遠超過其他任何概念。

Double-Check

- theory of evolution 進化理論
  [`θiərɪ] [ˌɛvə`luʃən]

- origin of species 物種起源
  [`ɔrədʒɪn] [`spiʃiz]

- natural selection 天擇，自然淘汰
  [`nætʃərəl][sə`lɛkʃən]

- a sound biological explanation 生物學上一套完整的解釋
  [ˌbaɪə`lɑdʒɪkl̩][ˌɛksplə`neʃən]

- multitudes of different organisms 眾多不同的生物體
  [`mʌltəˌtjudz] [`ɔrgənˌɪzm̩z]

- genetics and the mechanisms of inheritance 遺傳學和遺傳機制
  [dʒə`nɛtɪks] [`mɛkəˌnɪzm̩z] [ɪn`hɛrətəns]
  參 genetic(al) [dʒə`nɛtɪk(l̩)] (adj.) 遺傳學的，基因的
  gene [dʒin] (n.) 基因，遺傳因子

- become extinct 滅絕
  參 extinction [ɪk`stɪŋkʃən] (n.) 滅絕

Biology

Specifically Human Qualities
人類的特質

Key Sentences

MP3 076

1 The mode of adaptation of the animal to its world remains the same throughout.

動物對外在世界的**適應模式**，到哪裡都是一樣的。

2 If its instinctive equipment is no longer fit to cope successfully with a changing environment, the species will become extinct.

如果動物**天生的能力**不再能夠成功地應付環境的改變，這個物種就會滅絕。

3 The animal's inherited equipment makes it a fixed and unchanging part of its world.

經由遺傳獲得的能力，使動物成爲其生存環境中固定不變的一部分。

4 The emergence of man can be defined as occurring at the point in the process of evolution where instinctive adaptation has reached its minimum.

人類的出現，可以視爲演化過程中本能適應達最低點的時候。

Reading Focus 237字

MP3 077

The first element which differentiates human from animal existence is a negative one: the relative absence in man of instinctive regulation in the process of adaptation to the surrounding world. The mode of adaptation of the animal to its world remains the same throughout. If its instinctive equipment is no longer fit to cope successfully with a changing environment, the species will become extinct. The animal can adapt itself to changing conditions by changing itself. In this fashion it lives harmoniously, not in the sense of absence of struggle but in the sense that its inherited equipment makes it a fixed and unchanging part of its world; it either fits in or dies out.

The less complete and fixed the instinctive equipment of animals, the more developed is the brain and therefore the ability to learn. The emergence of man can be defined as occurring at the point in the process of evolution where instinctive adaptation has reached its minimum. But he emerges with new qualities which differentiate him from the animal: his awareness of himself as a separate entity, his ability to remember the past, to visualize the future, and to denote objects and acts by symbols; and his reason to conceive and understand the world. Man is the most helpless of all animals, but this very biological weakness is the basis for his strength, the prime cause for the development of his specifically human qualities.

Q Look at the word "mode" in paragraph 1. Find out the word or phrase in paragraph 1 that "mode" refers to.

A fashion

文章中譯

人類之所以異於動物，首要的因素其實是種負面的特質：人在適應周遭環境的過程中，比較缺乏本能性的調整。動物對外在世界的**適應模式**，到哪裡都是一樣的。如果動物**天生的能力**不再能夠成功地應付環境的改變，這個物種就會滅絕。動物可以藉由改變自己來適應環境的變化。藉由這種方式，動物可以和諧地生存，但並不是說動物不需要奮鬥掙扎，而是說**經由遺傳獲得的能力**，使動物成為其生存環境中固定不變的一部分；也就是說，適者生存，不適者淘汰。

動物天生的本能愈不完整、愈不固定，表示大腦愈發達，因此學習的能力就愈強。**人類的出現**，可以視為演化過程中本能適應達最低點的時候。但是人類也出現了新的特質，使得人與動物有所不同：人類意識到自己是獨立的存在，能夠記憶過往，展望未來，用符號指稱物體和動作，還能夠用理性去感知、了解這個世界。人類是所有動物中最無能的，但這項生物學上的弱點正是人類力量的基礎，是人類發展出獨有特質的主要原因。

Double-Check

- instinctive regulation　本能性的調整
  [ɪn`stɪŋktɪv] [ˌrɛgjə`leʃən]
  參 instinct [`ɪnstɪŋkt] (n.) 本能

- adaptation to the surrounding world　適應周遭環境
  [ˌædæp`teʃən] [sə`raʊndɪŋ]

- the mode of adaptation　適應的模式
  參 mode [mod] (n.) 模式，樣式 (= way/method/manner/fashion)

- instinctive equipment　天生的能力
  [ɪ`kwɪpmənt]

- inherited equipment　經由遺傳獲得的能力
  [ɪn`hɛrɪtɪd]

- the emergence of man　人類的出現
  [ɪ`mɝdʒəns]
  參 emerge [ɪ`mɝdʒ] (v.) 出現

- instinctive adaptation　本能的適應力

- a separate entity　獨立的存在
  [`sɛpərɪt] [`ɛntətɪ]

Biology

39 Human Aggression

人類的侵略行為

Key Sentences

MP3 078

1 To write about human aggression is a difficult task.

要談人類的侵略行為是一件困難的事。

2 When a child rebels against authority, it is being aggressive; but it is also manifesting a drive towards independence.

小孩子反抗權威是一種侵略的表現，但這同時也顯示出對於獨立的需求。

3 The desire for power has, in extreme form, disastrous aspects which we all acknowledge.

我們都知道，過度渴求權力會導致可怕的結果。

4 The drive to conquer difficulties underlies the greatest of human achievements.

克服困難的渴望，卻是人類偉大成就的基礎。

5 The aggressive part of human nature is not only a necessary safeguard against savage attack.

人類本性中具有侵略性的部分，這不僅僅是爲了抵抗粗暴攻擊的必要保衛機制。

6 He possessed a large amount of inborn aggressiveness.

人類天生具有強大的侵略性。

Reading Focus 236字

MP3 079

To write about human aggression is a difficult task because the term is used in so many different senses. Aggression is one of those words which everyone knows, but which is nevertheless hard to define. One difficulty is that there is no clear dividing line between those forms of aggression which we all deplore and those which we must not disown if we are to survive. When a child rebels against authority, it is being aggressive; but it is also manifesting a drive towards independence which is a necessary and valuable part of growing up. The desire for power has, in extreme form, disastrous aspects which we all acknowledge; but the drive to conquer difficulties, or to gain mastery over the external world, underlies the greatest of human achievements.

The aggressive part of human nature is not only a necessary safeguard against savage attack. It is also the basis of intellectual achievement, of the attainment of independence, and even of that proper pride which enables a man to hold his head high amongst his fellows. Without the aggressive, active side of his nature man would be even less able than he is to direct the course of his life or to influence the world around him. In fact, it is obvious that man could never have attained his present dominance, nor even have survived as a species, unless he possessed a large amount of inborn aggressiveness.

Q The word “inborn” in paragraph 2 is closest in meaning to:

(A) disastrous (B) aggressive (C) savage (D) innate

A (D)

文章中譯

要談**人類的侵略行為**是**一件困難的事**，因爲侵略這個詞彙帶有多種不同的涵義。侵略這個詞大家都聽過，但是卻很難定義。困難點之一在於，有的侵略行爲遭到同聲譴責，有的卻不可否認是生存所必須，而這兩種形式的侵略很難有個清楚的分界。小孩子**反抗權威**是一種侵略的表現，但這同時也**顯示出對於獨立的需求**，而這種需求是成長過程中必要且極爲珍貴的部分。我們都知道，過度**渴求權力**會導致**可怕的結果**；但是**克服困難**、掌控外在世界**的渴望**，卻是人類偉大成就的基礎。

人類本性中具有侵略性的部分，這不僅僅是爲了**抵抗粗暴攻擊的必要保衛機制**，也是人類智力成就及獲得獨立的基礎，甚至可以說是自尊的基礎，讓一個人得以在同儕之間抬頭挺胸。人類本質上若缺乏積極進取的一面，就無法像現在這樣能夠掌握生命，也不能影響周遭的世界。事實上，若不是**天生**具有強大的**侵略性**，人類根本不可能獲得現在擁有的優勢，甚至連人類這個種族都無法存續下來。

Double-Check

- human aggression 人類的侵略行爲
  [ə`grɛʃən]

- a difficult task 一件困難的事
  [tæsk]

- rebel against authority 反抗權威
  [rɪ`bɛl] [ə`θɔrətɪ]

- manifest a drive towards independence 顯示出對於獨立的需求
  [`mænə,fɛst] [,ɪndɪ`pɛndəns]

- the desire for power 渴求權力
  [dɪ`zaɪr]

- disastrous aspects 可怕的結果
  [dɪ`zæstrəs] [`æspɛkts]

- the drive to conquer difficulties 克服困難的渴望
  [`kaŋkɚ]

- a necessary safeguard against savage attack 抵抗粗暴攻擊的必要保衛機制
  [`sef,gard] [`sævɪdʒ]

- survive as a species 種族的存續
  [sɚ`vaɪv] [`spiʃiz]

- inborn aggressiveness 天生的侵略性
  [ə`grɛsɪvnɪs]

  參 inborn [`ɪnbɔrn] (adj.) 天生的，與生俱來的 (= natural/innate/inherent/native)

Biology

40 Aquaculture
水產養殖

Key Sentences

MP3 080

1 Raising animals and plants in the water is aquaculture.

在水中養殖動植物稱為水耕或水產養殖。

2 In animal aquaculture much effort has gone into controlling the breeding process.

在水產養殖中，必須花費很多心力控制育種的過程。

3 Some fish, such as trout, are easily bred in captivity.

有些魚類，例如鱒魚，在養殖的狀態下也能輕鬆繁衍。

4 Eggs are squeezed from the female and fertilized.

從雌魚體內擠壓出魚卵受精。

5 When the rice paddies are idle during the time between harvest and planting, farmers may buy young carp and fatten them in the paddies.

在稻田收割和種植之間的農閒時期，農夫可能會買小鯉魚放在田裡養肥。

6 The immature mussels float after hatching and attach themselves to the ropes.

幼小的貽貝孵化之後四處漂浮，然後附在繩子上。

7 In some areas fish are artificially bred.

有些地區的魚類是經由人工孵化。

Reading Focus 229字

MP3 081

The growing of plants and animals on land for food and other products is agriculture. Raising animals and plants in the water is aquaculture. In animal aquaculture much effort has gone into controlling the breeding process. Some fish, such as trout, are easily bred in captivity. Eggs are squeezed from the female and fertilized. Once hatched, immature fish are raised in tanks or ponds. Carp and catfish, which do not breed easily in captivity, are caught in the wild while young and then raised to maturity by aquaculturists. In Indonesia, for example, when the rice paddies are idle during the time between harvest and planting, farmers may buy young carp and fatten them in the paddies. Mussels are raised in France by a process that involves hanging ropes over natural mussel beds in the ocean. (A) The immature mussels, called spats, float after hatching and attach themselves to the ropes. (B) The spatcovered ropes are next wound around large stakes in the sea. (C) Similar methods are used to raise oysters in many parts of the world. (D)

Aquaculturists keep their animals captive by such means as ponds, tanks, and underwater enclosures. In some areas fish are artificially bred, released into the wild, and then recaptured as adults. This is done in enclosed areas such as the Caspian Sea, where sturgeon are raised for their flesh and their eggs.

Q The following sentence can be added to the passage.

There the mussels mature.

Where would it best fit in the passage? Choose the one best answer, (A), (B), (C) or (D).

A (C)

文章中譯

在陸地上種植或培育動植物以生產食物和其他產品，稱爲農業生產；**在水中養殖動植物，則稱為水耕或水產養殖**。在水產養殖中，必須花費很多心力**控制育種的過程**；有些魚類，例如鱒魚，**在養殖的狀態下也能輕鬆繁衍**，從雌魚體內擠壓出**魚卵受精**。孵化之後，把幼魚放在水槽或池塘中養殖。鯉魚和鯰魚則不容易在養殖池中繁殖，所以直接捕捉野生的小魚，再由養殖業者養大。以印尼爲例，在**稻田**收割和種植之間的**農閒時期**，農夫可能會買小鯉魚放在田裡養肥。法國的貽貝在養殖過程中，會把繩子掛在海中貽貝自然生長的地方；幼小的貽貝**孵化之後四處漂浮**，然後附著在繩子上。附滿貽貝的繩子，接著會被纏繞在海中的大柱子上。（貽貝就在那裡長大。）世界上很多地方都用類似的方法養殖牡蠣。

水產養殖業者利用池塘、水槽、水底圍欄等方法圈住養殖的動物。有些地區的魚類經由**人工孵化**之後野放，長大之後再捕捉回來；有些地形封閉的地區例如裏海，就是透過這種方式養殖鱘魚以取得魚肉和魚子。

Double-Check

- aquaculture (n.) 水耕，水產養殖
  [ˋækwəˏkʌltʃɚ]
  參 culture [ˋkʌltʃɚ] (n.) (v.) 養殖，培育，栽培

- the breeding process 育種的過程
  [ˋbridɪŋ]
  參 breed [brid] (v.) 繁殖，育種

- be easily bred in captivity 在養殖的狀態下輕鬆繁衍
  [brɛd]
  參 captivity [kæpˋtɪvətɪ] (n.) 監禁

- fertilize (v.) 使受精
  [ˋfɝtəˏlaɪz]
  參 fertilizer [ˋfɝtəˏlaɪzɚ] (n.)（化學）肥料
  fertile [ˋfɝtḷ] (adj.)（土地）肥沃的，多產的

- The rice paddies are idle. 在稻田的農閒時期。
  [ˋpædɪz]
  參 idle [ˋaɪdḷ] (adj.) 空閒的

- float after hatching 孵化之後四處漂浮
  [flot] [ˋhætʃɪŋ]

- be artificially bred 人工孵化
  [ˏɑrtəˋfɪʃəlɪ]

Biology

41 Flightless Birds

不會飛的鳥

Key Sentences

MP3 082

1 Certain birds whose ancient relatives once flew have lost the power of flight and have adapted to other modes of living.

有些鳥類的遠古親戚曾經會飛翔，但是牠們卻**失去了飛行的能力**，**採取了別種生活模式**。

2 Two extinct ratites are the elephant bird and the moa.

象鳥和恐鳥是**兩種已經絕種的平胸鳥**。

3 Birds are descended from reptiles that began to live in trees about 225 million years ago.

鳥類的**祖先是爬蟲類**，大約在 2 億 2 千 5 百萬年前開始生活在樹上。

4 The scales on the bodies of these reptiles are believed to have evolved into feathers.

一般認爲這種爬蟲類**身上的鱗片進化成羽毛**。

5 This was accompanied by the gradual modification of the forelimbs into membranous wings.

同時，伴隨著**前肢慢慢地變化**，**成為薄膜狀的翼**。

6 The first line of descent attained flight long ago.

第一條後代從很早以前**就會飛了**。

7 The other line, flightless birds, is at an early stage of evolution.

另外一條後代，也就是**不會飛的鳥**，**處於演化史上較早的階段**。

Reading Focus 259字

Certain birds whose ancient relatives once flew have lost the power of flight and have adapted to other modes of living. The largest such group of birds, called the ratites, includes the ostrich, rhea, emu, cassowary, and kiwi. Two extinct ratites are the elephant bird and the moa. Unrelated to the ratites are the penguin, whose flipperlike wings help it to swim, and the extinct dodo.

According to theory, birds are descended from pseudosuchians, reptiles that began to live in trees about 225 million years ago. With the passage of time, the scales on the bodies of these reptiles are believed to have evolved into feathers. This was accompanied by the gradual modification of the forelimbs into membranous wings, making it possible for these animals to leap from trees and glide to the ground. From these reptiles, Archaeopteryx ("ancient wing") evolved. According to theory, this warm-blooded animal could use its wings to rise up and move through the air. Archaeopteryx, the first true bird, probably appeared some 136 million years ago.

If all birds are descended from Archaeopteryx, where then do flightless birds come from? This question has puzzled scientists for a long time. Some suggest that modern birds have two common ancestors instead of one. The first line of descent, representing the majority, attained flight long ago.

The other line, flightless birds, is at an early stage of evolution. Most experts reject this view today. They say that flightless birds had flying ancestors but lost the use of their wings because they did not need them to survive.

文章中譯

有些鳥類的遠古親戚曾經會飛翔，但是牠們卻**失去了飛行的能力，採取了別種生活模式**。這種鳥類中最大的一群稱爲「平胸鳥」，包括鴕鳥、三趾鴕鳥、鷸鴕、食火雞、鶆鷞。象鳥和恐鳥則是**兩種已經絕種的平胸鳥**。另外還有不屬於平胸鳥的企鵝，翅膀像鰭一樣可以幫助游泳，以及已經絕種的多多鳥。

根據理論，鳥類的**祖先是**僞鱷類，一種大約在 2 億 2 千 5 百萬年前開始生活在樹上的**爬蟲類**。隨著時間過去，一般認爲這種爬蟲類**身上的鱗片進化成羽毛**。同時，伴隨著**前肢慢慢地變化，成為薄膜狀的翼**，使得這些動物能夠從樹上往下跳，滑行至地面。從這些爬蟲類進化出了「始祖鳥」；根據理論，這種溫血動物可以利用翅膀往上飛，在空中移動。始祖鳥是有史以來眞正可稱爲鳥類的鳥，可能出現在大約 1 億 3 千 6 百萬年前。

如果所有鳥類都是始祖鳥的後代，那爲什麼會有不會飛的鳥呢？這個問題讓科學家困擾了許久。有些科學家認爲，現在的鳥類有兩個共同的祖先，而非一個；大多數的鳥類屬於其中**第一條後代**，從很早以前**就會飛了**。

另外一條後代，也就是**不會飛的鳥**，則**處於演化史上較早的階段**。今日大部分專家都駁斥這種看法，他們認爲不會飛的鳥也是來自會飛的祖先，只是因爲不需要翅膀也可以生存，所以不再使用翅膀。

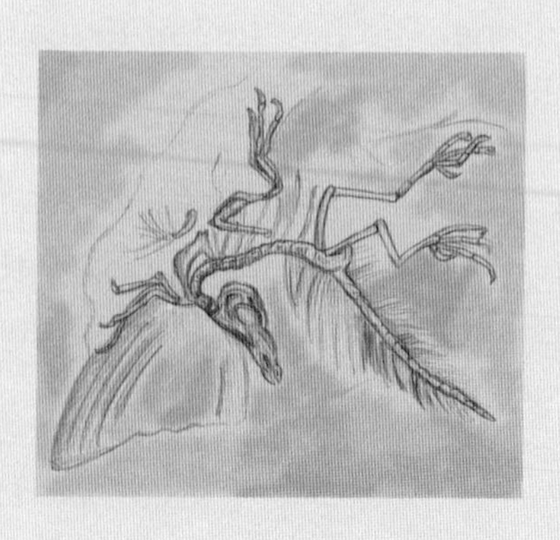

Double-Check

- lose the power of flight 失去飛行的能力
  [luz] [flaɪt]

- adapt to other modes of living 採取別種生活模式
  [ə`dæpt] [modz]

- two extinct ratites 兩種已經絕種的平胸鳥
  [ɪk`stɪŋkt][`rætaɪts]

- be descended from reptiles 祖先是爬蟲類
  [dɪ`sɛndɪd] [`rɛptl̩z]

- scale (n.) 鱗片
  [skel]

- evolve into feathers 進化成羽毛
  [ɪ`valv] [`fɛðɚz]

- the gradual modification 慢慢的變化
  [`grædʒuəl][ˌmadəfə`keʃən]

  參 modify [`madəˌfaɪ] (v.) 修正；變化

- the forelimbs into membranous wings 前肢變成薄膜狀的翼
  [`forˌlɪmz] [`mɛmbrənəs]

- the first line of descent 第一條後代
  [dɪ`sɛnt]

- attain flight 會飛
  [ə`ten]

- flightless birds 不會飛的鳥
  [`flaɪtlɪs]

- at an early stage of evolution 處於演化史上較早的階段
  [ˌɛvə`luʃən]

Symbiosis
共生

Key Sentences

1 Symbiosis is classified into: mutualism, commensalism, and parasitism.

共生關係可以分成：互利共生、片利共生和寄生。

2 Human beings, animals, and most plants need nitrogen to survive but cannot metabolize it from the air.

人類、動物和大部分的植物都需要氮氣才能生存，但是卻無法代謝空氣中的氮。

3 This compound is then converted into some organic form, such as amino acids.

這個化合物又被轉換成其他有機形式，例如氨基酸。

4 Lichens consist of fungi and algae.

地衣由真菌和藻類構成。

Reading Focus 247字

MP3 085

Close living arrangements between two different species is called symbiosis. The word comes from the Greek word meaning "state of living together." Usually the two organisms are in close physical contact, with one living on or in the other. In some cases, however, the relationship is less intimate. Symbiosis is classified into: mutualism (once called symbiosis), commensalism, and parasitism. These relationships range from mutually beneficial to harmful, or even fatal, for one of the species.

In mutualism both partners benefit from the relationship. One of the best-known mutual relationships is the one between "nitrogen-fixing" Rhizobium bacteria and several leguminous plants such as beans, peas, peanuts, and alfalfa.

Human beings, animals, and most plants need nitrogen to survive but cannot metabolize it from the air. Rhizobium bacteria, which live in the soil, enter the roots of legumes and produce nodules, or enlargements, in which they absorb nitrogen from the air and convert it into ammonia. This compound is then converted into some organic form, such as amino acids, which is shared by the bacteria and the host plant. By eating such leguminous plants, other organisms obtain a rich source of nitrogen-bearing compounds. The bacteria, in turn, benefit from the relationship by absorbing from the host plant nutrients that they cannot manufacture themselves.

Lichens, which consist of fungi and algae, are another well-known example of mutualism. Algae receive shelter and a moist environment by dwelling within the fungi. In turn, the algae provide the fungi with food through photosynthesis.

文章中譯

兩種不同的生物之間有密切的生存關係，稱為共生。共生的英文 symbiosis 源自希臘文，表示「一起生活的狀態」。通常這兩種生物會有密切的身體接觸，其中一種生物住在另一種生物的上面或裡面。不過，也有些共生關係並沒有那麼親密。**共生關係可以分成**：互利共生（一度被稱為共生）、片利共生和**寄生**。這些關係可能對雙方有利，也可能有害，甚至對其中一方造成致命傷害。

在互利共生中，雙方都從共生關係中獲利。互利關係最出名的一個例子，就是可進行「固氮作用」的根瘤菌和豆科植物如大豆、豌豆、花生、紫花苜蓿間的關係。

人類、動物和大部分的植物都**需要氮氣才能生存**，但是卻無法**代謝空氣中的氮**。根瘤菌是一種生存在土壤中的細菌，可以進入豆科植物的根部，形成「根瘤」，或是隆起，根瘤菌就在其中吸收空氣中的氮氣，轉化為氨。氨這個化合物又**被轉換成其他有機形式**，例如**氨基酸**，由根瘤菌和宿主植物共同享用。其他生物吃了這一類豆科植物，就可以獲得豐富的含氮化合物來源。至於根瘤菌從這種關係中得到的好處，則是從宿主身上吸取自己無法製造的養分。

由真菌和藻類構成的地衣，是互利共生另一個著名的例子。藻類住在眞菌的菌絲內，獲得庇護及濕潤的生活環境；在眞菌這一邊，則由藻類行光合作用提供養分。

Double-Check

- Symbiosis is classified into... 共生關係可以分成……
  [ˌsɪmbaɪˋosɪs] [ˋklæsəˌfaɪd]
- parasitism (n.) 寄生
  [ˋpærəsaɪtˌɪzm̩]
- need nitrogen to survive 需要氮氣才能生存
  [ˋnaɪtrədʒən]
- metabolize it from the air 代謝空氣中的氮
  參 metabolize [məˋtæbəˌlaɪz] (v.) 使新陳代謝
- be converted into some organic form 被轉換成其他有機形式
  [kənˋvɝtɪd] [ɔrˋgænɪk]
- amino acids 氨基酸
  [əˋmino]
- lichen (n.) 地衣
  [ˋlaɪkɪn]
- consist of fungi and algae 由眞菌和藻類構成
  [ˋfʌŋgaɪ] [ˋældʒi]

Biochemistry

43 Introduction

概論

Key Sentences

1 The organic compounds comprise the basic constituents of cells.

由基本細胞成分組成的有機化合物。

2 Biochemistry entails the study of all the complexly interrelated chemical changes that occur within the cell.

伴隨生化而來的研究是有關細胞內部各種錯綜複雜的化學變化。

3 The cell's degradation of substances that release energy, and its buildup of complex molecules that store energy or act as substrates or catalysts for biological chemical reactions are studied in detail by biochemists.

細胞物質分解（釋放能量）和細胞增生複雜分子（儲存能量或作爲生化反應的基質或催化劑），生化學家都會鉅細靡遺地研究。

4 Biochemists study the regulatory mechanisms within the body.

生化學家研究人體內的調節機制。

5 Molecular biology is a field closely allied to biochemistry.

分子生物學是與生化緊密結合的科學。

Reading Focus 248字

MP3 087

Biochemistry is the science concerned with the chemical substances and processes that occur in plants, animals, and microorganisms. Specifically, it involves the quantitative determination and structural analysis of the organic compounds that comprise the basic constituents of cells (proteins, carbohydrates, and lipids) and of those that play a key role in chemical reactions vital to life (nucleic acids, vitamins, and hormones). Biochemistry entails the study of all the complexly interrelated chemical changes that occur within the cell; for example, those relating to protein synthesis, the conversion of food to energy, and the transmission of hereditary characteristics. Both the cell's degradation of substances that release energy, and its buildup of complex molecules that store energy or act as substrates or catalysts for biological chemical reactions are studied in detail by biochemists. Biochemists also study the regulatory mechanisms within the body that govern these and other processes.

Biochemistry lies in the border area between the biological and physical sciences. Accordingly, it makes use of many of the techniques common to physiology and those integral to analytical, organic, and physical chemistry. The field of biochemistry has become so large that many subspecialties are recognized; for example, clinical chemistry and nutrition. Molecular biology, the study of large molecules—for example, proteins, nucleic acids, and carbohydrates—that are essential to life processes is a field closely allied to biochemistry. Taken as a whole, modern biochemistry has outgrown its earlier status as an applied science and has acquired a place among the pure sciences.

文章中譯

生物化學（生化）是研究動植物與微生物體內的化學物質和變化的科學。更精確地說，生化是量化和結構的分析，分析那些**由基本細胞成分**（蛋白質、碳水化合物、脂質）**組成的有機化合物**，也分析那些在生命不可或缺的化學反應中扮演關鍵角色的有機化合物（核酸、維生素、荷爾蒙）。**伴隨生化而來的研究**是有關細胞內部各種錯綜複雜的**化學變化**，例如蛋白質合成、食物轉換成能量、遺傳特質的傳播。不論是細胞**物質分解**（釋放能量），還是細胞增生複雜分子（儲存能量或作爲**生化反應的**基質或**催化劑**），生化學家都會鉅細靡遺地研究。生化學家也研究**人體內**掌控這些與其他過程**的調節機制**。

生物化學介於生物學和自然科學之間，因此利用了很多生理學常用的技術，以及分析化學、有機化學、物理化學中不可或缺的方法。生化領域已經變得相當廣泛，因此其下許多分支也被認可，例如臨床化學和營養學。分子生物學是研究生命不可或缺的大分子（例如蛋白質、核酸、碳水化合物）的科學，它**與生化緊密結合**。整體而言，現代生化學已經超出早先的應用科學地位，在正統科學中取得一席之地。

Double-Check

- the organic compounds [`kampaundz] — 有機化合物

- comprise the basic constituents of cells [kən`stɪtʃuənts] — 由基本細胞成分組成
  - 參 comprise [kəm`praɪz] (v.) 由…所構成；包含，包括

- Biochemistry entails the study of chemical changes. [͵baɪo`kɛmɪstrɪ] — 伴隨生化而來的是化學變化的研究。
  - 參 entail [ɪn`tel] (v.) 伴隨

- degradation of substances [͵dɛgrə`deʃən] [`sʌbstənsɪz] — 物質分解

- catalysts for biological chemical reactions [`kætəlɪsts] — 生化反應的催化劑

- biochemist [͵baɪo`kɛmɪst] — (n.) 生化學家

- the regulatory mechanisms within the body [`rɛgjələ͵torɪ] [`mɛkə͵nɪzm̩z] — 人體內的調節機制

- clinical chemistry and nutrition [`klɪnɪkl̩] [nju`trɪʃən] — 臨床化學和營養學

- molecular biology [mə`lɛkjələ˞] — 分子生物學
  - 參 molecule [`mɑlə͵kjul] (n.) 分子

- closely allied to biochemistry [ə`laɪd] — 與生化緊密結合的

Computer Science

44 Digital Computer

數位電腦

Key Sentences

MP3 088

1 A digital computer typically consists of a control unit, an arithmetic-logic unit, a memory unit, and input/output units.

數位電腦一般來說包括控制、**算術邏輯**、記憶、輸入／輸出等**單元**。

2 The main computer memory, usually high-speed random-access memory (RAM), stores instructions and data.

電腦主要的記憶單元，通常是**高速的隨機存取記憶體** (RAM)，儲存指令和資料。

3 The basic operation of the CPU is analogous to a computation carried out by a person using an arithmetic calculator.

CPU 的基本運作模式**和**人使用數學計算機進行**運算的方式類似**。

4 The CPU and fast memories are realized with transistor circuits.

電晶體迴路使得 CPU 和快速的記憶體成爲可能。

5 I/O units are commonly referred to as computer peripherals.

輸入／輸出單元通常**被稱為電腦週邊設備**。

6 Almost all computers contain a magnetic storage device known as a hard disk.

幾乎所有電腦都配備一種稱爲硬碟的**磁性儲存裝置**。

Reading Focus 251字

MP3 089

A digital computer typically consists of a control unit, an arithmetic-logic unit, a memory unit, and input/output units. The arithmetic-logic unit (ALU) performs simple addition, subtraction, multiplication, division, and logic operations, such as OR and AND. The main computer memory, usually high-speed random-access memory (RAM), stores instructions and data. The control unit fetches data and instructions from memory and affects the operations of the ALU. The control unit and ALU usually are referred to as a processor, or central processing unit (CPU). The operational speed of the CPU primarily determines the speed of the computer as a whole. The basic operation of the CPU is analogous to a computation carried out by a person using an arithmetic calculator. The control unit corresponds to the human brain and the memory to a notebook that stores the program, initial data, and intermediate and final computational results. In the case of an electronic computer, the CPU and fast memories are realized with transistor circuits.

I/O units, or devices, are commonly referred to as computer peripherals and consist of input units (such as keyboards and optical scanners) for feeding instructions and data into the computer and output units (such as printers and monitors) for displaying results. In addition to RAM, a computer usually contains some slower, but larger and permanent, secondary memory storage. Almost all computers contain a magnetic storage device known as a hard disk, as well as a disk drive to read from or write to removable magnetic media known as floppy disks.

文章中譯

數位電腦一般來說包括控制、**算術邏輯**、記憶、輸入／輸出等**單元**。算術邏輯單元 (ALU) 執行簡單的加、減、乘、除及邏輯運算，例如交集和聯集。電腦主要的記憶單元，通常是**高速的隨機存取記憶體** (RAM)，儲存指令和資料。控制單元從記憶體中取出資料和指令，左右 ALU 的運算。控制單元和 ALU 常常合稱爲處理器或中央處理單元 (CPU)；整台電腦的速度主要取決於 CPU 的作業速度。CPU 的基本運作模式**和**人使用數學計算機進行**運算的方式類似**；控制單元就像是人腦，記憶體則像是一本筆記本，記錄了程式、初始資料、演算的過程和最後的結果。在電子計算機中使用了**電晶體迴路**，使得 CPU 和快速的記憶體成爲可能。

輸入／輸出單元或裝置通常**被稱為電腦週邊設備**，由輸入單元（例如鍵盤、光學掃描器）和輸出單元（例如印表機、螢幕）所組成，輸入單元將指令與資料送進電腦，輸出單元則展示運算結果。除了 RAM，電腦通常還有一些比較慢，但是容量比較大的次級永久記憶儲存裝置。幾乎所有電腦都配備一種稱爲硬碟的**磁性儲存裝置**，另外還有軟碟機，可以在可取出的磁性媒介（一般稱爲軟碟）執行讀寫工作。

Double-Check

- a digital computer　數位電腦

　參 digital [ˋdɪʤətl̩] (adj.) 數位的，數碼的（反 analog (adj.) 類比的）

- an arithmetic-logic unit　算術邏輯單元

　[ˏærɪθˋmɛtɪk]

- high-speed random-access memory　高速的隨機存取記憶體

　[ˋrændəm]

- analogous to a computation　和運算類似

　[ˏkɑmpjʊˋteʃən]

　參 analogous [əˋnæləgəs] (adj.) 類似的

- transistor circuit　電晶體迴路

　[ˋsɜkɪt]

- be referred to as computer peripherals　被稱爲電腦週邊設備

　[pəˋrɪfərəlz]

　參 refer to ... as... 稱…爲…

- a magnetic storage device　磁性儲存裝置

　[mægˋnɛtɪk] [ˋstorɪʤ]

Earth Science

45 Four Seasons

四季

Key Sentences

1 Latitudinal variations in the input of solar energy are due to two factors.

緯度不同，接收到的太陽能也不同，原因有二。

2 The polar axis of the earth is tilted at an angle of 23.5° with respect to the ecliptic.

地球的南北極地軸與黃道（繞日軌道）呈 23.5 度傾斜。

3 In the Northern Hemisphere winter, no sunlight strikes the area around the North Pole during a full day's rotation of the earth.

北半球冬天時，地球自轉一整天也沒有任何日光照射到北極附近的地區。

4 As the seasons shift, the South Polar region eventually becomes plunged into 24-hour darkness.

隨著季節轉換，南極地區最後會陷入 24 小時的黑暗中。

5 Low-latitude regions near the equator undergo little seasonal change in the duration of daylight.

靠近赤道的低緯度地區，白晝時間長短很少隨著季節變化。

6 Because of seasonality, more annual radiation is received per unit area at lower as compared to higher latitudes.

因爲季節的關係，與高緯度地區比較，低緯度地區每單位面積整年所接收到的輻射能量較高。

Reading Focus 282字

MP3 091

Latitudinal variations in the input of solar energy are due to two factors. First, the earth is a sphere, and the angle at which the sun's rays hit its surface varies from 90° (or vertical) near the equator to 0° (or horizontal) near the poles. Less energy is received at the poles because the same amount of radiation is spread out over a much larger area at high latitudes and because at high latitudes the sun's rays must travel through a much greater thickness of atmosphere, where more absorption and reflection occur.

The second factor affecting latitudinal variations in heating is the duration of daylight. Because the polar axis of the earth is tilted at an angle of 23.5° with respect to the ecliptic, we have a progression of seasons where the angle of the sun's rays striking any given point varies over the year. In the Northern Hemisphere winter, no sunlight strikes the area around the North Pole during a full day's rotation of the earth because it is in the earth's shadow. Thus, little or no solar heating occurs in this area at this time. Conversely, at the South Pole there is continual daylight, but at a very low sun angle, during the Northern Hemisphere winter. As the seasons shift, the South Polar region eventually becomes plunged into 24-hour darkness, just as the North Pole had been earlier. Low-latitude regions near the equator, by contrast, undergo little seasonal change in the duration of daylight, whereas intermediate latitudes are subjected to changes intermediate between those of the poles and the equator. Thus, because of seasonality, more annual radiation is received per unit area at lower as compared to higher latitudes.

文章中譯

緯度不同，接收到的太陽能也不同，原因有二：第一，地球是個球體，太陽光線照射到地球表面的角度，可以從赤道附近的 90 度（垂直）到兩極地區的零度（水平）。極區接受到的能量較少，因爲在高緯度地區同樣的輻射能量分布的面積要廣大得多，而且在高緯度地區陽光必須穿過較厚的大氣層，導致更多能量被吸收、反射。

影響不同緯度溫度變化的第二個因素，是日照時間的長短。因爲**地球的南北極地軸與黃道（繞日軌道）呈 23.5 度傾斜**，所以在某些地方太陽入射的角度會隨著一年中不同時間而變化，因而有了四季的輪替。**北半球冬天**時，**地球自轉一整天**也沒有任何日光照射到北極附近的地區，因爲此時北極位於地球的陰影中。因此，這個地區在這段期間只能接收到一點點太陽能，甚至完全沒有。相反地，北半球冬天時南極卻是日照不斷，但是陽光入射的角度很低。**隨著季節轉換**，**南極地區**最後會陷入 24 小時的黑暗中，就跟之前的北極一樣。相對地，**靠近赤道的低緯度地區**，白晝時間長短**很少隨著季節變化**，而中緯度地區的變化則介於兩極和赤道之間。如此一來，因爲季節的關係，與高緯度地區比較，低緯度地區**每單位面積整年**所接收到的**輻射能量**較高。

Double-Check

- latitudinal variations [ˌlætəˋtjudənl̩] 緯度不同
- the duration of daylight [djuˋreʃən] 日照的時間
- the polar axis of the earth [ˋpolɚ] [ˋæksɪs] 地球的南北極地軸
- be tilted at an angle of 23.5° with respect to the ecliptic [ˋtɪltɪd] [ɪˋklɪptɪk] 與黃道（繞日軌道）呈 23.5 度傾斜
- the Northern Hemisphere winter [ˋhɛməˌsfɪr] 北半球的冬天
- during a full day's rotation of the earth [roˋteʃən] 地球自轉一整天
- as the seasons shift 隨著季節轉換
- the South Polar region [ˋridʒən] 南極地區
- low-latitude regions near the equator [ˋlætəˌtjud] [ɪˋkwetɚ] 靠近赤道的低緯度地區
- undergo little seasonal change [ˋsizn̩əl] 很少隨著季節變化
- annual radiation [ˋænjʊəl] [ˌredɪˋeʃən] 整年的輻射能量
- per unit area [ˋɛrɪə] 每單位面積

Earth Science

46 Ocean Water: Salinity

海水的鹽度

Key Sentences

MP3 092

1 The average ocean salinity is 35 parts per thousand (ppt).

海洋的平均鹽度是 35 ppt（千分之 35）。

2 The Black Sea is so diluted by river runoff, its average salinity is only 16 ppt.

黑海**因為河水匯入而被稀釋**，平均鹽度只有 16 ppt。

3 Estuaries (where fresh river water meets salty ocean water) are examples of brackish waters.

例如**河口（河流的淡水和有鹽分的海水交會處）**就是半鹹水。

4 The process by which water flows through a semi-permeable membrane (a material that lets only some things pass through it) such as the animal's skin from an area of low concentration (lots of water, little salt) to an area of high concentration (little water, lots of salt) is called osmosis.

水**穿透一種半滲透膜**（一種只讓某些東西穿透的物質），例如穿透動物的皮膚，從低濃度（多水少鹽）的地方流到高濃度（少水多鹽）的地方，這個過程稱爲**滲透**。

5 Your kidneys will try to flush the salts out of your body in urine, and in the process pump out more water than you are taking in.

你的腎臟會試圖**透過尿液把那些鹽分沖出你的體外**，在這個過程中所排出的水會多過於你所喝進的水。

Reading Focus 272字

MP3 093

The average ocean salinity is 35 parts per thousand (ppt). This number varies between about 32 and 37 ppt. Rainfall, evaporation, river runoff, and ice formation cause the variations. For example, the Black Sea is so diluted by river runoff, its average salinity is only 16 ppt.

Freshwater salinity is usually less than 0.5 ppt. Water between 0.5 ppt and 17 ppt is called brackish. Estuaries (where fresh river water meets salty ocean water) are examples of brackish waters.

Most marine creatures keep the salinity inside their bodies at about the same concentration as the water outside their bodies because water likes a balance. If an animal that usually lives in salt water were placed in fresh water, the fresh water would flow into the animal through its skin. If a fresh water animal found itself in the salty ocean, the water inside of it would rush out. The process by which water flows through a semi-permeable membrane (a material that lets only some things pass through it) such as the animal's skin from an area of low concentration (lots of water, little salt) to an area of high concentration (little water, lots of salt) is called osmosis.

This is also why humans (and nearly all mammals) cannot drink salt water. When you take in those extra salts, your body will need to expel them as quickly as possible. Your kidneys will try to flush the salts out of your body in urine, and in the process pump out more water than you are taking in. Soon you'll be dehydrated and your cells and organs will not be able to function properly.

（來源：Office of Naval Research, Science & Technology Focus）

文章中譯

海洋的平均鹽度是 35 ppt（千分之 35），這個數值會在 32 到 37 ppt 之間變動，降雨、蒸發、河水匯入、結冰都會造成影響。舉例來說，黑海**因為河水匯入而被稀釋**，平均鹽度只有 16 ppt。

淡水的鹽度通常不到 0.5 ppt。介於 0.5 ppt 到 17 ppt 之間的水稱爲半鹹水，例如**河口（河流的淡水和有鹽分的海水交會處）**就是半鹹水。

大部分海洋生物體內的鹽度會跟體外的海水維持同樣濃度，因爲水喜歡平衡。如果將平常生活在鹽水裡的動物放到淡水裡，淡水就會穿透皮膚流進牠的體內；如果某個淡水動物被放到海洋裡，牠體內的水就會快速流出來。水**穿透一種半滲透膜**（一種只讓某些東西穿透的物質），例如穿透動物的皮膚，從低濃度（多水少鹽）的地方流到高濃度（少水多鹽）的地方，這個過程稱爲**滲透**。

這也是人類（甚至幾乎是所有的哺乳類動物）爲什麼不能喝鹽水的原因。當你吸收過多鹽分，你的身體就得盡快排出鹽分。你的腎臟會試圖**透過尿液把那些鹽分沖出你的體外**，在這個過程中所排出的水會多過於你所喝進的水，不久你就會脫水，細胞和器官將無法正常運作。

Double-Check

■ the average ocean salinity [sə`lɪnətɪ]	海洋的平均鹽度
■ be diluted by river runoff [`rʌn͵ɔf] 參 dilute [dɪ`lut] (v.) 稀釋，沖淡	因爲河水匯入而被稀釋
■ estuaries (where fresh river water meets salty ocean water) 參 estuary [`ɛstʃu͵ɛrɪ] (n.) 河口，河川入海處	河口（河流的淡水和有鹽分的海水交會處）
■ flow through a semi-permeable membrane [`mɛmbren] 參 permeable [`pɜmɪəbl̩] (adj.) 可滲透的，可透過的	穿透一種半滲透膜
■ osmosis [ɑz`mosɪs]	(n.) 滲透
■ flush the salts out of your body in urine [flʌʃ] [`jurɪn]	透過尿液把那些鹽分沖出你的體外

Earth Science

47 How Rain Is Formed

雨水形成的過程

Key Sentences

MP3 094

1 The sun's heat evaporates the water.

太陽的熱度**使水蒸發**。

2 It remains in the atmosphere as an invisible vapor until it condenses, first into clouds and then into raindrops.

變成停留在大氣中**看不見的水汽**，之後水汽**凝結**，先是**形成雲**，然後變成雨滴。

3 Convergent lift occurs in cyclonic storms such as tornadoes.

在**氣旋風暴如龍捲風**當中，會出現**輻合抬升**。

4 Air whirling toward the center of a cyclone collides with itself and is forced upward.

空氣向氣旋的中心旋轉，**互相碰撞之下**被迫上升。

5 For raindrops to form there must be particulate matter in the air.

要形成雨滴，空氣中必須有**微粒狀物質**。

6 These particles are called condensation nuclei.

這些微粒稱爲**冷凝核**。

7 The precipitation falls as snow.

降下來的就是雪。

Reading Focus 269字

MP3 095

The oceans are the chief source of rain, but lakes and rivers also contribute to it. The sun's heat evaporates the water. It remains in the atmosphere as an invisible vapor until it condenses, first into clouds and then into raindrops. Condensation happens when the air is cooled.

Air cools either through expansion or by coming into contact with a cool object such as a cold landmass or an ice-covered expanse. When air passes over a cold object, it loses heat and its moisture condenses as fog, dew, or frost. Air also cools as it rises and expands. The water vapor in the cooling air condenses to form clouds and, sometimes, rain.

Air rises for several reasons. Convergent lift occurs in cyclonic storms such as tornadoes. Air whirling toward the center of a cyclone collides with itself and is forced upward. In convective lift, air coming into contact with a warm surface, such as a desert, is heated and becomes more buoyant than the surrounding air. In orographic lift, the air is forced upward as it encounters a cooler, denser body of air or when it meets raised landforms such as mountains.

For raindrops to form there must be particulate matter in the air, such as dust or salt, at temperatures above freezing. These particles are called condensation nuclei. When the nuclei are cooled to temperatures below the freezing point, water condenses around them in layers. The particles become so heavy they resist updrafts and fall through the clouds. When the air temperature is at or below freezing all the way to the ground, the precipitation falls as snow.

文章中譯

海洋是雨的主要來源，但是湖泊和河川同樣也功不可沒。太陽的熱度**使水蒸發**，變成停留在大氣中**看不見的水汽**，之後水汽**凝結**，先是**形成雲**，然後變成雨滴。空氣冷卻時，水汽就會凝結。

空氣之所以冷卻，可能是因爲氣團擴張，或是接觸到較冷的物體，例如寒冷的大陸或是冰層覆蓋的廣闊區域。空氣通過冷物體時熱氣會流失，其中的濕氣就會凝結成霧氣、露水、霜等。空氣上升膨脹時也會冷卻，冷卻的氣團中所含的水汽會凝結成雲，有時候就成了雨。

空氣上升有幾個原因。在**氣旋風暴如龍捲風**當中，會出現**輻合抬升**，空氣向氣旋的中心旋轉，**互相碰撞之下**被迫上升。在對流抬升之中，空氣接觸到溫暖的地表（例如沙漠地區）而受熱，變得比周圍的空氣更輕而上升。至於地形抬升，則是空氣遇到密度較高的一團冷空氣，或是碰到隆起的地形如山岳而被迫上升。

要形成雨滴，空氣中必須有**微粒狀物質**，例如灰塵或鹽分，而且溫度要高於冰點。這些微粒稱爲**冷凝核**。冷凝核的溫度降到冰點以下的時候，水汽就圍著冷凝核一層層地凝結，微粒愈來愈重，終於超過往上升的浮力時，就會穿過雲層往下降。如果一直到降至地表時的溫度都在冰點或冰點以下，**降下來的就是雪**。

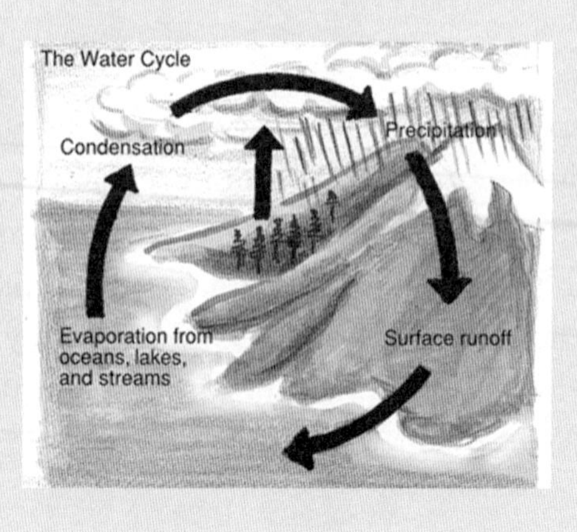

Double-Check

- evaporate the water 使水蒸發
  [ɪ`væpə͵ret]

- an invisible vapor 看不見的水汽
  [ɪn`vɪzəbḷ] [`vepɚ]

- condense into clouds 凝結成雲
  [kən`dɛns]

- convergent lift 輻合抬升
  參 convergent [kən`vɝdʒənt] (adj.) 聚合的，集中的

- cyclonic storms such as tornadoes 如龍捲風的氣旋風暴
  [saɪ`klɑnɪk] [tɔr`nedoz]

- collide with... 和…碰撞
  [kə`laɪd]

- convective lift 對流抬升
  [kən`vɛktɪv]

- orographic lift 地形抬升
  [͵ɔrə`græfɪk]

- particulate matter 微粒狀物質
  [pɑr`tɪkjəlɪt]

- condensation nuclei 冷凝核
  [͵kɑndɛn`seʃən] [`njuklɪ͵aɪ]

- precipitation (n.) 降雨（量），降雪（量）
  [prɪ͵sɪpə`teʃən]

Earth Science

48 Arctic Tundra

北極凍原

Key Sentences

1 Arctic tundra is located in the northern hemisphere, encircling the north pole and extending south to the coniferous forests of the taiga.

北極凍原位於北半球，環繞北極，向南延伸到針葉林地帶的針葉林。

2 The average summer temperature is 3 to 12°C which enables this biome to sustain life.

夏季平均溫度有攝氏 3 到 12 度，讓這裡的生物群落得以維持生命。

3 When water saturates the upper surface, bogs and ponds may form, providing moisture for plants.

當上層的表土水分飽和時，就會形成沼澤和池塘，提供水分給植物。

4 All of the plants are adapted to sweeping winds and disturbances of the soil.

這些植物全都能適應不斷吹襲的風以及土壤的變動。

5 Animals have adapted to handle long, cold winters and to breed and raise young quickly in the summer.

動物都能適應，知道如何對付又長又冷的冬天，也知道如何在夏天快速繁衍、養育下一代。

6 Animals such as mammals and birds also have additional insulation from fat.

哺乳類和鳥類等動物還能利用脂肪禦寒。

7 Because of constant immigration and emigration, the population continually oscillates.

由於不斷移入與移出，動物數量一直是起起伏伏的。

Reading Focus 284字

MP3 097

Arctic tundra is located in the northern hemisphere, encircling the north pole and extending south to the coniferous forests of the taiga. The arctic is known for its cold, desert-like conditions. The growing season ranges from 50 to 60 days. The average winter temperature is -34°C (-30°F), but the average summer temperature is 3 to 12°C (37 to 54°F) which enables this biome to sustain life. Rainfall may vary in different regions of the arctic. Yearly precipitation, including melting snow, is 15 to 25 cm (6 to 10 inches). Soil is formed slowly. A layer of permanently frozen subsoil called permafrost exists, consisting mostly of gravel and finer material. When water saturates the upper surface, bogs and ponds may form, providing moisture for plants. There are no deep root systems in the vegetation of the arctic tundra; however, there are still a wide variety of plants that are able to resist the cold climate. There are about 1,700 kinds of plants in the arctic and subarctic. All of the plants are adapted to sweeping winds and disturbances of the soil. Plants are short and cluster together to resist the cold temperatures and are protected by the snow during the winter. The fauna in the arctic is also diverse. Animals have adapted to handle long, cold winters and to breed and raise young quickly in the summer. Animals such as mammals and birds also have additional insulation from fat. Many animals hibernate during the winter because food is not abundant. Another alternative is to migrate south in the winter, like birds do. Reptiles and amphibians are few or absent because of the extremely cold temperatures. Because of constant immigration and emigration, the population continually oscillates.

（來源：UCMP/University of California Museum of Paleontology）

文章中譯

北極凍原位於北半球，**環繞北極**，**向南延伸到**針葉林地帶的**針葉林**。北極以寒冷、荒原般的環境著稱。植物的生長季節從 50 到 60 天不等，冬季平均溫度是攝氏零下 34 度（華氏零下 30 度），但夏季平均溫度有攝氏 3 到 12 度（華氏 37 到 54 度），**讓這裡的生物群落得以維持生命**。北極的降雨依區域而有所不同，年降雨量（包括融雪）在 150 到 250 毫米（6 到 10 英寸）之間。土壤的形成很緩慢。有一層永遠結凍的底土稱爲凍土，大多由砂礫和更細的物質組成。當**上層的表土水分飽和時**，**就會形成沼澤和池塘**，提供水分給植物。北極凍原沒有深根性植物，不過，仍然有很多各種能夠抵抗酷寒氣候的植物。北極和亞北極地帶有大約 1,700 種植物，這些植物全都能**適應不斷吹襲的風**以及**土壤的變動**。植物長得短小，聚集叢生以抵抗低溫，冬天則受到雪的保護。北極的動物群也很多樣化。動物都能適應，知道如何**對付又長又冷的冬天**，也知道如何在夏天**快速繁衍、養育下一代**。哺乳類和鳥類等動物**還能利用脂肪禦寒**。因爲食物短缺，許多動物在冬天會冬眠，或像鳥類一樣往南遷移。因爲酷寒氣候，爬蟲類和兩棲類動物很少見或完全沒有。由於不斷移入與移出，**動物數量一直是起起伏伏的**。

Double-Check

- arctic tundra 北極凍原
  [`ɑrktɪk] [`tʌndrə]
- encircle the north pole 環繞北極
  [ɪn`sɜkḷ]
- extend south to the coniferous forests 向南延伸到針葉林
  [kə`nɪfərəs]
- enable this biome to sustain life 讓這裡的生物群落得以維持生命
  [`baɪ͵om]
- water saturates the upper surface 上層的表土水分飽和
  參 saturate [`sætʃə͵ret] (v.) 浸透
- bogs and ponds may form 會形成沼澤和池塘
  [bɑgz]
- be adapted to sweeping winds 適應不斷吹襲的風
  [ə`dæptɪd]
- disturbances of the soil 土壤的變動
  [dɪ`stɜbənsɪz]
- handle long, cold winters 對付又長又冷的冬天
  參 handle [`hændḷ] (v.) 應付，對付，處理
- breed and raise young quickly 快速繁衍、養育下一代
  [brid]
- have additional insulation from fat 還能利用脂肪禦寒
  [͵ɪnsə`leʃən]
- the population continually oscillate 動物數量一直是起起伏伏的
  參 oscillate [`ɑsə͵let] (v.) 擺動，來回

Ecology

An Unintended Consequence

出乎意料的結果

Key Sentences

MP3 098

1 Scientists have discovered a disturbing unintended consequence of genetic engineering.

科學家發現**基因工程**有個**出乎意料**且令人不安**的後遺症**。

2 Monarchs are not an endangered species.

帝王蝶並不是**一種瀕臨絕種的蝶類**。

3 The genetically engineered corn might be killing other insects and doing other unseen damage to the food chain.

經過基因工程改造的玉米可能導致其他昆蟲死亡，**對食物鏈造成其他未知的傷害**。

4 The corn is genetically engineered to produce a natural pesticide that kills the corn-destroying European corn borer.

這種玉米**經過基因工程改造**，能夠分泌**一種天然的殺蟲劑**，殺死危害玉米的歐洲玉米螟。

5 Bt corn has been touted by the industry as a way to fight a major pest without using chemicals.

業界宣揚 Bt 玉米的**好處**是，不需使用任何化學藥劑就能抵抗主要的蟲害。

Reading Focus 188字

MP3 099

Scientists have discovered a disturbing unintended consequence of genetic engineering: pollen from a widely planted, laboratory-designed strain of corn can kill monarch butterflies.

Monarch caterpillars eating milkweed leaves dusted with pollen from the altered corn plants ate less, grew more slowly and died more quickly. After four days, 44 percent of them had died versus none of the caterpillars that did not feed on the pollen.

Monarchs are not an endangered species, but environmentalists fear that if the genetically engineered corn is killing the orange-and-black butterflies, it might be killing other insects and doing other unseen damage to the food chain.

The strain is called Bt corn and is manufactured by major agricultural companies. The corn is genetically engineered to produce a natural pesticide that kills the corn-destroying European corn borer.

It was approved in the U.S. by the Food and Drug Administration and hit the market in 1996. It accounted for more than 25 percent of the 40 million hectares of corn planted in the U.S. in 1998.

Bt corn has been touted by the industry as a way to fight a major pest without using chemicals.

Q The phrase "accounted for" in paragraph 5 is closest in meaning to:
(A) occupied (B) endangered (C) explained (D) altered

A (A)

文章中譯

科學家發現**基因工程**有個**出乎意料**且令人不安**的後遺症**：一種實驗室培養出來、大量種植的玉米，其花粉會殺害帝王蝶。

若在馬利筋葉子上沾上這種基因改造玉米的花粉，帝王蝶的幼蟲食用之後，食量會變小，生長速度減緩，而且比較容易死亡。四天後，有 44% 的幼蟲死亡，而沒有食用花粉的幼蟲則安然無恙。

帝王蝶並不是**一種瀕臨絕種的蝶類**，不過環境保護者擔憂，如果經過基因工程改造的玉米會殺害這種橘黑相間的蝴蝶，也可能導致其他昆蟲死亡，**對食物鏈造成其他未知的傷害**。

這種玉米稱爲「Bt 玉米[1]」，由各大農業公司生產製造。Bt 玉米**經過基因工程改造**，能夠分泌**一種天然的殺蟲劑**，殺死危害玉米的歐洲玉米螟。

Bt 玉米在美國經食品藥物管理局通過，於 1996 年上市；1998 年，全美種植的四千萬公頃玉米中，Bt 玉米占了超過 25%。

業界宣揚 Bt 玉米的**好處**是，不需使用任何化學藥劑就能抵抗主要的蟲害。

1 也稱爲「抗蟲玉米」。Bt 即 Bacillus thuringiensis（蘇力菌）。

Double-Check

- unintended consequence 出乎意料的結果
  [ˌʌnɪnˋtɛndɪd] [ˋkɑnsəˌkwɛns]

- genetic engineering 基因工程
  [dʒəˋnɛtɪk][ˌɛndʒəˋnɪrɪŋ]

- an endangered species 一種瀕臨絕種的物種
  [ɪnˋdendʒɚd]

- do unseen damage 造成未知的傷害
  [ˋdæmɪdʒ]

- food chain 食物鏈
  [tʃen]

- be genetically engineered 經過基因工程改造
  參 engineer [ˌɛndʒəˋnɪr] (v.) 處理，加工，控制

- a natural pesticide 天然的殺蟲劑
  參 pesticide [ˋpɛstɪˌsaɪd] (n.) 殺蟲劑 (= insecticide)

- be touted by the industry 業界宣揚（好處）
  [ˋtaʊtɪd] [ˋɪndəstrɪ]

Ecology

50 Conservation
生態保育

Key Sentences

1 In the 1980s a number of wildlife biologists and conservation groups fostered a movement to restore the gray wolf to Yellowstone National Park.

1980 年代，許多野生生物學家及保育團體發起一項運動，要恢復黃石國家公園內的灰狼生態。

2 Hunters would often poison the carcass of a downed elk in an attempt to decrease the wild canine population.

獵人常在麋鹿的屍體上下毒，試圖減少這種野生犬科動物的數目。

3 A bounty was placed on wolves by the government.

政府提供獵狼的獎金。

4 The animals would decimate area livestock.

這種動物會大量殺害地區內的家畜。

5 The wolves made a dramatic and beneficial impact on wildlife biodiversity in Yellowstone.

狼群對黃石公園裡野生動物的生物多樣性有極大的正面效應。

6 Coyotes had been the top predators in the ecosystem.

北美土狼成了生態系統中最上層的掠食者。

7 The decreased coyote population was a boon for rodent species.

土狼數目下降對齧齒類動物是一大福音。

Reading Focus 282字

MP3 101

In the 1980s a number of wildlife biologists and conservation groups fostered a movement to restore the gray wolf to Yellowstone National Park. In the late 19th century, wolves were considered a nuisance by park visitors; hunters would often poison the carcass of a downed elk in an attempt to decrease the wild canine population. A bounty was placed on wolves by the government, and by the 1920s the population was eliminated. The reintroduction program was strongly protested by local ranchers, who claimed that the animals would decimate area livestock. Despite the protests, the wolf restoration program began in 1995 with the release of 33 Canadian wolves into the park.

The wolf population thrived in their new home, with the population at the end of 1997 numbering approximately 97 and continuing to grow. In only two years after the wolves were transported from Canada to the Wyoming park, they reduced the Yellowstone coyote population by almost 50 percent. In doing so, the wolves made a dramatic and beneficial impact on wildlife biodiversity in Yellowstone. In the absence of the wolves, the coyotes had been the top predators in the ecosystem, at the top of the local food chain, along with grizzly bears. Their population had grown large but remained extremely stable. Part of the reason for the coyotes' decline after the wolves were reintroduced may be territorial shifts—some of the coyotes may have simply moved out of Yellowstone. But the main reason for the downsized coyote population was probably death at the jaws of the wolves. The decreased coyote population was a boon for rodent species, such as ground squirrels, voles, and pocket gophers, which constituted most of the coyote diet.

文章中譯

1980 年代，許多**野生生物學家**及**保育團體發起一項運動**，要**恢復**黃石國家公園內的**灰狼生態**。19 世紀晚期，來到公園的遊客對狼反感，而獵人常在**麋鹿的屍體**上下毒，試圖減少**這種野生犬科動物的數目**，政府也**提供**獵狼**的獎金**，於是到了 1920 年代便不見狼群的蹤跡。當地農牧業者大力反對復育狼群的計畫，他們表示狼這種動物會**大量殺害地區內的家畜**。儘管遭到抗議，灰狼復育計畫還是於 1995 年展開，在公園內野放了 33 匹從加拿大捕來的狼。

這批狼在新家繁衍茁壯，到了 1997 年底，數目約達 97 匹，而且仍持續成長中。這些狼從加拿大運送到位於美國懷俄明州的公園不過兩年的時間，就讓黃石公園內的北美土狼數目減少了 50%。因爲如此，狼群**對**黃石公園裡**野生動物的生物多樣性有極大的正面效應**。沒有狼群時，北美土狼成了**生態系統中最上層的掠食者**，和北美灰熊並列當地食物鏈的最高層。土狼數量大增，但是整體數目一直維持得非常穩定。重新引進灰狼後土狼的數目之所以減少，部分原因可能是因爲棲息地的轉換——有些土狼可能乾脆離開黃石公園。但是土狼數量縮減的主要原因，可能還是因爲死於灰狼的攻擊。土狼數目下降**對齧齒類動物**卻是**一大福音**，例如地松鼠、田鼠、金花鼠等，這些動物構成了土狼的主食。

灰狼

Double-Check

■ wildlife biologists [ˋwaɪld͵laɪf][baɪˋalədʒɪsts]	野生生物學家
■ conservation groups [͵kansəˋveʃən]	保育團體
■ foster a movement [ˋfɔstə]	發起一項運動
■ restore the gray wolf [rɪˋstɔr]	恢復灰狼生態
■ the carcass of a downed elk [ˋkarkəs] [ɛlk]	麋鹿的屍體
■ the wild canine population [ˋkenaɪn][͵papjəˋleʃən]	野生犬科動物的數目
■ a bounty was placed on… [ˋbaʊntɪ]	提供…的獎金
■ The population was eliminated. [ɪˋlɪmə͵netɪd]	這類動物被消滅了。
■ the reintroduction program [͵riɪntrəˋdʌkʃən]	復育計畫
■ decimate area livestock [ˋdɛsə͵met] [ˋlaɪv͵stak]	大量殺害地區內的家畜
■ make a beneficial impact on… [͵bɛnəˋfɪʃəl]	對…有正面效應
■ wildlife biodiversity [͵baɪodaɪˋvɝsətɪ]	野生動物的生物多樣性
■ the top predators in the ecosystem [ˋprɛdətəz] [ˋɛko͵sɪstəm]	生態系統中最上層的掠食者
■ a boon for rodent species [bun] [ˋrodn̩t]	對齧齒類動物是一大福音

Optics

Electron Microscopes
電子顯微鏡

Key Sentences

MP3 102

1 The electron microscope is so named because it directs a beam of electrons rather than light through a specimen.

電子顯微鏡之所以稱爲「電子顯微鏡」，是因爲使用時穿過標本的不是光線而是一束電子。

2 This beam then travels through the length of the microscope cylinder, which houses the lenses, the specimen chamber, and the image-recording system.

然後這束電子通過顯微鏡的鏡筒，鏡筒中含有透鏡、標本室以及影像紀錄系統。

3 The column and specimen chamber of the electron microscope are evacuated by pumps.

電子顯微鏡的鏡筒和標本室用幫浦抽成真空。

4 Living specimens cannot be examined with an electron microscope, since they will not survive in a vacuum.

活標本因爲在真空狀態下無法生存，不能使用電子顯微鏡來觀察。

5 In the optical microscope the image is determined by absorption of light by the specimen.

在光學顯微鏡中，成像品質由標本吸收的光線多寡決定。

6 The electron microscope, with its tremendous resolving power, can magnify specimens over 50,000 times.

電子顯微鏡由於解析力超強，可以放大標本五萬倍以上。

Reading Focus 268字

MP3 103

The electron microscope is so named because it directs a beam of electrons rather than light through a specimen. The beam of electrons is created in a hot tungsten filament in an electron gun. This beam then travels through the length of the microscope cylinder, which houses the lenses, the specimen chamber, and the image-recording system. Two types of electron lenses are used, electrostatic and electromagnetic. They create electric and electromagnetic fields to both concentrate and move the beam.

The electron microscope requires that the electron beam be in a vacuum, because electrons cannot travel far in air at atmospheric pressure. The column and specimen chamber of the electron microscope are evacuated by pumps. Living specimens cannot be examined with an electron microscope, since they will not survive in a vacuum. The magnification in magnetic electron microscopes is determined by the strength of the current passing through the electric and electromagnetic lens coils. The image is focused by changing the current through the objective lens coil. In the optical microscope the image is determined by absorption of light by the specimen; in the electron microscope the image results from a scattering of electrons by atoms of the specimen. Since an atom with a high atomic number scatters electrons more than does a light atom, it appears darker. As the beam passes through a specimen, each tiny variation in the structure of the specimen causes a variation in the electron stream. The image produced is then projected onto a fluorescent screen or recorded on film. The electron microscope, with its tremendous resolving power, can magnify specimens over 50,000 times.

文章中譯

電子顯微鏡之所以稱爲「電子顯微鏡」，是因爲**使用時穿過標本的**不是光線而是**一束電子**。電子槍中的熱鎢絲製造出一束電子，然後這束電子通過**顯微鏡的鏡筒**，鏡筒中**含有透鏡**、標本室以及影像紀錄系統。使用的電子透鏡有兩種，靜電透鏡和電磁透鏡。這兩種透鏡製造出電場和電磁場，具有集中和移動電子束的雙重功能。

電子顯微鏡中的電子束必須處於眞空狀態，因爲在大氣壓力下，電子無法移動太遠的距離。電子顯微鏡的鏡筒和標本室**用幫浦抽成真空**。活標本因爲**在真空狀態下**無法**生存**，不能使用電子顯微鏡來觀察。電磁型電子顯微鏡的放大倍率由電流通過靜電與電磁透鏡線圈的強度來決定。藉由改變通過物鏡線圈的電流讓影像聚焦。在**光學顯微鏡**中，成像品質由**標本吸收的光線**多寡決定；至於電子顯微鏡的成像則是由標本的原子對電子束的散射形成。和原子數較少的原子相較之下，原子數較大的原子對電子束的散射較強，因此顯得較暗。電子束穿過標本時，標本中每個細微的結構變化都會導致電子束跟著改變，產生的影像接著就被投射在螢光屏上，或記錄在底片上。電子顯微鏡由於**解析力超強**，可以**放大標本**五萬倍以上。

Double-Check

- the electron microscope 電子顯微鏡
  [ɪˋlɛktrɑn] [ˋmaɪkrə͵skop]
- direct a beam of electrons 使用一束電子
  [bim]
- through a specimen 穿過標本
  [ˋspɛsəmən]
- the microscope cylinder 顯微鏡的鏡筒
  [ˋsɪlɪndɚ]
- house the lenses 含有透鏡
  參 house [haʊs] (v.) 含有；收藏；提供房子給…
- atmospheric pressure 大氣壓力
  [͵ætməsˋfɛrɪk]
- be evacuated by pumps 用幫浦抽成真空
  [ɪˋvækjʊ͵etɪd] [pʌmps]
- survive in a vacuum 在眞空狀態下生存
  [ˋvækjʊəm]
- the optical microscope 光學顯微鏡
  [ˋɑptɪk!]
- absorption of light by the specimen 標本吸收的光線
  [əbˋsɔrpʃən]
- tremendous resolving power 超強的解析力
  [trɪˋmɛndəs] [rɪˋzɑlvɪŋ]
- magnify specimens 放大標本
  [ˋmægnə͵faɪ]

Printing

52 Offset Printing

平版印刷

Key Sentences

MP3 104

1 Offset printing (also called offset lithography) has replaced letterpress and intaglio methods almost entirely for commercial work.

在所有商業用途領域裡，**平版印刷**（又稱**平版印刷術**）幾乎完全取代了凸版印刷以及**凹版印刷**。

2 As the inked blanket cylinder rotates, it deposits the image onto the paper.

上了油墨的橡皮滾筒轉動時，把圖像複製到紙張上。

3 Offset does not depend on raised or etched surfaces to transfer images.

平版印刷不需要藉著突起或**蝕刻的表面**來**轉印圖像**。

4 The offset plate is chemically treated so that the area to which the ink is transferred retains the greasy ink and repels water.

平版印刷版**經過化學處理**，因此需要轉印墨水的地方會留住油墨、**排斥水分**。

5 Since there is no type to wear out, an offset plate can make a large number of impressions.

由於這種方法不會造成鉛字磨損，因此一塊平版印刷版可以**大量印刷**。

Reading Focus 276字

MP3 105

In the past few decades, offset printing (also called offset lithography) has replaced letterpress and intaglio methods almost entirely for commercial work. The name offset refers to the fact that the printing plates do not come into direct contact with the paper. Instead, the inked printing plates (which are attached to a cylinder) transfer, or offset, the image to a rubber blanket covering another cylinder. As the inked blanket cylinder rotates, it deposits the image onto the paper, which is fed from another set of rollers.

The offset technique was made possible at the beginning of the 20th century after the development of certain photographic processes and the rotary webfed press. Offset printing plates are usually made of steel, aluminum, or a chrome-copper alloy.

Unlike letterpress or intaglio printing, offset does not depend on raised or etched surfaces to transfer images. Instead it relies on the fact that grease and water do not mix. As the plate cylinder rotates, the plate passes first under watersoaked damping rollers and then under inking rollers that carry a grease-based ink. The offset plate is chemically treated so that the area to which the ink is transferred retains the greasy ink and repels water. The rest of the plate retains water and repels ink. As the cylinder continues to rotate, the plate presses against the rubber blanket, which accepts ink from the plate and transfers it to the paper. Since there is no type to wear out, an offset plate can make a large number of impressions. Offset presses can be designed to print both sides of the paper at once and to reproduce images with one or more colors.

文章中譯

過去幾十年間，在所有商業用途領域裡，**平版印刷**（又稱**平版印刷術**）幾乎完全取代了凸版印刷以及**凹版印刷**。所謂「平版」，指的是印刷版不直接接觸紙張，而是利用上了墨的印刷版（裝在滾筒上）將圖像轉印（或說「利用平版印刷術印刷」）到另一個裹著一層橡皮的滾筒上。**上了油墨的橡皮滾筒轉動時，把圖像複製**到由另一套滾筒送進來的紙張上。

平版印刷的技術在 20 世紀初出現，因為攝影及捲筒印刷技術的進步，使得平版印刷成為可能。平版的印刷版通常由鋼、鋁或鉻銅合金製成。

平版印刷和凸版或凹版印刷不同，不需要藉著突起或**蝕刻的表面**來**轉印圖像**，而是依靠油水不相容的原理。印版滾筒轉動時，印刷版首先從吸滿了水的潮濕滾輪下通過，然後再通過沾滿墨水的滾輪，滾輪上的墨水是有油脂成分的油墨。平版印刷版**經過化學處理**，因此需要轉印墨水的地方會留住油墨、**排斥水分**；印刷版的其餘部分則會留住水分、排斥油墨。滾筒繼續轉動時，印刷版壓在橡皮滾筒上，橡皮滾筒接收了版上的油墨，將其轉印到紙張上面。由於這種方法不會造成鉛字磨損，因此一塊平版印刷版可以**大量印刷**。平版印刷可以設計成一次完成紙張的雙面印刷，以及用一種以上的顏色印刷圖像。

Double-Check

- offset printing　平版印刷
  [`ɔf͵sɛt]

- lithography　(n.) 平版印刷術
  [lɪ`θɑgrəfɪ]

- intaglio methods　凹版印刷
  [ɪn`tæljo]

- cylinder rotates　滾筒轉動
  [`sɪlɪndɚ]　[`rotets]

- deposit the image　複製圖像
  參 **deposit** [dɪ`pɑzɪt] (v.) 放置，安置

- etched surfaces　蝕刻的表面
  [ɛtʃt]　[`sɝfɪsɪz]

- transfer images　轉印圖像
  [træns`fɝ]

- be chemically treated　經過化學處理
  [`kɛmɪkəlɪ]

- repel water　排斥水分
  參 **repel** [rɪ`pɛl] (v.) 排斥；驅逐

- make a large number of impressions　大量印刷
  [ɪm`prɛʃənz]

Geology

53 What Are Oil and Gas?

石油和天然氣是什麼？

Key Sentences

MP3 106

1 Oil and gas are primarily mixtures of compounds of carbon and hydrogen, known as hydrocarbons.

石油和天然氣主要是由**碳和氫的化合物**混合而成，**也就是碳氫化合物**。

2 A natural cycle begins with deposits of plant and animal remains and fine sediment.

自然循環一開始是**動植物遺骸**與**泥沙等細小沉積物的堆積**。

3 Any hydrocarbons remaining on the surface are soon oxidized by bacteria.

任何留在地表的碳氫化合物很快就會**被細菌氧化**。

4 Oil and gas may be trapped underneath curved layers of rock called anticlines, or by faults in the rock.

石油和天然氣可能被封閉在**弧狀的岩層**之下，也就是背斜層，或是封閉在**岩層斷層處**。

5 The term reservoir can be misleading, giving people the impression of large subterranean lakes full of oil.

儲油層這個詞彙容易造成誤解，給人一種印象，好像**地底**有一大片滿是石油的**湖泊**。

6 Oil and gas are trapped within porous sedimentary rocks.

石油和天然氣被封閉在**布滿孔隙的沉積岩**之中。

Reading Focus 217字

MP3 107

Oil and gas are primarily mixtures of compounds of carbon and hydrogen, known as hydrocarbons. They are formed as part of a natural cycle which begins with deposits of plant and animal remains and fine sediment. Trapped over millions of years, often deep beneath the ocean, this organic matter is transformed by the combined effect of temperature and pressure into oil and natural gas.

The formation of oil and gas deposits, or reservoirs, occurs when these hydrocarbons migrate upward through the rock layers towards the surface. These hydrocarbons often escape to the surface where they may form natural oil seeps or, in the case of gas, simply dissipate. Any hydrocarbons remaining on the surface are soon oxidized by bacteria. Sometimes oil and gas are trapped in deep underground structures which prevent them from reaching the surface. They may be trapped underneath curved layers of rock called anticlines, or by faults in the rock. Faults occur when layers of rock split and move, such as in an earthquake or during normal seismic events. The term reservoir can be misleading, giving people the impression of large subterranean lakes full of oil. In fact, oil and gas are trapped within porous sedimentary rocks such as sandstone or shale and may occupy as little as five percent of the rock volume.

文章中譯

石油和天然氣主要是由**碳和氫的化合物**混合而成，**也就是碳氫化合物**。石油和天然氣的形成是自然循環的一部分，一開始是**動植物遺骸**與**泥沙等細小沉積物的堆積**。這種生物有機體常常深埋於海底，經過數百萬年後，因爲溫度和壓力的雙重因素作用，轉變成石油和天然氣。

石油和天然氣蘊藏區（或稱儲油層）的形成，是這些碳氫化合物穿過岩層，往地表上升的結果。這些碳氫化合物往往從地表逸出，形成天然石油滲出，或形成天然氣直接消散。任何留在地表的碳氫化合物很快就會**被細菌氧化**。有時候石油和天然氣被封閉在深層的地下結構，無法到達地表。石油和天然氣可能被封閉在**弧狀的岩層**之下，也就是背斜層，或是封閉在**岩層斷層處**。岩層裂開、移動時（例如在大地震或平常的地震活動中）就會形成斷層。**儲油層這個詞彙容易造成誤解**，給人一種印象，好像**地底**有一大片滿是石油的**湖泊**。事實上，石油和天然氣被封閉在**布滿孔隙的沉積岩**如沙岩、頁岩之中，可能只有占岩層體積的 5%。

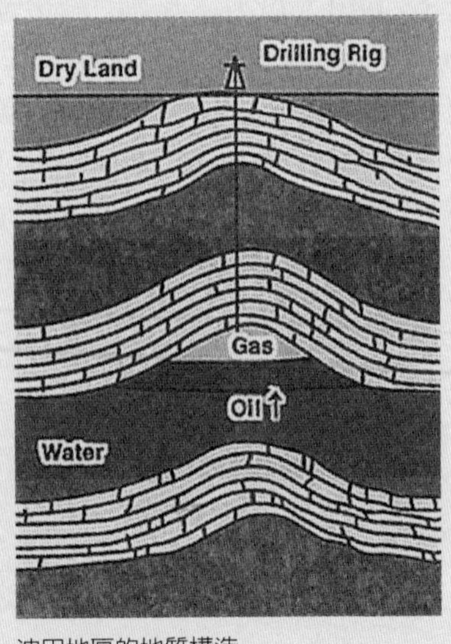

油田地區的地質構造

Double-Check

- compounds of carbon and hydrogen 碳和氫的化合物
  [`kampaʊndz] [`karbən] [`haɪdrədʒən]
- hydrocarbon (n.) 碳氫化合物
  [ˌhaɪdrə`karbən]
- deposits of plant and animal remains 動植物遺骸
  [dɪ`pazɪts] [rɪ`menz]
- fine sediment 細小沉積物
  [`sɛdəmənt]
- organic matter 有機體
  [ɔr`gænɪk]
- be oxidized by bacteria 被細菌氧化
  [`aksəˌdaɪzd] [bæk`tɪrɪə]
- curved layers of rock 弧狀的岩層
  [`leɚz]
- faults in the rock 岩層斷層處
  [fɔlts]
- seismic events 地震活動
  [`saɪzmɪk]
- reservoir (n.) 儲油層
  [`rɛzɚˌvɔr]
- misleading (adj.) 造成誤解的
  [mɪs`lidɪŋ]
- subterranean lakes 地底湖泊
  [ˌsʌbtə`renɪən]
- porous sedimentary rocks 布滿孔隙的沉積岩
  [ˌsɛdə`mɛntərɪ]

  參 porous [`pɔrəs] (adj.) 多孔隙的；能滲透的

Geology

54 Convergent Boundaries

聚合板塊邊緣

Key Sentences

MP3 108

1 Plates collide head-on along their convergent boundaries.

板塊沿著聚合板塊邊緣正面碰撞。

2 A profusion of geologic activities is associated with a plate collision.

許多地質活動都和板塊碰撞有關。

3 The edge of the overriding plate is crumpled and uplifted to form a mountain chain roughly parallel to the trench.

位在上方的板塊的邊緣因褶曲而隆起，形成一條大致與海溝平行的山脈。

4 Materials may be scraped off the descending slab and incorporated into the adjacent mountains.

下沉板塊上面的物質可能會被刮掉，併入毗鄰的山脈中。

5 Magma formed where plates sink into the mantle floats upwards, and can reach the surface and erupt from volcanoes.

板塊沉入地函之處形成岩漿，岩漿往上冒，可能到達地表，從火山噴出。

6 Divergent zones are sources of new lithosphere.

分歧帶製造出新的岩石圈。

Reading Focus 199字

MP3 109

Because the plates cover the globe, if they separate in one place, they must converge somewhere else; and they do. Plates collide head-on along their convergent boundaries.

A profusion of geologic activities is associated with a plate collision. One plate sinks beneath the other, a process called subduction. Ocean lithosphere thus descends into the asthenosphere. This downbuckling produces a long, narrow deep-sea trench (about 100 km wide), where the ocean floor reaches its greatest depths (about 10 km below sea level). The edge of the overriding plate is crumpled and uplifted to form a mountain chain roughly parallel to the trench. The enormous forces of collision and subduction produce great earthquakes. Materials may be scraped off the descending slab and incorporated into the adjacent mountains. Imagine yourself as a geologist attempting to figure out the meaning of such tangled evidence. Furthermore, during subduction, parts of the descending plate may begin to melt. Magma formed where plates sink into the mantle floats upwards, and can reach the surface and erupt from volcanoes.

Recall that divergent zones are sources of new lithosphere. Subduction zones at boundaries of convergence are sinks in which lithosphere is consumed by being returned to the mantle.

! 特別注意 lithosphere [`lɪθə͵sfɪr] 與 asthenosphere [æs`θinə͵sfɪr] 的發音。

文章中譯

由於板塊覆蓋在地球表面，如果板塊在某個地方分開，一定會在另一個地方聚合，事實上也是如此。**板塊**沿著**聚合板塊邊緣正面碰撞**。

許多地質活動都和板塊碰撞有關。板塊沒入另一個板塊之下，這個過程稱為隱沒。海洋岩石圈因此下沉至軟流圈；這種向下彎曲的過程產生了一條狹長的深海海溝（寬約 100 公里），海床在此達到最深（低於海平面約 10 公里）。**位在上方的板塊的邊緣因褶曲而隆起**，形成一條大致**與海溝平行**的山脈。碰撞和隱沒產生極大的力量，造成大地震。下沉板塊上面的物質可能會被刮掉，**併入毗鄰的山脈中**。試著想像你是一名地質學家，正試圖理解這種混雜跡象的意義。而且，在隱沒的過程中，部分的下沉板塊可能會開始融化。**板塊沉入地函**之處形成岩漿，岩漿往上冒，可能到達地表，**從火山噴出**。

回想先前提到的，**分歧帶**製造出新的岩石圈。位於聚合板塊邊緣的隱沒帶則是沉沒的地區，岩石圈由此重新進入地函而消失。

Double-Check

- Plates collide head-on. 板塊正面碰撞。
  [kə`laɪd]

- convergent boundaries 聚合板塊邊緣
  [kən`vɝdʒənt] [`baʊndərɪz]

- a profusion of geologic activities 許多地質活動
  [prə`fjuʒən] [ˌdʒiə`lɑdʒɪk]

- the overriding plate 位在上方的板塊
  [ˌovə`raɪdɪŋ]

- crumple (v.) 弄皺，扭曲
  [`krʌmpḷ]

- uplift (v.) 上升，隆起
  [ʌp`lɪft]

- parallel to the trench 與海溝平行
  [`pærəˌlɛl] [trɛntʃ]

- be incorporated into the adjacent mountains 併入毗鄰的山脈中
  [ə`dʒesənt]

  參 incorporate [ɪn`kɔrpəˌret] (v.) 使併入

- Plates sink into the mantle. 板塊沉入地函。
  [`mæntḷ]

- erupt from volcanoes 從火山噴出
  [ɪ`rʌpt] [vɑl`kenoz]

- divergent zones 分歧帶

  參 divergent [də`vɝdʒənt] (adj.) 分歧的（反 convergent (adj.) 聚合的）

Geology

Energy and Resources

能源與資源

Key Sentences

MP3 110

1 The earth's crust consists of a relatively thin layer of rock lying above the mantle, a region of high temperatures and pressures.

地殼由一層相較之下較薄的岩層構成，位於溫度與壓力均高的地函之上。

2 Geologists call the rate of increase the "geothermal gradient," and measure it in degrees per unit of depth.

地質學家把這種溫度增加的比例稱爲「地溫梯度」，以每單位深度測量其度數。

3 Geothermal energy schemes go back thousands of years.

地熱能的利用可以回溯至數千年前。

4 Such reservoirs occur in permeable rocks, most commonly in seismically active regions.

這種蘊藏產生於具有滲透性的岩層，尤其在地震活動頻繁的區域最爲常見。

5 The first generator driven by geothermal steam began operating in Italy in 1904.

1904 年，第一部由地熱蒸汽驅動的發電機在義大利開始運作。

6 Decaying radioactive elements give the rocks extra heat.

放射衰退元素給了岩層額外的溫度。

Reading Focus 252字

MP3 111

The earth's crust consists of a relatively thin layer of rock lying above the mantle, a region of high temperatures and pressures. Geologists call the rate of increase the "geothermal gradient," and measure it in degrees per unit of depth.

The geothermal gradient varies from place to place, but it is usually higher in crust beneath the sea than in thicker continental crust. Engineers can exploit the heat wherever they can reach it.

Geothermal energy schemes go back thousands of years. Reservoirs of hot water can lie close to the surface where local geological conditions allow. Such reservoirs occur in permeable rocks, most commonly in seismically active regions. These are often close to the boundaries of crustal plates, for example in Iceland, New Zealand and Italy. Converting the energy to electricity is also not a new idea. The first generator driven by geothermal steam began operating in Italy in 1904. Today, geothermal power plants around the world have a capacity of more than two thousand megawatts. Together with geothermal projects that supply only warmth for space heating rather than electricity generation, this adds up to at least 10,000 MW of geothermal energy already in use. Engineers could extract more of this heat if they could find ways to drill economically through impermeable rock to depths at which temperatures are high enough. In a development project run by Britain's Central Electricity Generating Board in Cornwall in South-West England, the geothermal gradient is normal, but decaying radioactive elements give the rocks extra heat.

文章中譯

地殼由一層相較之下較**薄的岩層**構成，**位於**溫度與壓力均高的**地函之上**。地質學家把這種溫度增加的比例稱爲「**地溫梯度**[1]」，以**每單位深度**測量其度數。

地溫梯度隨著地方不同而變化，不過海洋地殼的地溫梯度通常高於較厚的大陸地殼。在可以獲得地熱的地方，工程師就可以利用這股熱能。

地熱能的利用可以回溯至數千年前。如果當地的地質狀況允許，熱水可能就會蘊藏在接近地表的地方。這種蘊藏**產生於具有滲透性的岩層**，尤其在**地震活動頻繁的區域**最爲常見，通常在地殼板塊邊緣的附近，例如冰島、紐西蘭、義大利。把地熱能轉換成電力也不是新想法。1904 年，**第一部由地熱蒸汽驅動的發電機**在義大利開始運作。今日，全球地熱發電廠的發電功率超過 20 億瓦特。如果連僅提供暖氣使用、不提供發電的地熱利用計畫也算進去，目前已經在使用的地熱能可以達到至少 100 億瓦特。如果能夠找到經濟的方法鑽過不透水層，到達溫度夠高的深度，工程師就可以取得更多的地熱能。英國的中央發電局在英格蘭西南部康瓦爾地區進行的一個發展計畫中，地溫梯度雖然只有一般的程度，但**放射衰退元素**卻給了岩層**額外的溫度**。

1 即深入地下每單位的溫度變化幅度。以大陸地殼來說，地溫梯度平均是 30°C/km，也就是深度每增加一公里，溫度就升高攝氏 30 度。

Double-Check

- the earth's crust [krʌst] — 地殼
- thin layer of rock [θɪn] — 薄的岩層
- lying above the mantle [`mæntḷ] — 位於地函之上的
- geothermal gradient [ˌdʒio`θɝmḷ] [`gredɪənt] — 地溫梯度
- per unit of depth [dɛpθ] — 每單位深度
- geothermal energy schemes [skimz] — 地熱能的利用
- occur [ə`kɝ] — (v.) 發生
- permeable rocks [`pɝmɪəbḷ] — 具有滲透性的岩層
- seismically active regions [`saɪzmɪkəlɪ] [`ridʒənz] — 地震活動頻繁的區域
- driven by geothermal steam [`drɪvən] — 由地熱蒸汽驅動的
- decaying radioactive elements [dɪ`keɪŋ] [ˌredɪo`æktɪv] — 放射衰退元素
- extra heat — 額外的溫度

Medicine

56 Massage
按摩

Key Sentences

MP3 112

1. Massage is a proven cure to stress.
   按摩**經證實對解除壓力有效**。

2. The massaging of flesh quiets the stress response.
   按摩肌肉能夠**平撫壓力的反應症狀**。

3. Massage can improve lung function in asthmatics and increase the immune function in men with HIV.
   按摩可以**改善氣喘患者的肺功能**並**提升**愛滋病帶原者的**免疫力**。

4. There are many other options, from yoga to biofeedback to music therapy.
   還有很多其他的選擇，從瑜伽、生物反饋療法到**音樂療法**。

5. People with asthma or rheumatoid arthritis could ease their sickness by writing about the most stressful events in their lives.
   罹患**氣喘或風濕性關節炎**的病患，藉由寫下**生活中使他們感到壓力最大的事件**，可以舒緩病情。

Reading Focus 236字

MP3 113

Massage is a proven cure to stress. No one knows precisely how the massaging of flesh quiets the stress response, but the effects can be dramatic. Over the past 23 years psychologist Tiffany Field of the University of Miami's Touch Research Institute has published studies suggesting it can hasten weight gain in early birth babies, improve lung function in asthmatics and increase the immune function in men with HIV. Healthy people may benefit too. In a 1996 study, medical workers who got 10 biweekly massages outscored their colleagues who didn't receive massages on timed math tests.

There are many other options, from yoga to biofeedback to music therapy, and none of them excludes the others. So do what works for you. And whether you go to church, join a support group or start a diary, find a way to talk about your feelings. Studies suggest that group support can extend the lives of people with skin or breast cancer. And researchers showed recently that people with asthma or rheumatoid arthritis could ease their sickness by writing about the most stressful events in their lives. How can such different exercises have such similar benefits? The key, experts agree, is that they fight feelings of helplessness. Anything that encourages a sense of control—putting a terrible memory into words, calming a racing heart through breathing exercises, even planning your own funeral—lets you stop feeling like a victim.

! 特別注意 So do what works for you. 的意思。

文章中譯

按摩經證實對解除壓力有效。沒有人確切了解按摩肌肉如何**平撫壓力的反應症狀**，但是按摩的效果可以是非常驚人的。過去 23 年以來，邁阿密大學觸覺研究中心的心理學家蒂芬妮．菲爾德發表了一連串的研究，結果顯示按摩可以提高早產兒體重增加的速度、**改善氣喘患者的肺功能**並**提升**愛滋病帶原者的**免疫力**。健康的人也可以受惠。在 1996 年的一項研究中，接受每兩週一次、共 10 次按摩的醫療從業人員在限時數學測驗中，成績高於沒有接受按摩的同仁。

還有很多其他的選擇，從瑜伽、生物反饋療法到**音樂療法**，沒有一種可以和其他療法完全劃清界限，所以選擇對自己有用的方式吧。不論是上教堂、加入互助團體還是開始寫日記，找個方法談論你的感受。研究顯示，團體的支持可以延長皮膚癌或乳癌患者的生命。研究人員最近還發現，罹患**氣喘或風濕性關節炎**的病患，藉由寫下**生活中使他們感到壓力最大的事件**，可以舒緩病情。這些活動差異這麼大，爲什麼能夠帶來這麼相似的好處呢？專家一致同意，關鍵是這些活動能夠抵抗無助感。只要能夠提高掌控的感覺，任何活動（例如把一段恐怖的記憶化爲文字、透過呼吸吐納平緩心跳，甚至是計畫自己的葬禮）都有助於使你不再感覺自己是個受害者。

Double-Check

- a proven cure to stress — 經證實對解除壓力有效
  [ˋpruvən]

- quiet the stress response — 平撫壓力的反應症狀
  [rɪˋspɑns]

  參 quiet [ˋkwaɪət] (v.) 減輕；使安靜

- improve lung function in asthmatics — 改善氣喘患者的肺功能
  [lʌŋ] [ˋfʌŋkʃən] [æzˋmætɪks]

- the immune function — 免疫力
  [ɪˋmjun]

  參 immune [ɪˋmjun] (adj.) 免疫的

- music therapy — 音樂療法
  [ˋθɛrəpɪ]

- asthma — (n.) 氣喘
  [ˋæzmə]

- rheumatoid arthritis — 風濕性關節炎
  [ˋruməˏtɔɪd] [ɑrˋθraɪtɪs]

- the most stressful events — 壓力最大的事件
  [ˋstrɛsfəl]

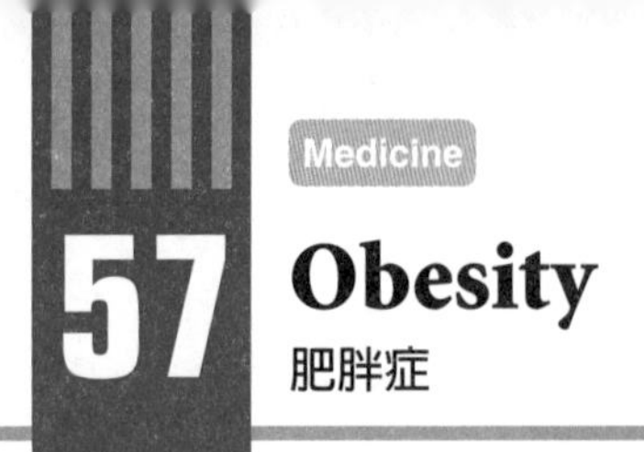

Obesity
肥胖症

Key Sentences

MP3 114

1 Obesity is the principal nutritional disease.

肥胖成了主要的營養性疾病。

2 Obesity itself is merely a form of hunger in disguise.

肥胖本身就是一種經過偽裝的飢餓型態。

3 The specter of overweight stalks some of us the way starvation stalks others.

體重過重的陰影威脅我們之中的某些人，正如飢餓威脅另一些人一樣。

4 The stomach bears witness.

胃就是最好的見證。

5 Bulky meals of 10,000 or more calories pose no mechanical or physiological problems.

一萬卡路里以上的大量進食，也不會造成物理性或生理上的問題。

6 We have an almost irresistible urge to eat.

對於吃，我們有種幾乎是無法抗拒的衝動。

7 We also have at least some built-in controls that reduce our appetite for food and that limit the accumulation of excess fat.

我們至少還是有些內建的控制機制，可以降低我們對食物的慾望，限制過量脂肪堆積。

Reading Focus 207字

MP3 115

In a society in which obesity is the principal nutritional disease, one easily forgets the horrible things that lack of food and drink can do to the human body. Yet obesity itself is merely a form of hunger in disguise. The specter of overweight stalks some of us the way starvation stalks others. That is because we humans have long developed the ability both to eat and to overeat. The stomach bears witness. Though it is a small muscular sac when empty, it readily expands to take in several pounds of food at a time; bulky meals of 10,000 or more calories pose no mechanical or physiological problems.

Healthy people who have endured considerable weight loss over a number of months as a result of food deprivation can eat in great volume. After volunteers in a famous laboratory hunger study returned to eating freely, their daily consumption rose to 10,000 calories.

Yet, no matter how hungry at the outset, human beings do not ordinarily continue to stuff themselves so resolutely that they swell to gigantic proportions. We have an almost irresistible urge to eat, but we also have at least some built-in controls that reduce our appetite for food and that limit the accumulation of excess fat.

Q The phrase "stuff" in paragraph 3 is closest in meaning to:

(A) feed (B) block (C) endure (D) starve

A (A)

文章中譯

在一個**肥胖**成了主要**營養性疾病**的社會中，大家很容易就會忘記缺乏食物和飲水對人體會造成多大的危害。而肥胖本身就是一種**經過偽裝的飢餓**型態，**體重過重的陰影威脅我們之中的某些人**，正如飢餓威脅另一些人一樣。這是因爲我們人類很早就發展出飲食和飲食過量這兩種能力，我們的胃**就是最好的見證**。胃裡面空空的時候，只是個由肌肉構成的小小囊袋，但它可以輕易擴張，一次容納好幾磅重的食物；就算是一萬卡路里以上的**大量進食**，也**不會造成物理性或生理上的問題**。

健康的人如果在幾個月之內因爲缺乏食物造成體重相當程度的減輕，可以吃下大量的食物。有個實驗室進行知名的飢餓研究，志願參與實驗的受試者恢復正常飲食之後，每日的食物攝取量提升至一萬卡路里。

然而，不論一開始有多餓，人類一般不會一直往嘴巴裡塞進食物、讓自己腫大到不成比例。對於吃，我們有種幾乎是**無法抗拒的衝動**，可是我們至少還是有些**內建的控制機制**，可以**降低我們**對食物**的慾望**，限制**過量脂肪堆積**。

Double-Check

- obesity (n.) 肥胖
  [o`bisətɪ]

- nutritional disease 營養性疾病
  [nju`trɪʃənḷ] [dɪ`ziz]

- hunger in disguise 經過偽裝的飢餓
  參 disguise [dɪs`gaɪz] (n.)(v.) 偽裝

- the specter of overweight 體重過重的陰影
  [`spɛktɚ]

- stalk (v.) 偷偷靠近
  [stɔk]

- bear witness 見證，證明
  [bɛr] [`wɪtnɪs]

- bulky meals 大量進食
  [`bʌlkɪ]

- pose no mechanical or physiological problems 不會造成物理性或生理上的問題
  [mə`kænɪkḷ] [ˌfɪzɪə`lɑdʒɪkḷ]

- irresistible urge 無法抗拒的衝動
  [ˌɪrɪ`zɪstəbḷ] [ɝdʒ]

- built-in controls 內建的控制機制
  [kən`trolz]

- reduce our appetite 降低我們的食慾
  [`æpəˌtaɪt]

- the accumulation of excess fat 過量脂肪的堆積
  [əˌkjumjə`leʃən] [ɪk`sɛs]

Medicine

Sports Medicine
運動醫學

Key Sentences

MP3 116

1 Sports medicine encompasses four areas.

運動醫學**包含四個領域**。

2 Physical preparation involves a program of conditioning exercises designed to develop certain muscle groups and to increase cardiac output and oxygen intake.

身體的準備包括一整套訓練運動，用以強化某些肌肉群、**增加心輸出量及攝氧量**。

3 Athletic shoes are continually improved to boost athletes' speed and endurance.

運動鞋一直不斷改進以**提升運動員的速度與耐力**。

4 New materials can increase performance by decreasing friction and resistance.

新的材質可以藉由**減少摩擦力和阻力**提高運動員的表現。

5 Nutrition is a critical aspect of sports medicine.

營養是運動醫學**一個非常重要的面向**。

6 The wrong diet can seriously impair an athlete's performance and health.

不當的飲食可能**嚴重影響運動員的表現**與健康。

Reading Focus 239字

MP3 117

Sports medicine encompasses four areas: preparation of the athlete, prevention of injury or illness, diagnosis and treatment of injury, and rehabilitation. Physical preparation involves a program of conditioning exercises designed to develop certain muscle groups and to increase cardiac output and oxygen intake. Mental preparation focuses on building self-image, maintaining motivation and discipline to train regularly, avoiding undue risks, and learning to accept whatever changes in life-style may be necessary. Mental preparation also helps athletes to handle the psychological stress associated with the risk of injury or illness. Practitioners of sports medicine advise manufacturers on the development of equipment that enhances performance and promotes the health and safety of athletes. Athletic shoes, for instance, are continually improved to boost athletes' speed and endurance while providing comfort and protection from injury. New materials make sportswear more comfortable and protective and can increase performance by decreasing friction and resistance.

Nutrition is a critical aspect of sports medicine. The wrong diet can seriously impair an athlete's performance and health. Nutritional counseling by trained professionals can ensure that athletes have what they need in terms of nutrient adequacy, energy requirements, protein and carbohydrate distribution, timing of meals, and fluid intake. In the late 20th century, increasing attention was given to athletes' use of so-called performance-enhancing drugs such as amphetamines and anabolic steroids. Today, practitioners of sports medicine must be prepared to advise athletes about the serious health risks associated with such drug use.

文章中譯

運動醫學**包含四個領域**：運動員的準備工作、傷害或疾病的預防、運動傷害的診斷與治療以及復健。身體的準備包括一整套訓練運動，用以強化某些肌肉群、**增加心輸出量及攝氧量**。心理的準備則集中在建立自我定位、維持固定訓練的動機及紀律、避免不必要的風險、學習接受任何可能必須的生活型態轉變。心理準備也可以幫助運動員面對受傷或生病的風險帶來的心理壓力。運動醫學專家及醫生針對運動器材的改善向製造商提出建議，以提升運動員的表現並促進運動員的健康和安全。以運動鞋爲例，一直不斷改進以**提升運動員的速度與耐力**，同時也提供舒適性，保護運動員免受運動傷害。新的材質使得運動服飾更舒適、更具保護性，還可以藉由**減少摩擦力和阻力**提高運動員的表現。

營養是運動醫學**一個非常重要的面向**。不當的飲食可能**嚴重影響運動員的表現**與健康。由受過訓練的專家提供營養諮詢，可以確保運動員在適當的營養、能量需求、蛋白質與碳水化合物分配比例、進食時間、流體攝取等方面獲得所需。在 20 世紀晚期，愈來愈多的注意力集中在運動員使用所謂「加強表現」的藥品上，例如安非他命和同化類固醇。今日，運動醫學專家和醫生必須做好準備，告訴運動員使用這類藥品會對健康造成嚴重的威脅。

Double-Check

- encompass four areas 包含四個領域
  [ɪn`kʌmpəs]

- increase cardiac output and oxygen intake 增加心輸出量及攝氧量
  [`kɑrdɪˌæk] [`ɑksədʒən]
  參 intake [`ɪnˌtek] (n.) 吸入（量），攝取（量）

- enhance performance 提升表現
  [ɪn`hæns]

- promote the health 促進健康
  [prə`mot]

- boost athletes' speed and endurance 提升運動員的速度與耐力
  [ɪn`djʊrəns]
  參 boost [bust] (v.) 增加，提高
  athlete [`æθlit] (n.) 運動員

- decrease friction and resistance 減少摩擦力和阻力
  [`frɪkʃən] [rɪ`zɪstəns]

- Nutrition is a critical aspect. 營養是一個非常重要的面向。
  [nju`trɪʃən] [`krɪtɪkl]

- seriously impair an athlete's performance 嚴重影響運動員的表現
  參 impair [ɪm`pɛr] (v.) 危害，損害

Physics

59 Conversion of Energy
能量的轉換

Key Sentences

MP3 118

1 James Joule performed a long series of experiments to study the conversion of mechanical energy to heat.

詹姆士．焦耳進行了一長串的實驗，研究**機械能如何轉換成熱能**。

2 In one experiment he used a barrel to heat water by rotating a paddle wheel inside the barrel.

在一項實驗中，他藉著**旋轉一個放在大桶內的槳輪**來加熱水。

3 The principle—known as the law of conservation of energy—is one of the fundamental laws of classical physics.

這個原理稱爲**能量不滅定律**，是古典物理學的基礎定律之一。

4 If all our autos ran on electricity, that energy could be supplied only by burning additional fossil or nuclear fuel at our electricity generating plants.

如果我們所有的汽車都依靠電力，所需的能量只能靠**發電廠**燃燒額外的**石油或核燃料**來提供。

5 This advantage might well be offset by the weight of the batteries to be carried about.

這項優點可能會**因為**所攜帶的**電池的重量而抵銷**。

Reading Focus 293字

MP3 119

Beginning in the year 1840, James Joule performed a long series of experiments to study the conversion of mechanical energy to heat. In one experiment he used a barrel to heat water by rotating a paddle wheel inside the barrel. He measured the work done in turning the wheel and the heat produced in the water, and found that a given amount of work always produced the same amount of heat. Later experiments showed that heat and mechanical energy are always converted back and forth in precisely the same ratio. We now know that the same rule is true for all forms of energy. In everyday terms, energy is never lost: When it disappears in one form, it always shows up in an equal amount in another form. The principle—known as the law of conservation of energy—is one of the fundamental laws of classical physics and is a very cornerstone of modern science and technology.

When it comes to the subject of energy, we should understand why a nation like the United States cannot solve its energy problems by operating automobiles on electricity instead of gasoline. It should be clear by now that electrical energy is no easier to come by than the chemical energy in gasoline. Neglecting engine efficiency for the moment, it takes the same amount of energy to move an automobile a given distance regardless of the initial source of that energy. If all our autos ran on electricity, that energy could be supplied only by burning additional fossil or nuclear fuel at our electricity generating plants. It is true, of course, that electric motors are more efficient than gasoline engines. But this advantage might well be offset by the weight of the batteries to be carried about.

文章中譯

從 1840 年開始，詹姆士．焦耳進行了一長串的實驗，研究**機械能如何轉換成熱能**。在一項實驗中，他藉著**旋轉一個放在大桶內的槳輪**來加熱水。他測量了轉動槳輪所做的功以及水中產生的熱，發現定量的功總是產生定量的熱。之後的實驗證明，熱能和機械能總是以完全相同的比率來回轉換。我們現在都知道，同樣的原則適用於所有形式的能量。在日常生活中，能量永遠不滅：一種形式的能量消失，一定會以等量的另一種能量形式出現。這個原理稱爲**能量不滅定律**，是古典物理學的基礎定律之一，也是現代科學與科技最重要的基石。

談到能量這個主題，我們應該了解爲什麼像美國這樣的國家無法藉著讓汽車由汽油改用電力這個方法來解決能源問題。現在看來應該很清楚，電能並沒有比汽油中的化學能來得容易取得。若暫時不考慮引擎效能的問題，要使得一輛汽車移動固定的距離，不管能量最初的來源爲何，都需要消耗等量的能量。如果我們所有的汽車都依靠電力，所需的能量只能靠**發電廠**燃燒額外的**石油或核燃料**來提供。當然，電動車的效能確實比汽油引擎來得好，但是這項優點也可能會**因為**所攜帶的**電池的重量而抵銷**。

Double-Check

- the conversion of mechanical energy to heat 機械能轉換成熱能
  [kən`vɜʃən]

  參 convert [kən`vɜt] (v.) 轉換

- rotate a paddle wheel inside the barrel 旋轉一個放在大桶內的槳輪
  [`rotet] [`pædl̩] [`bærəl]

- be converted back and forth 來回轉換
  [kən`vɜtɪd]

- the same ratio 相同的比率
  [`reʃo]

- the law of conservation of energy 能量不滅定律
  [ˌkɑnsɚ`veʃən]

- fossil or nuclear fuel 石油或核燃料
  [`fɑsl̩] [`njuklɪɚ] [`fjuəl]

- electricity generating plants 發電廠
  [ɪˌlɛk`trɪsətɪ]

  參 generate [`dʒɛnəˌret] (v.) 發電；產生

- be offset by the weight of the batteries 被電池的重量抵銷
  [ɔf`sɛt] [wet]

Physics

Analysis and Mechanics

分析與力學

Key Sentences

MP3 120

1 The scientific revolution had bequeathed to mathematics a major program of research in analysis and mechanics.

科學革命**帶給數學**一套研究分析與力學的重要程式。

2 "The century of analysis" witnessed the consolidation of the calculus and its extensive application to mechanics.

「分析的世紀」見證了**微積分的發展**以及**其在力學上的廣泛應用**。

3 The applications of analysis were also varied, including the theory of the vibrating string, particle dynamics, the theory of rigid bodies, the mechanics of flexible and elastic media, and the theory of compressible and incompressible fluids.

分析的應用也是變化多端，包括震動弦理論、**粒子動力學**、剛體理論、柔性及**彈性介質**力學、**可壓縮及不可壓縮的流體理論**。

4 The modern disciplinary division between physics and mathematics and the association of the latter with logic had not yet developed.

物理學與數學間**現代學科的分類**，以及數學與邏輯的關係在當時尚未發展完全。

Reading Focus 224字

MP3 121

The scientific revolution had bequeathed to mathematics a major program of research in analysis and mechanics. The period from 1700 to 1800, "the century of analysis," witnessed the consolidation of the calculus and its extensive application to mechanics. With expansion came specialization, as different parts of the subject acquired their own identity: ordinary and partial differential equations, calculus of variations, infinite series, and differential geometry. The applications of analysis were also varied, including the theory of the vibrating string, particle dynamics, the theory of rigid bodies, the mechanics of flexible and elastic media, and the theory of compressible and incompressible fluids. Analysis and mechanics developed in close association, with problems in one giving rise to concepts and techniques in the other, and all the leading mathematicians of the period made important contributions to mechanics.

The close relationship between mathematics and mechanics in the 18th century had roots extending deep into Enlightenment thought. In the organizational chart of knowledge at the beginning of the preliminary discourse to the Encyclopedie, d'Alembert distinguished between "pure" mathematics (geometry, arithmetic, algebra, calculus) and "mixed "mathematics (mechanics, geometric astronomy, optics, art of conjecturing). Mathematics generally was classified as a "science of nature" and separated from logic, a "science of man." The modern disciplinary division between physics and mathematics and the association of the latter with logic had not yet developed.

文章中譯

科學革命**帶給數學**一套研究分析與力學的重要程式。1700 至 1800 年這段期間是「分析的世紀」，見證了**微積分的發展**以及**其在力學上的廣泛應用**。隨著科目擴張而來的是專業分工，這個學科的不同部分獲得各自不同的定位：常微分方程式與偏微分方程式、變動微積分、無窮級數以及微分幾何。分析的應用也是變化多端，包括震動弦理論、**粒子動力學**、剛體理論、柔性及**彈性介質**力學、**可壓縮及不可壓縮的流體理論**。分析與力學的發展緊密相關，其中一個領域所產生的問題，往往引發出另一個領域的觀念及技術，那段時期所有主要的數學家都對力學做出了重大的貢獻。

18 世紀數學和力學之間密切的關係，其根源可以追溯至啓蒙時代的思想。在百科全書初步論述一開始的知識組織圖表中，達朗伯特將數學區分爲「純」數學（幾何學、算術學、代數、微積分）以及「混合」數學（力學、幾何天文學、光學、猜測的藝術）。數學一般被分類爲「自然科學」，脫離邏輯而獨立，因爲邏輯是「人的科學」。物理學與數學間**現代學科的分類**，以及數學與邏輯的關係在當時尚未發展完全。

Double-Check

- bequeath ... to mathematics [ˌmæθəˋmætɪks] — 帶給數學…
  - 參 bequeath [bɪˋkwið] (v.) 留下，送給
- the consolidation of the calculus [ˋkælkjələs] — 微積分的發展
  - 參 consolidation [kənˌsɑləˋdeʃən] (n.) 強化，鞏固
- extensive application to mechanics [ɪkˋstɛnsɪv] [ˌæpləˋkeʃən] [məˋkænɪks] — 在力學上的廣泛應用
- differential equations [ˌdɪfəˋrɛnʃəl] [ɪˋkweʃənz] — 微分方程式
- calculus of variations [ˌvɛrɪˋeʃənz] — 變動微積分
- infinite series [ˋɪnfənɪt] — 無窮級數
- differential geometry [dʒɪˋɑmətrɪ] — 微分幾何
- particle dynamics [ˋpɑrtɪkl̩] [daɪˋnæmɪks] — 粒子動力學
- elastic media [ɪˋlæstɪk] — 彈性介質
- incompressible fluids [ˌɪnkəmˋprɛsəbl̩] [ˋfluɪdz] — 不可壓縮的流體
- geometry [dʒɪˋɑmətrɪ] — (n.) 幾何學
- arithmetic [əˋrɪθmətɪk] — (n.) 算術學
- algebra [ˋældʒəbrə] — (n.) 代數
- the modern disciplinary division [ˋdɪsəplɪˌnɛrɪ] [dəˋvɪʒən] — 現代學科的分類

Part 2
Classified Word List
托福分類字彙

01 Agriculture
農業

MP3 122

agrarian [ə`grɛrɪən]	(adj.) 土地的，耕地的；農業的 ● an agrarian movement 農業改革運動
agronomist [ə`granəmɪst]	(n.) 農（藝）學家
barley [`barlɪ]	(n.) 大麥
barn [barn]	(n.) 穀倉
basil [`bæzl̩]	(n.) 羅勒（一種帶香味可用於烹調的植物）
★**crop** [krap]	(n.) 農作物；收成 ● crop rotation 輪作 ● the main crops of a country 一個國家的主要作物
cropland [`krap͵lænd]	(n.) 農地，農田
★**grain** [gren]	(n.) 穀物 ● a grain elevator 穀倉
millet [`mɪlɪt]	(n.) 小米，粟
★**sow** [so]	(v.) 播種 反 reap (v.) 收割，收穫
wheat [hwit]	(n.) 小麥
windmill [`wɪnd͵mɪl]	(n.) 風車
cultivation [͵kʌltə`veʃən]	(n.) 耕作，耕種 ● out of cultivation 休耕中

★**soil** [sɔɪl]	(n.) 土壤 • poor soil 貧瘠的土壤 • good/fertile/rich soil 肥沃的土壤
★**soil fertility** [sɔɪl fɝ`tɪlətɪ]	(n.) 土壤肥沃度
soil conservation [sɔɪl ˏkɑnsɚ`veʃən]	(n.) 土壤保持
vegetation [ˏvɛdʒə`teʃən]	(n.)（一地區的）植物；植被 • tropical vegetation 熱帶植物
★**exhaustion** [ɪg`zɔstʃən]	(n.) 耗盡，枯竭
weed [wid]	(v.) 除草 (n.) 雜草 • weed a garden 除去花園的雜草
★**regenerate** [rɪ`dʒɛnəˏret]	(v.) 再生
fallow [`fælo]	(adj.) 休耕的 (n.) 休耕地 • lay land fallow 土地休耕
the slash-and-burn [slæʃ] **method** [`mɛθəd]	(n.) 刀耕火種法（砍伐土地上的草木並燒成灰當肥料、播種後不再施肥的耕作法） 參 slash (n.) (v.) 砍，砍伐
hoe [ho]	(n.) 鋤頭
plow [plaʊ]	(v.) 犁，耕 (= cultivate/furrow)
degrade [dɪ`gred]	(v.) 使（土地）退化、劣化
★**region** [`ridʒən]	(n.) 地區，區域 • tropical regions 熱帶地區
agrichemical [ˏægrɪ`kɛmɪkl̩]	(n.) 農藥 參 insecticide (n.) 殺蟲劑 (= pesticide)
★**fertilizer** [`fɝtəˏlaɪzɚ]	(n.) 肥料（尤指化學肥料）

★**herbicide** [ˋhɝbə͵saɪd]	(n.) 除草劑
nutrient [ˋnjutrɪənt]	(n.) 養分
★**livestock** [ˋlaɪv͵stɑk]	(n.) 家畜 (= stock/domestic animals)
dairy [ˋdɛrɪ]	(adj.) 乳製的 ● dairy products 乳製品
★**intensive** [ɪnˋtɛnsɪv]	(adj.) 密集的，集中的 ● intensive agriculture 集約農業
prune [prun]	(v.) 修剪（樹枝），修整（花木）
deplete [dɪˋplit]	(v.) 使枯竭，耗盡（資源等） ● Our supplies of food are rather depleted. 我們的糧食供給已經消耗殆盡。
★**depletion** [dɪˋpliʃən]	(n.) 枯竭，用盡

02 American Studies

美國研究

MP3 123

*Puritan [`pjʊrətn̩]	(n.) 清教徒 (adj.) 清教徒的
cooperation [ko͵apə`reʃən]	(n.) 合作；合作社 (= cooperative)
*diversity [daɪ`vɝsətɪ]	(n.) 多樣性 ● the diversity policy of American university 美國大學的多樣化政策 參 diversify (v.) 使多樣化
*proponent [prə`ponənt]	(n.) 擁護者，支持者
*integrate [`ɪntə͵gret]	(v.) 使融入，使整合 (= combine)；廢除種族差別待遇
*bison [`baɪsn̩]	(n.) 北美野牛 ! 經常出現在與原住民狩獵相關的文章中。
*nomadic [no`mædɪk]	(adj.) 遊牧的
*verge [vɝdʒ]	(n.) 邊緣 ● on the verge of bankruptcy 瀕臨破產
*Pueblo [`pwɛblo]	(n.) 普埃布羅族（美國西南部及墨西哥北部的印地安部落）
subterranean [͵sʌbtə`renɪən]	(adj.) 地下的 ● subterranean rooms 地下室
adobe [ə`dobɪ]	(n.) 泥磚
*immigrant [`ɪməgrənt]	(n.)（自外國移入的）移民
plantation [plæn`teʃən]	(n.)（熱帶的）大農場，農園；造林地

★**colonial** [kə`lonɪəl]	(adj.) 殖民地的；英屬殖民地時代的
★**declare** [dɪ`klɛr]	(v.) 宣告，宣布 ● declare war on/upon/against... 對…宣戰
★**declaration** [ˌdɛklə`reʃən]	(n.) 宣言，宣告，發表 ● the Declaration of Independence（美國）獨立宣言
patriot [`petrɪət]	(n.) 愛國者
★**patriotism** [`petrɪətɪzm̩]	(n.) 愛國心，愛國精神
★**act** [ækt]	(n.)〔字首常大寫〕法案，法令 ● the Act of Congress 國會法案
★**legislation** [ˌlɛdʒɪs`leʃən]	(n.) 立法 ㊂ legislator (n.) 立法委員；國會議員
provision [prə`vɪʒən]	(n.) 條款，規定 ! 也可當「糧食」解釋，用複數形，請注意前後文。
★**delegate** [`dɛləgɪt]	(n.) 代表 ● the U.S. delegates to the conference 會議上的美國代表
delegation [ˌdɛlə`geʃən]	(n.)〔集合用法〕代表團，派遣團
★**consent** [kən`sɛnt]	(n.) (v.) 同意，贊成
★**abolish** [ə`bɑlɪʃ]	(v.) 廢除（法律、制度、習俗等）(= abrogate/do away with) ● abolish the death penalty 廢除死刑
★**abolition** [ˌæbə`lɪʃən]	(n.) 廢除 ㊂ abolitionist (n.) 主張廢除奴隸制度的人
repeal [rɪ`pil]	(n.)（法令）廢除
★**fort** [fort]	(n.) 要塞，堡壘

raid [red]	(n.) **襲擊，突擊** • make a raid on an enemy's camp 對敵營展開突擊
* **surrender** [sə`rɛndɚ]	(v.) **棄守，讓與，投降** • surrender the fort to the enemy 棄守要塞給敵人
* **recession** [rɪ`sɛʃən]	(n.)（一時的）**景氣衰退**（depression 的委婉說法）
* **depression** [dɪ`prɛʃən]	(n.) **不景氣** • the Depression 1929 年的世界經濟大恐慌 (= the Great Depression) 參 recession (n.)（一時的）景氣衰退
halt [hɔlt]	(n.) **停止，休止** • The economic depression of 1930's brought the population expansion to a halt. 1930 年代的經濟恐慌使得人口擴張停止下來。
the New Deal (policy) [dil]	(n.) **新政**（美國於 1929 年進入經濟大恐慌，當時的小羅斯福總統實施一連串經濟、社會政策，統稱為新政）
* **tackle** [`tækl̩]	(v.) **處理，應付**
* **melting pot** [`mɛltɪŋ pɑt]	(n.) **大熔爐**（指不同種族的人融合在一起）
mobilize [`mobə͵laɪz]	(v.)（軍事）**動員** • In 1941 the US entered WWII and began to mobilize. 1941 年美國參加二次世界大戰，並開始動員起來。
abolitionism [͵æbə`lɪʃə͵nɪzm̩]	(n.) **廢除奴隸制度**
* **eradicate** [ɪ`rædɪ͵ket]	(v.) **根除，消滅**
nullify [`nʌlə͵faɪ]	(v.) **使無效** • nullify a treaty 使條約失效
* **desegregation** [di͵sɛgrə`geʃən]	(n.) **廢除種族隔離**

Civil Rights Movement [`sɪvḷ raɪts `muvmənt]	(n.) 民權運動（50、60 年代美國黑人為廢除種族隔離制度、爭取平等權利而展開的運動，促成了 1964 年民權法的通過）
★**racial** [`reʃəl]	(adj.) 人種的，種族的 ● racial prejudice 種族偏見
racism [`resɪzṃ]	(n.) 種族歧視
racist [`resɪst]	(n.) 種族主義者
★**integration** [ˏɪntə`greʃən]	(n.) 統合，（種族的）融合
barrier [`bærɪɚ]	(n.) 障礙，壁壘 ● a deep-rooted barrier between peoples 不同民族間根深蒂固的壁壘
disparity [dɪs`pærətɪ]	(n.) 差異，不同 ● disparity in prestige 身分懸殊
hotbed [ˏhɑt`bɛd]	(n.) 溫床 ● a hotbed of crime 犯罪的溫床
poverty line [`pɑvɚtɪ laɪn]	(n.) 貧窮線（區分是否貧困的最低收入）
★**remedy** [`rɛmədɪ]	(n.) 對策，補救方法；治療法 ● find a remedy for air pollution 找出解決空氣汙染的方法
★**alienate** [`eljəˏnet]	(v.) 使疏離，使疏遠；讓渡（土地、財產等） ● alienate liberals from society 使自由主義者和社會疏離
mobility [mo`bɪlətɪ]	(n.)（階級、職業等的）流動，流動性
★**congress** [`kɑŋgrəs]	(n.) 議會，國會；〔字首大寫〕美國國會（由參議院和衆議院所組成） 參 congressional (adj.) 議會的，國會的

★**the Senate** [ˋsɛnɪt]	(n.) 美國參議院 參 the House of Representatives 美國眾議院（常簡稱為 the House）
★**Democrat** [ˋdɛmə͵kræt]	(n.) 民主黨員
★**Republican** [rɪˋpʌblɪkən]	(adj.) 共和黨的 (n.) 共和黨員
★**nomination** [͵nɑməˋneʃən]	(n.) 提名；任命 參 nominee (n.) 被提名人
presidency [ˋprɛzədənsɪ]	(n.) 總統的職務、任期
★**inauguration** [ɪn͵ɔgjəˋreʃən]	(n.)（總統）就職典禮
inaugural address [ɪnˋɔgjərəl əˋdrɛs]	(n.) 就職演說

Anthropology & Archaeology
人類學與考古學

MP3 124

anthropologist [ˌænθrəˋpɑlədʒɪst]	(n.) 人類學家 ! anthropo- 是表示「人，人類」的字根。
mound [maʊnd]	(n.) 塚；土石堆，小丘
burial [ˋbɛrɪəl]	(n.) 埋葬
cannibalism [ˋkænəbəˌlɪzm̩]	(n.) 食人；同類相食 參 cannibal (n.) 食人肉者 (adj.) 食人的
coffin [ˋkɔfɪn]	(n.) 棺材
connoisseur [ˌkɑnəˋsɝ]	(n.)（藝術品的）鑑賞家，鑑定家
*__corpse__ [kɔrps]	(n.) 屍體 ! 容易和 corps（兵團；團體，發音為 [kor]）的發音搞混，請小心。
marital [ˋmærətl̩]	(adj.) 婚姻的
extramarital [ˌɛkstrəˋmærɪtl̩]	(adj.) 婚姻外的 • extramarital relations 婚外情
fabric [ˋfæbrɪk]	(n.) 織物，紡織品
seal [sil]	(n.) 印鑑；封印
*__weave__ [wiv]	(v.) 編織
ritual [ˋrɪtʃʊəl]	(n.)（宗教的）儀式 (= ceremony/rite)
*__aborigine__ [ˌæbəˋrɪdʒəni]	(n.) 原住民

arch [ɑrtʃ]	(n.) 足背，足弓
★**ethnic** [`ɛθnɪk]	(adj.) 種族的，民族的 ● ethnic minority 少數民族
primitive [`prɪmətɪv]	(adj.) 原始的 (n.) 原始人
★**excavate** [`ɛkskəˏvet]	(v.) 發掘，挖出 ● The archaeologist excavated a Stone-Age tomb. 那名考古學家發掘出一座石器時代的墳墓。
ruin [`ruɪn]	(n.)〔可數〕廢墟，遺跡；〔不可數〕毀壞，破敗 (v.) 破壞，毀壞 ● the ruins of Rome 羅馬的遺跡
artifact [`ɑrtɪˏfækt]	(n.) 人工製品；工藝品
★**conservation** [ˏkɑnsɚ`veʃən]	(n.)（自然資源等的）保護，保存 ● conservation area（建築、史蹟等的）保護區 反 destruction (n.) 破壞
★**conserve** [kən`sɝv]	(v.) 保護，保存 ● conserve energy 保存能源
demography [dɪ`mɑgrəfɪ]	(n.) 人口統計學
demographic transition [ˏdimə`græfɪk træn`zɪʃən]	(n.) 人口轉型
horticulture [`hɔrtɪˏkʌltʃɚ]	(n.) 園藝
incise [ɪn`saɪz]	(v.) 切，切開
outcrop [`aʊtˏkrɑp]	(n.)（岩石或岩層的）露出
pictograph [`pɪktəˏgræf]	(n.) 象形文字
Pleistocene [`plaɪstəˏsin]	(n.) 更新世（地質時代第四紀的前半期） (adj.) 更新世的

★**prehistoric** [ˌprihɪsˋtɔrɪk]	(adj.) 史前的，有歷史記載之前的
provenience [proˋvinɪəns]	(n.) 起源，出處 (= provenance)
quartzite [ˋkwɔrtsaɪt]	(n.) 石英岩（玻璃、耐火磚、陶瓷器的原料）
★**date** [det]	(v.) 推斷、鑑定…的年代；（藝術等）屬於某時期 ● We date the custom from the colonial days. 我們推斷這個習俗來自殖民地時期。
radiocarbon dating [ˌredɪoˋkɑrbən ˋdetɪŋ]	(n.) 放射性碳定年法
sedentary [ˋsɛdn̩ˌtɛrɪ]	(adj.) 定居性的，不遷徙的 反 migratory (adj.) 移居性的
ethnography [ɛθˋnɑgrəfɪ]	(n.) 人種誌，人種論
★**subsistence** [səbˋsɪstəns]	(n.) 生存；（最低限度的）生活，生計

美國新墨西哥州的印地安部落土屋

04 Architecture
建築學

MP3 125

baroque
[bə`rok]
(adj.)（建築、音樂、藝術等）巴洛克風格的
● the Baroque 巴洛克式建築；巴洛克音樂

canopy
[`kænəpɪ]
(n.)（罩在床鋪或寶座上面的）罩篷，華蓋

railing
[`relɪŋ]
(n.) 圍欄，欄杆

residence
[`rɛzədəns]
(n.) 住宅
參 reside (v.) 居住

abbey
[`æbɪ]
(n.) 大修道院

acropolis
[ə`krɑpəlɪs]
(n.)（古希臘城市的）衛城（通常蓋在山丘上）

★**aisle**
[aɪl]
(n.)（教堂的）側廊（中殿 (nave) 側面的走廊）；通道

ambulatory
[`æmbjələˌtorɪ]
(n.)（修道院等的）走廊，迴廊

spacious
[`speʃəs]
(adj.) 寬敞的

spatial
[`speʃəl]
(adj.)（關於）空間的

★**antique**
[æn`tik]
(adj.) 古式的，古董的
參 antiquarian (adj.) 古物的，研究、收藏古物的

arcade
[ɑr`ked]
(n.) 拱廊

atrium
[`etrɪəm]
(n.)（古羅馬建築的）中庭，主廳

baptistery
[`bæptɪstrɪ]
(n.) 洗禮堂，浸禮池

basilica [bə`sɪlɪkə]	(n.)（古羅馬的）長方形會堂；長方形廊柱大廳式教堂
buttress [`bʌtrɪs]	(n.) 拱壁，扶牆
chancel [`tʃænsḷ]	(n.) 高壇，聖壇（通常在教堂東側，牧師和唱詩班所坐的地方）
choir [kwaɪr]	(n.)（尤指教堂的）唱詩班；合唱團
clerestory [`klɪr͵storɪ]	(n.) 高窗，縱向天窗（教堂側廊頂端供採光和通風之用的窗戶）
cloister [`klɔɪstɚ]	(n.)（教堂、修道院等的）迴廊；修道院
coffer [`kɔfɚ]	(n.)（天花板或圓屋頂的）裝飾用鑲板；保險箱
colonnade [͵kɑlə`ned]	(n.) 柱廊，列柱
★**column** [`kɑləm]	(n.) 柱，圓柱
beam [bim]	(n.) 橫樑，桁
corbel [`kɔrbḷ]	(n.) 樑托（從牆上伸出用來支撐的支柱）
girder [`gɝdɚ]	(n.) 大樑
cornice [`kɔrnɪs]	(n.) 飛簷（牆或柱頂突出的裝飾）
crypt [krɪpt]	(n.) 教堂地下室
dome [dom]	(n.) 圓屋頂 • the dome of the Capitol Building 美國國會大廈的圓頂
dormer [`dɔrmɚ]	(n.) 天窗，老虎窗 (= dormer window)（突出於斜面屋頂的窗戶）

engraving [ɪn`grevɪŋ]	(n.) 雕刻（術）；版畫
★**facade** [fə`sɑd]	(n.)（建築物的）正面；外觀
finial [`fɪniəl]	(n.)（屋頂或家具頂部的）尖頂裝飾
fluting [`flutɪŋ]	(n.)（柱子等的）凹槽裝飾
fresco [`frɛsko]	(n.) 壁畫
gable [`gebl̩]	(n.) 山形牆，三角牆 (= pediment) ● gable roof 山形屋頂，人字型屋頂
gargoyle [`gɑrgɔɪl]	(n.) 石像鬼（哥德式建築屋頂的怪物狀滴水嘴，作用是將雨水導離屋頂）
groin [grɔɪn]	(n.) 交叉穹稜，交叉拱頂（拱狀的穹肋於頂端交叉所形成的屋頂）
lintel [`lɪntl̩]	(n.) 過樑（門或窗上面的橫木）
mosaic [mo`zeɪk]	(n.) 鑲嵌工藝（品）；馬賽克
narthex [`nɑr͵θɛks]	(n.)（古教堂的）前廊；（通往中殿的）教堂門廳
pagoda [pə`godə]	(n.)（佛教等的）塔，寶塔
pantheon [`pænθɪən]	(n.) 萬神殿，殿堂；諸神
pediment [`pɛdəmənt]	(n.) 山形牆，三角牆 (= gable)
pilaster [pə`læstɚ]	(n.) 壁柱，半露方柱（部分嵌在牆中、作為裝飾之用的扁平方柱）
pyramid [`pɪrəmɪd]	(n.) 金字塔

quoin [kɔɪn]	(n.)（建築物的）外角，隅石
rib [rɪb]	(n.)（圓拱的）彎樑，肋樑
rotunda [roˋtʌndə]	(n.)（有圓屋頂的）圓形建築物，圓形大廳
sanctuary [ˋsæŋktʃʊˌɛrɪ]	(n.) 聖殿，聖所；保護區
spandrel [ˋspændrəl]	(n.) 三角壁，拱肩
stupa [ˋstupə]	(n.) 佛塔
sublime [səˋblaɪm]	(adj.) 莊嚴的，雄偉的
picturesque [ˌpɪktʃəˋrɛsk]	(adj.) 如畫的，美麗的
tracery [ˋtresərɪ]	(n.) 窗花格（哥德式窗戶上方的裝飾窗格）
transept [ˋtrænsɛpt]	(n.) 袖廊，兩側走廊（十字型教堂的左右翼部，與中殿成直角）
vault [vɔlt]	(n.)（教堂等的）拱型圓屋頂；地窖
★**urban** [ˋɝbən]	(adj.) 都市的 ● urban planning 都市計畫
★**urban congestion** [ˋɝbən kənˋdʒɛstʃən]	(n.) 都市密集 參 traffic congestion 交通壅塞
urban fringe [ˋɝbən frɪndʒ]	(n.) 都市周邊
flat [flæt]	(n.) 公寓 (= apartment house) 參 flat roof 平屋頂
tenement [ˋtɛnəmənt]	(n.)（尤指都市貧民區的）廉價公寓 (= tenement house)；租地

tenant [ˋtɛnənt]	(n.) 房客，承租人
★**amenity** [əˋmɛnətɪ]	(n.)〔常用複數〕生活福利設施，便利設施（如公園、圖書館等）
apartment [əˋpartmənt]	(n.) 公寓 ● furnished apartment 附家具的公寓
★**occupancy** [ˋakjəpənsɪ]	(n.)（土地、住宅等的）占有，居住
cooperative [koˋapəˌretɪv]	(n.) 合作公寓，共同產權公寓（住戶無獨立產權，只有公寓使用權）；合作社
condominium [ˌkandəˋmɪnɪəm]	(n.) 公寓大樓（住戶擁有獨立產權）
★**property** [ˋprapətɪ]	(n.) 財產
Gothic [ˋgaθɪk]	(n.) 哥德式建築 (adj.) 哥德式的
Romanesque [ˌroməˋnɛsk]	(n.) 羅馬式，羅馬風格 (adj.) 羅馬式的，羅馬風格的
spire [spaɪr]	(n.)（教堂的）尖塔
arch [artʃ]	(n.) 拱型結構，拱門
★**renovation** [ˌrɛnəˋveʃən]	(n.)（建築物的）裝修，翻新 (= restoration)

05 Art History
美術史

MP3 126

bead [bid]	(n.) 珠子 • Beads were probably the first durable ornaments humans possessed. 珠子可能是人類最早擁有能長久保存的裝飾品。
coterie [ˋkotərɪ]	(n.)（有共同興趣、嗜好或專業的人組成的）小團體，小圈子 • a literary coterie 文藝圈
laureate [ˋlɔrɪɪt]	(adj.) 享有殊榮的 (n.) 桂冠詩人 (= poet laureate)；獲獎者
★**legacy** [ˋlɛgəsɪ]	(n.) 遺產 (= heritage)
patron [ˋpetrən]	(n.) 贊助者，資助人
★**workshop** [ˋwɝkˏʃap]	(n.) 工作坊；研討會
★**festive** [ˋfɛstɪv]	(adj.) 節日的，喜慶的 • the festive season 有節慶的季節（通常指耶誕節與新年那段期間）
fiesta [fɪˋɛstə]	(n.)（宗教的）節日，假日
easel [ˋizl̩]	(n.) 畫架
★**authentic** [ɔˋθɛntɪk]	(adj.) 原作的，真的 (= genuine/real)
★**conspicuous** [kənˋspɪkjʊəs]	(adj.) 顯著的，出色的 • His works cut a conspicuous figure in artistic circles. 他的作品在藝術圈大放異彩。
★**counterfeit** [ˋkaʊntɚˏfɪt]	(n.) 贗品，仿造品 (adj.) 假的，仿造的 • The "Picasso" turned out to be a counterfeit. 那幅「畢卡索」後來證明是贗品。

delusion [dɪˋluʒən]	(n.) 妄想；錯覺 ● delusions of persecution 被害妄想
empathy [ˋɛmpəθɪ]	(n.) 移情；同理心
emulate [ˋɛmjə͵let]	(v.) 和…競爭；效法
enchant [ɪnˋtʃænt]	(v.) 迷惑，蠱惑，迷住 參 enchanting (adj.) 迷人的，使人陶醉的
fascinate [ˋfæsə͵net]	(v.) 使著迷 參 fascination (n.) 魅力；著迷，入迷
flawless [ˋflɔlɪs]	(adj.) 完美無瑕的 ● flawless works 完美的作品
ineffable [ɪnˋɛfəbl̩]	(adj.) 無法言喻的 ● ineffable beauty 言語無法形容的美
infatuate [ɪnˋfætʃʊ͵et]	(v.) 使迷戀，使著迷 參 infatuation (n.) 迷戀
mold [mold]	(v.) 塑形，用模子做出某種形狀 (= mould) ● mold the soft clay into a figure 將柔軟的黏土捏成人的樣子
mystic [ˋmɪstɪk]	(adj.) 神祕的
★**priceless** [ˋpraɪslɪs]	(adj.) 非常貴重的，無價的 ! 常考單字。
spectacular [spɛkˋtækjələ˞]	(adj.) 壯觀的
adorn [əˋdɔrn]	(v.) 裝飾 (= decorate)
★**bestow** [bɪˋsto]	(v.) 授予 ● The queen bestowed knighthood on the artist. 女王授予那位藝術家爵位。
disfigure [dɪsˋfɪgjə˞]	(v.) 使變得難看；損毀…的外形

ornamental [ˌɔrnəˋmɛntḷ]	(adj.) 裝飾用的
embedded [ɪmˋbɛdɪd]	(adj.) 嵌入的 ● a crown embedded with jewels 鑲嵌寶石的王冠
glitter [ˋglɪtɚ]	(v.) 閃閃發亮
array [əˋre]	(n.) 整齊排列的展示
★**duplicate** [ˋdjupləˌket]	(v.) 複製，複寫 (adj.) 複製的，複寫的 ! 形容詞發音爲 [ˋdjupləkɪt]。
fleeting [ˋflitɪŋ]	(adj.) 短暫的，飛逝的 ● for a fleeting moment 一瞬間，短暫的時間
★**hue** [hju]	(n.) 顏色，色調 ● the hues of a rainbow 彩虹的顏色
intricately [ˋɪntrəkɪtlɪ]	(adv.) 複雜地
sizable [ˋsaɪzəbḷ]	(adj.) 非常大的
★**symmetry** [ˋsɪmɪtrɪ]	(n.) 對稱 (= balance/proportion/equilibrium)
★**Renaissance** [ˋrɛnəˌsɑns]	(n.) 文藝復興（14 至 16 世紀歐洲的古典文藝、學術復興運動）
★**perspective** [pɚˋspɛktɪv]	(n.) 透視畫法
★**Impressionism** [ɪmˋprɛʃəˌnɪzṃ]	(n.) 印象派，印象主義
portrait [ˋportret]	(n.) 肖像畫
Realism [ˋriəˌlɪzṃ]	(n.) 寫實主義（繼 19 世紀浪漫主義之後，在文學藝術上的流派）
Cubism [ˋkjubɪzṃ]	(n.) 立體派，立體主義（20 世紀一種藝術流派，多以幾何圖形來表現主題）

★**school** [skul]	(n.) 學派；流派 ● painters of the Impressionist school 印象派畫家
movement [`muvmənt]	(n.)（政治、社會的）運動 (= campaign)
abstract [`æbstrækt]	(adj.) 抽象（派）的 (n.) 抽象畫
manner [`mænɚ]	(n.)（藝術等的）手法，風格
★**enhance** [ɪn`hæns]	(v.) 提高，增加 ● The soft evening light enhanced her beauty. 夜晚輕柔的燈火增添她的美麗。
sculpture [`skʌlptʃɚ]	(n.) 雕刻 (= carving)
★**medium** [`midɪəm]	(n.) 媒介；媒體 ! 複數形是 mediums 或 media。
★**aesthetic** [ɛs`θɛtɪk]	(adj.) 美學的，美感的 參 aesthetics (n.) 美學
chisel [`tʃɪzl]	(n.) 鑿子，雕刻刀
plaster [`plæstɚ]	(n.) 石膏
bronze [brɑnz]	(n.) 青銅 (adj.) 青銅（製）的 ● cast bronze into a statue 用青銅鑄造雕像
★**carving** [`kɑrvɪŋ]	(n.) 雕刻藝術；雕刻作品 (= sculpture)
cast [kæst]	(v.) 鑄造 ● a statue cast in bronze 用青銅鑄成的雕像
★**weld** [wɛld]	(v.) 焊接 ● weld metal sheets 焊接金屬薄板
★**inspiration** [ˌɪnspə`reʃən]	(n.) 靈感
★**prodigy** [`prɑdədʒɪ]	(n.) 天才

execution [ˌɛksɪˋkjuʃən]	(n.) 技巧，手法
collection [kəˋlɛkʃən]	(n.) 收藏（品）
stylize [ˋstaɪlaɪz]	(v.) 使…（手法等）符合某種風格

06 Astronomy
天文學

MP3 127

whirl [hwɜl]	(v.) 快速旋轉
***manned** [mænd]	(adj.) 載人的；由人駕駛的 ● manned flights 載人的飛行
flash [flæʃ]	(n.) 閃爍；閃光（燈）
***launch** [lɔntʃ]	(v.) 發射 ● launch a spaceship into orbit 發射太空船上軌道
***galaxy** [ˋgæləksɪ]	(n.) 銀河系；星系
***the solar system** [ˋsolɚ] [ˋsɪstəm]	(n.) 太陽系（以太陽為中心的天文體系，包含九大行星和約 50 個衛星，及將近 4,000 個小行星和彗星）
Mercury [ˋmɜkjərɪ]	(n.) 水星
Venus [ˋvinəs]	(n.) 金星
Earth [ɜθ]	(n.) 地球
Mars [mɑrz]	(n.) 火星
Jupiter [ˋʤupətɚ]	(n.) 木星
Saturn [ˋsætən]	(n.) 土星
Uranus [ˋjʊrənəs]	(n.) 天王星
Neptune [ˋnɛptjun]	(n.) 海王星

Pluto [`pluto]	(n.) 冥王星
★**sphere** [sfɪr]	(n.) 球體
★**celestial** [sə`lɛstʃəl]	(adj.) 天體的，天空的 ● celestial bodies 天體 參 terrestrial (adj.) 地球的；陸地的
★**axis** [`æksɪs]	(n.) 軸 ● the axis of the earth 地軸
★**orbit** [`ɔrbɪt]	(n.) 軌道 ！常考單字。 ● The spaceship has been put in orbit round the earth. 太空船進入環繞地球的軌道上。
lunar module [`lunɚ `mɑdʒul]	(n.) 登月小艇，登月艙
★**meteor** [`mitɪɚ]	(n.) 流星 參 meteoroid (n.) 流星體
meteorite [`mitɪə,raɪt]	(n.) 隕石
★**satellite** [`sætə,laɪt]	(n.) 衛星 ● The satellite was repaired in orbit by astronauts from the space shuttle in 1984. 1984 年，太空船上的太空人在軌道上修復那個衛星。
★**astronaut** [`æstrə,nɔt]	(n.) 太空人
★**detect** [dɪ`tɛkt]	(v.) 偵測，察覺，發現 ● These satellite instruments have detected frequent, small variations in the Sun's energy output. 這些衛星儀器偵測到太陽釋放的能量經常有小變化。
★**register** [`rɛdʒɪstɚ]	(v.)（機器等）自動記錄 ● These instruments registered a 0.3 percent drop in the solar energy reaching the Earth. 根據這些儀器的紀錄，抵達地球的太陽能減少了 0.3%。

binary star [ˋbaɪnərɪ stɑr]	(n.) **雙子星**
variable star [ˋvɛrɪəbḷ stɑr]	(n.) **變星**
sight [saɪt]	(v.) **看到，發現；觀測** (= observe) ● sight a new star 發現新星
the big bang theory [bæŋ] [ˋθiərɪ]	(n.) **霹靂說，宇宙爆炸起源論**（即宇宙的誕生來自於一次大爆炸）
★**spiral** [ˋspaɪrəl]	(adj.) **螺旋狀的** ● a spiral galaxy 螺旋星系
★**spacecraft** [ˋspes͵kræft]	(n.) **太空船** (= spaceship)
★**eclipse** [ɪˋklɪps]	(n.) **（太陽、月球的）蝕** ● a solar/lunar eclipse 日／月蝕
quarters of the Moon [ˋkwɔrtɚz]	(n.) **（上、下）弦月**
lunar month [ˋlunɚ mʌnθ]	(n.) **太陰月**（月球繞地球一周所需時間，約 29.5 日）
black hole [blæk hol]	(n.) **黑洞**（大質量恆星死亡後所呈現的狀態，密度極高、重力極為強大，連光線都會被吸進去）
Polaris [poˋlɛrɪs]	(n.) **北極星**
vernal equinox [ˋvɝnḷ ˋikwə͵nɑks]	(n.) **春分**
autumnal equinox [ɔˋtʌmnḷ ˋikwə͵nɑks]	(n.) **秋分**
★**apex** [ˋepɛks]	(n.) **頂點** ● the apex of a triangle 三角形的頂點

★**configuration** [kən,fɪgjə`reʃən]	(n.)（行星的）組態，位形；（原子的）排列組合 ❗常考單字。 ● Twice each month, the Sun, Moon and Earth lie at the apexes of triangular configuration. 每個月兩次，太陽、月球和地球會位在三角形星位的頂點。
accretion [ə`kriʃən]	(n.) 添加，增長
Alpha Centaurus [`ælfə sɛn`tɔrəs]	(n.) 半人馬座阿爾法星（太陽系之外距離地球最近的恆星系統）
angstrom [`æŋstrəm]	(n.) 埃（表示光波波長的單位）
asteroid [`æstə,rɔɪd]	(n.) 小行星 (= planetoid)
★**atmosphere** [`ætməs,fɪr]	(n.) 大氣；氣壓 ● pollute the earth's atmosphere 汙染地球的大氣層
aurora [ɔ`rorə]	(n.) 極光（高緯度地區天空發光現象）
basalt [bə`sɔlt]	(n.) 玄武岩（由火山岩漿所形成的暗色岩石）
bolide [`bolaɪd]	(n.) 火流星（和空氣摩擦而產生光亮的流星）
bow shock [bo ʃɑk]	(n.) 弓形震波（物體在超音速運動時，前端所產生的撞擊波）
breccia [`brɛtʃɪə]	(n.) 角礫岩
★**calcium** [`kælsɪəm]	(n.) 鈣
caldera [kæl`dɛrə]	(n.) 破火山口，巨火山口（火山爆發後地表下陷而產生的大規模窪地）
carbonate [`kɑrbə,net]	(n.) 碳酸鹽 (v.) 使變為碳酸鹽；使含有二氧化碳

chromosphere [ˋkromə͵sfɪr]	(n.) **色球層**（為太陽最外層三層氣體中的第二層氣體，肉眼可觀測的機會只有在日全蝕時，出現於太陽周圍的玫瑰色光環）
cinder [ˋsɪndɚ]	(n.) **火山渣**
cinder cone [ˋsɪndɚ kon]	(n.) **火山碎屑錐，火山渣錐**
coma [ˋkomɑ]	(n.) **彗髮**（彗星周圍的星雲狀物） ! 在非天文學相關的文章中多當「昏迷」解釋。
composite volcano [kəmˋpɑzɪt vɑlˋkeno]	(n.) **複式火山**（由火山的熔岩流與碎屑物質堆積而成的火山）
★**cosmos** [ˋkɑzmos]	(n.) **（井然有序的）宇宙** 參 chaos (n.) 混亂
cosmic ray [ˋkɑzmɪk re]	(n.) **宇宙射線**（由外太空射入地球的放射線）
craton [ˋkretɑn]	(n.) **穩定地塊**（大陸內部相對而言較為穩定的地塊）
cretaceous period [krɪˋteʃəs ˋpɪrɪəd]	(n.) **白堊紀**（約自 1 億 3 千 5 百萬年前開始至 6 千 5 百萬年前結束）
dielectric constant [͵daɪəˋlɛktrɪk ˋkɑnstənt]	(n.) **介電常數**
Doppler Effect [ˋdɑplɚ ɪˋfɛkt]	(n.) **都卜勒效應**（即波源與觀察者有相對運動時，觀察者接收到的頻率和波源發出的頻率不同的現象）
eccentricity [͵ɛksənˋtrɪsətɪ]	(n.) **離心率，偏心率**
★**ecliptic** [ɪˋklɪptɪk]	(n.) **黃道**
ellipse [ɪˋlɪps]	(n.) **橢圓（形）**
fissure [ˋfɪʃɚ]	(n.) **裂縫，裂隙**

flare [flɛr]	(n.) 火焰；太陽閃焰（太陽釋放大量能量時，於表層出現的強光噴射現象）
granulation [ˌgrænjəˋleʃən]	(n.) 米粒組織（太陽光球層上的顆粒狀組織）
***gravity** [ˋgrævətɪ]	(n.) 重力 ● zero gravity 無重力狀態
***gravitation** [ˌgrævəˋteʃən]	(n.) 引力
gravitational collapse [ˌgrævəˋteʃənḷ kəˋlæps]	(n.) 引力塌縮（由星球自身的引力所引起）
heliocentric [ˌhilɪoˋsɛntrɪk]	(adj.) 以太陽為中心的
hummock [ˋhʌmək]	(n.) 圓丘，小山
igneous [ˋɪgnɪəs]	(adj.) 火的；火成的
***inclination** [ˌɪnkləˋneʃən]	(n.) 傾斜，斜面；傾向
inferior planet [ɪnˋfɪrɪɚ ˋplænɪt]	(n.) 內行星（運行於地球軌道內的行星，即水星和金星）
ion [ˋaɪən]	(n.) 離子
***lava** [ˋlɑvə]	(n.) 熔岩，火山岩 ! 常考單字。
***light year** [laɪt jɪr]	(n.) 光年（距離單位，即光走一年的距離，約為 9 兆 4 千 6 百億公里）
magma [ˋmægmə]	(n.) 岩漿
***magnetic field** [mægˋnɛtɪk fild]	(n.) 磁場
magnetosphere [mægˋnitəˌsfɪr]	(n.) 磁層（地球大氣層的外圈，受地球磁場控制，充滿帶電粒子）

magnitude [`mægnə͵tjud]	(n.) 星等（星的亮度）；（地震的）震級
neutrino [nju`trino]	(n.) 微中子
nuclear fusion [`njuklɪɚ `fjuʒən]	(n.) 核融合
obliquity [ə`blɪkwətɪ]	(n.) 傾斜度，斜角
Paleozoic era [͵pelɪə`zoɪk `ɪrə]	(n.) 古生代
penumbra [pɪ`nʌmbrə]	(n.) 半影；明暗交界部分
perigee [`pɛrə͵ʤi]	(n.) 近地點（月球繞地球公轉的軌道上距離地球最近的點）
perihelion [͵pɛrɪ`hilɪən]	(n.) 近日點（地球繞太陽公轉的軌道上距離太陽最近的點）
perturb [pɚ`tɜb]	(v.) 擾亂
photosphere [`fotə͵sfɪr]	(n.) 光球層（肉眼可見太陽表面發光的部分）
plasma [`plæzmə]	(n.) 等離子；電漿
polarization [͵polərə`zeʃən]	(n.) 極化
Precambrian era [pri`kæmbrɪən `ɪrə]	(n.) 前寒武紀
prominence [`prɑmənəns]	(n.) 日珥（太陽表面噴出的熾熱氣流，有如火舌狀紅色火焰）
pyroclastic flow [͵paɪrə`klæstɪk flo]	(n.) 火山碎屑流
pumice [`pʌmɪs]	(n.) 輕石，浮石

★**resolution** [ˌrɛzəˋluʃən]	(n.) 溶解；分解
retrograde [ˋrɛtrəˏgred]	(adj.)（行星等）逆行的 (v.)（行星等）逆行
rhyolite [ˋraɪəˏlaɪt]	(n.) 流紋岩（火山岩的一種）
★**rift** [rɪft]	(n.) 裂口，裂縫，裂痕
scarp [skɑrp]	(n.) 陡坡，險坡
gully [ˋgʌlɪ]	(n.) 小峽谷
shatter cone [ˋʃætɚ kon]	(n.) 碎裂圓錐石，破裂錐（錐狀的岩石碎片，以放射狀裂紋為其特徵）
shield [ʃild]	(n.) 地盾
shield volcano [ʃild vɑlˋkeno]	(n.) 盾狀火山
silicate [ˋsɪlɪkɪt]	(n.) 矽酸鹽
sinus [ˋsaɪnəs]	(n.) 彎曲（處）；凹陷（處）
★**sunspot** [ˋsʌnˏspɑt]	(n.) 太陽黑子 ● These fluctuations of the Sun's energy output coincide with the appearance and disappearance of large groups of sunspots on the Sun's disk. 太陽能釋放的變動，與太陽表面大量黑子的出現和消失同時發生。
superior planet [səˋpɪrɪɚ ˋplænɪt]	(n.) 外行星（運行於地球軌道外的行星，即土星、火星、木星、天王星、海王星等）
★**tectonic** [tɛkˋtɑnɪk]	(adj.) 地殼構造的
terra [ˋtɛrə]	(n.) 土地，大地

tuff [tʌf]	(n.) 凝灰岩
umbra [`ʌmbrə]	(n.) 陰影部，太陽黑子的中央黑暗部分
vent [vɛnt]	(n.) 火山口；通氣孔
volatile [`valətḷ]	(adj.) 易揮發的；不安定的
aphelion [æ`filɪən]	(n.) 遠日點（地球繞太陽公轉的軌道上距離太陽最遠的點）
apogee [`æpə͵ʤi]	(n.) 遠地點（月球繞地球公轉的軌道上距離地球最遠的點）
astro- [`æstro; `æstrə]	表示「太空、星、天體」的字根
astrophysics [͵æstro`fɪzɪks]	(n.) 天體物理學
★**luminosity** [͵lumə`nasətɪ]	(n.) 光度
calibration [͵kælə`breʃən]	(n.) 口徑測定；（測量器上的）刻度
★**corona** [kə`ronə]	(n.) 日冕（日全蝕時可見的太陽周圍的白色光環） ! 複數形是 coronae。
cosmology [kaz`malədʒɪ]	(n.) 宇宙論（研究宇宙的起源和構造等，為哲學或天文學的一部分）
declination [͵dɛklə`neʃən]	(n.)（磁針的）偏角，偏差
disk [dɪsk]	(n.)（天體的）表面
extragalactic [͵ɛkstrəgə`læktɪk]	(adj.) 銀河系外的
galactic halo [gə`læktɪk `helo]	(n.) 銀河系暈

gamma ray [`gæmə re]	(n.) 伽瑪射線
globular cluster [`glɑbjələ˞ `klʌstə˞]	(n.) 球狀星團
Hubble's law [`hʌbəlz lɔ]	(n.) 哈伯定律（遙遠星系的後退速度隨著與觀測者的距離增加而增加）
★**hydrogen** [`haɪdrədʒən]	(n.) 氫 ! hydro- 是表示「水、氫」的字根。
implosion [ɪm`ploʒən]	(n.) 內爆
★**interstellar** [ˌɪntə˞`stɛlə˞]	(adj.) 星際的
Kepler's laws [`kɛplə˞z lɔz]	(n.) 克卜勒定律（關於行星環繞太陽運行的三大定律）
★**laser** [`lezə˞]	(n.) 雷射（也稱為 optical maser）
magnetic pole [mæg`nɛtɪk pol]	(n.) 磁極
mass [mæs]	(n.) 質量
quasar [`kwesɑr]	(n.) 類星體
microwave [`maɪkrəˌwev]	(n.) 微波
★**NASA** [`næsə]	(n.) 美國國家航空暨太空總署（全名為 National Aeronautics and Space Administration）
★**nebula** [`nɛbjələ]	(n.) 星雲 ! 複數形是 nebulae。
Newtonian mechanics [nju`tonɪən mə`kænɪks]	(n.) 牛頓力學
★**nova** [`novə]	(n.) 新星 ! 複數形是 novae。

★**opacity** [o`pæsətɪ]	(n.) 不透明
photon [`fotɑn]	(n.) 光子
photoelectric effect [ˌfotoɪ`lɛktrɪk ɪ`fɛkt]	(n.) 光電效應
Planck's constant [plaŋks `kɑnstənt]	(n.) **普朗克常數**（量子力學中的一種基本常數）
planetary nebula [`plænəˌtɛrɪ `nɛbjələ]	(n.) **行星狀星雲**（恆星死亡時散逸出的雲氣所形成貌似行星的星雲）
positron [`pɑzɪˌtrɑn]	(n.) **陽電子**（跟電子質量相同，但所帶電荷相反）
pulsar [`pʌlsɑr]	(n.) **脈衝星；波霎**（恆星演化到末期的一種狀態，以高速自轉，並發出強烈電波）
radial velocity [`redɪəl və`lɑsətɪ]	(n.) **視向速度**（物體或天體在觀察者視線方向的運動速度）
radian [`redɪən]	(n.) **弧度**（角度單位）
right ascension [raɪt ə`sɛnʃən]	(n.) **赤經**（以春分點為基準，向東測量出春分點與天體間的角度）
singularity [ˌsɪŋgjə`lærətɪ]	(n.) **奇點**（位於黑洞中心，為所有質量集中之處）
spectrometer [ˌspɛk`trɑmətɚ]	(n.) 分光計，光譜儀
spectrum [`spɛktrəm]	(n.) 光譜 ! 複數形是 spectra。
stellar [`stɛlɚ]	(adj.) 星的，星球的
supernova [ˌsupɚ`novə]	(n.) 超新星
visible [`vɪzəbḷ]	(adj.) 可見的 反 invisible (adj.) 看不見的

wavelength [ˋwev͵lɛŋθ]	(n.) 波長
white dwarf [hwaɪt dwɔrf]	(n.) 白矮星（一種低光度、高密度、高溫度的恆星，為恆星演化的老年期）
*__wax__ [wæks]	(v.)（月亮）盈，漸滿
*__wane__ [wen]	(v.)（月亮）虧，缺

07 Biology

生物學

MP3 130

★**species** [ˋspiʃiz]	(n.) 種（生物學上的分類名稱）
★**tissue** [ˋtɪʃʊ]	(n.)（動植物細胞的）組織 ● brain/nervous tissues 腦／神經細胞
coexist [ˌkoɪgˋzɪst]	(v.) 共存，同時存在
scout [skaʊt]	(n.) 偵察兵 (v.)（為了獲得某物而）搜尋，偵察 ● Formic scouts locate a new nesting site. 負責偵察的兵蟻找到新的築巢地點。
bite [baɪt]	(v.) 叮，螫，咬 ● He was bitten by mosquitoes several times. 他被蚊子叮了好幾下。
★**bloom** [blum]	(v.) 開花 (n.)（尤指觀賞用植物的）花
burrow [ˋbɝo]	(n.) 巢穴，洞穴 (v.) 挖洞穴，挖掘
carnivorous [kɑrˋnɪvərəs]	(adj.) 肉食性的 參 carnivore (n.) 肉食動物
★**prey** [pre]	(v.) 捕食 (n.) 獵物 ● prey on the plant-eaters 獵捕草食動物 ! 容易和 pray 搞混，動詞 pray 是「祈禱，禱告」的意思。
chameleon [kəˋmilɪən]	(n.) 變色龍；反覆無常的人
camouflage [ˋkæməˌflɑʒ]	(n.) 偽裝（生物改變身體的顏色，與周遭環境一致，以達到自我保護的作用）；保護色
mimicry [ˋmɪmɪkrɪ]	(n.) 擬態（生物改變身體結構模擬其他生物，以躲避天敵的捕食）
chirp [tʃɝp]	(v.)（小鳥）發出啁啾聲，（昆蟲）發出唧唧聲

cobweb [ˋkɑbˏwɛb]	(n.) 蜘蛛網
cocoon [kəˋkun]	(n.) 繭（裡面包著蛹 (pupa)）
crawl [krɔl]	(v.)（蟲、蛇等）爬行；（人）匍匐前進 ● There is a lizard crawling on the window. 窗戶上有一隻蜥蜴在爬。
***zoology** [zoˋɑlədʒɪ]	(n.) 動物學
***cub** [kʌb]	(n.) 動物（熊、獅、狼、虎等）的幼獸
fang [fæŋ]	(n.)（肉食動物的）犬齒；（蛇的）毒牙
***feed** [fid]	(v.) 餵食 ● Horses are fed oats. 馬被餵食燕麥。
flock [flɑk]	(n.) 羊群，鳥（鴨、鵝等）群 參 herd (n.) 牛（豬等家畜）群 pack (n.) 狼群 school/shoal (n.) 魚群 drove (n.) 走動的畜群
***fungus** [ˋfʌŋgəs]	(n.) 菌類 ! 複數形是 fungi，發音爲 [ˋfʌndʒaɪ]。要記住單複數的拼法和發音。
genus [ˋdʒinəs]	(n.) 屬（生物學上的分類名稱） ● the genus Homo 人類
gourd [gord]	(n.) 結葫蘆的攀緣植物
graze [grez]	(v.)（牛、羊等）吃草；放牧
heath [hiθ]	(n.) 石南屬灌木
***herd** [hɝd]	(n.)（動物的）群 ● A herd of antelopes was grazing in the field. 一群羚羊在原野上吃草。

hornet [ˋhɔrnɪt]	(n.) 大黃蜂
★**invertebrate** [ɪnˋvɜtəbrɪt]	(adj.) 無脊椎（動物）的 (n.) 無脊椎動物
ivory [ˋaɪvərɪ]	(n.) 象牙
lush [lʌʃ]	(adj.)（草木）茂盛的，繁茂的
ox [ɑks]	(n.) 公牛 ! 複數形是 oxen。
paw [pɔ]	(n.)（動物的）腳掌
★**plume** [plum]	(n.)（大又顯眼的）羽毛（小的羽毛稱為 feather）
★**poultry** [ˋpoltrɪ]	(n.)〔集合用法〕家禽；家禽肉
primate [ˋpraɪmet]	(n.) 靈長類動物
progeny [ˋprɑdʒənɪ]	(n.) 後代 (= offspring)
★**prowl** [praʊl]	(v.) (n.)（動物為覓食而）潛行
swarm [swɔrm]	(n.)（昆蟲的）群 (v.) 群集；成群移動 ● a swarm of ants 一群螞蟻
biochemistry [ˌbaɪoˋkɛmɪstrɪ]	(n.) 生物化學 參 biochemical (adj.) 生物化學的
rattle [ˋrætl̩]	(v.) 發出嘎嘎聲 (n.) 嘎嘎聲 參 rattlesnake (n.) 響尾蛇
extant [ɪkˋstænt]	(adj.) 現存的 ● the only species extant 現存的唯一品種
gamut [ˋgæmət]	(n.) 整個範圍

hardy
[`hardɪ]
(adj.)（人、動物）強壯的；（植物）耐寒的

proximity
[prak`sɪmətɪ]
(n.)（時間、距離或血緣關係）接近
- proximity of blood 近親

transform
[træns`fɔrm]
(v.) 變形；改變
參 transformative (adj.) 變化的；有變形能力的

★**pathogen**
[`pæθədʒən]
(n.) 病原（體）

phenotype
[`finə,taɪp]
(n.) 表現型，顯型（一生物體的基因表現呈現外顯的特徵或性狀，為遺傳和環境相互作用的結果）

phylogenetic tree
[,faɪlədʒɪ`nɛtɪk tri]
(n.) 系統樹 (= genealogical tree)（描繪生物系統關係的樹狀圖）

phylum
[`faɪləm]
(n.) 門（生物學上的分類名稱，主要用於動物的分類；植物要用 division）

★**population**
[,papjə`leʃən]
(n.) 群體；（動物的）總數
- the elephant population of Kenya 肯亞的象群

★**predator**
[`prɛdətɚ]
(n.) 捕食其他動物的動物
參 predatory (adj.) 以捕食其他動物為生的

★**predator control**
[`prɛdətɚ kən`trol]
(n.) 捕食動物控制（即 p. 198 Conservation 一文中 gray wolf 和 coyote 的關係）

species diversity
[`spiʃiz daɪ`vɝsətɪ]
(n.) 物種的多樣性

★**stability**
[stə`bɪlətɪ]
(n.) 穩定，安定
- the stability of the plant community 植物群落的穩定性

參 stabilize (v.) 使安定

subspecies
[sʌb`spiʃiz]
(n.) 亞種（生物分類上的位階，位於「種」之下）

succession
[sək`sɛʃən]
(n.) 演替（新的生物群落不斷取代舊生物群落的現象）；連續；繼承

★**specimen**
[`spɛsəmən]
(n.) 標本
- specimens of rare insects 稀有昆蟲的標本

taxonomy [tæk`sanəmɪ]	(n.) 分類法；分類學
★**clone** [klon]	(n.) 單性生殖體由無性生殖而繁殖的有機體群；生物體複製
★**cloning** [`klonɪŋ]	(n.) 由無性生殖之繁殖
★**chromosome** [`kromə͵som]	(n.) 染色體
vascular plant [`væskjələ plænt]	(n.) 維管植物（具有維管組織來運輸水分和養分的植物，例如蕨類）
★**paleontology** [͵pelɪan`talədʒɪ]	(n.) 古生物學
chromatin [`kromətɪn]	(n.)（染色體的）染色質
★**breed** [brid]	(v.)（動物）生育；繁殖；改良（品種） (n.)（動植物的）品種，種類
breeding [`bridɪŋ]	(n.) 繁殖，飼育 ● the breeding grounds 繁殖地
★**wildlife** [`waɪld͵laɪf]	(n.)〔集合用法〕野生生物
skeleton [`skɛlətn̩]	(n.) 骨骼；骸骨；葉脈
★**ecosystem** [`iko͵sɪstəm]	(n.) 生態系統
★**botany** [`batn̩ɪ]	(n.) 植物學
botanist [`batn̩ɪst]	(n.) 植物學家
★**genetics** [dʒə`nɛtɪks]	(n.) 遺傳學
genetic engineering [dʒə`nɛtɪk ͵ɛndʒə`nɪrɪŋ]	(n.) 遺傳工程，基因工程

genetic manipulation [ʤə`nɛtɪk mə,nɪpjə`leʃən]	(n.) 遺傳操控，基因控制
★**gene** [ʤin]	(n.) 基因，遺傳因子
gene bank [ʤin bæŋk]	(n.) 基因銀行
★**anatomy** [ə`nætəmɪ]	(n.) 解剖學；解剖；分析
★**physiology** [,fɪzɪ`ɑləʤɪ]	(n.) 生理學
capillary [`kæpḷ,ɛrɪ]	(adj.) 毛細管（現象）的 ● capillary attraction 毛細管引力
capillary vessel [`kæpḷ,ɛrɪ `vɛsḷ]	(n.) 毛細血管 (= capillary tube)，微血管
cell [sɛl]	(n.) 細胞
cytology [saɪ`tɑləʤɪ]	(n.) 細胞學
meiosis [maɪ`osɪs]	(n.) 減數分裂 (= reduction division)
★**evolution** [,ɛvə`luʃən]	(n.) 進化（論） ● the theory of evolution 進化論
★**fossil** [`fɑsḷ]	(n.) 化石 (adj.) 化石的 ● a fossil shell 貝殼化石 ● fossil fuel 化石燃料（如石油、煤炭、天然氣等）
amber [`æmbɚ]	(n.) 琥珀（色）
★**survival** [sɚ`vaɪvḷ]	(n.) 生存 ● the survival of the fittest 適者生存
natural selection [`nætʃərəl sə`lɛkʃən]	(n.) 自然淘汰
fermentation [,fɝmɛn`teʃən]	(n.) 發酵

ferment [`fɜmɛnt]	(n.) 發酵；酵素 (v.) 發酵 ● natural ferment (= fermentation) of food 食品的發酵
algae [`ældʒi]	(n.) 海藻，藻類 ! 單數形是 alga。 ● algae bloom 藻華（河川營養素過多造成藻類過量繁殖的現象）
★**bacteria** [bæk`tɪrɪə]	(n.) 細菌 ! 單數形是 bacterium。
bacteriophage [bæk`tɪrɪə,fedʒ]	(n.) 噬菌體
protozoa [,protə`zoə]	(n.) 原生動物類
★**metabolism** [mə`tæbl̩,ɪzm̩]	(n.) 新陳代謝
replication [,rɛplə`keʃən]	(n.) 再生 參 replicate (v.) 複製
conjugation [,kandʒə`geʃən]	(n.)（生殖細胞的）結合，接合
★**transformation** [,trænsfɚ`meʃən]	(n.) 變形，變態 ● the transformation of a tadpole into a frog 由蝌蚪變成青蛙
recombination [,rikambə`neʃən]	(n.)（基因）重組
★**microbe** [`maɪkrob]	(n.) 微生物；病菌
embryo [`ɛmbrɪ,o]	(n.) 胚胎；胚芽
★**germinate** [`dʒɜmə,net]	(v.) 發芽 (= sprout/bud)
★**mineral** [`mɪnərəl]	(adj.) 含礦物的，礦物性的 (n.) 礦物 ● a mineral vein 礦脈
★**nutrition** [nju`trɪʃən]	(n.) 營養

***photosynthesis** [ˌfotə`sɪnθəsɪs]	(n.) 光合作用
chemosynthesis [ˌkimo`sɪnθəsɪs]	(n.) 化學合成
***carbon dioxide** [`kɑrbən daɪ`ɑksaɪd]	(n.) 二氧化碳 ● Absorption of carbon dioxide occurs mainly in areas of thick forests. 二氧化碳的吸收主要發生在濃密的森林中。
biome [`baɪˌom]	(n.) 生物群落
***pollen** [`pɑlən]	(n.) 花粉 ● pollen count 花粉數
***petal** [`pɛtl̩]	(n.) 花瓣
stem [stɛm]	(n.)（草木的）莖，幹，梗
trunk [trʌŋk]	(n.) 樹幹；軀幹
annual ring [`ænjʊəl rɪŋ]	(n.) 年輪
coniferous tree [kə`nɪfərəs tri]	(n.) 針葉樹
broadleaf tree [`brɔdˌlif tri]	(n.) 闊葉樹
***defoliation** [diˌfolɪ`eʃən]	(n.) 落葉
deciduous tree [dɪ`sɪdʒʊəs tri]	(n.) 落葉樹 參 deciduous teeth 乳牙
evergreen tree [`ɛvɚˌgrin tri]	(n.) 常綠樹
moss [mɔs]	(n.) 苔蘚

***fern** [fɝn]	(n.) 羊齒植物，蕨類 ● fern seed 羊齒植物的孢子 ! 聽力和閱讀測驗常考單字，特別是與繁殖 (reproduction) 相關的主題。
***vertebrate** [ˋvɝtə͵bret]	(n.) 脊椎動物 反 invertebrate (n.) 無脊椎動物
***mammal** [ˋmæml̩]	(n.) 哺乳動物
viviparity [͵vɪvɪˋpærətɪ]	(n.) 胎生 參 viviparous (adj.) 胎生的
oviparity [͵ovɪˋpærətɪ]	(n.) 卵生 參 oviparous (adj.) 卵生的
***migration** [maɪˋgreʃən]	(n.) 遷徙，移居 ● the migration of birds 鳥類的遷徙
migrant [ˋmaɪgrənt]	(n.) 候鳥，洄游魚，有遷移習性的動物 (adj.) 移居性的
***reptile** [ˋrɛptaɪl]	(n.) 爬蟲類
carapace [ˋkærə͵pes]	(n.)（蝦、蟹、烏龜等的）背甲，甲殼
***hibernation** [͵haɪbɚˋneʃən]	(n.) 冬眠
***dinosaur** [ˋdaɪnə͵sɔr]	(n.) 恐龍 ! 聽力測驗常考單字。
demise [dɪˋmaɪz]	(n.) 滅絕，死亡 ● It is not clear what other factors led to an auk's demise around 1844. 我們並不清楚還有哪些因素造成 1844 年左右一種北極海鳥的滅絕。
***amphibian** [æmˋfɪbɪən]	(n.) 兩棲類；水陸兩用飛機 (adj.) 兩棲類的；水陸兩用飛機的
***metamorphosis** [͵mɛtəˋmɔrfəsɪs]	(n.) 變態；蛻變，演變

gill [gɪl]	(n.) 鰓
★**scale** [skel]	(n.)（魚類、爬蟲類等的）鱗
★**insect** [ˋɪnsɛkt]	(n.) 昆蟲 ● an insect net 捕蟲網
★**antenna** [ænˋtɛnə]	(n.) 觸角，觸鬚 (= feeler)；天線
★**larva** [ˋlɑrvə]	(n.) 幼蟲
★**pupa** [ˋpjʊpə]	(n.) 蛹 ! 常考單字。
★**nucleus** [ˋnjuklɪəs]	(n.) 核；細胞核
chloroplast [ˋklorə͵plæst]	(n.) 葉綠體
sperm [spɜm]	(n.) 精子；精液
fertilization [͵fɜtələˋzeʃən]	(n.) 受精；施肥
★**biotechnology** [͵baɪotɛkˋnɑlədʒɪ]	(n.) 生物科技
★**subject** [ˋsʌbdʒɪkt]	(n.)（實驗）受試者，實驗對象 ! 常考單字。
★**DNA**	(n.) 去氧核糖核酸（即 deoxyribonucleic acid）
★**RNA**	(n.) 核糖核酸（即 ribonucleic acid）
★**enzyme** [ˋɛnzaɪm]	(n.) 酵素 ● enzyme engineering 酵素工程
amino acid [əˋmino ˋæsɪd]	(n.) 氨基酸
★**protein** [ˋprotiɪn]	(n.) 蛋白質

amoeba [ə`mibə]	(n.) 阿米巴原蟲，變形蟲 ! 複數形是 amoebae 或 amoebas。
★**parasite** [`pærə,saɪt]	(n.) 寄生生物，寄生蟲
parasitic [,pærə`sɪtɪk]	(adj.) 寄生的；寄生生物引起的
★**parasitism** [`pærəsaɪt,ɪzṃ]	(n.) 寄生現象；寄生蟲病
host [host]	(n.)（寄生生物的）宿主
★**rear** [rɪr]	(v.) 養育 (= raise/bring up) ! 常考單字。
★**forage** [`fɔrɪdʒ]	(v.)（動物）覓食 (n.) 覓食；糧草，飼料 • animals foraging for food 覓食的動物
★**mate** [met]	(n.) 配偶，伴侶
★**habitat** [`hæbə,tæt]	(n.) 棲息地 • the natural habitat of the Bengal tigers 孟加拉虎的天然棲息地
★**occur** [ə`kɜ]	(v.) 存在，出現；發生 • Bats occur almost everywhere. 幾乎到處都有蝙蝠。
foliage [`folɪɪdʒ]	(n.)〔集合用法〕葉子
bark [bɑrk]	(n.) 樹皮
stump [stʌmp]	(n.)（砍樹或樹倒之後留下的）殘株
★**organic** [ɔr`gænɪk]	(adj.) 生物的，有機體的；有機的 • organic remains 生物遺骸
pollinate [`pɑlə,net]	(v.) 授粉
nectar [`nɛktɚ]	(n.) 花蜜

sponge [spʌndʒ]	(n.) 海綿動物
★**coral** [\`kɔrəl]	(n.) 珊瑚，珊瑚蟲；珊瑚製品
jellyfish [\`dʒɛlɪˌfɪʃ]	(n.) 水母
starfish [\`stɑrˌfɪʃ]	(n.) 海星
arthropod [\`ɑrθrəˌpɑd]	(n.) 節肢動物（包括甲殼類、蛛形類和昆蟲類動物等）
reef [rif]	(n.) 礁，暗礁 ● coral reef 珊瑚礁
clam [klæm]	(n.) 蛤，蚌
snail [snel]	(n.) 蝸牛
★**nocturnal** [nɑk\`tɝnəl]	(adj.) 夜行性的 反 diurnal (adj.) 日行性的
★**pest** [pɛst]	(n.) 害蟲；有害的動植物
★**pesticide** [\`pɛstɪˌsaɪd]	(n.) 殺蟲劑
★**hatch** [hætʃ]	(v.) 孵化 ● The duck hatched five ducklings. 那隻鴨子孵出五隻小鴨。
★**caterpillar** [\`kætəˌpɪlə]	(n.) 毛蟲（蝶或蛾的幼蟲）
★**mature** [mə\`tʃʊr]	(adj.) 成熟的 (v.) 成熟
locust [\`lokəst]	(n.) 蝗蟲
cricket [\`krɪkɪt]	(n.) 蟋蟀

cicada [sɪ`kedə]	(n.) 蟬 ! 複數形是 cicadae。
centipede [`sɛntə,pid]	(n.) 蜈蚣
eel [il]	(n.) 鰻魚
trout [traʊt]	(n.) 鱒魚
toad [tod]	(n.) 蟾蜍
tadpole [`tæd,pol]	(n.) 蝌蚪 (= polliwog)
venom [`vɛnəm]	(n.)（蛇、蜘蛛等所分泌的）毒液 ● a venom fang 毒牙
crane [kren]	(n.) 鶴
pheasant [`fɛznṭ]	(n.) 雉，野雞
owl [aʊl]	(n.) 貓頭鷹
skylark [`skaɪ,lɑrk]	(n.) 雲雀
thrush [θrʌʃ]	(n.) 畫眉鳥，鶇
vulture [`vʌltʃɚ]	(n.) 兀鷹
***bill** [bɪl]	(n.) 鳥嘴，喙 (= beak)
beak [bik]	(n.) 鳥嘴，喙 (= bill)
***deft** [dɛft]	(adj.) 靈巧的，敏捷的 ● A crossbill is deft at removing the seeds. 交嘴鳥在取出種子時很靈巧。

earthworm [`ɜθ͵wɜm]	(n.) 蚯蚓
nostril [`nαstrəl]	(n.) 鼻孔
***nesting** [`nɛstɪŋ]	(n.) 築巢
***reproduction** [͵riprə`dʌkʃən]	(n.) 繁殖，生殖
chick [tʃɪk]	(n.) 幼雛，小雞
reproduce [͵riprə`djus]	(v.) 繁殖，生殖
***brood** [brud]	(n.) 一窩孵出的幼雛 (v.) 孵蛋
***incubate** [`ɪnkjə͵bet]	(v.) 孵化 ● Hummingbirds need six weeks to build a nest, incubate their eggs, and raise the chicks. 蜂鳥需要六週的時間築巢、孵蛋和撫養幼鳥。
***protective coloring** [prə`tɛktɪv `kʌlərɪŋ]	(n.) 保護色 (= protective coloration)
perch [pɜtʃ]	(v.)（鳥）棲息 (n.)（鳥的）棲木
flap [flæp]	(v.) 拍動（翅膀）；振翅飛翔
aerial [`ɛrɪəl]	(adj.) 空中的 ● aerial attacks 空中攻擊
claw [klɔ]	(n.)（動物或鳥類的）爪；（蟹等的）螯
weasel [`wizl̩]	(n.) 鼬鼠，黃鼠狼
squirrel [`skwɜəl]	(n.) 松鼠

★**prairie dog** [ˋprɛrɪ dɔg]	(n.)（北美的）草原犬鼠，草原土撥鼠 參 prairie (n.) 草原地帶；美國密西西比河流域的大草原
coyote [kaɪˋoti]	(n.)（北美大草原的）土狼，郊狼
cougar [ˋkugɚ]	(n.) 美洲豹，美洲獅（主要棲息於北美山區）
grizzly bear [ˋgrɪzlɪ bɛr]	(n.)（產於北美洛磯山脈的）大灰熊
hyena [haɪˋinə]	(n.) 鬣狗，土狼（產於亞洲和非洲，嗜吃腐肉）
meerkat [ˋmɪrkæt]	(n.) 狐獴（產於南非的貓鼬類動物）
omnivorous [ɑmˋnɪvərəs]	(adj.) 雜食性的
omnivore [ˋɑmnəˏvɔr]	(n.) 雜食動物
ruminant [ˋrumənənt]	(n.) 反芻動物
roost [rust]	(v.) 棲息 (n.) 鳥巢，棲木
★**school** [skul]	(n.) 魚群 (v.) 成群結隊 ● a school of whales 一群鯨魚
goat [got]	(n.) 山羊
mole [mol]	(n.) 鼴鼠
otter [ˋɑtɚ]	(n.) 水獺
rat [ræt]	(n.) 鼠（體型較 mouse 大）
rhinoceros [raɪˋnɑsərəs]	(n.) 犀牛

hippopotamus [ˌhɪpə`patəməs]	(n.) 河馬 ! 簡稱 hippo。
hoof [hʊf]	(n.) 蹄
tusk [tʌsk]	(n.)（大象、海象等的）長牙
★**microorganism** [ˌmaɪkro`ɔrgəˌnɪzm̩]	(n.) 微生物
★**interact** [ˌɪntɚ`ækt]	(v.) 交互作用，互相影響
★**adapt** [ə`dæpt]	(v.) 適應 (= adjust/accommodate) 參 adaptation (n.) 適應，順應
★**offspring** [`ɔfˌsprɪŋ]	(n.) 子孫，後代
genotype [`dʒɛnəˌtaɪp]	(n.) 基因型，遺傳型
★**hybridization** [ˌhaɪbrɪdə`zeʃən]	(n.)（異種）交配 參 hybrid (n.)（動植物的）混種
inbreeding [`ɪnˌbridɪŋ]	(n.) 近親交配，同種繁殖
★**inherit** [ɪn`hɛrɪt]	(v.) 遺傳；繼承 • Ron inherited his father's nose. 朗遺傳到他父親的鼻子。 參 inheritance (n.) 繼承；遺產
★**synthesis** [`sɪnθəsɪs]	(n.) 合成，綜合
genesis [`dʒɛnəsɪs]	(n.) 起源，創始，發生 • the genesis of life 生命的起源
★**vermin** [`vɝmɪn]	(n.) 害蟲；有害的動物
mutant [`mjutənt]	(n.) 突變種 參 mutation (n.) 突變

mollusk [`maləsk]	(n.) 軟體動物
herbivore [`hɝbə͵vor]	(n.) 草食動物
accession [æk`sɛʃən]	(n.) 接近，到達；增加
assemblage [ə`sɛmblɪdʒ]	(n.) 聚集的人或物；集會，聚集
★**biodiversity** [͵baɪodaɪ`vɝsətɪ]	(n.) 生物多樣性
biogeography [͵baɪodʒɪ`ɑgrəfɪ]	(n.) 生物地理學
biotic [baɪ`ɑtɪk]	(adj.) 生命的，與生命相關的
buffer zone [`bʌfɚ zon]	(n.) 緩衝地帶，中立地區
★**endemic** [ɛn`dɛmɪk]	(adj.) 某地特有的 ● endemic species 某地特有的品種
community [kə`mjunətɪ]	(n.) 生物群落；社區；團體
climax community [`klaɪmæks kə`mjunətɪ]	(n.) 巔峰群落，極峰群落（生物演替到最後所出現的相當穩定的族群組合）
cosmopolitan [͵kɑzmə`pɑlətn̩]	(adj.)（動植物）分布於世界大部分地區的 ● cosmopolitan species 廣泛分布的品種
cryogenics [͵kraɪə`dʒɛnɪks]	(n.) 低溫學 參 cryogenic (adj.) 低溫的；需要低溫儲存的
★**decomposition** [͵dikɑmpə`zɪʃən]	(n.) 分解；腐爛
ecotype [`ikətaɪp]	(n.) 生態型
★**fauna** [`fɔnə]	(n.)（某區域或某時代的）動物群

★**flora** [ˋflorə]	(n.)（某區域或某時代的）植物群
★**cellular** [ˋsɛljələ˞]	(adj.) 細胞的；由細胞組成的
hemophilia B [ˌhiməˋfɪlɪə bi]	(n.) B 型血友病
inject [ɪnˋʤɛkt]	(v.) 注入，注射

08 Chemistry
化學

MP3 134

★**carbohydrate** [ˌkɑrboˋhaɪdret]	(n.) 碳水化合物，醣
yeast [jist]	(n.) 酵母
component [kəmˋponənt]	(n.) 成分，構成要素
dilute [dɪˋlut]	(adj.) 稀薄的，淡的 (v.) 稀釋 • He filled his car battery with dilute acid. 他將汽車電池注滿稀釋過的酸。
emanate [ˋɛməˌnet]	(v.) 發出，散發 • a strong odor of sulfur emanated from the spring 一股強烈的硫磺氣味從溫泉中散發出來
★**sulfur** [ˋsʌlfɚ]	(n.) 硫磺
foil [fɔɪl]	(n.) 箔 • aluminum foil 鋁箔
neon [ˋniɑn]	(n.) 氖（化學元素的一種，符號為 Ne）
sparkle [ˋspɑrkḷ]	(v.)（使）發出火光；閃耀
substance [ˋsʌbstəns]	(n.) 物質
particle [ˋpɑrtɪkḷ]	(n.) 粒子 • particle physics 粒子物理學
atom [ˋætəm]	(n.) 原子
atomic nucleus [əˋtɑmɪk ˋnjuklɪəs]	(n.) 原子核

element [`ɛləmənt]	(n.) 元素
***compound** [`kampaʊnd]	(n.) 化合物
***molecule** [`maləˏkjul]	(n.) 分子
***property** [`prapɚtɪ]	(n.) 性質，特性，屬性 ● the chemical properties of alcohol 酒精的化學性質
***chemical reaction** [`kɛmɪkḷ rɪ`ækʃən]	(n.) 化學反應
carbon [`karbən]	(n.) 碳（化學元素的一種，符號為 C）
analyze [`ænḷˏaɪz]	(v.) 分解；分析 ● Water can be analyzed into oxygen and hydrogen. 水可以分解為氧和氫。 反 synthesize (v.) 使合成
oxygen [`aksədʒən]	(n.) 氧
***catalyst** [`kætəlɪst]	(n.) 觸媒，催化劑
catalyze [`kætḷˏaɪz]	(v.) 催化
structural formula [`strʌktʃərəl `fɔrmjələ]	(n.)（化學）結構式
***synthetic** [sɪn`θɛtɪk]	(adj.) 合成的 ● synthetic resin 合成樹脂 ● synthetic fiber 合成纖維
proton [`protan]	(n.) 質子
neutron [`njutran]	(n.) 中子
***electron** [ɪ`lɛktran]	(n.) 電子

charge [tʃardʒ]	(n.) 電荷 (= electric charge)
★**nitrogen** [ˋnaɪtrədʒən]	(n.) 氮（化學元素的一種，符號為 N）
nitrogen fixation [ˋnaɪtrədʒən fɪkˋseʃən]	(n.) 固氮（作用）
nitric acid [ˋnaɪtrɪk ˋæsɪd]	(n.) 硝酸
★**sulfuric acid** [sʌlˋfjʊrɪk ˋæsɪd]	(n.) 硫酸
zinc [zɪŋk]	(n.) 鋅（化學元素的一種，符號為 Zn）
brass [bræs]	(n.) 黃銅（銅鋅合成的金屬）
★**uranium** [jʊˋrenɪəm]	(n.) 鈾（化學元素的一種，符號為 U）
★**alloy** [ˋælɔɪ]	(v.) 使成為合金 (n.) 合金 ● alloy tin with copper 把錫和銅混成合金
copper [ˋkapɚ]	(n.) 銅（化學元素的一種，符號為 Cu）
★**lead** [lɛd]	(n.) 鉛（化學元素的一種，符號為 Pb）
sodium [ˋsodɪəm]	(n.) 鈉（化學元素的一種，符號為 Na）
tin [tɪn]	(n.) 錫（化學元素的一種，符號為 Sn）
★**compression** [kəmˋprɛʃən]	(n.) 壓縮
★**nylon** [ˋnaɪlan]	(n.) 尼龍 ● Nylon is a synthetic made from a combination of water, air, and a by-product of coal. 尼龍是混合水、空氣和一種煤的副產品而成的合成物。

polyester [ˌpɑlɪˋɛstɚ]	(n.) 聚酯纖維
brew [bru]	(v.) 釀造，釀酒 參 brewery (n.) 釀造廠，啤酒廠
★**solution** [səˋluʃən]	(n.) 溶液；溶解
solvent [ˋsɑlvənt]	(n.) 溶劑，溶媒
★**density** [ˋdɛnsətɪ]	(n.) 濃度，密度
★**dissolve** [dɪˋzɑlv]	(v.)（使）溶解 ● Water dissolves salt. 水溶解鹽。
★**extract** [ɪkˋstrækt]	(v.)（用壓榨、蒸餾等方式）抽出，提煉，萃取 (n.) 萃取物 ！名詞發音爲 [ˋɛkstrækt]。
tallow [ˋtælo]	(n.) 獸脂（可用於製作蠟燭）
★**wick** [wɪk]	(n.) 燭芯，燈芯
charcoal [ˋtʃɑrˌkol]	(n.) 木炭
explosive [ɪkˋsplosɪv]	(adj.) 爆炸性的 (n.) 爆炸物
★**distill** [dɪˋstɪl]	(v.) 蒸餾；抽取 ● distill the impurities out of water 用蒸餾方式除去水中雜質
★**feasible** [ˋfizəbl̩]	(adj.) 可行的 (= practicable) ● a feasible project 可行的計畫
★**odor** [ˋodɚ]	(n.) 氣味；臭味
antimony [ˋæntəˌmonɪ]	(n.) 銻（化學元素的一種，符號為 Sb）
bauxite [ˋbɔksaɪt]	(n.) 鋁礬土（煉鋁的原料）

chromite [`kromaɪt]	(n.) 亞鉻酸鹽；鉻鐵礦
cobalt [`kobɔlt]	(n.) 鈷（化學元素的一種，符號為 Co，用於多種合金）
iron ore [`aɪɚn ɔr]	(n.) 鐵礦石
manganese [`mæŋgə͵nis]	(n.) 錳（化學元素的一種，符號為 Mn）
molybdenum [mə`lɪbdənəm]	(n.) 鉬（化學元素的一種，符號為 Mo）
nickel [`nɪkḷ]	(n.) 鎳（化學元素的一種，符號為 Ni）
palladium [pə`ledɪəm]	(n.) 鈀（化學元素的一種，符號為 Pd）
platinum [`plætɪnəm]	(n.) 鉑，白金（化學元素的一種，符號為 Pt）
titanium [taɪ`tenɪəm]	(n.) 鈦（化學元素的一種，符號為 Ti）
tungsten [`tʌŋstən]	(n.) 鎢（化學元素的一種，符號為 W）

Computer & Information Technology

電腦與資訊科技

MP3 135

unzip [ʌn`zɪp]	(v.) 解壓縮
configuration [kən,fɪgjə`reʃən]	(n.) 系統組成，配置
slot [slɑt]	(n.) 插槽
upgrade [`ʌp,gred]	(v.) 升級
★**site** [saɪt]	(n.) 網站
★**browser** [`braʊzɚ]	(n.) 瀏覽器
operating system [`ɑpə,retɪŋ `sɪstəm]	(n.) 作業系統
display [dɪ`sple]	(n.) 顯示器，電腦螢幕
keyboard [`ki,bord]	(n.) 鍵盤
mouse [maʊs]	(n.) 滑鼠
★**CPU**	(n.) 中央處理器（即 central processing unit）
ROM	(n.) 唯讀記憶體（即 read-only memory）
RAM	(n.) 隨機存取記憶體（即 random-access memory）
hard disk [hɑrd dɪsk]	(n.) 硬碟
floppy disk [`flɑpɪ dɪsk]	(n.) 軟碟
drive [draɪv]	(n.) 驅動裝置

directory [də`rɛktərɪ]	(n.) 目錄
★**file** [faɪl]	(n.) 檔案
file compression [faɪl kəm`prɛʃən]	(n.) 檔案壓縮
★**folder** [`foldɚ]	(n.) 檔案夾
★**cursor** [`kɜsɚ]	(n.) 游標
dragging [`drægɪŋ]	(n.) 拖曳（滑鼠）
function key [`fʌŋkʃən ki]	(n.) 功能鍵，F 鍵
★**save** [sev]	(v.) 儲存
log on [lɑg ɑn]	(v.) 登入 (= log in)
log off [lɑg ɔf]	(v.) 登出
access [`æksɛs]	(v.) 存取
password [`pæs,wɜd]	(n.) 密碼
★**account** [ə`kaʊnt]	(n.) 帳號
cache memory [kæʃ `mɛmərɪ]	(n.) 快取記憶體
★**the Internet** [ðə `ɪntɚ,nɛt]	(n.) 網際網路
★**world wide web** [wɜld waɪd wɛb]	(n.) 全球資訊網（簡稱 WWW）
hardware [`hard,wɛr]	(n.) 硬體

software [`sɔft,wɛr]	(n.) 軟體
the assembly line [ə`sɛmblɪ]	(n.)（電腦產業的）系統組裝線
incompatible [,ɪnkəm`pætəbḷ]	(adj.) 不相容的
authentication [ɔ,θɛntɪ`keʃən]	(n.) 認證（確認是否具有讀取資訊的資格）
resolution [,rɛzə`luʃən]	(n.)（螢幕、印表機的）解析度
information retrieval [,ɪnfɚ`meʃən rɪ`trivḷ]	(n.) 資訊檢索
*__boot__ [but]	(v.) 開機
software virus [`sɔft,wɛr `vaɪrəs]	(n.) 軟體病毒
ASP	(n.) 應用服務供應商（即 application service provider）
applet [`æplɪt]	(n.) 附屬功能程式（用 java 程式語言寫成的小型應用程式）
cookie [`kʊkɪ]	(n.) 儲存在硬碟中的特殊辨識檔案，可記錄使用者的資料
CG	(n.) 電腦圖像（即 computer graphics）
CGI	(n.) 共通閘道介面（即 common gateway interface）
domain name [do`men nem]	(n.) 網域名稱（用來區分網際網路網址，如 com, edu, gov 等）
FAQ	(n.) 常見問題集（即 frequently asked questions）
GIF [ʤɪf]	(n.) 圖形交換格式（即 graphics interchange format，一種儲存影像的格式）
HTML	(n.) 超文件標示語言（即 hypertext markup language）

★**interactive** [ˌɪntəˋæktɪv]	(adj.) 互動式的
Java [ˋʤɑvə]	(n.) 一種程式設計語言
NIC	(n.) 網路資訊中心（即 network information center，掌管 IP 位址和網域名稱的機構）
URL	(n.) 網址，統一資源定位器（即 uniform resource locator，指全球資訊網上某一頁的位址）
bandwidth [ˋbændˌwɪθ]	(n.) 頻寬
firewall [ˋfaɪrˌwɔl]	(n.) 防火牆
login [ˋlɔgˌɪn]	(n.) 登入
online [ˋɑnˌlaɪn]	(adj.) 連線的 (adv.) 連線中，在線上
offline [ˋɔfˌlaɪn]	(adj.) 離線的 (adv.) 離線，不在線上
★**server** [ˋsɝvɚ]	(n.) 伺服器
streaming [ˋstrimɪŋ]	(n.) 影音串流技術
protocol [ˋprotəˌkɑl]	(n.) 通訊協定
TCP/IP	(n.) 網路通訊協定
hacker [ˋhækɚ]	(n.) 駭客
store [stor]	(v.) 儲存
process [ˋprɑsɛs]	(v.)（資料的）處理
★**retrieve** [rɪˋtriv]	(v.)（資料）檢索

★**retrieval** [rɪ`trivḷ]	(n.)（電腦）資料檢索
encode [ɪn`kod]	(v.) 編碼
modem [`modəm]	(n.) 數據機
feed [fid]	(v.) 輸入 (= input/enter) ● feed the data into a computer 將資料輸入電腦中
binary [`baɪnərɪ]	(adj.) 二進位的 ● binary digits 位元
bit [bɪt]	(n.) 位元（即 binary digits 的簡稱，為電腦傳遞或儲存資料的最小單位）
byte [baɪt]	(n.) 位元組（由八個位元 (bit) 組成）
command [kə`mænd]	(n.) 指令
insert [ɪn`sɜt]	(v.) 插入
★**undo** [ʌn`du]	(v.) 回復，復原
sophisticated [sə`fɪstɪˌketɪd]	(adj.) 精密的；複雜的
★**delete** [dɪ`lit]	(v.) 刪除
algorithm [`ælgəˌrɪðm]	(n.) 演算法
★**artificial intelligence** [ˌartə`fɪʃəl ɪn`tɛlədʒəns]	(n.) 人工智慧（簡稱 AI）
★**cognitive science** [`kagnətɪv `saɪəns]	(n.) 認知科學
cybernetics [ˌsaɪbɚ`nɛtɪks]	(n.) 模控學

fuzzy logic [`fʌzɪ `ladʒɪk]	(n.) 模糊邏輯理論，乏晰邏輯
heuristic [hjʊ`rɪstɪk]	(adj.) 啓發式的 ● heuristic approach 啓發式的方法
infiltration [ˌɪnfɪl`treʃən]	(n.) 滲透；侵入

10 Earth Science

地球科學

MP3 136

dash [dæʃ]	(v.) 衝擊，碰撞 • The waves dashed against the rocks. 波浪衝擊著岩石。
revolve [rɪˋvalv]	(v.) 旋轉 • The earth revolves on its axis. 地球以地軸為中心旋轉。
magnitude [ˋmægnə͵tjud]	(n.) 大小；（地震的）震度 • the magnitude of a swamp 沼澤地的大小
* **meteorite** [ˋmitɪə͵raɪt]	(n.) 隕石
meteoroid [ˋmitɪə͵rɔɪd]	(n.) 流星體
infrared [͵ɪnfrəˋrɛd]	(adj.) 紅外線的
* **infrared ray** [͵ɪnfrəˋrɛd re]	(n.) 紅外線
summer solstice [ˋsʌmɚ ˋsalstɪs]	(n.) 夏至
winter solstice [ˋwɪntɚ ˋsalstɪs]	(n.) 冬至
meteorological [͵mitɪərəˋladʒɪkl]	(adj.) 氣象的 • a meteorological observatory 氣象觀測站
* **crude oil** [krud ɔɪl]	(n.) 原油 (= crude petroleum)
* **observatory** [əbˋzɝvə͵torɪ]	(n.) 觀測站，氣象站；天文台
abyss [əˋbɪs]	(n.) 深淵

aquaculture [ˋækwə͵kʌltʃɚ]	(n.)（魚類、海藻類的）水產養殖
aquanaut [ˋækwə͵nɔt]	(n.) 海底觀察員
aquatic [əˋkwatɪk]	(adj.) 水的，水生的，水上的
aquarium [əˋkwɛrɪəm]	(n.) 水族箱；水族館
ballast [ˋbæləst]	(n.)（船上讓船保持平衡的）壓艙物；（穩定熱氣球的）沙袋；（鋪設道路或鐵路用的）碎石
bathometer [bəˋθamɪtɚ]	(n.)（測水深用的）深度計
brig [brɪg]	(n.) 一種雙桅方帆的帆船；（艦上的）禁閉室
buoy [bɔɪ]	(n.) 浮標 (v.) 使浮起
capelin [ˋkæpəlɪn]	(n.) 柳葉魚，毛鱗魚
clipper [ˋklɪpɚ]	(n.) 快速帆船
cod [kad]	(n.) 鱈魚
coxswain [ˋkaksən]	(n.)（賽船的）舵手；艇長
crabwise [ˋkræb͵waɪz]	(adv.) 橫向地，蟹行地
craft [kræft]	(n.) 船，船舶 ● a pleasure craft 遊艇，觀光船
crayfish [ˋkre͵fɪʃ]	(n.) 淡水螯蝦
crew [kru]	(n.)（船或飛機上的）全體工作人員 ● All the crew were saved. 機組人員全部獲救。

crustacean [krʌs`teʃən]	(n.) 甲殼類動物（例如蟹 (crab) 和龍蝦 (lobster)） (adj.) 甲殼類的
eelgrass [`il,græs]	(n.) 大葉藻，苦草（一種海草）
★**endangered** [ɪn`dendʒəd]	(adj.) 瀕臨絕種的 ● endangered species 瀕臨滅絕的物種
estuary [`ɛstʃʊ,ɛrɪ]	(n.)（廣闊的）河口，河川入海處 ● the Hudson estuary 哈得遜河口
fin [fɪn]	(n.) 鰭 ● fin, fur, and feathers 魚類、獸類與鳥類
fishery [`fɪʃərɪ]	(n.) 漁業，水產業；漁場，養殖場
fishmonger [`fɪʃ,mʌŋgə]	(n.) 魚販 (= fish dealer)
flounder [`flaʊndə]	(n.) 比目魚
forecastle [`foksl̩]	(n.) 水手艙
frigate [`frɪgɪt]	(n.) 巡防艦；（反潛、護航用的）小型驅逐艦
haddock [`hædək]	(n.) 黑線鱈（鱈魚的一種）
hook [hʊk]	(n.) 釣魚鉤
houseboat [`haʊs,bot]	(n.) 船屋
hydrofoil [`haɪdrə,fɔɪl]	(n.) 水翼船，水上飛機
inboard [`ɪn,bord]	(adj.)（船或飛機）艙內的
Indian Ocean [`ɪndɪən `oʃən]	(n.) 印度洋

inshore [ˋɪn͵ʃor]	(adj.) 沿岸的；近海的
intertidal [͵ɪntɚˋtaɪdḷ]	(adj.) 潮間帶的
keel [kil]	(n.)（船的）龍骨
lateen [læˋtin]	(n.) 大三角帆船
★**longitude** [ˋlanʤə͵tjud]	(n.) 經度 ● 20 degrees 15 minutes of east longitude 東經 20 度 15 分
leeward [ˋliwɚd]	(adj.) 下風的 (adv.) 向下風，在下風 (n.) 下風處 反 windward (adj.) 迎風的 (adv.) 迎風 (n.) 迎風面
littoral [ˋlɪtərəl]	(adj.) 海岸的，沿岸的 (n.) 沿岸地區
longitudinal [͵lanʤəˋtjudənḷ]	(adj.) 經度的，經線的；縱的
alongshore [əˋlɔŋ͵ʃor]	(adv.) 沿著海岸
menhaden [mɛnˋhedṇ]	(n.) 油鯡（鯡魚的一種）
mercantile [ˋmɝkən͵taɪl]	(adj.) 商業的；重商主義的
mercantile marine [ˋmɝkən͵taɪl məˋrin]	(n.)（一國的）商船隊
mermaid [ˋmɝ͵med]	(n.) 人魚
★**molt** [molt]	(n.) 蛻皮；換毛
narwhal/narwal [ˋnarwəl]	(n.) 獨角鯨（齒鯨的一種，棲息於北極海）
★**navigation** [͵nævəˋgeʃən]	(n.) 航海

navy [ˋnevɪ]	(n.) 海軍
oceanarium [ˏoʃəˋnɛrɪəm]	(n.)（大型的）海洋水族館
Oceania [ˏoʃɪˋænɪə]	(n.) 大洋洲
***oceanography** [ˏoʃɪəˋnɑgrəfɪ]	(n.) 海洋學
oyster bed [ˋɔɪstɚ bɛd]	(n.) 牡蠣養殖場
pelagic [pəˋlædʒɪk]	(adj.) 遠洋的
platypus [ˋplætəpəs]	(n.) 鴨嘴獸 (= duckbill)（一種產於澳洲的卵生哺乳動物）
pod [pɑd]	(n.)（海豹、鯨等的）一小群
punt [pʌnt]	(n.) 平底小船
quay [ki]	(n.) 碼頭 (= wharf)
quintal [ˋkwɪntḷ]	(n.) 一百磅；一百公斤
***raft** [ræft]	(n.) 木筏；浮台；橡皮艇
red tide [rɛd taɪd]	(n.) 紅潮
refit [riˋfɪt]	(n.)（船舶的）修理，改裝
rigging [ˋrɪgɪŋ]	(n.)（船上的繩索、鍊子等）索具
schooner [ˋskunɚ]	(n.)（兩桅以上的）縱帆船

seaquake [ˋsiˏkwek]	(n.) 海底地震
sea urchin [si ˋɜtʃɪn]	(n.) 海膽
sea wall [si wɔl]	(n.) 防波堤
seaweed [ˋsiˏwid]	(n.) 海草，海藻
seaworthy [ˋsiˏwɝðɪ]	(adj.) 適合航海的
sextant [ˋsɛkstənt]	(n.) 六分儀（測量距離和角度的儀器，用來定位船隻或飛機）
shoal [ʃol]	(n.) 淺灘，沙洲；潛在危險
tentacle [ˋtɛntəkl̩]	(n.) 觸鬚，觸角，觸毛
tide [taɪd]	(n.) 潮流，潮汐
tide rip [taɪd rɪp]	(n.)（潮流互撞而成的）潮激浪
trawl [trɔl]	(n.) 拖網
upriver [ˋʌpˋrɪvɚ]	(n.) 上游地區
upstream [ˋʌpˋstrim]	(adv.) 向上游，逆流地 (adj.) 上游的
upwind [ˋʌpˋwɪnd]	(adv.) 迎風地 (adj.) 迎風的
★**vessel** [ˋvɛsl̩]	(n.) 船隻 ● an observation vessel 觀測船
wale knot [wel nɑt]	(n.) 繩端結（一種打在繩子尾端的大結，又稱作 wall knot）

waterway [ˋwɔtɚˏwe]	(n.) 水路，河道，運河
watery grave [ˋwɔtərɪ grev]	(n.) 溺斃
wharf [wɔrf]	(n.) 碼頭
xebec [ˋzibɛk]	(n.)（航行於地中海的）三桅小帆船
zoophyte [ˋzoəˏfaɪt]	(n.) 植蟲類（類似植物的動物，如海葵、珊瑚等）
zooplankton [ˏzoəˋplæŋktən]	(n.)〔集合用法〕浮游動物
zoospore [ˋzoəˏspor]	(n.) 游動孢子
★**spring tide** [sprɪŋ taɪd]	(n.)（新月及滿月時的）滿潮
★**flood tide** [flʌd taɪd]	(n.) 漲潮，滿潮
★**ebb tide** [ɛb taɪd]	(n.) 退潮，落潮 參 ebb (n.) 退潮 ● The tide is now at the lowest ebb. 目前處於最低潮。
fathom [ˋfæðəm]	(n.) 噚（表水深的單位，相當於 6 英尺 (feet) 或 1.8 公尺 (meter)）

11 Ecology
生態學

MP3 138

★**penetrate** [ˋpɛnə͵tret]	(v.) 穿過，貫穿
encroach [ɪnˋkrotʃ]	(v.)（海水）侵蝕
encompass [ɪnˋkʌmpəs]	(v.) 包圍，圍繞
★**emission** [ɪˋmɪʃən]	(n.) 排出，排放；發射 • an emission-free automobile 不會排放廢氣的汽車
★**emission control** [ɪˋmɪʃən kənˋtrol]	(n.) 廢氣排放管制
★**environment** [ɪnˋvaɪrənmənt]	(n.) 環境
★**environmental disruption** [ɪn͵vaɪrənˋmɛntḷ dɪsˋrʌpʃən]	(n.) 環境破壞 參 disruption (n.) 混亂；（國家等）分裂，瓦解
environmentalist contingent [ɪn͵vaɪrənˋmɛntḷɪst kənˋtɪndʒənt]	(n.) 環保團體 參 contingent (n.) 代表團；（軍隊、艦隊的）分遣隊
★**acid rain** [ˋæsɪd ren]	(n.) 酸雨
★**deforestation** [͵difɔrəsˋteʃən]	(n.) 砍伐森林，破壞森林
★**disaster** [dɪˋzæstɚ]	(n.) 災害，災難 • the Chernobyl nuclear plant disaster 車諾比核電廠災難
niche [nɪtʃ]	(n.) 區位，棲位（生態系中適合個別物種生存或發展的環境）；利基 • ecological niche 生態區位

★**extinction** [ɪk`stɪŋkʃən]	(n.) 滅絕，絕種 參 extermination (n.) 消滅，根絕
★**extinct** [ɪk`stɪŋkt]	(adj.) 滅絕的，絕種的 !常考單字。 ● become extinct 滅絕 參 exterminate (v.) 消滅
★**catastrophe** [kə`tæstrəfɪ]	(n.) 大災難，浩劫
consume [kən`sum]	(v.) 毀滅，燒毀；消費 ● The fire consumed the whole forest. 大火吞噬了整座森林。
★**radioactive** [ˌredɪo`æktɪv]	(adj.) 放射性的 ● radioactive substance 放射性物質
★**atmospheric pollution** [ˌætməs`fɛrɪk pə`luʃən]	(n.) 大氣汙染
★**contamination** [kənˌtæmə`neʃən]	(n.) 汙染 (= pollution) !常考單字。 參 contaminate (v.) 汙染
★**contaminant** [kən`tæmənənt]	(n.) 汙染物
food chain [fud tʃen]	(n.) 食物鏈
insectivore [ɪn`sɛktəˌvor]	(n.) 食蟲動物，食蟲植物
★**insecticide** [ɪn`sɛktəˌsaɪd]	(n.) 殺蟲劑
★**global warming** [`globḷ `wɔrmɪŋ]	(n.) 全球暖化（由溫室效應 (greenhouse effect) 所引起）
★**greenhouse effect** [`grinˌhaʊs ɪ`fɛkt]	(n.) 溫室效應
★**petroleum** [pə`trolɪəm]	(n.) 石油
coal [kol]	(n.) 煤

tropical rain forest [`trɑpɪkl̩ ren `fɔrɪst]	(n.) 熱帶雨林
***fertile** [`fɝtl̩]	(adj.)（土地）肥沃的；（動植物）多產的 • land fertile in fruit and crops 盛產水果和穀物的沃土
***radiation** [ˌredɪ`eʃən]	(n.) 放射線，輻射
***desert** [`dɛzɚt]	(n.) 沙漠
***flood** [flʌd]	(n.) 洪水 • a flood gate 水門，水閘
***energy conservation** [`ɛnɚdʒɪ ˌkɑnsɚ`veʃən]	(n.) 節約能源
***toxic** [`tɑksɪk]	(adj.) 有毒的
toxin [`tɑksɪn]	(n.) 毒素，有毒物質
***waste** [west]	(n.) 廢棄物 • toxic waste 有毒廢棄物
***dump** [dʌmp]	(v.) 傾倒（垃圾等）(n.) 垃圾場
***disposal** [dɪ`spozl̩]	(n.) 處理，處置 • the disposal of nuclear waste 核廢料的處理
***pollution** [pə`luʃən]	(n.) 汙染 參 pollutant (n.) 汙染物
biosphere [`baɪəˌsfɪr]	(n.) 生物圈（地球上生命可生存的區域）
***trash** [træʃ]	(n.) 垃圾
***garbage** [`gɑrbɪdʒ]	(n.)〔集合用法〕垃圾 (= trash/rubbish/refuse/dust)
***rubbish** [`rʌbɪʃ]	(n.) 垃圾

★**litter** [`lɪtɚ]	(n.) 紙屑，垃圾 • No Litters 禁止亂丟垃圾
★**evacuation** [ɪˌvækjʊ`eʃən]	(n.) 疏散，撤離
smog [smɑg]	(n.) 煙霧
ozone [`ozon]	(n.) 臭氧
★**ozone layer** [`ozon `leɚ]	(n.) 臭氧層（可吸收對動植物有害的太陽紫外線）
★**ozone depletion** [`ozon dɪ`pliʃən]	(n.) 臭氧層破壞，臭氧層耗竭
oxidization [ˌɑksədaɪ`zeʃən]	(n.) 氧化
corrosion [kə`roʒən]	(n.) 腐蝕
★**erode** [ɪ`rod]	(v.)（酸等）腐蝕，（波浪等）侵蝕 • Acids erode certain metals. 酸會腐蝕某些金屬。
★**precipitation** [prɪˌsɪpɪ`teʃən]	(n.) 降雨（量），降雪（量）
★**erosion** [ɪ`roʒən]	(n.) 侵蝕，腐蝕
acid [`æsɪd]	(n.) 酸 (adj.) 酸性的 • acid reaction 酸性反應
alkaline [`ælkəˌlaɪn]	(adj.) 鹼性的
alluvium [ə`luvɪəm]	(n.) 沖積層；沖積土
aqueduct [`ækwɪˌdʌkt]	(n.) 輸水道，導水管
★**aquifer** [`ækwəfɚ]	(n.)（可供鑿井取水的）含水層

★**artesian well** [ɑr`tiʒən wɛl]	(n.) 自流井
bedrock [`bɛd,rɑk]	(n.) 基岩，床岩
★**capillary action** [`kæpə,lɛrɪ `ækʃən]	(n.) 毛細管現象
★**condense** [kən`dɛns]	(v.) 使凝結；濃縮 ● condense steam into water 使蒸汽凝結成水
condensation [,kandɛn`seʃən]	(n.) 凝結；濃縮
cubic feet per second [`kjubɪk]	(n.) 每秒立方英尺 (= cfs)
desalinization [di,sælənə`zeʃən]	(n.) 除鹽，脫鹽 (= desalination)
★**irrigation** [,ɪrə`geʃən]	(n.) 灌溉
drawdown [`drɔ,daʊn]	(n.) 減少，削減
effluent [`ɛflʊənt]	(n.)（河川、湖泊等分出的）支流；（工廠排出的）廢水，汙水
★**evaporation** [ɪ,væpə`reʃən]	(n.) 蒸發
★**evaporate** [ɪ`væpə,ret]	(v.) 蒸發 ● The small pool of water evaporated in the sunshine. 那一小池水在陽光下蒸發了。
★**geyser** [`gaɪzɚ]	(n.) 間歇泉，噴泉
★**ground water** [graʊnd `wɔtɚ]	(n.) 地下水
hardness [`hardnɪs]	(n.)（水的）硬度
headwater [`hɛd,wɔtɚ]	(n.) 上游，源流

★**hydroelectric power** [ˌhaɪdroɪ`lɛktrɪk `paʊɚ]	(n.) 水力發電
★**harness** [`harnɪs]	(v.) 利用 ● harness solar energy 利用太陽能
impermeable layer [ɪm`pɝmɪəbl̩ `leɚ]	(n.) 不透水層
leach [litʃ]	(v.) (n.) 過濾
levee [`lɛvɪ]	(n.) 河堤
osmosis [ɑz`mosɪs]	(n.) 滲透
outfall [`aʊtˌfɔl]	(n.) 河口；出水口
★**percolation** [ˌpɝkə`leʃən]	(n.) 過濾 (= filtration)
★**permeability** [ˌpɝmɪə`bɪlətɪ]	(n.) 滲透性
★**permeate** [`pɝmɪˌet]	(v.) 滲透 (= penetrate/soak)
reclaimed wastewater [rɪ`klemd `westˌwɔtɚ]	(n.) 回收再利用的廢水
reservoir [`rɛzɚˌvɔr]	(n.) 蓄水池；水庫
★**runoff** [`rʌnˌɔf]	(n.)（雨水等未被土地吸收而在地表流動的）徑流
★**saline water** [`selaɪn `wɔtɚ]	(n.) 鹽水 ㊜ salinity (n.) 鹽分，鹽度
★**sediment** [`sɛdəmənt]	(n.) 沉澱，沉積（物） ㊜ sedimentary rocks 沉積岩
seepage [`sipɪdʒ]	(n.) 滲出，滲漏

sewage [`suɪdʒ]	(n.) 下水道的汙物，汙水
sewage treatment plant [`suɪdʒ `tritmənt plænt]	(n.) 汙水處理廠
★**sewer** [`suɚ]	(n.) 下水道 參 sewerage (n.) 汙水處理
subsidence [səb`saɪdəns]	(n.) 沉澱，堆積
★**surface tension** [`sɝfɪs `tɛnʃən]	(n.) 表面張力
thermal pollution [`θɝml̩ pə`luʃən]	(n.) 熱汙染，熱公害（發電廠等排出溫水而使水質惡化）
transpiration [ˌtrænspə`reʃən]	(n.) 蒸騰（水分從植物表面散失的現象）
★**tributary** [`trɪbjəˌtɛrɪ]	(adj.) 支流的 ● tributary streams 支流
turbidity [tɝ`bɪdətɪ]	(n.) 混濁；濁度
unsaturated zone [ʌn`sætʃəˌretɪd zon]	(n.) 不飽和帶，未飽和層
★**water cycle** [`wɔtɚ `saɪkl̩]	(n.) 水循環
water table [`wɔtɚ `tebl̩]	(n.) 地下水位
watershed [`wɔtɚˌʃɛd]	(n.) 分水嶺

12 Economics & Management
經濟學與經營學

MP3 140

analyst [`ænəlɪst]	(n.) 分析者，分析師
***bankrupt** [`bæŋkrʌpt]	(adj.) 破產的 ● go bankrupt 破產 (= go broke)
***bankruptcy** [`bæŋkrʌptsɪ]	(n.) 破產
broker [`brokɚ]	(n.) 經紀人，仲介
***curtailment** [kɜ`telmənt]	(n.) 削減，縮減
devalue [di`vælju]	(v.) 使貶值；貶低
exhortation [ˌɛgzɔr`teʃən]	(n.) 力勸，勸告
***exploit** [ɪk`splɔɪt]	(v.)（資源等）開發，利用；剝削 ● Many children were exploited as cheap labor in factories. 許多兒童被剝削，成為工廠的廉價勞工。
***imbalance** [ɪm`bæləns]	(n.) 不平均，失衡 (= disproportion)
ledger [`lɛdʒɚ]	(n.) 分類帳
nationalize [`næʃənḷˌaɪz]	(v.) 使國有化
***personnel** [ˌpɜsə`nɛl]	(n.)〔集合用法〕全體職員，員工；人事部門 ● cutbacks in personnel 縮減人員
***productivity** [ˌprodʌk`tɪvətɪ]	(n.) 生產力 ● high costs and low productivity 高成本低生產力
proviso [prə`vaɪˌzo]	(n.)（合約中的）但書，條件

★**retail** [ˋritel]	(v.) 零售 ● These socks retail at/for $5 a pair. 襪子每雙零售價五美元。
retailer [ˋritelɚ]	(n.) 零售商
★**storage** [ˋstorɪdʒ]	(n.) 貯藏；保管
★**transaction** [trænsˋækʃən]	(n.) 交易，買賣 ● have business transactions with someone 和某人有生意往來
★**valid** [ˋvælɪd]	(adj.) 有效的 參 validity (n.) 效力；正當性
★**warehouse** [ˋwɛrˌhaʊs]	(n.) 倉庫
★**wholesale** [ˋholˌsel]	(n.) 批發 反 retail (n.) 零售 參 wholesaler (n.) 批發業者
★**assessment** [əˋsɛsmənt]	(n.) 評估；(財產、收入等的) 估計，估價 ● environmental assessment 環境影響評估
★**sluggish** [ˋslʌgɪʃ]	(adj.) 遲緩的，不振的，疲軟的 ● a sluggish economy 疲弱的經濟
repercussion [ˌripɚˋkʌʃən]	(n.) (不好的) 影響，結果
★**boost** [bust]	(v.) 增加，提高；促進 ● boost sales 增加銷售額
★**consolidate** [kənˋsɑləˌdet]	(v.) 合併；鞏固 ● consolidate one's debts 合併債務
★**remit** [rɪˋmit]	(v.) 匯款 ● remit the balance to him by money order 用匯票將餘額匯給他
★**spur** [spɝ]	(n.) 刺激，激勵，動力

★**deduction** [dɪ`dʌkʃən]	(n.) 扣除（額） ● income tax deduction 所得稅扣除額
downright [`daʊn,raɪt]	(adj.) 徹底的，完全的
★**enumerate** [ɪ`njumə,ret]	(v.) 列舉
joint [dʒɔɪnt]	(adj.) 共同的，共有的 ● joint owners of a business 企業的共同擁有者
★**manifold** [`mænə,fold]	(adj.) 種種的，多樣的，多方面的 ● a manifold operation 多方面的計畫
★**margin** [`mɑrdʒɪn]	(n.) 保證金；利潤 ● margin transaction 保證金交易，信用交易
★**multilateral** [,mʌltɪ`lætərəl]	(adj.) 多邊的，多國參加的 ● a multilateral agreement 多邊協議
multiple [`mʌltəpl̩]	(adj.) 多重的，多樣的
prolong [prə`lɔŋ]	(v.) 延長
★**superfluous** [sʊ`pɝflʊəs]	(adj.) 多餘的，過剩的，不必要的
tardiness [`tɑrdɪnɪs]	(n.) 緩慢，遲滯
foreign exchange market [`fɔrɪn ɪks`tʃendʒ `mɑrkɪt]	(n.) 外匯市場
★**lay off** [le ɔf]	(v.)（暫時）解雇，裁員 ● We were laid off (work) for three weeks. 我們被暫時解雇三星期。
★**executive** [ɪg`zɛkjʊtɪv]	(n.) 管理者，經理，主管 ● He is an executive in the airlines. 他是航空公司的主管。
stock [stɑk]	(n.) 股票

stock price index [stɑk praɪs `ɪndɛks]	(n.) 股價指數
★**stock market** [stɑk `mɑrkɪt]	(n.) 股票市場
stockholder [`stɑk,holdɚ]	(n.) 股東
★**shareholder** [`ʃɛr,holdɚ]	(n.) 股東
exchange rate [ɪks`tʃendʒ ret]	(n.) 匯率
principal [`prɪnsəpḷ]	(n.) 本金
capital gain [`kæpətḷ gen]	(n.) 資本利得（出售土地、股票等資產所得的利益）
★**surplus** [`sɝplʌs]	(n.) 盈餘 反 deficit (n.) 赤字
★**affiliation** [ə,fɪlɪ`eʃən]	(n.) 聯合；聯繫 ● hospitals in affiliation with University of Washington 隸屬於華盛頓大學的醫院
★**affiliate** [ə`fɪlɪ,et]	(v.)（使）加入（團體）(n.) 分會，支會；附屬機構
high-interest rate [haɪ `ɪntərɪst ret]	(n.) 高利率
★**high yield** [haɪ jild]	(n.) 高收益
official discount rate [ə`fɪʃəl `dɪskaʊnt ret]	(n.) 官方貼現率 參 discount rate 貼現率
★**arbitrage** [`ɑrbətrɪdʒ]	(n.)〔集合用法〕（股票等的）套利
★**fund** [fʌnd]	(n.) 資金；基金 ● a reserve fund 準備金
subcontractor [,sʌbkən`træktɚ]	(n.) 轉包商

★**consume** [kən`sum]	(v.) 消費；消耗 ● This machine consumes 10 percent of all the power we use. 這部機器消耗我們所使用電力的 10%。
consumer goods [kən`sumə gʊdz]	(n.) 消費性商品
consumer price index [kən`sumə praɪs `ɪndɛks]	(n.) 消費者物價指數
★**consumption** [kən`sʌmpʃən]	(n.) 消費 ● consumption tax 消費稅
securities industry [sɪ`kjʊrətɪz `ɪndəstrɪ]	(n.) 證券業
★**output** [`aʊt,pʊt]	(n.) 產量
★**equilibrium** [,ikwə`lɪbrɪəm]	(n.) 均衡，平衡 ● Supply and demand are in equilibrium. 供需平衡。
★**aggregate** [`ægrɪgɪt]	(adj.) 總計的，合計的 ● aggregate demand 總需求
break-even point [`brek`ivən pɔɪnt]	(n.) 損益平衡點
★**tax evasion** [tæks ɪ`veʒən]	(n.) 逃漏稅
★**merger** [`mɝdʒə]	(n.) 合併 ● merger and acquisition (M&A) 併購
morale [mə`ræl]	(n.) 士氣 ● boost the morale of workers 提高員工的士氣
★**mortgage** [`mɔrgɪdʒ]	(n.) 抵押；房屋貸款 ● place a mortgage on one's land 以土地來抵押
★**languish** [`læŋgwɪʃ]	(v.) 變得疲弱、沒有生氣
commission [kə`mɪʃən]	(n.) 佣金；委任，委託

investment [ɪn`vɛstmənt]	(n.) 投資
investment trust [ɪn`vɛstmənt trʌst]	(n.) 投資信託
monopoly [mə`napəlɪ]	(n.) 獨占，專賣，壟斷 ● the monopoly prohibition law 禁止壟斷法
dealing [`dilɪŋ]	(n.) 交易，往來 ● have dealings with... 和…有商業往來
★**business transaction** [`bɪznɪs træn`sækʃən]	(n.) 商業交易 參 cash transaction 現金交易
★**dividend** [`dɪvə͵dɛnd]	(n.) 股息 ● pass a dividend 不發股息
bargain [`bargɪn]	(n.)（買賣等的）協議 ● close/settle/arrange/strike/conclude/make a bargain with someone over the price 和某人就價格達成協議
blue chip [blu tʃɪp]	(n.) 藍籌股，績優股
head office [hɛd `ɔfɪs]	(n.) 總公司，總部
board of directors [bord] [də`rɛktɚz]	(n.) 董事會；理事會
depositor [dɪ`pazɪtɚ]	(n.) 存款人
rate hike [ret haɪk]	(n.) 利率上揚
labor union [`lebɚ `junjən]	(n.) 工會
employment [ɪm`plɔɪmənt]	(n.) 雇用
unemployment [͵ʌnɪm`plɔɪmənt]	(n.) 失業；失業人數 ● disguised unemployment 隱藏性失業

unemployment benefits [ˌʌnɪm`plɔɪmənt `bɛnəfɪts]	(n.) 失業救濟金
★**analysis** [ə`næləsɪs]	(n.) 分析 ！複數形是 analyses。 • logical analyses of human behavior 對人類行為的邏輯分析
analytic [ˌænə`lɪtɪk]	(adj.) 分析的 參 synthetic (adj.) 綜合的
★**equitable** [`ɛkwɪtəbḷ]	(adj.) 公平的 • distribute the money in an equitable manner 以公平的方法分配金錢
commodity [kə`mɑdətɪ]	(n.) 商品；日用品 • staple commodity 主要商品
★**allocate** [`æləˌket]	(v.) 分配，撥出 • allocate $300,000 for the facilities of a library 撥出 30 萬美元給圖書館增添設備
★**subsidize** [`sʌbsəˌdaɪz]	(v.) 資助，補助 • The project is heavily subsidized by the government. 這項計畫受到政府鉅額補助。
★**subsidy** [`sʌbsədɪ]	(n.) 補助金
★**subsidiary** [səb`sɪdɪˌɛrɪ]	(adj.) 補助的；附屬的 (n.) 子公司
auditor [`ɔdɪtɚ]	(n.) 查帳員，稽核員 參 audit (v.) 查帳，稽核帳目
seniority system [sin`jɔrətɪ `sɪstəm]	(n.) 年功序列制（指薪資隨年資的增加而成長的制度）
★**revenue** [`rɛvəˌnju]	(n.) 歲入，稅收；收益 • internal revenue 國內稅收
★**fiscal** [`fɪskḷ]	(adj.) 財政的，會計的 • a fiscal year 會計年度

★**stagnant** [`stægnənt]	(adj.) 停滯的；不景氣的 參 stagnation (n.) 停滯；不景氣
★**per capita** [pɚ `kæpətə]	(adj.) (adv.) 按人計算的，每人
★**dismiss** [dɪs`mɪs]	(v.) 解雇 (= discharge/fire) ● dismiss half the employees 解雇一半的員工
★**distribution** [ˌdɪstrə`bjuʃən]	(n.) 分配；分布 ● distribution curves（統計的）分布曲線
★**distribute** [dɪ`strɪbjut]	(v.) 分配；分布 ● distribute to each employee the benefits due to him 分配給每一位員工其應得的利益
★**pension** [`pɛnʃən]	(n.) 年金；養老金 ● collect an old age pension 領取老人年金
★**entrepreneur** [ˌɑntrəprə`nɝ]	(n.) 企業家
withholding tax [wɪð`holdɪŋ tæks]	(n.) 預扣所得稅（即雇主代替政府從受雇者薪水中預扣的所得稅）
★**tariff** [`tærɪf]	(n.) 關稅 (= customs/duty)
savings account [`sevɪŋz ə`kaunt]	(n.) 儲蓄存款帳戶
checking account [`tʃɛkɪŋ ə`kaunt]	(n.) 支票存款帳戶
★**depreciation** [dɪˌpriʃɪ`eʃən]	(n.) 貶值，跌價；折舊 ● depreciation reserves 折舊準備金
★**appreciation** [əˌpriʃɪ`eʃən]	(n.) 升值，漲價 ● the appreciation of the yen 日圓升值
vicious [`vɪʃəs]	(adj.) 惡性的；惡意的 ● vicious circle 惡性循環
developing country [dɪ`vɛləpɪŋ `kʌntrɪ]	(n.) 開發中國家 (= emerging nation)

developer [dɪˋvɛləpɚ]	(n.) 開發者
human rights [ˋhjumən raɪts]	(n.) 人權
★**indigenous people** [ɪnˋdɪdʒɪnəs ˋpipl̩]	(n.) 原住民
industrial country [ɪnˋdʌstrɪəl ˋkʌntrɪ]	(n.) 工業國
logging [ˋlɔgɪŋ]	(n.) 伐木，木材採運業 ● a logging railroad 木材運輸鐵路
★**materialize** [məˋtɪrɪəl͵aɪz]	(v.) 實現，具體化 ● materialize one's dream 實現某人的夢想
nonprofit [͵nanˋprafɪt]	(adj.) 非營利的
sustainable [səˋstenəbl̩]	(adj.) 永續的，可持續的
World Bank [wɝld bæŋk]	(n.) 世界銀行
firm [fɝm]	(n.) 公司，商號 ● a law firm 法律事務所
★**asset** [ˋæsɛt]	(n.) 財產，資產 ● He is a great asset to our company. 他是我們公司的重要資產。
★**liable** [ˋlaɪəbl̩]	(adj.)（法律上）應負責的；有義務的 ● be liable to taxation 應繳稅的
★**register** [ˋrɛdʒɪstɚ]	(v.) 登記，註冊
★**agency** [ˋedʒənsɪ]	(n.) 機構；代理店 ● Central Intelligence Agency (CIA) 美國中央情報局
loan [lon]	(n.) 借款，貸款；公債 ● raise/issue a loan 發行公債

income [`ɪn,kʌm]	(n.) 收入 ● gross/net income 總 / 淨收入
★**currency** [`kɜənsɪ]	(n.) 貨幣，通貨 ● foreign currency 外幣
income tax [`ɪn,kʌm tæks]	(n.) 所得稅
★**soar** [sor]	(v.)（物價等）高漲，飆漲 ● The price of gold is soaring. 金價飆漲。
competitiveness [kəm`pɛtətɪvnɪs]	(n.) 競爭力
competition [,kampə`tɪʃən]	(n.) 競爭 參 compete with/against... 和…競爭
★**competent** [`kampətənt]	(adj.) 有能力的，能勝任的 ● The new section chief is a man competent for the task. 新來的課長可以勝任那項任務。
retirement [rɪ`taɪrmənt]	(n.) 退休 ● take early retirement 提前退休
retirement benefits [rɪ`taɪrmənt `bɛnəfɪts]	(n.) 退休金
supply [sə`plaɪ]	(n.) 供給 ● supply and demand 供需
★**deficit** [`dɛfɪsɪt]	(n.) 赤字，不足額 ● deficit financing 赤字財政 參 be in the red 虧損，負債
★**incentive** [ɪn`sɛntɪv]	(n.) 刺激，誘因，動機
★**interest rate** [`ɪntərɪst ret]	(n.) 利率
★**innovation** [,ɪnə`veʃən]	(n.) 革新，創新 ● technological innovation 技術革新
multinational [,mʌltɪ`næʃənḷ]	(adj.) 多國的，跨國的 (n.) 跨國企業 (= multinational corporation)

antitrust law [ˌæntɪ`trʌst lɔ]	(n.) 反托拉斯法
balance [`bæləns]	(n.)（收支等的）差額，餘額 ● a favorable/unfavorable balance of trade 貿易出超 / 入超
creditor [`krɛdɪtɚ]	(n.) 債權人，債主 反 debtor (n.) 債務人 ● Creditors have better memories than debtors. 債主的記性比欠錢的好。〔諺語〕
foreign exchange reserves [`fɔrɪn ɪks`tʃendʒ rɪ`zɝvz]	(n.) 外匯存底
★**curb** [kɝb]	(v.) 抑制，限制 ！常考單字。 ● curb one's spending 節制開支
★**diversify** [daɪ`vɝsəˌfaɪ]	(v.) 使多樣化，增加（產品等的）種類
★**stake** [stek]	(n.) 利害關係；股份；賭注
denomination [dɪˌnɑmə`neʃən]	(n.)（貨幣等的）面額；單位 ● Bonds were issued in denomination of $500. 債券以 500 美元的面額發行。
flier [`flaɪɚ]	(n.) 廣告傳單
★**alliance** [ə`laɪəns]	(n.) 聯合，聯盟 ● a triple alliance 三國聯盟
book [bʊk]	(n.) 帳簿
★**tax return** [tæks rɪ`tɝn]	(n.) 報稅單
ordinance [`ɔrdɪnəns]	(n.) 法令，條例 ● a cabinet/government ordinance 政令
premium [`primɪəm]	(n.) 保險費；獎金

list [lɪst]	(v.)（股票等）上市
★**expenditure** [ɪk`spɛndɪtʃɚ]	(n.) 支出，費用 ● annual expenditure 年度支出
expire [ɪk`spaɪr]	(v.) 期滿，終止 ● My license **expires** on the first day of March. 我的執照在 3 月 1 日到期。 參 expiration (n.)（期限等的）屆滿，期滿
venture [`vɛntʃɚ]	(n.) 企業；投機活動
maturity [mə`tjʊrətɪ]	(n.)（支票的）到期
★**finance** [faɪ`næns]	(n.) 財務；財政學 (v.) 融資，提供資金 ● a finance bill 財政法案
financial market [faɪ`nænʃəl `mɑrkɪt]	(n.) 金融市場
★**liabilities** [ˌlaɪə`bɪlətɪz]	(n.)〔用複數形〕負債，債務
equity [`ɛkwətɪ]	(n.)（無固定利息的）普通股票；公正 ● equity capital 股本
financial reform [faɪ`nænʃəl rɪ`fɔrm]	(n.) 財政改革
cash flow [kæʃ flo]	(n.) 現金流轉，現金流量 ● have cash flow problems 有現金流量的問題
liquidity [lɪ`kwɪdətɪ]	(n.) 資產變現能力；流動力
leverage [`lɛvərɪdʒ]	(n.) 手段；槓桿作用，財務槓桿（即預期利潤會高過利息而借款作投機生意）
return [rɪ`tɝn]	(n.) 利潤，收益
interest [`ɪntərɪst]	(n.) 利益，利害關係；同業者；利息 ● the shipbuilding interests 造船業者

bond [band]	(n.) 債券，公債；束縛 ● corporate/government bonds 公司債 / 公債
capital [`kæpətl]	(n.) 資本，資金 ● financial capital 金融資本
★**trade-off** [`tred,ɔf]	(n.) 交換；(在無法兩相兼顧時所做的) 權衡
accounting [ə`kaʊntɪŋ]	(n.) 會計；會計學 參 bookkeeping (n.) 簿記
lease [lis]	(n.) 租賃契約
inventory [`ɪnvən,torɪ]	(n.) 庫存；目錄

13 Education
教育學

MP3 143

★**browse** [brauz]	(n.) (v.) 瀏覽，翻閱
console [kən`sol]	(v.) 安慰，慰問 • console someone for/on his misfortune 安慰某人的不幸
★**embody** [ɪm`badɪ]	(v.)〔常用被動〕體現，使具體化 • His opinions are embodied in this essay. 他的想法在這篇文章中具體地表現出來。
★**enlightenment** [ɪn`laɪtn̩mənt]	(n.) 啓發，啓蒙，教化 • the Enlightenment（17 到 18 世紀發生於歐洲的）啓蒙運動
★**intelligible** [ɪn`tɛlədʒəbl̩]	(adj.) 可理解的，明白易懂的
ambivalent [æm`bɪvələnt]	(adj.) 懷有矛盾情感的 • an ambivalent feeling toward religion 對於宗教有矛盾的情感
★**aptitude** [`æptə,tjud]	(n.) 資質，才能 • a remarkable aptitude for language 在語言方面顯著的才能
★**certificate** [sə`tɪfəkɪt]	(n.) 證書，證照 • a teacher's/teaching certificate 教師證照
certify [`sɜtə,faɪ]	(v.) 證明；保證 • It has been certified that the documents are correct. 那些文件經證明是正確無誤的。
compulsion [kəm`pʌlʃən]	(n.) 強制；〔心理學〕不可抗拒的衝動 • feel a compulsion to steal 感覺到偷竊的衝動
★**disinterestedness** [dɪs`ɪntərəstɪdnɪs]	(n.) 公正無私 (= impartiality)

★**eligible** [`ɛlɪdʒəbḷ]	(adj.) 合適的，合格的
★**eliminate** [ɪ`lɪmə,net]	(v.) 刪除，消掉 • eliminate slang words from one's writings 刪掉某人作品中的俚語
engross [ɪn`gros]	(v.) 使全神貫注 • engross oneself with... 全神貫注於…
★**evaluate** [ɪ`vælju,et]	(v.) 評估，評價 • It is difficult to evaluate him as a teacher. 很難評斷他為人師表的表現。
forbear [fɔr`bɛr]	(v.) 忍住，克制 • forbear one's anger 抑制某人的怒氣
★**indebted** [ɪn`dɛtɪd]	(adj.) 感激的 • I am indebted to him for his help with my research. 我很感激他對我研究上的協助。
★**persevere** [,pɝsə`vɪr]	(v.) 努力不懈，不屈不撓 • persevere in one's efforts 堅持努力不懈
statement of purpose [`stetmənt] [pɝpəs]	(n.) 讀書計畫（申請國外大學、研究所入學許可時的文件）
★**entail** [ɪn`tel]	(v.) 需要；引起 • Writing a philosophy book entails a great deal of work. 寫哲學書很花功夫。
lull [lʌl]	(v.) 哄（小孩）入睡 • She lulled her baby to/into sleep. 她哄她的寶寶入睡。
★**adept** [ə`dɛpt]	(adj.) 熟練的 (n.) 專家 • be adept at... 熟練於…
eligibility for entrance [,ɛlɪdʒə`bɪlətɪ] [`ɛntrəns]	(n.) 入學資格
entrance ceremony [`ɛntrəns `sɛrə,monɪ]	(n.) 入學典禮
university entrance examination	(n.) 大學入學考試

admission procedure [əd`mɪʃən prə`sidʒɚ]	(n.) 入學申請手續 參 admission (n.)（入場、入學等的）許可；入場費；承認
★**admission requirement** [əd`mɪʃən rɪ`kwaɪrmənt]	(n.) 入學資格
★**enrollment** [ɪn`rolmənt]	(n.) 註冊人數；註冊，登記入學 • Women's enrollment in engineering schools has risen/dropped. 工學院的女性登記入學人數已經上升／下降。
foster [`fɔstɚ]	(v.) 促成，培養；養育 • foster many social reforms 促成許多次社會改革
informative [ɪn`fɔrmətɪv]	(adj.) 增廣見聞的
★**prerequisite** [ˌpri`rɛkwəzɪt]	(n.) 先修科目 • "Prerequisite—see University Catalogue" 「先修科目——請參照大學目錄」
★**requisite** [`rɛkwəzɪt]	(adj.) 必要的 (n.) 必要條件 • He lacks the requisite credentials for that job. 他缺乏那項工作必要的資格。
intermediate [ˌɪntɚ`midɪət]	(adj.) 中級的，中間的 • the intermediate level 中級程度
★**adolescent** [ˌædə`lɛsənt]	(n.) 青少年 (adj.) 青少年的
★**puberty** [`pjubɚtɪ]	(n.) 青春期，發育期
★**commute** [kə`mjut]	(v.) 通學，通勤 • a commuter pass 通勤車票
★**dormitory** [`dɔrməˌtorɪ]	(n.) 宿舍（簡稱 dorm） • When you enter as first year students, the university will assign you to a dorm and a roommate. 如果你是大一新生，學校會分配一間宿舍和一名室友給你。
boarding house [`bordɪŋ haʊs]	(n.) 供餐的宿舍 參 room and board 食宿

★**bully** [ˋbʊlɪ]	(n.) 欺負，霸凌；欺負弱小者 (v.) 欺負，霸凌 • play the bully 欺負弱小
courtesy [ˋkɝtəsɪ]	(n.) 禮貌；好意
governess [ˋgʌvənɪs]	(n.)（尤指住在雇主家中教導幼兒的）女家教
inquisitor [ɪnˋkwɪzətɚ]	(n.) 調查者；訊問者
naughty [ˋnɔtɪ]	(adj.) 調皮的，淘氣的
★**qualification** [ˌkwɑləfəˋkeʃən]	(n.) 資格，條件；資格證明，執照 • paper qualifications 學歷證明文件
qualify [ˋkwɑləˌfaɪ]	(v.) 使有資格 • be qualified for teaching/to teach music 有教音樂的資格 • be qualified as a teacher of music 具有音樂教師的資格
★**reunion** [riˋjunjən]	(n.) 重聚，團聚 • a class reunion 同學會 參 alumni association 校友會
★**tease** [tiz]	(v.) 嘲弄 (= mock)；欺負 (= bully)
toddler [ˋtɑdlɚ]	(n.) 學步的幼兒
vocational school [voˋkeʃənl̩ skul]	(n.) 職業學校
★**vocational education** [voˋkeʃənl̩ ˌɛdʒʊˋkeʃən]	(n.) 職業教育
★**requirement** [rɪˋkwaɪrmənt]	(n.) 必修科目 (= required subject)；必要條件
★**elective** [ɪˋlɛktɪv]	(adj.) 選修的；選舉的 (n.) 選修科目

★**quiz**
[kwɪz]

(n.) 小考

- She gave us two pop quizzes in spelling last week.
  上禮拜她給我們兩次拼字的臨時小考。

★**handout**
[`hændaʊt]

(n.) 講義

★**paper**
[`pepɚ]

(n.) 報告

- I submitted the term paper to Professor Smith yesterday. 昨天我把期末報告交給史密斯教授。

★**take-home exam**

(n.) 可帶回家寫的考試

cheating
[`tʃitɪŋ]

(n.) 作弊

參 cheat (v.) 作弊；欺騙；出軌

- cheat in/on the examination 在考試中作弊

unit
[`junɪt]

(n.) 學分 (= credit)；單元

audit
[`ɔdɪt]

(v.) 旁聽（課程）

★**faculty**
[`fækḷtɪ]

(n.)（大學的）全體教職員；學院

- the Faculty of Comparative Culture 比較文化學院

faculty meeting
[`fækḷtɪ `mitɪŋ]

(n.) 教職員會議

★**grade**
[gred]

(n.) 成績，分數；年級

- have/gain outstanding grades in science
  在科學方面成績優異

★**GPA**

(n.) 平均分數，成績點數與學分的加權平均值 (= grade point average)

- If your grade point average is 3.0 or above, you are exempt from submitting test scores.
  如果你的 GPA 達到三以上，就不需要提出考試成績。

★**transcript**
[`træn͵skrɪpt]

(n.) 成績單

★**graduation**
[͵grædʒʊ`eʃən]

(n.) 畢業；畢業典禮 (= graduation ceremony/ commencement)

graduation thesis [ˌgrædʒuˋeʃən ˋθisɪs]	(n.) 畢業論文
★**diploma** [dɪˋplomə]	(n.) 畢業證書；文憑 ● a high school diploma 中學畢業證書
★**degree** [dɪˋgri]	(n.) 學位 ● He got/took his master's degree in Comparative Literature. 他取得比較文學的碩士學位。
★**resume** [ˌrɛzjuˋme]	(n.) 履歷，個人簡歷 (= curriculum vitae)
★**graduate school** [ˋgrædʒuɪt skul]	(n.) 研究所（可攻讀碩士學位 (master's degree) 和博士學位 (doctor's degree)）
★**probation** [proˋbeʃən]	(n.) 留校察看期 (= academic probation)
dropout [ˋdrapˌaut]	(n.) 休學者，輟學者
honor student [ˋanɚ ˋstjudn̩t]	(n.) 榮譽學生
★**alumni** [əˋlʌmnaɪ]	(n.) 校友 ! 男校友是 alumnus，女校友則是 alumna，都是單數。alumni 是 alumnus 的複數形，可以指男女校友。
aging society [ˋedʒɪŋ səˋsaɪətɪ]	(n.) 高齡化社會
calligraphy [kəˋlɪgrəfɪ]	(n.) 書法；字跡優美 反 cacography (n.) 字跡拙劣
coeducation [ˌkoɛdʒəˋkeʃən]	(n.) 男女合校（簡稱 coed）
College of Liberal Arts [ˋlɪbərəl]	(n.) 文學院 ! college 在此指學院。
★**compulsory** [kəmˋpʌlsərɪ]	(adj.) 強制的，義務的；必修的 ● compulsory education 義務教育
multiple-choice [ˋmʌltəpl̩ tʃɔɪs]	(adj.) 選擇題的

correspondence [ˌkɔrə`spɑndəns]	(n.) 通信；信件 ● correspondence course 函授課程
cram [kræm]	(n.) 填塞；(為了考試) 填鴨式學習、死記硬背 (= cramming) ● pass the exam by cram alone 單靠死記硬背通過考試
★**credit** [`krɛdɪt]	(n.) 學分 (= unit) ● Community college credit is allowed up to a maximum of 70 semester units. 社區大學學分的認可上限為 70 個學期學分。
curriculum [kə`rɪkjələm]	(n.) 課程
Dean of the faculty [din] [`fækl̩tɪ]	(n.) 學院院長
★**dissertation** [ˌdɪsɚ`teʃən]	(n.) 論文（尤指博士論文） ● write a dissertation for a PhD 寫博士論文
final oral defense [`faɪnl̩ `orəl dɪ`fɛns]	(n.)（學位審查）最後的答辯
★**doctor's degree** [`dɑktɚz dɪ`gri]	(n.) 博士學位（簡稱 Dr. 或 D.）(= PhD) ● take one's doctor's degree 取得博士學位
★**master's degree** [`mæstɚz dɪ`gri]	(n.) 碩士學位（簡稱 MA 或 MS）
education-conscious [`kɑnʃəs] **society**	(n.) 重視學歷的社會
educational administration [ˌɛdʒʊ`keʃənl̩ ədˌmɪnə`streʃən]	(n.) 教育行政
elementary school [ˌɛlə`mɛntərɪ skul]	(n.) 小學 (= grade school)
equal opportunity [`ikwəl ˌɑpɚ`tjunətɪ]	(n.)（不分種族、性別）機會均等

★**extracurricular activity** [ˌɛkstrəkəˋrɪkjələ ækˋtɪvətɪ]	(n.) 課外活動 參 extracurricular (adj.) 課外的
fine arts [faɪn ɑrts]	(n.) 美術，藝術 ! 單數 fine art 是指「美術品」。
fire drill [faɪr drɪl]	(n.) 消防演習
★**higher education** [ˋhaɪə ˌɛdʒʊˋkeʃən]	(n.) 高等教育（指專科學校、大學、研究所的教育）
★**junior college** [ˋdʒunjə ˋkɑlɪdʒ]	(n.) 二年制學院 (= community college)
preschool-education [ˋpriˋskul ˌɛdʒʊˋkeʃən]	(n.) 學前教育
★**kindergarten** [ˋkɪndəˌgɑrtn̩]	(n.) 幼稚園 ! 注意拼字。
★**nursery school** [ˋnɝsərɪ skul]	(n.) 托兒所 (= day care center) ! nursery 有「育兒室」和「苗圃」等意思。
★**medical checkup** [ˋmɛdɪkl̩ ˋtʃɛkˌʌp]	(n.) 健康檢查 (= medical examination)
intelligence test [ɪnˋtɛlədʒəns tɛst]	(n.) 智力測驗 (= IQ test)
mentally handicapped [ˋhændɪˌkæpt] **children education**	(n.) 弱智兒童教育
physically and mentally handicapped children	(n.) 身心障礙兒童
★**mentally retarded** [ˋmɛntəlɪ rɪˋtɑrdɪd]	(adj.) 智能不足的，智能遲緩的 ● a mentally retarded pupil 智能不足的學生
emotional disorder [ɪˋmoʃənl̩ dɪsˋɔrdə]	(n.) 情緒障礙
anxiety disorder [æŋˋzaɪətɪ dɪsˋɔrdə]	(n.) 焦慮症
autistic [ɔˋtɪstɪk]	(n.) 自閉症患者 (adj.) 患有自閉症的 參 autism (n.) 自閉症

visual disturbance [`vɪʒuəl dɪs`tɜbəns]	(n.) 視覺障礙
acoustic disturbance [ə`kustɪk dɪs`tɜbəns]	(n.) 聽覺障礙
communication disorder [kə,mjunə`keʃən dɪs`ɔrdɚ]	(n.) 溝通障礙
amentia [ə`mɛnʃɪə]	(n.)（先天性）精神衰弱，智力缺陷
★**peer group** [pɪr grup]	(n.) 同儕團體 參 peer pressure 同儕壓力
★**physical education** [`fɪzɪkḷ ,ɛdʒʊ`keʃən]	(n.) 體育 ! 簡稱 PE，經常出現在聽力測驗。
physical fitness test [`fɪtnɪs]	(n.) 體適能測驗
★**president** [`prɛzədənt]	(n.)（大學）校長 參 vice-president (n.) 副校長
principal [`prɪnsəpḷ]	(n.) 校長
public school [`pʌblɪk skul]	(n.) 公立學校（在英國指「公學」，為私立的貴族學校，如著名的伊頓公學 (Eton College)）
school excursion [skul ɪk`skɜʒən]	(n.) 學校遠足
school for deaf and dumb [dʌm]	(n.) 聾啞學校
★**self evaluation** [sɛlf ɪ,vælju`eʃən]	(n.) 自我評量
★**self-discipline** [sɛlf `dɪsəplɪn]	(n.) 自律；自我訓練
★**quarter** [`kwɔrtɚ]	(n.)（四學期制的）學期（一學期通常是 10-12 週）

***semester system** [sə`mɛstɚ `sɪstəm]	(n.) 二學期制（通常分 9-1 月和 2-6 月兩個學期）
seminar [`sɛmə,nɑr]	(n.) 研討會
***syllabus** [`sɪləbəs]	(n.)（授課的）摘要，進度表，課程大綱
***transfer** [`trænsfɝ]	(n.) 轉學
***tuition** [tjʊ`ɪʃən]	(n.) 學費 (= fees) ● Legal residents of California are not charged tuition. 加州的合法居民不必繳學費。
***tutorial mode** [tu`torɪəl mod]	(n.)（大學）個別指導模式
***uniformity** [ˌjunə`fɔrmətɪ]	(n.) 統一，一致

Engineering
工程學

MP3 145

*maneuver [mə`nuvɚ]	(v.) 巧妙地操縱
*specify [`spɛsə,faɪ]	(v.) 指定 ● Tile roofing was specified. 屋頂指定要用瓦片。
*aviation [,evɪ`eʃən]	(n.) 航空，飛行
dashboard [`dæʃ,bɔrd]	(n.)（汽車、飛機的）儀表板
*blur [blɝ]	(v.) 使模糊不清；弄髒 ● Static blurred the television screen. 靜電干擾使得電視畫面模糊不清。
*breakdown [`brek,daʊn]	(n.) 故障 ● the breakdown of machine 機器故障
*fiber [`faɪbɚ]	(n.) 纖維 ● synthetic fiber 合成纖維
*cog [kɑg]	(n.) 齒輪；（齒輪的）輪齒
*combustion [kəm`bʌstʃən]	(n.) 燃燒；（有機體的）氧化 ● spontaneous combustion 自燃
*install [ɪn`stɔl]	(v.) 安裝；安置 ● have a telephone installed 安裝電話
*malfunction [mæl`fʌŋkʃən]	(n.) 故障
*manipulation [mə,nɪpjʊ`leʃən]	(n.) 操作；巧妙運用，操縱 參 manipulative (adj.) 操作的；巧妙處理的
mechanization [,mɛkənaɪ`zeʃən]	(n.) 機械化

modulate [ˋmɑdʒə͵let]	(v.) 調節，調整
shaft [ʃæft]	(n.) 軸
ventilate [ˋvɛntḷ͵et]	(v.) 使通風，使換氣
★**voltage** [ˋvoltɪdʒ]	(n.) 電壓，伏特數
watt [wɑt]	(n.) 瓦特（功率單位）
compact [kəmˋpækt]	(adj.) 緊密的；小巧的
interchangeable [͵ɪntɚˋtʃendʒəbḷ]	(adj.) 可交換的，可交替的
★**absorber** [əbˋsɔrbɚ]	(n.) 吸收裝置；減震器 (= shock absorber)
absorption coefficient [əbˋsɔrpʃən ͵koɪˋfɪʃənt]	(n.) 吸收係數
★**air mass** [ɛr mæs]	(n.) 氣團（水平方向溫度、濕度差異微小的大空氣團）
★**alternating current** [ˋɔltɚ͵netɪŋ ˋkɝənt]	(n.) 交流電 (= AC)
ampere [ˋæmpɪr]	(n.) 安培（電流量單位，簡稱為 A）
★**cell** [sɛl]	(n.) 電池（cell 組合而成 battery）
fuel cell [ˋfjuəl sɛl]	(n.) 燃料電池
photovoltaic cell [͵fotovɑlˋteɪk sɛl]	(n.) 光電池
★**charging** [ˋtʃɑrdʒɪŋ]	(n.) 充電

★**battery** [ˋbætərɪ]	(n.) 電池 ● a dry/storage battery 乾／蓄電池
grid [grɪd]	(n.) 柵極（三極真空管陰陽極之間的金屬格子，為調節電流的裝置）
antireflection [ˌæntɪrɪˋflɛkʃən]	(n.) 防止反射的塗料
diode [ˋdaɪod]	(n.) 二極體，二極管
boron [ˋborɑn]	(n.) 硼（礦物元素）
cadmium [ˋkædmɪəm]	(n.) 鎘（金屬元素）
★**chlorofluorocarbon** [ˌklorəˌfluərəˋkɑrbən]	(n.) 氟氯碳化物（用於冷媒等，因為會破壞臭氧層已被禁用）
conduction band [kənˋdʌkʃən bænd]	(n.) 傳導帶
★**conversion** [kənˋvɝʃən]	(n.) 換算，變換 ● a conversion table 換算表 ! conversion 還有「改變信仰」的意思，也是常考單字。
dendrite [ˋdɛndraɪt]	(n.) 樹枝狀晶體
diffusion [dɪˋfjuʒən]	(n.)（原子、離子、氣體等的）擴散；（光的）漫射
direct current [dəˋrɛkt ˋkɝənt]	(n.) 直流電 (= DC)
★**discharge** [dɪsˋtʃɑrdʒ]	(n.) (v.) 放電
donor [ˋdonɚ]	(n.) 施體（半導體材料中提供電子者）
dopant [ˋdopənt]	(n.) 摻雜物（摻雜製程 (doping) 中加入半導體的物質）

doping [`dopɪŋ]	(n.) 摻雜（製程）（在半導體中加入雜質或摻雜物 (dopant) 以改變其電子特性）；使用藥物以提高體育競賽成績
electric charge [ɪ`lɛktrɪk tʃɑrdʒ]	(n.) 電荷
★**electric circuit** [ɪ`lɛktrɪk `sɝkɪt]	(n.) 電路
★**electric current** [ɪ`lɛktrɪk `kɝənt]	(n.) 電流
electrodeposition [ɪˌlɛktrəˌdɛpə`zɪʃən]	(n.) 電沉積法
electrolyte [ɪ`lɛktrəˌlaɪt]	(n.) 電解液，電解質
★**semiconductor** [ˌsɛmɪkən`dʌktɚ]	(n.) 半導體
intrinsic semiconductor [ɪn`trɪnsɪk ˌsɛmɪkən`dʌktɚ]	(n.) 本質半導體
gallium [`gælɪəm]	(n.) 鎵（金屬元素）
giga- [`gɪgə]	表示「10 的九次方，10 億」的字首 ● gigameter (n.) 百萬公里 ● gigawatt (n.) 10 億瓦特
glaze [glez]	(n.) 釉 (v.) 給（陶瓷）上釉
★**hetero-** [`hɛtəro]	表示「其他的，不同的」的字首 ● heterogeneous strain 不均勻變形
★**homo-** [`homo]	表示「相同的」的字首 ● homogeneous reaction 相同的反應
indium [`ɪndɪəm]	(n.) 銦（金屬元素）

★**insulation** [ˌɪnsə`leʃən]	(n.) 絕緣；絕緣體，絕緣材料 ! 常考單字。
inverter [ɪn`vɜtɚ]	(n.) 交流器，變流器（使直流電變交流電的裝置）
★**patent** [`pætn̩t]	(n.) 專利（權）(v.) 取得專利 ● file a patent for laser 申請雷射的專利
junction [`dʒʌŋkʃən]	(n.)（半導體的）接合，接面
★**load** [lod]	(n.) 負載，負荷
module [`mɑdʒul]	(n.) 模組
monolithic [ˌmɑnə`lɪθɪk]	(adj.) 單一的 反 hybrid (adj.) 混合的
★**nuclear energy** [`njuklɪɚ `ɛnɚdʒɪ]	(n.) 核能
parallel connection [`pærəˌlɛl kə`nɛkʃən]	(n.) 並聯
polycrystalline [ˌpɑlɪ`krɪstəlɪn]	(adj.) 多晶的
★**radioactive waste** [ˌredɪo`æktɪv west]	(n.) 放射性廢棄物
rectifier [`rɛktəˌfaɪɚ]	(n.) 整流器
silicon [`sɪlɪkən]	(n.) 矽
★**solar constant** [`solɚ `kɑnstənt]	(n.) 太陽常數（到達地球的太陽能量單位）
★**solar cell** [`solɚ sɛl]	(n.) 太陽能電池
★**solar energy** [`solɚ `ɛnɚdʒɪ]	(n.) 太陽能

transmission line [træns`mɪʃən laɪn]	(n.) 傳輸線
★**ultraviolet ray** [ˌʌltrə`vaɪəlɪt re]	(n.) 紫外線 參 infrared (ray) 紅外線
ultraviolet radiation [ˌʌltrə`vaɪəlɪt ˌredɪ`eʃən]	(n.) 紫外線輻射

15 Essays & Term Papers

論文與學期報告

MP3 146

***explicit** [ɪk`splɪsɪt]	(adj.) 明確的，明白的 ● explicit directions 明確的指示
***inference** [`ɪnfərəns]	(n.) 推論，推斷 ● inductive/deductive inference 歸納 / 演繹推論
terse [tɝs]	(adj.)（文體、用字等）簡潔的
***conversely** [kən`vɝslɪ]	(adv.) 相反地
expository [ɪk`spɑzɪˌtɔrɪ]	(adj.) 說明的，解釋的 ● expository writing 說明文 ! 美國各大學新生必修的「基礎英語課」(English 101) 一定會出現這個單字。
interpretative [ɪn`tɝprɪˌtetɪv]	(adj.) 解釋的，說明的
***style** [staɪl]	(n.) 文體，（寫作）風格 ● write in the style of Hemingway 用海明威的風格寫作
***descriptive approach** [dɪ`skrɪptɪv ə`protʃ]	(n.) 採描述的方式
explanatory approach [ɪk`splænəˌtɔrɪ ə`protʃ]	(n.) 採說明的方式
***documentation** [ˌdɑkjəmɛn`teʃən]	(n.) 證明文件；證明文件的提供
citation [saɪ`teʃən]	(n.)〔可數〕引文；〔不可數〕引用 參 quotation (n.) 引文；引用
***bibliography** [ˌbɪblɪ`ɑgrəfɪ]	(n.) 參考書目
index card [`ɪndɛks kɑrd]	(n.) 索引卡

★**plagiarism** [ˋpledʒə͵rɪzm̩]	(n.) 剽竊，抄襲
footnote [ˋfʊt͵not]	(n.) 註腳，註解 (v.) 加註腳
★**reference** [ˋrɛfərəns]	(n.) 參考資料；參考 ● the most relevant references to the topic 和該主題最相關的參考資料
★**reasoning** [ˋriznɪŋ]	(n.) 推論，推理
★**assumption** [əˋsʌmpʃən]	(n.) 假設，假定，前提 ● on the assumption that... 在…的假設之下
★**deduction** [dɪˋdʌkʃən]	(n.) 演繹；推論
deductive reasoning [dɪˋdʌktɪv ˋriznɪŋ]	(n.) 演繹法
★**induction** [ɪnˋdʌkʃən]	(n.) 歸納
inductive reasoning [ɪnˋdʌktɪv ˋriznɪŋ]	(n.) 歸納法
★**logic** [ˋlɑdʒɪk]	(n.) 邏輯
logical fallacy [ˋlɑdʒɪkl̩ ˋfæləsɪ]	(n.) 邏輯上的謬誤 參 fallacy (n.) 謬誤，謬論
★**stereotype** [ˋstɛrɪə͵taɪp]	(n.) 刻板印象 ● hold stereotypes about women 對女性有刻板印象
redundant [rɪˋdʌndənt]	(adj.) 冗長的，多餘的
circular argument [ˋsɝkjəlɚ ˋɑrgjəmənt]	(n.) 循環論證
disjoint [dɪsˋdʒɔɪnt]	(v.) 弄亂，使雜亂 ● Too many digressions disjoint his writings. 太多離題之處使他的文章顯得雜亂不堪。

★**abstract** [ˋæbstrækt]	(n.) 摘要 (= summary) ● make an abstract of... 將…做成摘要
★**outline** [ˋaʊtˏlaɪn]	(n.) 概要，大綱
table of contents [ˋkɑntɛnts]	(n.) 目錄 (= contents)

16 Geography

地理學

MP3 147

beacon [ˋbikn̩]	(n.) 烽火台；燈塔；信號燈
★**basin** [ˋbesn̩]	(n.) 盆地；流域 • an ocean/a lake basin 海 / 湖盆地 • the Mississippi basin 密西西比河流域
cave [kev]	(n.) 洞穴（比 hollow 大，比 cavern 小）
cavern [ˋkævɚn]	(n.) 大洞穴
cliff [klɪf]	(n.)（尤指海邊的）懸崖，峭壁
hinterland [ˋhɪntɚˏlænd]	(n.)（海岸、河岸的）後方地區；腹地，內地
inland [ˋɪnlənd]	(adj.)（遠離海洋的）內陸的，內地的
meridian [məˋrɪdɪən]	(n.) 子午線 • the celestial meridian 天體子午線
mountainous [ˋmaʊntənəs]	(adj.) 多山的 • mountainous districts 山區
★**sporadic** [spəˋrædɪk]	(adj.) 零星的，時有時無的；分散的 • sporadic earthquakes 零星的地震
sprawl [sprɔl]	(v.)（都市等）無計畫地擴展 • The city sprawled (out) in all directions. 都市向四面八方擴展。
stretch [strɛtʃ]	(n.)（土地等）綿延 • a stretch of desert 一片綿延無盡的沙漠
contour [ˋkɑntʊr]	(adj.) 等高線的 (n.)（山脈等的）輪廓 • a contour line 等高線

isotherm [`aɪsə͵θɝm]	(n.) 等溫線
★**steppe** [stɛp]	(n.) 沒有樹的大草原 ● the Steppes 西伯利亞、中亞的大草原
subtropical [sʌb`trɑpɪkḷ]	(adj.) 亞熱帶的
Mediterranean [͵mɛdətə`renɪən]	(n.) 地中海 (adj.) 地中海的
savanna [sə`vænə]	(n.)（熱帶地區的無樹）大草原
★**equator** [ɪ`kwetɚ]	(n.) 赤道
tundra [`tʌndrə]	(n.)（北極和其附近的）凍原
taiga [`taɪgə]	(n.) 歐亞大陸和北美洲北方的大面積針葉林
ice cap [aɪs kæp]	(n.)（長年冰雪覆蓋的）冰原
★**circumpolar** [͵sɝkəm`polɚ]	(adj.) 極地附近的
★**Arctic** [`ɑrktɪk]	(adj.) 北極的 (n.) 北極
★**Antarctic** [æn`tɑrktɪk]	(adj.) 南極的 (n.) 南極 ● an Antarctic expedition 南極探險隊
subarctic [sʌb`ɑrktɪk]	(adj.) 靠近北極的，亞北極的
★**saturate** [`sætʃə͵ret]	(v.) 浸透，滲透 (= soak) ! 常考單字。
permafrost [`pɝmə͵frɔst]	(n.) 永久凍土層
★**boggy land** [`bɑgɪ lænd]	(n.) 沼澤地 (= swamp/moor/marsh/bog) ! 常出現在生物學、氣象學、地質學、地理學相關的聽力和閱讀測驗中。

***Atlantic** [ət`læntɪk]	(n.) 大西洋 (adj.) 大西洋的 • the Atlantic 大西洋 • a trans-Atlantic flight 橫越大西洋的飛行
***strait** [stret]	(n.) 海峽；困境 • the Bering Strait 白令海峽
***trade wind** [tred wɪnd]	(n.) 信風，貿易風
***front** [frʌnt]	(n.) 鋒面 • a cold/warm front 冷 / 暖鋒
hot spot [hɑt spɑt]	(n.) 熱點；不安定區域
***mouth** [maʊθ]	(n.) 河口 (= estuary)
delta [`dɛltə]	(n.)（河口的）三角洲
fold [fold]	(n.) 山谷的坑窪；彎曲褶皺
***glaciation** [͵gleʃɪ`eʃən]	(n.) 冰河作用
weathering [`wɛðərɪŋ]	(n.) 風化作用
***deposition** [͵dɛpə`zɪʃən]	(n.) 堆積；堆積物 • deposition of topsoil from a river in flood 洪水引發河川泛濫而造成的表土堆積
focal point [`fokḷ pɔɪnt]	(n.) 焦點，中心
colonialism [kə`lonɪəl͵ɪzṃ]	(n.) 殖民主義，殖民政策
heterogeneity [͵hɛtərədʒə`niətɪ]	(n.) 異質性
ethnocentrism [͵ɛθnə`sɛntrɪzṃ]	(n.) 種族中心論，民族優越感

★**social stratification** [ˋsoʃəl ˏstrætəfəˋkeʃən]	(n.) 社會階層
pluralism [ˋplʊrəlɪzm̩]	(n.)（國家、社會的）多元性（不同種族、政治立場或宗教信仰並存的狀態）
★**drought** [draʊt]	(n.) 乾旱，旱災
★**tribalism** [ˋtraɪbl̩ɪzm̩]	(n.) 部落意識，部落制度
nepotism [ˋnɛpəˏtɪzm̩]	(n.) 重用親戚，裙帶關係
★**coup d'etat** [ku deˋtɑ]	(n.) 政變
★**starvation** [stɑrˋveʃən]	(n.) 飢餓
★**life expectancy** [laɪf ɪkˋspɛktənsɪ]	(n.) 平均餘命
★**malnutrition** [ˏmælnjuˋtrɪʃən]	(n.) 營養不良
★**famine** [ˋfæmɪn]	(n.) 饑荒，飢餓 (= starvation) ● a region ravaged by famine 饑荒嚴重的地區
★**infrastructure** [ˋɪnfrəˏstrʌktʃɚ]	(n.) 基礎建設
soil exhaustion [sɔɪl ɪgˋzɔstʃən]	(n.) 土地耗竭
★**soil erosion** [sɔɪl ɪˋroʒən]	(n.) 土壤侵蝕
★**topsoil** [ˋtɑpˏsɔɪl]	(n.) 表土（土壤的最上層，一般由風化造成，含有機物，對作物栽培很重要）
★**desertification** [dɪˏzɝtəfɪˋkeʃən]	(n.) 沙漠化（過度放牧或過分砍伐森林使得森林、草原等變成沙漠的現象）
★**affluence** [ˋæflʊəns]	(n.) 湧入，流入；豐富，富裕 ● an affluence of refugees 難民湧入

17 Geology
地質學

MP3 148

★**collide** [kə`laɪd]	(v.) 碰撞；衝突 ● Plates sometimes collided head-on. 板塊有時會正面互撞。 參 collision (n.) 碰撞；衝突
crush [krʌʃ]	(v.) 擠壓，壓碎 ● crush stone into gravel 把石頭壓碎成沙礫
elevation [ˌɛlə`veʃən]	(n.) 高度，海拔 ● at an elevation of 3,000 meters 在海拔 3,000 公尺的高度
immerse [ɪ`mɝs]	(v.) 浸入，泡進（液體等）
★**jolt** [dʒolt]	(v.) 激烈搖晃；顛簸
shatter [`ʃætɚ]	(v.) 粉碎
★**soak** [sok]	(v.) 浸，泡
★**tilt** [tɪlt]	(v.) 傾斜 (= slant)
unleash [ʌn`liʃ]	(v.) 釋放，鬆開 ● tsunami unleashed by the earthquake 地震引起的海嘯
★**chasm** [`kæzəm]	(n.)（地面上的）裂口，裂縫；小峽谷 (= gorge)
clay [kle]	(n.) 黏土 ● clay soil 黏土質土壤
crack [kræk]	(n.) 裂縫；龜裂

ditch [dɪtʃ]	(n.) 溝，渠
★**drench** [drɛntʃ]	(v.) 浸濕 (= saturate/soak) ● get drenched 濕透
droplet [ˋdraplɪt]	(n.)（液體的）小滴
gutter [ˋgʌtɚ]	(n.) 溝
pebble [ˋpɛbl̩]	(n.) 小圓石
precipitous [prɪˋsɪpətəs]	(adj.) 陡峭的，險峻的
★**terrain** [təˋren]	(n.)（地理、軍事上的）地形，地勢
★**trail** [trel]	(n.)（荒野或山中由人或動物踏出來的）小徑；足跡 ● a deer trail 鹿的小徑
glossy [ˋglɔsɪ]	(adj.) 有光澤的，光滑的
glow [glo]	(v.) 發光，發熱
granite [ˋgrænɪt]	(n.) 花崗岩，花崗石
marble [ˋmarbl̩]	(n.) 大理石
★**opaque** [oˋpek]	(adj.) 不透明的；（對於熱、電等）不傳導的
pigment [ˋpɪgmənt]	(n.) 色素
★**fragile** [ˋfrædʒəl]	(adj.) 易碎的，脆弱的 ● a fragile fossil 易碎的化石
★**crust** [krʌst]	(n.) 地殼 ● The weight of the huge mass of ice depressed the crust of the Earth. 巨大冰塊的重量壓迫著地殼。

***mantle** [ˋmæntḷ]	(n.) 地函（位於地殼和地核之間，占地球體積 80% 以上）
***core** [kɔr]	(n.) 地核；核心，中心
seafloor [ˋsiˏflor]	(n.) 海底，海床
***hemisphere** [ˋhɛməsˏfɪr]	(n.)（地球的）半球
***pole** [pol]	(n.)（地球的）極，極地 • the North/South Pole 北 / 南極
***latitude** [ˋlætəˏtjud]	(n.) 緯度 • south latitude 35 degrees (= latitude 35 degrees south) 南緯 35 度
***altitude** [ˋæltəˏtjud]	(n.) 高度，海拔，標高 • We are cruising at an altitude of 10,000 feet. 我們在海拔一萬英尺處巡航。
***gulf** [gʌlf]	(n.) 灣 • the Gulf Stream（墨西哥）灣流
***peninsula** [pəˋnɪnsələ]	(n.) 半島，岬
***channel** [ˋtʃænḷ]	(n.) 海峽（比 strait 大） • the English Channel 英吉利海峽
***plateau** [plæˋto]	(n.) 高原，台地
***plate** [plet]	(n.) 板塊
***mountain range** [ˋmaʊntn̩ rendʒ]	(n.) 山脈
***archipelago** [ˏarkəˋpɛləˏgo]	(n.) 群島，列島；群島周圍海域
***eruption** [ɪˋrʌpʃən]	(n.)（火山的）爆發；（熔岩等的）噴出 • eruptions of ashes and lava 火山灰和熔岩的噴出

★**crater** [ˋkretə˞]	(n.) 火山口；(月球表面的) 環形山；隕石坑 ● a crater lake 火口湖
★**volcano** [valˋkeno]	(n.) 火山 ● an active/extinct volcano 活 / 死火山 ● a dormant/submarine volcano 休 / 海底火山
★**seism-** [ˋsaɪzəm]	表示「地震」的字根 參 seismic (adj.) 地震的 ● seismic sea waves（地震引起的）海嘯 (= tsunami)
seismology [saɪzˋmalədʒɪ]	(n.) 地震學
★**sedimentary** [ˌsɛdəˋmɛntərɪ]	(adj.) 沉積的，沉澱的 ● sedimentary rocks 沉積岩
limestone [ˋlaɪmˌston]	(n.) 石灰岩
shale [ʃel]	(n.) 頁岩，泥板岩
★**strata** [ˋstretə]	(n.) 地層 ! 單數形是 stratum。
★**glacier** [ˋgleʃə˞]	(n.) 冰河
★**iceberg** [ˋaɪsˌbɝg]	(n.) 冰山
moraine [moˋren]	(n.) 冰磧石（冰河中的土石沉積物）
★**fault** [fɔlt]	(n.) 斷層 (v.) 產生斷層 ! 常考單字。 ● an active fault 活斷層
★**ridge** [rɪdʒ]	(n.) 山脊，山脈
trench [trɛntʃ]	(n.) 海溝
subduction [səbˋdʌkʃən]	(n.)（板塊的）隱沒作用（一板塊沒入另一個板塊之下）

★**undulate** [ˋʌndjə͵let]	(v.)（地面等）起伏 (adj.) 起伏不平的 ● the undulating landscape 起伏的景色
★**margin** [ˋmɑrʤɪn]	(n.) 邊緣 (= edge) ● the margin of a glacier 冰河的邊緣
★**debris** [dəˋbri]	(n.) 岩屑，碎石 ● a lot of debris after the eruption 火山噴發後產生大量碎屑 ❗ 注意最後的 -s 不發音。
★**deposit** [dɪˋpɑzɪt]	(n.) 沉澱物；礦床 ● a coal deposit 煤礦床
slab [slæb]	(n.) 厚板，平板 ● a stone slab 石板
★**depression** [dɪˋprɛʃən]	(n.) 窪地；下陷
★**summit** [ˋsʌmɪt]	(n.) 山頂，山峰；頂點 (v.) 登頂
★**pass** [pæs]	(n.) 山路，隘路
★**peak** [pik]	(n.) 山頂，山峰 (= summit)
dale [del]	(n.) 谷 ● go over hills and dales 越過山谷
★**damp** [dæmp]	(adj.) 潮濕的 (n.) 潮溼，濕氣 (= moisture) ● damp weather 潮濕的天氣
moor [mʊr]	(n.) 沼澤地；荒野
★**marsh** [mɑrʃ]	(n.) 濕地，沼澤地 (= swamp/bog) ❗常考單字。 ● marsh fever 沼澤熱，瘧疾
lagoon [ləˋgun]	(n.) 潟湖，環礁湖
★**drain** [dren]	(v.)（土地）排水 (n.) 排水，流出 ● drain water from a swamp 排掉沼澤中的水 參 drainage (n.) 排水；排水系統

18 History
歷史學

MP3 149

*bequeath [bɪˋkwið]	(v.) 留下，留給；遺贈 • Numerous discoveries were bequeathed to us. 許多發現被遺留下來給我們。
*centennial [sɛnˋtɛnɪəl]	(adj.) 一百年的 • a centennial anniversary 一百週年紀念
entrench [ɪnˋtrɛntʃ]	(v.) 確立（權利、習慣、信仰等），根深蒂固 • be entrenched in one's beliefs 深植於某人的信念中
*fugitive [ˋfjudʒətɪv]	(n.) 逃亡者，逃犯 (adj.) 逃亡的 • fugitives from Hungary 來自匈牙利的逃犯
*recurrent [rɪˋkɜənt]	(adj.) 一再發生的
*threshold [ˋθrɛʃold]	(n.)（事物的）開端；門檻
throng [θrɔŋ]	(n.) 一大群人，群眾；群集
abscond [æbˋskɑnd]	(v.)（為躲避罪責等）潛逃，逃亡 • The suspect absconded from the country. 嫌犯潛逃出國。
*artillery [ɑrˋtɪlərɪ]	(n.) 大砲；砲兵部隊
assassin [əˋsæsɪn]	(n.) 暗殺者，刺客 參 assassination (n.) 暗殺 assassinate (v.) 暗殺，行刺
*assault [əˋsɔlt]	(n.) 襲擊，攻擊 • make a violent assault on a fortress 對一個要塞發動猛烈攻擊
*barter [ˋbɑrtɚ]	(v.) (n.) 以物易物
*bounty [ˋbaʊntɪ]	(n.) 賞金，獎金 • a bounty hunter 賞金獵人（追捕逃犯以獲取賞金的人）

brigade [brɪˋged]	(n.)（為了某個目的而成立的）隊，組；〔軍隊用語〕旅 ● a fire brigade 消防隊
capitulation [kəˏpɪtʃəˋleʃən]	(n.)（有條件投降的）降書，投降協定
captive [ˋkæptɪv]	(adj.) 被俘的；被迷住的 (n.) 俘虜 (= prisoner)
★**commonwealth** [ˋkɑmənˏwɛlθ]	(n.) 聯邦；共和國 ● the Commonwealth of Australia 澳大利亞聯邦
★**confederation** [kənˏfɛdəˋreʃən]	(n.) 同盟，聯盟；邦聯 ● the Confederation（美國獨立前由東部 13 個殖民地組成的）十三州邦聯
★**dictator** [ˋdɪktetɚ]	(n.) 獨裁者
★**dynasty** [ˋdaɪnəstɪ]	(n.) 朝代，王朝 ● the Tang dynasty 唐朝
★**emancipation** [ɪˏmænsəˋpeʃən]	(n.)（奴隸、女性等的）解放 ● Emancipation Proclamation 解放奴隸宣言
emblem [ˋɛmbləm]	(n.) 象徵，標誌；徽章 ● The eagle is the emblem of the United States. 老鷹是美國的象徵。
empower [ɪmˋpaʊɚ]	(v.) 授權 ● The police are empowered by the law to search private houses. 法律授予警察搜索私人住宅的權利。
enshrine [ɪnˋʃraɪn]	(v.) 奉祀；神聖化 ● enshrine the nation's ideals 將國家的理想神聖化
forewarn [forˋwɔrn]	(v.) 預先警告
holocaust [ˋhɑləˏkɔst]	(n.) 大屠殺（尤指二次世界大戰時德國納粹黨對猶太人的大屠殺）
imperialism [ɪmˋpɪrɪəˏlɪzm̩]	(n.) 帝國主義，擴張主義 參 imperial (adj.) 帝國的

★**mercenary** [ˋmɝsn̩ˏɛrɪ]	(n.) 傭兵 (adj.) 被（外國軍隊）雇用的
oligarchy [ˋalɪˏgarkɪ]	(n.) 寡頭政治；實行寡頭政治的國家
★**oppression** [əˋprɛʃən]	(n.) 壓迫，壓制
ordain [ɔrˋden]	(v.)（法律等）規定；（命運）注定
★**propaganda** [ˏprapəˋgændə]	(n.)（組織的）宣傳，宣傳活動
repulse [rɪˋpʌls]	(v.) 擊退 ● repulse the enemy 擊退敵人
★**revolt** [rɪˋvolt]	(n.) (v.) 反抗，叛亂，造反 ● rise in revolt 起而反抗
scaffold [ˋskæfəld]	(n.) 絞刑台，斷頭台 ● die on the scaffold 死於斷頭台，處絞刑而死
shipwreck [ˋʃɪpˏrɛk]	(n.) 船難 (= wreck)；遇難船，失事船隻的殘骸 ● suffer shipwreck 遭遇船難
★**subdue** [səbˋdju]	(v.) 征服，鎮壓；抑制
subjugate [ˋsʌbʤəˏget]	(v.) 征服，使服從
★**summon** [ˋsʌmən]	(v.) 召喚，召集 ● be summoned into the President's office 被召喚到總統府
thrall [θrɔl]	(n.) 奴隸；〔集合用法〕奴隸身分；束縛
★**trigger** [ˋtrɪgɚ]	(v.) 引起，觸發 (n.)（槍砲的）扳機 ● The economic expansion prompted by the Second World War triggered a spectacular population boom in the West. 二次世界大戰之後的經濟成長促使西方人口激增。

★**tyranny** [`tɪrənɪ]	(n.) 暴政，專制政治 ● be oppressed by tyranny 受到暴政的壓迫
★**tyrant** [`taɪrənt]	(n.) 暴君，專制君主
underdog [`ʌndɚ͵dɔg]	(n.)（政治、社會上或比賽中）居於劣勢的一方，弱勢族群；失敗者 ● side with the underdog 支持弱勢者 反 top dog 勝利者
★**unify** [`junə͵faɪ]	(v.) 統一，統合，使一致 ● unify the factions of a political party 統合政黨裡各個派系
upheaval [ʌp`hivl̩]	(n.)（社會等的）大變動；劇變；動亂
uprising [`ʌp͵raɪzɪŋ]	(n.) 暴動 ● a student uprising 學生暴動
warrior [`wɔrɪɚ]	(n.) 戰士，勇士
★**wreck** [rɛk]	(n.) 船難；（失事船隻的）殘骸 (v.) 破壞
honorific [͵ɑnə`rɪfɪk]	(adj.) 尊敬的 ● honorific titles 敬稱
★**inscription** [ɪn`skrɪpʃən]	(n.) 碑文；銘刻，刻印文字
★**outlook** [`aʊt͵lʊk]	(n.) 前景；看法，觀點 ● the outlook for a negotiated-settlement of the war 以談判交涉來結束戰爭的前景
pagan [`pegən]	(n.) 異教徒 (adj.) 異教的
parchment [`partʃmənt]	(n.) 羊皮紙；寫在羊皮紙上的文件

postulate [ˋpastʃə͵let]
(v.) 假定；主張
● The economist postulates that full employment is an impossible goal.
該經濟學家主張，完全就業是不可能達到的目標。

revere [rɪˋvɪr]
(v.) 尊敬

★**scripture** [ˋskrɪptʃɚ]
(n.)（一宗教的）聖書，經典
● the Scripture(s) 聖經

★**astrology** [əˋstrɑlədʒɪ]
(n.) 占星術

audacious [ɔˋdeʃəs]
(adj.) 大膽的；魯莽的

brutal [ˋbrutl̩]
(adj.) 殘酷的，不人道的
參 brute (n.) 禽獸，野獸 (adj.) 野蠻的，殘忍的

candor [ˋkændɚ]
(n.) 坦白，坦率；公平
● state a problem with candor 坦率地說出問題

caprice [kəˋpris]
(n.) 反覆無常，善變

clement [ˋklɛmənt]
(adj.) 仁慈的；（個性或氣候）溫和的

covert [ˋkovɚt]
(adj.) 隱藏的，隱密的，暗地的
反 overt (adj.) 明白的，公開的

★**crucial** [ˋkruʃəl]
(adj.) 決定性的，關鍵的 (= decisive/important)
● a crucial decision 關鍵的決定

elegant [ˋɛləgənt]
(adj.) 優雅的，高貴的；洗練的

embolden [ɪmˋboldn̩]
(v.) 給予勇氣，壯膽
● Her smile emboldened him to speak to her.
她的微笑使他鼓起勇氣跟她說話。

enrage [ɪnˋredʒ]
(v.) 激怒

★**foresee** [fɔr`si]	(v.) 預見，預知 ● We cannot foresee what will happen in the next century. 我們無法預知下個世紀會發生什麼事。
★**futile** [`fjutḷ]	(adj.) 徒勞的，無益的；瑣碎的 ● He made a futile attempt to resist. 他試圖反抗，但徒勞無功。
humiliate [hju`mɪlɪˌet]	(v.) 羞辱，使丟臉
★**invincible** [ɪn`vɪnsəbḷ]	(adj.) 無敵的，所向披靡的 ● the Invincible Armada（西班牙）無敵艦隊
majesty [`mædʒɪstɪ]	(n.) 雄偉；威嚴；〔字首大寫〕陛下
notorious [no`torɪəs]	(adj.) 惡名昭彰的，聲名狼藉的
★**prominent** [`prɑmənənt]	(adj.) 突出的，顯眼的；卓越的，傑出的 ● The case received prominent coverage in *Time*. 該事件獲得《時代雜誌》大篇幅的報導。
★**trait** [tret]	(n.) 特徵，特質，特色 ● American traits 美國國民性
debase [dɪ`bes]	(v.) 降低（品質、價值、地位等） ● debase the currency 使貨幣貶值
★**mutation** [mju`teʃən]	(n.) 變化；（人生的）浮沉；（基因）突變 ● the mutations of life 人生的起起伏伏
★**outbreak** [`aʊtˌbrek]	(n.)（戰爭、疾病等的）爆發 ● the outbreak of war 戰爭爆發
★**renounce** [rɪ`naʊns]	(v.) 放棄（權利、地位、頭銜等） ● renounce one's claim to the throne 放棄王位繼承權
★**transition** [træn`zɪʃən]	(n.) 轉移，變化，過渡（期） ● be in transition 處於過渡時期
★**unveil** [ʌn`vel]	(v.) 揭露，公布 ● The new project was unveiled at the conference. 新企劃於會議上公開。

★**dazzle** [ˋdæzl̩]	(v.) 使目眩，使迷惑；使驚豔
★**coincide** [ˏkoɪnˋsaɪd]	(v.) 同時發生；一致
concurrent [kənˋkɝənt]	(adj.) 同時發生的，同時存在的 (= coincident) ● a concurrent resolution（上下議院）同時決議
incessant [ɪnˋsɛsn̩t]	(adj.) 不間斷的，不停的
★**invasion** [ɪnˋveʒən]	(n.) 侵略，入侵；（權利等的）侵害 ● the Soviet invasion of Afghanistan 蘇聯侵略阿富汗
kinship [ˋkɪnʃɪp]	(n.) 親族關係；（性質等）相似
maiden [ˋmedn̩]	(adj.) 初次的；未婚的，處女的 ● a maiden voyage 處女航
★**millennium** [məˋlɛnɪəm]	(n.) 一千年；千禧年；（幻想中的）黃金時代
precursor [prɪˋkɝsɚ]	(n.) 前導，先驅，先鋒 (= pioneer)
★**prevalent** [ˋprɛvələnt]	(adj.) 普遍的，盛行的 ● a prevalent belief 普遍的信仰
remnant [ˋrɛmnənt]	(n.) 殘餘，殘留
★**witness** [ˋwɪtnɪs]	(v.) 目擊；〔以事件為主詞〕是…的發生地或發生時間 ● The decade after the First World War witnessed another major surge of people pouring into the West. 第一次世界大戰後 10 年間，是大批人潮再一次湧入西方的時期。 ! 動詞 see 也有類似用法。
retribution [ˏrɛtrəˋbjuʃən]	(n.) 報復；懲罰，報應 ● suffer terrible retribution 遭受可怕的報復
treacherous [ˋtrɛtʃərəs]	(adj.) 背叛的，不忠的；危險的 ● a treacherous deed 背叛的行為

★**ally** [ə`laɪ]	(n.) 同盟，盟國，盟友 ● the Allies（第一次世界大戰的）協約國，（第二次世界大戰的）同盟國
★**heritage** [`hɛrətɪdʒ]	(n.) 遺產，繼承物 ● cultural heritage 文化遺產
★**feudalism** [`fjudḷ͵ɪzṃ]	(n.) 封建制度
lord [lɔrd]	(n.) 領主，主人；〔字首大寫〕上帝 ● the lord of the manor 莊園領主
vassal [`væsḷ]	(n.)（封建時代的）諸侯，附庸
★**chivalry** [`ʃɪvḷrɪ]	(n.) 騎士精神 ● Chivalry was satirized by Cervantes. 塞萬提斯撰文諷刺騎士精神。
knight [naɪt]	(n.) 騎士，武士
★**peasant** [`pɛzṇt]	(n.) 農民；鄉下人
★**the Middle Ages**	(n.) 中世紀 參 medieval (adj.) 中世紀的
manor [`mænɚ]	(n.) 莊園，領地；領主的宅第
★**bureaucracy** [bjʊ`rɑkrəsɪ]	(n.) 官僚政治（主義、制度）；繁文縟節
bureau [`bjʊro]	(n.) 局，處 ● Federal Bureau of Investigation (FBI) （美國）聯邦調查局 ● the Bureau of the Mint（美國財政部的）造幣局
manufacturing [͵mænjə`fæktʃərɪŋ]	(n.) 製造（業）(= manufacture)
trade [tred]	(n.) 貿易，商業，交易 ● foreign/free/protected trade 國外 / 自由 / 保護貿易

trade barrier [tred `bærɪɚ]	(n.) 貿易壁壘
★**trade friction** [tred `frɪkʃən]	(n.) 貿易摩擦
★**trade deficit** [tred `dɛfəsɪt]	(n.) 貿易逆差
★**the Industrial Revolution**	(n.) 工業革命
★**reign** [ren]	(n.) 統治（期間），支配 ● Queen Victoria's reign 維多利亞女王的統治 ! 注意發音。
★**unprecedented** [ʌn`prɛsə͵dɛntɪd]	(adj.) 史無前例的，空前的 ● an unprecedented victory 空前的勝利
renown [rɪ`naʊn]	(n.) 名聲，聲望 ● win renown 贏得名聲

1863 年 11 月 19 日，林肯於蓋茲堡發表著名的《蓋茲堡演說》(Gettysburg Address)

19 International Relations

國際關係

MP3 151

hegemonic [ˌhɛdʒə`manɪk]	(adj.) 握有主導權的 參 hegemony (n.) 霸權
ransom [`rænsəm]	(n.) 贖金 ● exact a ransom of 100 million dollars for the hostage release 勒索一億美元的贖金以釋放人質
trajectory [trə`dʒɛktərɪ]	(n.)（子彈等的）彈道
warfare [`wɔrˌfɛr]	(n.) 交戰狀態，戰爭
*** designate** [`dɛzɪgˌnet]	(adj.) 指定好的，選定的 (v.) 標明，指定；指派，任命 ● an ambassador designate 已指定（但尚未就任）的大使
*** avert** [ə`vɜt]	(v.) 避免，防止，避開 ● avert a tragic end by prompt action 以迅速的行動避免悲劇的發生
*** compatible** [kəm`pætəbḷ]	(adj.) 能共存的，相容的 ● Both countries are trying to gain compatible ends. 兩國都在努力達到可相容共存的結果。
*** comply** [kəm`plaɪ]	(v.) 遵守，服從 ● comply with the law 遵守法律的規定
pertinent [`pɜtənənt]	(adj.) 適當的 (= appropriate)
*** emigration** [ˌɛmə`greʃən]	(n.)（往外國）移民 參 immigration (n.)（自外國）移居入境
bilateral [baɪ`lætərəl]	(adj.) 雙邊的，雙方的 ● a bilateral treaty 雙邊條約
courier [`kurɪɚ]	(n.)（傳遞信件或官方文件的）信使

★**intervention** [ˌɪntɚˋvɛnʃən]	(n.) 介入；調停，斡旋
minimize [ˋmɪnəˌmaɪz]	(v.) 使減至最小量或最低限度；輕視
★**synchronize** [ˋsɪŋkrəˌnaɪz]	(v.) 同時發生；使同步
★**national interest** [ˋnæʃənḷ ˋɪntərɪst]	(n.) 國家利益 參 national affairs 國事
★**national security** [ˋnæʃənḷ sɪˋkjʊrətɪ]	(n.) 國家安全 參 national defense 國防
★**deterrent** [dɪˋtɝənt]	(adj.) 遏止的，阻止的 (n.) 制止物；嚇阻武力 ● the nuclear deterrent 核防禦力（用來嚇阻其他國家的核子攻擊）
military buildup [ˋmɪləˌtɛrɪ ˋbɪldˌʌp]	(n.) 加強軍備
★**economic sanction** [ˌikəˋnɑmɪk ˋsæŋkʃən]	(n.) 經濟制裁
economic superpower [ˌikəˋnɑmɪk ˋsupɚˌpaʊɚ]	(n.) 經濟超級強國
global standard [ˋglobḷ ˋstændɚd]	(n.) 國際標準
★**advanced nation** [ədˋvænst ˋneʃən]	(n.) 先進國家，已開發國家 參 a developing nation 開發中國家
★**multiculturalism** [ˌmʌltɪˋkʌltʃərəlɪzṃ]	(n.) 多元文化主義
cross-cultural [krɔs ˋkʌltʃərəl]	(adj.) 跨文化的，涉及多國文化的 ● cross-cultural studies 跨文化研究
★**prejudice** [ˋprɛdʒədɪs]	(n.) 偏見，成見 (= bias) ● racial prejudice 種族偏見
asylum [əˋsaɪləm]	(n.)（尤指對外國政治犯的）庇護，保護 ● political asylum 政治庇護

biological and [ˌbaɪəˋlɑdʒɪkl̩] **chemical weapons** [ˋkɛmɪkl̩] [ˋwɛpənz]	(n.) 生化武器
genocide [ˋdʒɛnəˌsaɪd]	(n.) **集體屠殺，種族滅絕** ! -cide 是表示「殺」之意的字根，例如 homicide（殺人）、suicide（自殺）、pesticide（殺蟲劑）。
★**persecute** [ˋpɝsɪˌkjut]	(v.) **迫害** ● He was persecuted for his religion. 他受到宗教迫害。
★**persecution** [ˌpɝsɪˋkjuʃən]	(n.) **迫害**
★**refugee** [ˌrɛfjʊˋdʒi]	(n.) **難民，流亡者** ● a refugee camp 難民營
★**territory** [ˋtɛrəˌtorɪ]	(n.) **領土，領域** 參 territorial (adj.) 領土的 ● territorial dispute 領土紛爭
★**conflict** [ˋkɑnflɪkt]	(n.) **衝突，爭執** ● a conflict between two countries 兩國之間的衝突 ● a conflict of opinions 意見衝突
★**hostage** [ˋhɑstɪdʒ]	(n.) **人質** ● The guerrillas took the ambassador hostage. 游擊隊劫持大使作為人質。
★**peace treaty** [pis ˋtritɪ]	(n.) **和平條約** 參 peace talks 和平會談
martial law [ˋmɑrʃəl lɔ]	(n.) **戒嚴令** ● place the capital under martial law 在首都實施戒嚴
truce [trus]	(n.) **休戰，停戰；停戰協定** ● call a truce 宣布休戰
★**purge** [pɝdʒ]	(v.) **整肅，清除（政敵等）** (n.) **清除異己，整肅** ● purge the party of radicals (= purge the radicals from the party) 清除黨內的激進分子

convoy [`kɑnvɔɪ]	(n.) 護送，護衛；護航艦 ● a Navy convoy 海軍護航艦
★**seize** [siz]	(v.) 占領，奪取 ● seize a castle 占領城堡
★**embassy** [`ɛmbəsɪ]	(n.) 大使館 ● the Japanese Embassy 日本大使館
aide [ed]	(n.)（尤指政府部長的）助理，助手 ● a presidential/White House aide 總統 / 白宮助理
microcredit [`maɪkro͵krɛdɪt]	(n.) 微型貸款
ICJ	(n.) 國際法院 (= International Court of Justice)
OECD	(n.) 經濟合作暨發展組織 (= Organization for Economic Cooperation and Development)

20 Journalism
新聞學

MP3 152

forum [ˋforəm]	(n.) 論壇
charismatic [ˏkærɪzˋmætɪk]	(adj.) 有魅力的 ㊫ charisma (n.) 魅力；(能使人效忠的) 領袖氣質
★**digest** [ˋdaɪdʒɛst]	(n.) 摘要，文摘 (v.) 理解；消化 ● This book contains a digest of several articles on psychology. 這本書有好幾篇心理學相關文章的摘要。
purveyor [pɚˋveɚ]	(n.) (食物或消息等的) 提供者
editorial [ˏɛdəˋtorɪəl]	(n.) 社論
confidentiality [ˏkɑnfəˏdɛnʃɪˋælətɪ]	(n.) 保密，機密
★**incorporate** [ɪnˋkɔrpəˏret]	(v.) 合併，包含 ● The book incorporates his earlier essays. 這本書收錄他早期的文章。
tactics [ˋtæktɪks]	(n.) 戰術，策略 (= strategy) ● strong-arm tactics 建立在暴力基礎上的策略
gazette [gəˋzɛt]	(n.) 公報；…報 (用於報刊名稱)
handwriting [ˋhændˏraɪtɪŋ]	(n.) 手寫；筆跡
★**jargon** [ˋdʒɑrgən]	(n.) 術語，專門用語 (= terminology)，行話 ● official jargon 官方用語
baffle [ˋbæfl̩]	(v.) 使困惑 (= perplex)
deem [dim]	(v.) 認為，以為 ● The extinction of the alligators was deemed almost inevitable. 短吻鱷的滅絕被認為是幾乎無法避免的。

broadcasting
[ˋbrɔdˏkæstɪŋ]
(n.) 廣播
● a broadcasting station 廣播電台

televise
[ˋtɛləˏvaɪz]
(v.) 由電視播放

★**coverage**
[ˋkʌvərɪdʒ]
(n.)（新聞的）取材範圍；新聞報導
● This press gave her adequate coverage.
這個媒體對她做完整的報導。

deadline
[ˋdɛdˏlaɪn]
(n.) 截止日期，最後期限；（報紙等）截稿時間
● meet a deadline for submitting a paper
在最後期限前交報告

★**supplement**
[ˋsʌpləmənt]
(n.) 補充；（書籍的）附錄；（報章雜誌的）副刊，增刊

★**article**
[ˋartɪkl]
(n.) 文章
● a newspaper article 報紙的文章

★**literacy**
[ˋlɪtərəsɪ]
(n.) 讀寫的能力，識字
● the literacy rate 識字率
反 illiteracy (n.) 不識字

★**illiterate**
[ɪˋlɪtərɪt]
(adj.) 不識字的；未受教育的

liberal
[ˋlɪbərəl]
(adj.) 進步的，自由主義的；大方的 (= generous)

★**conservative**
[kənˋsɝvətɪv]
(adj.) 保守的，保守主義的；謹慎的
● a conservative attitude toward marriage
對婚姻抱持保守的態度

press conference
[prɛs ˋkanfərəns]
(n.) 記者會
參 the press corps 記者團

correspondent
[ˏkɔrəˋspandənt]
(n.) 通訊記者
● a special correspondent 特派員

speech balloon
[spitʃ bəˋlun]
(n.)（漫畫中用以標示人物對白的）汽球狀圈圈，對話泡泡 (= speech bubble)

★**comic strip** [`kamɪk strɪp]	(n.) 連載漫畫 ● The modern comic strip started out as ammunition in a newspaper war. 現代漫畫一開始是報紙戰爭的彈藥庫。
★**syndicate** [`sɪndɪket]	(v.) 經由報紙雜誌聯盟發出（新聞稿、漫畫等） (n.) 報紙雜誌聯盟 ❗名詞發音爲 [`sɪndɪkɪt]。 ● That comic strip is syndicated in over 30 papers. 那個漫畫經報紙雜誌聯盟發出，在 30 幾份報紙上連載。
★**restrict** [rɪ`strɪkt]	(v.) 限制，限定 ● restrict freedom of speech 限制言論自由 參 restrictive (adj.) 限制的
prototype [`protə͵taɪp]	(n.) 原型
★**staple** [`stepl̩]	(n.) 重要元素 ● By 1915 comic strips had become a staple of daily newspaper. 到了 1915 年，連載漫畫已經成為日報的重要內容。
tabloid [`tæblɔɪd]	(n.) 小報（版面較小，常報導八卦新聞）
muckrake [`mʌk͵rek]	(v.) 揭發醜聞
sensational [sɛn`seʃənl̩]	(adj.) 煽情的，訴諸感官的
the penny press	(n.) 一分錢報，便士報（以八卦報導為主要內容的廉價報紙）
★**circulation** [͵sɜkjə`leʃən]	(n.)（報紙、期刊等的）發行量
★**avid** [`ævɪd]	(adj.) 熱切的；貪心的 ● Americans are avid readers of periodicals. 美國人熱愛看期刊。
★**emerge** [ɪ`mɝdʒ]	(v.) 出現，浮現 ● The true fact began to emerge. 事情的真相開始浮上檯面。

agent [ˋedʒənt]	(n.) 起因，原因 ● The agent of trouble was his style. 問題出在於他的寫作風格。
★**foreshadow** [fɔrˋʃædo]	(v.) 預示
disseminate [dɪˋsɛmə͵net]	(v.) 傳播，散布（消息、思想等） ● disseminate information 傳播資訊

21 Law
法律

MP3 153

*justice [ˋdʒʌstɪs]	(n.) 司法，審判；公平，正義
*juvenile [ˋdʒuvən!]	(adj.) 青少年的 • juvenile delinquency 青少年犯罪 • juvenile offender 青少年罪犯
*delinquent [dɪˋlɪŋkwənt]	(adj.) 犯法的；怠忽職守的 (n.) 青少年罪犯 • a delinquent boy 犯罪少年
*abide by [əˋbaɪd baɪ]	(v.) 遵守 • abide by the rule 遵守規則
prostitution [ˌprastəˋtjuʃən]	(n.) 賣淫 參 prostitute (n.) 賣淫者，娼妓
codify [ˋkadəˌfaɪ]	(v.) 將…編成法典
*confiscate [ˋkanfɪsˌket]	(v.) 沒收，將…充公
extort [ɪkˋstɔrt]	(v.) 逼迫；敲詐，勒索 • extort a confession from someone 逼迫某人招供
*penalize [ˋpɛn!ˌaɪz]	(v.) 處罰；宣告有罪
*testimony [ˋtɛstəˌmonɪ]	(n.) 證詞 • call someone in testimony 傳某人作證
*identification [aɪˌdɛntəfəˋkeʃən]	(n.) 確認，識別；身分證明
*identify [aɪˋdɛntəˌfaɪ]	(v.) 確認，識別，鑑定 • The body has been identified at once. 屍體的身分馬上就獲得確認。
intimidate [ɪnˋtɪməˌdet]	(v.) 威嚇，脅迫

★**prohibit** [pro`hɪbɪt]	(v.)（以法令規定等）禁止 ● The law prohibits child labor. 法律禁止童工。
★**tolerate** [`tɑlə,ret]	(v.) 忍受，容忍 (= endure/bear/stand/swallow/put up with)
★**verify** [`vɛrə,faɪ]	(v.) 證明，證實
slaughter [`slɔtɚ]	(n.) (v.) 屠殺
expertise [,ɛkspɚ`tiz]	(n.) 專門知識
intermediary [,ɪntɚ`midɪ,ɛrɪ]	(adj.) 中間的，媒介的 (n.) 中間者，媒介
★**suspend** [sə`spɛnd]	(v.) 暫時取消；暫緩執行（刑罰等） ● suspend a license 吊銷執照
★**prosecution** [,prɑsɪ`kjuʃən]	(n.) 起訴，告發
★**supreme court** [sə`prim kɔrt]	(n.) 最高法院
★**death penalty** [dɛθ `pɛnḷtɪ]	(n.) 死刑 (= capital punishment) ● abolish the death penalty 廢除死刑
★**capital punishment** [`kæpətḷ `pʌnɪʃmənt]	(n.) 死刑
★**life imprisonment** [laɪf ɪm`prɪzṇmənt]	(n.) 無期徒刑 ● He was under life imprisonment. 他被判無期徒刑。
previous conviction [`privɪəs kən`vɪkʃən]	(n.) 前科 參 ex-con (n.) 前科犯（con 是從已定罪的囚犯 convict 一字省略而來）
search warrant [sɝtʃ `wɔrənt]	(n.) 搜查令
★**lawsuit** [`lɔ,sut]	(n.) 訴訟（尤指民事案件）(= suit)
★**defense attorney** [dɪ`fɛns ə`tɝnɪ]	(n.) 被告律師，辯護律師

gallery [`gælərɪ]	(n.) 旁聽席 ● the press gallery（法院的）記者席
civil lawsuit [`sɪvḷ `lɔˌsut]	(n.) 民事訴訟
*** convict** [kən`vɪkt]	(v.) 判決有罪 (n.)（已判決有罪的）犯人 ! 名詞的發音爲 [`kanvɪkt]。 ● convict the accused of murder 判決被告謀殺罪成立
*** conviction** [kən`vɪkʃən]	(n.) 定罪 ● a conviction for murder 判決謀殺罪
code [kod]	(n.) 法規，法典 ● the civil code 民法 ● the criminal code 刑法
*** crime** [kraɪm]	(n.)（法律上的）犯罪 ! crime 和 offense 指法律上的罪，sin 和 vice 則指道德、宗教上的罪。 ● commit a crime 犯罪
court [kɔrt]	(n.) 法院；法庭 ● go to court 訴諸法律，打官司
trial [`traɪəl]	(n.) 審判
*** jury** [`dʒʊrɪ]	(n.) 陪審團 (= panel)
defendant [dɪ`fɛndənt]	(n.) 被告
plaintiff [`plentɪf]	(n.) 原告
lawyer [`lɔjɚ]	(n.) 律師 (= attorney)
prosecutor [`prɑsɪˌkjutɚ]	(n.) 檢察官；原告
burden of proof [`bɝdṇ] [pruf]	(n.) 舉證責任

disprove [dɪsˋpruv]	(v.) 證明…是錯的，駁斥
circumstantial evidence [ˏsɜkəmˋstænʃəl ˋɛvədəns]	(n.) 間接證據
***sentence** [ˋsɛntəns]	(n.) 判決 ❗常考單字。 ● The sentence was a fine of $80. 判決是罰款 80 美元。
***witness** [ˋwɪtnɪs]	(n.) 證人；目擊者 (v.) 為…作證；目擊 ● He was a witness for prosecution. 他是檢方的證人。
***fine** [faɪn]	(v.) 處以罰金 (n.) 罰金，罰鍰 ● fine a person 30 dollars for speeding 超速者被處以 30 美元罰款
***probation** [proˋbeʃən]	(n.) 緩刑
***imprisonment** [ɪmˋprɪzn̩mənt]	(n.) 監禁
***enforce** [ɪnˋfɔrs]	(v.) 實施（法律等），執行 ● enforce the law 執法
***violation** [ˏvaɪəˋleʃən]	(n.) 違反；侵犯
***sanction** [ˋsæŋkʃən]	(n.)〔常用複數〕國際制裁；認可
***detective** [dɪˋtɛktɪv]	(n.) 偵探 (adj.) 偵探的；偵察用的 ● a private detective 私家偵探
***murder** [ˋmɜdɚ]	(n.) (v.) 謀殺
homicide [ˋhaməˏsaɪd]	(n.) 殺人（正式法律用語）
***robbery** [ˋrabərɪ]	(n.) 搶劫，搶案
***armed** [armd]	(adj.) 武裝的，持有武器的 ● an armed robbery 持械搶劫

rape [rep]	(n.) (v.) 強姦 ● statutory rape 法定強姦罪（與未達合法性行為同意年齡 (age of consent) 的人發生性行為）
***theft** [θɛft]	(n.) 偷竊
***arson** [`ɑrsn̩]	(n.) 縱火（罪） 參 arsonist (n.) 縱火犯
***abduct** [æb`dʌkt]	(v.) 誘拐，綁架 (= kidnap)
abduction [æb`dʌkʃən]	(n.) 誘拐，綁架
***kidnap** [`kɪdnæp]	(v.) 誘拐，綁架（小孩）
***fraud** [frɔd]	(n.) 詐騙；騙子 ● practice fraud 進行詐騙行為
***bribery** [`braɪbərɪ]	(n.) 行賄，受賄 參 bribe (n.) 行賄物，賄款 (v.) 賄賂，收買
misappropriation [ˌmɪsəˌproprɪ`eʃən]	(n.) 侵吞
narcotic [nɑr`kɑtɪk]	(n.) 麻醉劑；〔常用複數〕迷幻毒品
***smuggle** [`smʌgl̩]	(v.) 走私，偷運 ! 常考單字。
FBI	(n.)（美國）聯邦調查局 (= Federal Bureau of Investigation)
***inmate** [`ɪnmet]	(n.) 囚犯 (= prisoner/convict)
bail [bel]	(n.) 保釋；保釋金 (v.) 保釋 ● He was out on bail. 他被保釋了。
libel [`laɪbl̩]	(n.) 誹謗 (= defamation)；誹謗文字 (v.) 發表誹謗他人的文字，中傷

acquit [ə`kwɪt]	(v.) 宣告無罪
★**perjury** [`pɝdʒərɪ]	(n.) 偽證（罪） 參 perjure (v.) 作偽證
penal code [`pinḷ kod]	(n.) 刑法
★**infringement** [ɪn`frɪndʒmənt]	(n.) 違反；侵害（權利）
★**piracy** [`paɪrəsɪ]	(n.) 盜版，侵害著作權
intellectual property right [ˌɪntə`lɛktʃuəl `prɑpətɪ raɪt]	(n.) 智慧財產權
★**arrest** [ə`rɛst]	(v.) (n.) 逮捕 • The policeman arrested the man for drunken driving. 警察以酒醉駕車的罪名逮捕那名男子。
apprehend [ˌæprɪ`hɛnd]	(v.) 逮捕
arrest warrant [ə`rɛst `wɔrənt]	(n.) 逮捕令
★**looting** [`lutɪŋ]	(n.) 掠奪，洗劫
swindler [`swɪndlɚ]	(n.) 詐騙的人，騙子
★**reformatory** [rɪ`fɔrməˌtorɪ]	(n.) 少年感化院
insurance [ɪn`ʃurəns]	(n.) 保險；保險理賠金；保險費 • insurance premium 保險費
insurance claim [ɪn`ʃurəns klem]	(n.) 保險索賠
★**settle** [`sɛtḷ]	(v.) 解決（問題等），結束（紛爭） • settle the claim with the insurance company 和保險公司解決賠償問題

optimum [ˋɑptəməm]	(adj.) 最佳的，最理想的 (n.) 最大限度；最適宜條件
***attorney** [əˋtɝnɪ]	(n.) 律師 (= lawyer)
***mediator** [ˋmidɪˏetɚ]	(n.) 調停者，斡旋者 參 mediation (n.) 調停，斡旋
mandatory arbitration [ˋmændəˏtorɪ ˏɑrbəˋtreʃən]	(n.) 強制仲裁 ● refer a wage dispute to mandatory arbitrations 將薪資的紛爭提請強制仲裁
litigation [ˏlɪtəˋgeʃən]	(n.) 訴訟，爭訟
deposition [ˏdɛpəˋzɪʃən]	(n.) 宣誓作證，證詞
interrogatory [ˏɪntəˋrɑgəˏtorɪ]	(n.) 質詢 (adj.) 質問的；疑問的
***production of document** [prəˋdʌkʃən əv ˋdɑkjəmənt]	(n.) 書面文件的提出
expert witness [ˋɛkspɝt ˋwɪtnɪs]	(n.) 專家證人
jury verdict [ˋdʒurɪ ˋvɝdɪkt]	(n.) 陪審團裁決
***eyewitness** [ˋaɪˏwɪtnɪs]	(n.) 目擊者 (= witness)
***offender** [əˋfɛndɚ]	(n.) 違法者
perpetrator [ˋpɝpəˏtretɚ]	(n.) 犯罪者，加害者
culprit [ˋkʌlprɪt]	(n.) 罪犯 (= criminal)；(刑事) 被告 (= defendant/accused)
***detain** [dɪˋten]	(v.) 拘留，留住 ● Three suspects were detained at the police station. 三名嫌犯被拘留在警察局。

elicit [ɪ`lɪsɪt]	(v.) 引出；誘出 ● elicit a confession from the criminal 誘使罪犯招供
***suspect** [`sʌspɛkt]	(n.) 嫌犯 ● The suspect is still at large. 嫌犯依然在逃。
allege [ə`lɛdʒ]	(v.)（無充分證據而）斷言，宣稱 參 allegedly (adv.) 依傳聞，據聲稱
***file a suit** [faɪl ə sut]	(v.) 提出訴訟 ● file a suit for divorce against someone 對某人提起離婚訴訟
***charge** [tʃɑrdʒ]	(v.) 控告，指控 ● He was charged with assault and battery. 他被控犯下傷害罪。
***testify** [`tɛstə,faɪ]	(v.) 作證
oath [oθ]	(n.) 宣誓
***plead** [plid]	(v.) 辯稱，辯護；承認 ● plead not guilty 辯稱無罪
***confess** [kən`fɛs]	(v.) 坦白，承認，供認 (= break/own up)
exonerate [ɪg`zɑnə,ret]	(v.) 證明…無罪，免除責任 ● He was exonerated from responsibility for the accident. 他被證明不用為那個事故負責。
cross-examine [krɔs ɪg`zæmɪn]	(v.)（向對方證人）質問，反覆詢問
clemency [`klɛmənsɪ]	(n.)（指施罰時的）寬容，仁慈；溫和 參 clement (adj.)（施罰等）寬大的
retaliation [rɪ,tælɪ`eʃən]	(n.) 報復 (= revenge/requital)
indictment [ɪn`daɪtmənt]	(n.) 起訴，告發

22 Linguistics
語言學

MP3 155

*linguistic [lɪŋ`gwɪstɪk]	(adj.) 語言的；語言學的
*abbreviation [əˌbrivɪ`eʃən]	(n.) 縮寫 參 acronym (n.) 首字母縮略字（由數個字的開頭字母所組成的字，如 AIDS）
*dictate [`dɪktet]	(v.) 口述（讓他人聽寫或記錄） ● The teacher dictated a short paragraph to us. 老師唸了一段短文讓我們聽寫。
syllable [`sɪləbḷ]	(n.) 音節 參 phoneme (n.) 音素（構成音節的最小語音單位）
*ambiguous [æm`bɪgjuəs]	(adj.) 引起歧義的，模稜兩可的（例如 The girl killed the old man with a knife. 一句有兩個可能意思：「少女持刀將老翁殺死」及「少女殺死持刀的老翁」）
intercultural [ˌɪntɚ`kʌltʃərəl]	(adj.) 不同文化間的
*bilingual [baɪ`lɪŋgwəl]	(adj.) 雙語的 (n.) 能說兩種語言的人 ● She is bilingual in English and French. 她會說英、法兩種語言。
*vowel [`vaʊəl]	(n.) 母音 參 consonant (n.) 子音
*dialect [`daɪəˌlɛkt]	(n.) 方言 (adj.) 方言的 ● They were speaking in Southern dialect. 他們用南部方言在交談。
phonetics [fə`nɛtɪks]	(n.) 語音學 參 phonology (n.) 音韻學
morphology [mɔr`fɑlədʒɪ]	(n.) 構詞學

grammar [ˋgræmɚ]	(n.) 文法，語法 ● transformational grammar 生成語法
★**semantics** [səˋmæntɪks]	(n.) 語意學（研究字義、句義的學問）
syntax [ˋsɪntæks]	(n.) 語法學；句法（研究句子的組成方法）
★**arbitrary** [ˋɑrbəˏtrɛrɪ]	(adj.) 任意的，獨斷的；反覆無常的
★**acquisition** [ˏækwəˋzɪʃən]	(n.) 習得 ● language acquisition 語言的習得
cued speech [kjud spitʃ]	(n.) 口手標音法，提示法（藉由手語或符號提供線索，幫助聽障兒童發音）
★**interaction** [ˏɪntɚˋækʃən]	(n.) 互動；互相影響 ! 常考單字。
lexicon [ˋlɛksɪkən]	(n.) 詞彙；詞典
pragmatics [prægˋmætɪks]	(n.) 語用學 ! 容易和 pragmatism（實用主義）的拼字搞混，請小心。
subliminal perception [sʌbˋlɪmənl̩ pɚˋsɛpʃən]	(n.) 閾下知覺，潛意識知覺
★**pitch** [pɪtʃ]	(n.) 音高
★**inflection** [ɪnˋflɛkʃən]	(n.) 音調變化；字形變化 參 derivative (n.) 衍生語
★**conjugation** [ˏkandʒəˋgeʃən]	(n.) 動詞變化 參 declension (n.)（名詞、代名詞、形容詞的）語尾變化
idiolect [ˋɪdɪəlɛkt]	(n.) 個人習慣用語
sociolinguistics [ˏsoʃɪolɪŋˋgwɪstɪks]	(n.) 社會語言學

pidgin [ˋpɪdʒən]	(n.) **洋涇濱語**（混用一經簡化的語言和一個當地語言而成，通常是為了方便溝通），**混成語** ● pidgin English 洋涇濱英語（看似英文，但不符合英文語法規則，例如將「人山人海」說成 people mountain people sea）
Creole [ˋkriol]	(n.) **克里奧語**（混合歐洲語言和西印度群島當地語言而成，當做母語使用），**混語**
register [ˋrɛdʒɪstɚ]	(n.) **語域**（不同場合使用的語言和文體等）
referent [ˋrɛfərənt]	(n.) **文字或符號所指涉的對象**

23 Literature
文學

MP3 156

*haunted [`hɔntɪd]	(adj.) 鬧鬼的；困擾的
homely [`homlɪ]	(adj.)（外表）普通、不好看的 反 attractive (adj.) 吸引人的
*infusion [ɪn`fjuʒən]	(n.) 注入，灌輸
*innate [ɪ`net]	(adj.) 與生俱來的，天生的 (= inborn/natural/inherent)
*behold [bɪ`hold]	(v.) 看，注視 (interj.) 看呀
*mimic [`mɪmɪk]	(v.) 模仿 (= imitate/copy) (n.) 善於模仿的人 (adj.) 模仿的
*naive [nɑ`iv]	(adj.) 天真的 (= ingenuous/simple/childlike)，輕易相信他人的
sensual [`sɛnʃuəl]	(adj.) 感官的，官能的；肉體上的
entrapment [ɪn`træpmənt]	(n.) 圈套，陷阱
villain [`vɪlən]	(n.) 壞人，惡棍 (= wretch/rogue)，反派角色
*ensure [ɪn`ʃur]	(v.) 保證，確保 ● You must ensure that children will wash their hands. 你必須確保孩子們會洗手。
*extravagant [ɪk`strævəgənt]	(adj.) 浪費的，奢侈的 (= luxurious)；過度的
kingdom [`kɪŋdəm]	(n.) 王國
*throne [θron]	(n.) 王位，王座 ● mount the throne 登上王位

★**allude** [ə`lud]	(v.) 暗示，間接提及，略微提到 ● He alluded to the possibility of cooperation with the ruling party. 他暗示和執政黨合作的可能性。
★**articulation** [ɑr͵tɪkjə`leʃən]	(n.)（清楚的）發音；（思想、情感的）表達 參 articulate (v.) 清楚地發音；明白地表達 (adj.) 發音清晰的；表達力強的
construe [kən`stru]	(v.) 解釋為，理解 ● His poem can be construed as a confession. 他的詩可以被解釋為是他的告白。
★**contradiction** [͵kɑntrə`dɪkʃən]	(n.) 矛盾，不一致，牴觸 (= incoherence/paradox/discrepancy) 參 contradict (v.) 與…矛盾
★**depict** [dɪ`pɪkt]	(v.) 描寫，描繪，刻劃 ● fairy tales depicted in pen-and-ink drawing 鋼筆畫中描繪的童話故事
divine [də`vaɪn]	(adj.) 神的；神聖的；天賜的
★**fallacy** [`fæləsɪ]	(n.) 謬論，謬誤
flesh [flɛʃ]	(n.) 肉；肉體 ● They are of the same flesh as you and I. 他們和你我一樣都是血肉之軀。
folklore [`fok͵lɔr]	(n.) 民間傳說，民俗
hymn [hɪm]	(n.) 讚美詩，聖歌
mythical [`mɪθɪkḷ]	(adj.) 神話的；虛構的
mythology [mɪ`θɑlədʒɪ]	(n.)〔集合用法〕神話；神話學
★**narrative** [`nærətɪv]	(n.) 故事；敘述 (adj.) 敘事的 ● a historical narrative 歷史故事

pastoralism
[ˋpæstərəl͵ɪzm̩]
(n.) 田園風格；牧歌體
參 pastoral poetry 田園詩；牧歌

★**portray**
[pɔrˋtre]
(v.) 描繪，描寫

recount
[riˋkaunt]
(v.) 敘述，講述 (= narrate)

revamp
[riˋvæmp]
(v.) 改寫；改造，修補 (= improve)

★**revision**
[rɪˋvɪʒən]
(n.) 修改，修訂；修訂本

saga
[ˋsɑgə]
(n.) 傳說，英雄事蹟，冒險故事

scribble
[ˋskrɪbl̩]
(v.) 草草寫下，草率創作
(n.) 草草寫下的東西，潦草的筆跡

succinct
[səkˋsɪŋkt]
(adj.) 簡潔的 (= brief)，簡明的 (= precise)

★**verbal**
[ˋvɝbl̩]
(adj.) 口頭的，言語的
- The writer has great verbal skill.
這個作家有高超的語言技巧。

wording
[ˋwɝdɪŋ]
(n.) 措辭，用語

★**worldly**
[ˋwɝldlɪ]
(adj.) 世俗的 (= secular/earthly/material)

adore
[əˋdor]
(v.) 崇拜，仰慕，敬重
- His readers adored him. 他的讀者崇拜他。

★**authoritative**
[əˋθɔrə͵tetɪv]
(adj.)（消息、書籍等）權威的，可信賴的；官方的；命令式的
- an authoritative book on Shakespeare
談論莎士比亞的權威著作

authorize
[ˋɔθə͵raɪz]
(v.) 授權，批准，認可

beguile [bɪˋgaɪl]	(v.) 欺騙，向…騙取；使陶醉 ● be beguiled (= cheated) of one's money 被人騙取了金錢
beloved [bɪˋlʌvd]	(adj.) 摯愛的；受人喜愛的 (n.) 心愛的人 (= sweetheart)
★**bizarre** [bɪˋzɑr]	(adj.) 詭異的，不尋常的
★**disillusion** [ˌdɪsɪˋluʒən]	(v.) 使幻滅，使清醒 ● Many young people are disillusioned with his new novel. 許多年輕人對他的新小說感到幻滅。
drawback [ˋdrɔˌbæk]	(n.) 缺點，短處 ● There are many drawbacks to his method of describing the event. 他敘述該事件的方式有許多缺點。
★**elusive** [ɪˋlusɪv]	(adj.) 難以捉摸的，難以理解的
enigma [əˋnɪgmə]	(n.) 謎，難以理解的事物
exquisite [ˋɛkskwɪzɪt]	(adj.) 精緻的；優雅的；絕妙的 ● exquisite manners 優雅的舉止
ghastly [ˋgæstlɪ]	(adj.) 可怕的，恐怖的 (adv.) 可怕地
grotesque [groˋtɛsk]	(adj.) 詭異的，怪誕的
★**grudge** [grʌdʒ]	(v.) 不願意給，吝惜；嫉妒 (n.) 怨恨 參 grudging (adj.) 吝惜的
horrify [ˋhɔrəˌfaɪ]	(v.) 使感到恐懼
★**intuition** [ˌɪntjuˋɪʃən]	(n.) 直覺，敏銳的洞察力 ● by intuition 憑直覺
languish [ˋlæŋgwɪʃ]	(v.) 衰弱，凋萎；因渴望而憔悴

monotonous [mə`natṇəs]	(adj.) 單調的，無變化的 ● in a monotonous tone 用單調的語調
ominous [`amənəs]	(adj.) 不祥的 (= inauspicious)；預兆的
sinister [`sɪnɪstɚ]	(adj.) 惡兆的；惡意的，陰險的
★**perplex** [pɚ`plɛks]	(v.) 使感到困惑 參 perplexing (adj.) 令人困惑的，費解的
★**plausible** [`plɔzəbḷ]	(adj.) 看似有理的 (= likely/feasible)；很會說話的
★**preoccupation** [pri͵akjə`peʃən]	(n.) 全神貫注，入神
preposterous [prɪ`pastərəs]	(adj.) 荒謬的，可笑的 (= absurd)
reminiscence [͵rɛmə`nɪsṇs]	(n.) 回憶 (= retrospect/recollection/memory)；引人想起相似事物的東西；〔複數〕回憶錄
retrospect [`rɛtrə͵spɛkt]	(n.) (v.) 回顧，回想 ● in retrospect 回想起來
★**resentment** [rɪ`zɛntmənt]	(n.) 憤怒，憤慨，怨恨
indignation [͵ɪndɪg`neʃən]	(n.) 憤怒，憤慨 ● stir indignation 激起憤怒
★**rudimentary** [͵rudə`mɛntərɪ]	(adj.) 初步的，基本的；發展未完全的
sneer [snɪr]	(v.) (n.) 冷笑，輕蔑地笑
★**spontaneous** [span`tenɪəs]	(adj.) 自發的；不由自主的；自然的
★**surpass** [sɚ`pæs]	(v.) 勝過，優於，超越 ● Hemingway surpasses Faulkner in a short story. 海明威在一篇短篇故事中超越福克納。

*modify [ˋmɑdə͵faɪ]	(v.) 修改，稍微修正；修飾
*obliterate [əˋblɪtə͵ret]	(v.) 擦掉，塗掉 (= erase/blot out)；消滅
odyssey [ˋɑdəsɪ]	(n.) 長途冒險的旅程 ● the Odyssey 奧德賽（相傳為荷馬 (Homer) 所作的史詩）
idyll [ˋaɪdḷ]	(n.) 田園詩；田園散文 ● a prose idyll 散文田園詩
beast [bist]	(n.) 野獸；如野獸般粗暴的人 ● man and beast 人畜
appendix [əˋpɛndɪks]	(n.) 附錄，附件；附加物 ! 也有「闌尾」（俗稱盲腸）的意思。
pedantic [pɪˋdæntɪk]	(adj.) 好賣弄學問的，學究的
courtship [ˋkortʃɪp]	(n.) 求愛，追求
*miscellaneous [͵mɪsəˋlenɪəs]	(adj.) 多才多藝的；五花八門的，混雜的 ● a miscellaneous writer 多才多藝的作家
revenge [rɪˋvɛnʤ]	(n.) (v.) 報仇，報復 ● revenge oneself on one's enemy 向敵人報復
affront [əˋfrʌnt]	(v.) 侮辱 (= insult)，冒犯
*anecdote [ˋænɪk͵dot]	(n.) 奇聞軼事
clown [klaʊn]	(n.) 小丑，丑角；愛開玩笑的人 (= jester)
duel [ˋdjuəl]	(n.) 決鬥 ● fight a duel with someone 和某人決鬥
dwarf [dwɔrf]	(n.) 小矮人，侏儒 (= pygmy) 反 giant (n.) 巨人
*embrace [ɪmˋbres]	(v.) 擁抱；欣然接受（建議等）；包含 (n.) 擁抱，懷抱

★**endow** [ɪn`daʊ]	(v.) 賦予（才能、權利等）；捐贈，資助 ● be endowed with talent/resources/right 天生具有才能 / 被賦予資源 / 被賦予權利
★**allegory** [`ælə͵gɔrɪ]	(n.) 寓言，諷喻，象徵
alliteration [ə͵lɪtə`reʃən]	(n.) 頭韻法，押頭韻
★**rhyme** [raɪm]	(n.) 韻，韻腳；韻文 (v.) 押韻
★**adaptation** [͵ædæp`teʃən]	(n.) 改編，改寫 ● This film is an adaptation of a novel. 這部電影改編自一部小說。
★**allusion** [ə`luʒən]	(n.) 暗示，間接提到；引述，典故
★**anachronism** [ə`nækrə͵nɪzm̩]	(n.) 不合時宜，落伍的人事物；時代錯誤 ● Slavery is a sheer anachronism in the modern age. 奴隸制度在現代完全是不合時宜的。
anagram [`ænə͵græm]	(n.) 回文構詞法（改變單字的順序而構成新的單字，例如 time 變成 emit）
★**analogous** [ə`næləgəs]	(adj.) 類似的 (= similar)，可比擬的 ● The major poems of Frost and Robinson are somewhat analogous in conception. 佛洛斯特和羅賓森的主要詩作在概念上多少有些類似。
★**analogy** [ə`nælədʒɪ]	(n.) 類似，相似；比擬，類推 ● an analogy between the computer and the brain 電腦和人腦的相似性
annotation [͵æno`teʃən]	(n.) 註解，註釋
antagonist [æn`tægənɪst]	(n.) 敵手，對手 (= adversary/opponent/enemy)
anthology [æn`θalədʒɪ]	(n.) 選集，文選

*antihero [ˋæntaɪˏhɪro]	(n.) 反英雄，非正統派主角（指文學作品中缺乏傳統英雄品格的主角）
antithesis [ænˋtɪθəsɪs]	(n.) 對照，相反；對語，對句
*archetype [ˋɑrkəˏtaɪp]	(n.) 原型 (= prototype)，典型
blank verse [blæŋk vɝs]	(n.) 無韻詩
bowdlerize [ˋbaʊdləˏraɪz]	(v.) 刪節，刪改
cacophony [kəˋkɑfənɪ]	(n.) 雜音，不和諧音
carpe diem [ˋkɑrpe ˋdiəm]	(n.)〔拉丁文〕抓住今天，及時行樂 (= seize the day)
catharsis [kəˋθɑrsɪs]	(n.) 淨化，洗滌（尤指透過觀賞悲劇作品達到淨化感情的作用）
*cliché [kliˋʃe]	(n.) 陳腔濫調 ● An epigram will become a cliché soon. 警句很快就會變成陳腔濫調。
criticism [ˋkrɪtəˏsɪzm̩]	(n.) 批評，評論 ● be above/beyond criticism 無可非議，無可挑剔 參 critic (n.) 批評家
*critical [ˋkrɪtɪkl̩]	(adj.) 批評的，吹毛求疵的；緊要的；危急的 ● critical works 評論
*dialogue [ˋdaɪəˏlɔg]	(n.) 對話，交談；（戲劇或小說中的）對白；對話式文學作品 ● After that, a short dialogue took place between them. 在那之後，他們之間有一段短暫的談話。
didactic [daɪˋdæktɪk]	(adj.) 有教訓意味的，說教的
elegy [ˋɛlədʒɪ]	(n.) 哀歌，輓歌

epigraph
[ˋɛpɪ͵græf]
(n.) 碑文，題詞

epilogue
[ˋɛpə͵lɔg]
(n.) 結語，跋，收場白
反 prologue (n.) 序言，開場白

epithet
[ˋɛpə͵θɛt]
(n.) 稱號；綽號，表示特徵的形容詞
- The Lion-Hearted is an epithet for Richard I.
  獅心是對理查一世的稱號。

existentialism
[͵ɛgzɪsˋtɛnʃəlɪzm̩]
(n.) 存在主義
- Existentialism had a great influence on Camus.
  存在主義對卡繆有很大的影響。

★**fable**
[ˋfebl̩]
(n.) 寓言；虛構的故事
- Aesop's Fables 伊索寓言

★**genre**
[ˋʒɑnrə]
(n.) 文類（文藝作品的類型）

haiku
[ˋhaɪkʊ]
(n.) 俳句（日本傳統詩歌的一種，由排列成三行的五、七、五共 17 個字音組成）
! tsunami（海嘯）也是來自日文的英文。

icon
[ˋaɪkɑn]
(n.) 畫像；聖像；偶像；（電腦螢幕上的）圖像

invective
[ɪnˋvɛktɪv]
(n.) 謾罵，辱罵 (= insult)

modernism
[ˋmɑdɚn͵ɪzm̩]
(n.) 現代主義；現代思想

★**myth**
[mɪθ]
(n.) 神話；迷思
- ancient Greek myths 古希臘神話

naturalism
[ˋnætʃərəl͵ɪzm̩]
(n.) 自然主義，自然論

ode
[od]
(n.) 頌歌，賦

★**onomatopoeia**
[͵ɑnə͵mætəˋpiə]
(n.) 擬聲法；擬聲詞

★**pathos**
[ˋpeθɑs]
(n.)（文學、戲劇、音樂或演講等的）感染力（使人產生憐憫、同情、哀愁等情緒）

persona [pɚ`sonə]	(n.)（小說、戲劇中的）人物 (= character)；外在性格（表現在他人面前的性格和特質，與本性相去甚遠）
structuralism [`strʌktʃərəˌlɪzm̩]	(n.) 結構主義
***rhetoric** [`rɛtərɪk]	(n.) 修辭學；修辭；言論
***satire** [`sætaɪr]	(n.) 諷刺；諷刺文學 ● The play was a satire on political circles. 那齣戲是在諷刺政治圈。
immortal [ɪ`mɔrtl̩]	(adj.) 不朽的 ● immortal masterpieces 不朽的傑作
***epigram** [`ɛpəˌgræm]	(n.) 警句，雋語；機智的短詩
***irony** [`aɪrənɪ]	(n.) 諷刺，反諷 ● a dramatic irony 戲劇性反諷（劇中人物不知情，而觀眾卻對台詞的言外之意心領神會的一種戲劇手法）
***medieval** [ˌmɛdɪ`ivl̩]	(adj.) 中世紀的，中古的 ● medieval literature 中古文學
***paradox** [`pærəˌdɑks]	(n.) 似非而是的議論；自相矛盾的話 (= contradiction/discrepancy)
scansion [`skænʃən]	(n.)（詩的）韻律分析
semiology [ˌsimɪ`ɑlədʒɪ]	(n.) 符號學 (= semiotics)
***play** [ple]	(n.) 戲劇 (= drama)；劇本
theater of the absurd [`θiətɚ] [əb`sɝd]	(n.) 荒謬劇（1940–50 年代興起於巴黎的一種前衛的戲劇形式，藉由違背常理和習慣的演出，反映出人類生活的單調與不合理性。代表作品為貝克特 (Samuel Beckett) 的《等待果陀》(Waiting for Godot)）

★**poetry** [ˋpoɪtrɪ]	(n.)〔集合用法〕詩的總稱；韻文 (= verse) ! 一首詩、兩首詩要用可數的 poem，如 a poem, two poems。
★**treatise** [ˋtritɪs]	(n.)（學術）論文，專著
★**prose** [proz]	(n.) 散文；平凡，單調
★**verse** [vɝs]	(n.) 韻文，詩歌 ● blank verse 無韻詩
★**chronicle** [ˋkrɑnɪkl̩]	(n.) 編年史，年代記 (v.) 依發生時間記錄下來
★**metaphor** [ˋmɛtəˏfɔr]	(n.) 隱喻，暗喻 反 simile (n.) 明喻
epic [ˋɛpɪk]	(n.) 史詩，敘事詩；史詩般的作品 (adj.) 史詩的；壯麗的；英雄的 ● an epic novel 史詩般的小說
lyric [ˋlɪrɪk]	(n.) 抒情詩；歌詞 (adj.) 抒情的 ● lyric prose 抒情的散文
★**biography** [baɪˋɑgrəfɪ]	(n.) 傳記 參 autobiography (n.) 自傳
★**tragedy** [ˋtrædʒədɪ]	(n.) 悲劇
★**comedy** [ˋkɑmədɪ]	(n.) 喜劇
tragicomedy [ˏtrædʒɪˋkɑmədɪ]	(n.) 悲喜劇
★**playwright** [ˋpleˏraɪt]	(n.) 劇作家 (= dramatist)
★**perspective** [pɚˋspɛktɪv]	(n.) 觀點，看法；展望
platitude [ˋplætəˏtjud]	(n.) 陳腔濫調 參 platitudinous (adj.) 陳腐的，老掉牙的

incongruous [ɪn`kaŋgruəs]	(adj.) 不合適的；不協調的
★**appreciate** [ə`priʃɪ͵et]	(v.) 欣賞，領會 ● His novel was appreciated by his own generation. 他的小說受到同一時代的人的喜愛。
prod [prɑd]	(v.) 驅使，刺激
★**advocate** [`ædvə͵ket]	(v.) 提倡，擁護，主張 (n.) 提倡者，擁護者 ● advocate free speech 倡導言論自由
★**ridicule** [`rɪdɪ͵kjul]	(v.) (n.) 嘲笑，揶揄 (= mock)

Mathematics
數學

MP3 159

commensurate [kə`mɛnʃərɪt]	(adj.) 同數量的，同等的
abacus [`æbəkəs]	(n.) 算盤
***formula** [`fɔrmjələ]	(n.) 公式，方程式；配方 ● a binomial formula 二項式
***formulate** [`fɔrmjə͵let]	(v.) 使公式化，以公式表示 ● formulate a hypothesis 將假設化為公式
***dimension** [daɪ`mɛnʃən]	(n.) 維度，次元；（長、寬、高等）尺寸 ● A plane has two dimensions. 平面是二次元的。
***minimal** [`mɪnɪml̩]	(adj.) 最小的
quadruple [`kwɑdrupl̩]	(adj.) 四倍的 (n.) 四倍數 (v.)（使）成四倍
***remainder** [rɪ`mendɚ]	(n.) 差數，餘數；剩餘物
equilateral triangle [͵ikwə`lætərəl `traɪ͵æŋgl̩]	(n.) 等邊三角形，正三角形
***cube** [kjub]	(n.) 立方體；三次方 (v.) 自乘兩次；求…的體積
***cylinder** [`sɪlɪndɚ]	(n.) 圓柱（體），柱面
***cone** [kon]	(n.) 圓錐體，圓錐形
***prism** [`prɪzm̩]	(n.) 稜柱體，角柱體；稜鏡
development [dɪ`vɛləpmənt]	(n.) 展開（圖）；發展，進展；沖洗（照片等）

★**circle** [ˋsɝkḷ]	(n.) 圓，圓圈 ● draw a circle with compasses 用圓規畫一個圓
★**oval** [ˋovḷ]	(n.) 橢圓形 (adj.) 橢圓形的
sector [ˋsɛktɚ]	(n.) 扇形；扇形面；部分
★**square** [skwɛr]	(n.) 正方形；平方 (v.) 自乘；求…的面積
★**root** [rut]	(n.) 根，根數 ● 3 is the square root of 9. 三是九的平方根。
★**rectangle** [ˋrɛk͵tæŋgḷ]	(n.) 矩形，長方形
parallelogram [͵pærəˋlɛlə͵græm]	(n.) 平行四邊形
diamond [ˋdaɪəmənd]	(n.) 菱形，鑽石形 (adj.) 菱形的
★**pentagon** [ˋpɛntə͵gɑn]	(n.) 五角形，五邊形 ● the Pentagon 五角大廈（美國國防部，因其建築物的形狀而得名）
hexagon [ˋhɛksə͵gɑn]	(n.) 六角形，六邊形
octagon [ˋɑktə͵gɑn]	(n.) 八角形，八邊形
★**equation** [ɪˋkweʒən]	(n.) 方程式，等式；相等 ● a linear equation 一次方程式
quadratic equation [kwɑdˋrætɪk ɪˋkweʒən]	(n.) 二次方程式
cubic equation [ˋkjubɪk ɪˋkweʒən]	(n.) 三次方程式
★**function** [ˋfʌŋkʃən]	(n.) 函數 ● a trigonometric function 三角函數
factor [ˋfæktɚ]	(n.) 因數 (v.) 分解…的因數 ● a common factor 公因數

★**integer** [`ɪntədʒɚ]	(n.) 整數
variable [`vɛrɪəbḷ]	(n.) 變數
greatest common divisor [`gretɪst `kɑmən də`vaɪzɚ]	(n.) 最大公因數
lowest common multiple [`loɪst `kɑmən `mʌltəpḷ]	(n.) 最小公倍數
★**million** [`mɪljən]	(n.) 百萬 (adj.) 百萬的 ● five million, four hundred and two thousand 540 萬 2 千
★**billion** [`bɪljən]	(n.)〔美〕十億，〔英〕兆
★**trillion** [`trɪljən]	(n.)〔美〕兆，〔英〕百萬兆
★**odd number** [ɑd `nʌmbɚ]	(n.) 奇數
★**even number** [`ivən `nʌmbɚ]	(n.) 偶數
round [raʊnd]	(adj.) 整數的
★**round off** [raʊnd ɔf]	(v.) 四捨五入 ● round 7.828 off two decimal places 將 7.828 小數點後第三位四捨五入
round up [raʊnd ʌp]	(v.) 無條件進位
round down [raʊnd daʊn]	(v.) 無條件捨去
theorem [`θiərəm]	(n.) 定理 ● the Pythagorean theorem 畢達哥拉斯定理，畢氏定理

★**width** [wɪdθ]	(n.) 寬，寬度 ● a room 10 feet wide by 20 feet long 一個寬 10 英尺長 20 英尺的房間
★**height** [haɪt]	(n.) 高；高度
★**depth** [dɛpθ]	(n.) 深度
length [lɛŋθ]	(n.) 長度
direct proportion [də`rɛkt prə`porʃən]	(n.) 正比 反 inverse proportion 反比
weight [wet]	(n.) 重量
area [`ɛrɪə]	(n.) 面積
★**volume** [`vɑljəm]	(n.) 體積；容積
base [bes]	(n.) 基數；底邊
★**circumference** [sɚ`kʌmfərəns]	(n.) 圓周，周長 ● The circumference of the pond is almost 3 miles. 那個池塘的周長大約三英里。
★**radius** [`redɪəs]	(n.) 半徑
★**diameter** [daɪ`æmətɚ]	(n.) 直徑 ● That circle is 10 inches in diameter. = That circle has a diameter of 10 inches. 那個圓的直徑是 10 英寸。
★**right angle** [raɪt `æŋgl]	(n.) 直角
vertical [`vɜtɪkl]	(n.) 垂直線 (adj.) 垂直的
★**parabola** [pə`ræbələ]	(n.) 拋物線

perpendicular line [ˌpɜpən`dɪkjələ˞ laɪn]	(n.) 垂直線
diagonal [daɪ`ægənḷ]	(adj.) 對角線的 ● diagonal line 對角線
parallel line [`pærəˌlɛl laɪn]	(n.) 平行線
★**diagram** [`daɪəˌgræm]	(n.) 圖表；圖解 ● This book has diagrams showing the parts of a car engine. 這本書有汽車引擎零件的圖解。
★**approximation** [əˌprɑksə`meʃən]	(n.) 近似值；概算
★**ratio** [`reʃo]	(n.) 比，比例，比率 (= proportion)
polygon [`pɑlɪˌgɑn]	(n.) 多角形，多邊形
circumscribe [`sɜkəmˌskraɪb]	(v.) 畫外接圓，使外切
surface area [`sɜfɪs `ɛrɪə]	(n.) 表面積
volume of a sphere [`vɑljəm] [sfɪr]	(n.) 球體體積
★**figure** [`fɪgjə˞]	(n.) 圖形；圖表；數字 ● a plane figure 平面圖形
★**addition** [ə`dɪʃən]	(n.) 加法
★**subtraction** [səb`trækʃən]	(n.) 減法 參 subtract (v.) 減去，扣除
★**multiplication** [ˌmʌltəplə`keʃən]	(n.) 乘法 ● multiplication tables 九九乘法表
★**multiply** [`mʌltəˌplaɪ]	(v.) 乘 ● multiply 5 by 3 五乘以三
★**division** [də`vɪʒən]	(n.) 除法

divide [də`vaɪd]	(v.) 除 ● divide 9 by 3 九除以三
★**geometry** [dʒɪ`amətrɪ]	(n.) 幾何學 ● solid geometry 立體幾何學
★**probability** [ˌprabə`bɪlətɪ]	(n.) 機率，或然率
cardinal number [`kardṇəl `nʌmbɚ]	(n.) 基數
ordinal number [`ɔrdṇəl `nʌmbɚ]	(n.) 序數
★**differential calculus** [ˌdɪfə`rɛnʃəl `kælkjələs]	(n.) 微分學
★**integral calculus** [`ɪntəgrəl `kælkjələs]	(n.) 積分學
★**fraction** [`frækʃən]	(n.) 分數 ● a mixed fraction 帶分數
permutation [ˌpɜmjə`teʃən]	(n.) 排列
combination [ˌkambə`neʃən]	(n.) 組合
★**set** [sɛt]	(n.) 集合 ● a negative integer set 負整數的集合
★**statistics** [stə`tɪstɪks]	(n.) 統計學；統計資料
deviation value [ˌdivɪ`eʃən `vælju]	(n.) 偏差值
★**decimal** [`dɛsəml̩]	(adj.) 小數的；十進位的 (n.) 小數 ● a decimal point 小數點 ● a decimal system 十進位制
imaginary number [ɪ`mædʒəˌnɛrɪ `nʌmbɚ]	(n.) 虛數
logarithm [`lagəˌrɪðəm]	(n.) 對數

★**proportion** [prəˋporʃən]	(n.) **比例，比率** 參 direct/inverse proportion 正／反比
ounce [aʊns]	(n.) **盎司**（縮寫為 oz.，等於 28.35 公克）
pint [paɪnt]	(n.) **品脫**（容量單位，等於 1/2 夸脫，相當於 473 毫升〔美〕或 568 毫升〔英〕）
quart [kwɔrt]	(n.) **夸脫**（容量單位，等於 2 品脫，相當於 946 毫升〔美〕或 1136 毫升〔英〕）
★**gallon** [ˋgælən]	(n.) **加侖**（容量單位，1 加侖等於 3.785 公升〔美〕或 4.546 公升〔英〕）
bushel [ˋbʊʃəl]	(n.) **蒲式耳**（計算穀物和水果的單位，1 蒲式耳相當於 35.24 公升〔美〕或 36.37 公升〔英〕）

25 Medicine
醫學

MP3 161

★**pierce** [pɪrs]	(v.) 刺，穿
★**impalpable** [ɪm`pælpəbḷ]	(adj.) 無法感觸到的；無形的
★**moderation** [ˌmɑdə`reʃən]	(n.) 溫和；緩和；適度
stupor [`stjupɚ]	(n.) 不省人事；恍惚；麻木
★**susceptible** [sə`sɛptəbḷ]	(adj.) 易受…感染的；易受…影響的 ● be susceptible to colds 容易感冒的
★**abstain** [əb`sten]	(v.) 禁絕，戒除 (= refrain) ● abstain from drinking 戒酒
★**refrain** [rɪ`fren]	(v.) 避免；抑制，忍住 ● Please refrain from smoking in the car. 請不要在車上抽菸。
★**breakthrough** [`brekˌθru]	(n.)（科學等的）突破，突破性進展 ● make a breakthrough in medicine 在醫學上有所突破
★**impair** [ɪm`pɛr]	(v.) 損傷，傷害 ● Overwork impaired his health. 工作過度損害他的健康。
★**mitigate** [`mɪtəˌget]	(v.) 緩和，減輕
★**squeeze** [skwiz]	(v.) 壓榨，擠
stretch [strɛtʃ]	(v.) 伸展，延伸；扭傷
★**chronically** [`krɑnɪklɪ]	(adv.) 慢性地；長期地

protrude [pro`trud]	(v.) 伸出，突出 ● protrude (= put out) one's tongue 伸出舌頭
★**abuse** [ə`bjuz]	(v.) 濫用；虐待 ● abuse one's health 損害健康
★**alcoholic** [ˌælkə`hɔlɪk]	(n.) 酒精中毒者；酗酒者
★**bruise** [bruz]	(n.) 瘀傷；擦傷
★**choke** [tʃok]	(v.) 使窒息；阻塞
★**contagious** [kən`tedʒəs]	(adj.) 傳染性的 (= infectious/epidemic/taking/pestilent) ● a contagious disease 傳染病
cramp [kræmp]	(n.) 抽筋，痙攣 ● a cramp in the calf 小腿抽筋
cripple [`krɪpl̩]	(v.) 使跛，使殘廢
★**disabled** [dɪs`ebl̩d]	(adj.) 殘廢的；有缺陷的
★**dose** [dos]	(n.)（藥物等）一次服用量，一劑 (v.)（按劑量）開藥
tablet [`tæblɪt]	(n.) 錠劑，藥片 (= pill)
epilepsy [`ɛpəlɛpsɪ]	(n.) 癲癇症，羊癲瘋
gland [glænd]	(n.) 腺體 ● the sweat gland 汗腺
innocuous [ɪ`nɑkjʊəs]	(adj.)（藥等）無害的；無毒的
insomniac [ɪn`sɑmnɪˌæk]	(n.) 失眠症患者
★**itchy** [`ɪtʃɪ]	(adj.) 癢的

★**longevity** [lɑn`dʒɛvətɪ]	(n.) 長壽
malign [mə`laɪn]	(adj.) 惡性的 (= malignant) 反 benign (adj.) 良性的
★**medication** [ˌmɛdɪ`keʃən]	(n.) 藥物治療；藥物
crystalline [`krɪstḷaɪn]	(adj.) 結晶的；結晶狀的 ● crystalline lens（眼球的）水晶體
★**myopia** [maɪ`opɪə]	(n.) 近視
★**nurture** [`nɝtʃɚ]	(v.) (n.) 養育，教養
olfactory [ɑl`fæktərɪ]	(adj.) 嗅覺的
★**perceptible** [pɚ`sɛptəbḷ]	(adj.) 可感知的，可察覺的 ● There is no perceptible change in her condition. 她的狀況沒有什麼變化。
★**perceptive** [pɚ`sɛptɪv]	(adj.) 可察覺的，可感知的
★**perspire** [pɚ`spaɪr]	(v.) 出汗，流汗 參 perspiration (n.) 流汗 (= sweat)
physiognomy [ˌfɪzɪ`ɑgnəmɪ]	(n.) 面相，面容
physique [fɪ`zik]	(n.) 體格，體形
★**posture** [`pɑstʃɚ]	(n.) 姿勢；立場，態度
practitioner [præk`tɪʃənɚ]	(n.) 開業者（尤指醫生、律師） 參 practice the medicine 醫師開業
★**prescribe** [prɪ`skraɪb]	(v.) 開藥方；規定
★**quarantine** [`kwɔrənˌtin]	(n.) 檢疫；隔離 ● keep a patient in quarantine 將一名病患隔離

refrigeration [rɪˏfrɪʤəˋreʃən]	(n.) 冷藏；冷凍
★**sensory** [ˋsɛnsərɪ]	(adj.) 知覺的，感覺的 ● sensory memory 感官記憶
★**sore** [sor]	(adj.) 痛的 ● have sore shoulders 肩膀疼痛
★**surgical** [ˋsɜʤɪkl̩]	(adj.) 外科的；外科（手術）用的
tactile [ˋtæktaɪl]	(adj.) 觸覺的；能觸知的
★**therapist** [ˋθɛrəpɪst]	(n.) 治療師
urinal [ˋjʊrənl̩]	(n.) 尿壺；男子小便斗
★**virus** [ˋvaɪrəs]	(n.) 病毒
wrinkle [ˋrɪŋkl̩]	(n.) 皺紋
★**allergy** [ˋælɚʤɪ]	(n.) 過敏症 ● pollen allergy 花粉過敏；花粉熱 (= hay fever)
allergen [ˋælɚˏʤɛn]	(n.) 過敏原
★**germ** [ʤɜm]	(n.) 細菌；微生物 ● a room free of germs 無菌室
★**paralyze** [ˋpærəˏlaɪz]	(v.) 使麻痺；使癱瘓 ● the traffic paralyzed by the snowstorm 被暴風雪癱瘓的交通
★**hygienic** [ˏhaɪʤɪˋɛnɪk]	(adj.) 衛生的
★**sanitary** [ˋsænəˏtɛrɪ]	(adj.) 公共衛生的 ● a bad sanitary condition 衛生條件不良
atopic dermatitis [əˋtɑpɪk ˏdɜməˋtaɪtɪs]	(n.) 異位性皮膚炎

adrenaline [æd`rɛnl̩ɪn]	(n.) 腎上腺素 (= epinephrine)；一陣激動
*****implant** [ɪm`plænt]	(v.) 移植 ● implant a piece of bone 植入一塊骨頭
genetic code [ʤə`nɛtɪk kod]	(n.) 基因碼，遺傳密碼
*****influenza** [ˌɪnflu`ɛnzə]	(n.) 流行性感冒 (= flu)
*****complication** [ˌkɑmplə`keʃən]	(n.) 併發症；混亂
diarrhea [ˌdaɪə`riə]	(n.) 腹瀉 ! 注意發音。
acrophobia [ˌækrə`fobɪə]	(n.) 懼高症 參 -phobia …恐懼症
cholera [`kɑlərə]	(n.) 霍亂
relapse [rɪ`læps]	(v.)（疾病等）復發 (= return/reappear) (n.) 舊疾復發
*****symptom** [`sɪmptəm]	(n.) 症狀；徵兆 ● subjective symptom 自覺症狀
dietary therapy [`daɪəˌtɛrɪ `θɛrəpɪ]	(n.) 飲食療法
midwife [`mɪdˌwaɪf]	(n.) 助產士
medical examination [`mɛdɪkl̩ ɪgˌzæmə`neʃən]	(n.) 健康檢查
heartbeat [`hartˌbit]	(n.) 心跳 (= pulse)
*****heart disease** [hart dɪ`ziz]	(n.) 心臟病 (= heart trouble)
heart attack [hart ə`tæk]	(n.) 心臟病發作

★**Medicare** [ˋmɛdɪˏkɛr]	(n.)（美國）高齡者醫療保險（制度） 參 Medicaid（美國）貧民的醫療補助（medical aid 的簡寫）
★**diagnosis** [ˏdaɪəgˋnosɪs]	(n.) 診斷 ● make a diagnosis on the case of... 對…的病患作診斷
lifestyle-related disease [ˋlaɪfˏstaɪl rɪˋletɪd dɪˋziz]	(n.) 生活習慣導致的疾病
★**asthma** [ˋæzmə]	(n.) 氣喘，哮喘 參 asthmatic (adj.) 氣喘的 (n.) 氣喘患者
★**remove** [rɪˋmuv]	(v.) 取出，切除 (= extirpate)
★**sunstroke** [ˋsʌnˏstrok]	(n.) 中暑
heatstroke [ˋhitˏstrok]	(n.) 中暑 (= heat exhaustion)
★**brain death** [bren dɛθ]	(n.) 腦死 (= cerebral death) 參 euthanasia (n.) 安樂死 (= mercy killing)
★**pneumonia** [njuˋmonjə]	(n.) 肺炎
fertility drug [fɝˋtɪlətɪ drʌg]	(n.) 受孕藥；刺激排卵劑
pneumoconiosis [ˏnjuməˏkonɪˋosɪs]	(n.) 塵肺病，肺塵埃沉著病
★**leukemia** [luˋkimɪə]	(n.) 白血病，血癌
cystitis [sɪsˋtaɪtɪs]	(n.) 膀胱炎 參 cyst (n.) 囊腫；囊胞
folk medicine [fok ˋmɛdəsn̩]	(n.) 民俗療法
★**immune** [ɪˋmjun]	(adj.) 免疫的 ● immune response 免疫反應 參 immunity (n.) 免疫

immune system [ɪˋmjun ˋsɪstəm]	(n.) 免疫系統
★**immunization** [ˌɪmjənəˋzeʃən]	(n.) 免疫；預防接種 ● The Student Health Center can provide the immunization free of charge. 學生健康中心提供免費的預防接種。
★**depression** [dɪˋprɛʃən]	(n.) 憂鬱症
★**preventive medicine** [prɪˋvɛntɪv ˋmɛdəsn̩]	(n.) 預防醫學
clinical test [ˋklɪnɪkl̩ tɛst]	(n.) 臨床測試
★**appetite** [ˋæpəˌtaɪt]	(n.) 食慾，胃口
stethoscope [ˋstɛθəˌskop]	(n.) 聽診器
★**thermometer** [θɚˋmɑmətɚ]	(n.) 體溫計；溫度計
★**urine** [ˋjʊrɪn]	(n.) 尿
urinary organ [ˋjʊrəˌnɛrɪ ˋɔrgən]	(n.) 泌尿器官
shot [ʃɑt]	(n.) 注射
drip [drɪp]	(n.) 點滴 (= infusion) ● be put on a drip 打點滴
★**pharmacy** [ˋfɑrməsɪ]	(n.) 製藥業；藥房 (= drugstore)
★**prescription** [prɪˋskrɪpʃən]	(n.) 藥方，處方 參 prescribe (v.) 開（藥方）
gastritis [gæsˋtraɪtɪs]	(n.) 胃炎
★**mumps** [mʌmps]	(n.) 腮腺炎

★**ulcer** [`ʌlsɚ]	(n.) 潰瘍 (= canker) ● a stomach ulcer 胃潰瘍
★**hay fever** [he `fivɚ]	(n.) 花粉熱 (= pollen allergy)
slipped disk [slɪpt dɪsk]	(n.) 脊椎錯節，椎間盤突出
dislocated finger [`dɪslə͵ketɪd `fɪŋgɚ]	(n.) 手指脫臼
tuberculosis [tju͵bɝkjə`losɪs]	(n.) 結核病 (= TB)
hemorrhoids [`hɛmə͵rɔɪdz]	(n.) 痔瘡
hives [haɪvz]	(n.) 蕁麻疹
★**measles** [`mizl̩z]	(n.) 麻疹
chicken pox [`tʃɪkɪn pɑks]	(n.) 水痘
burn [bɝn]	(n.) 燒傷，灼傷 ● a burn on the finger 手指燒傷
★**nervous system** [`nɝvəs `sɪstəm]	(n.) 神經系統
★**nerve** [nɝv]	(n.) 神經 ● nerve strain 神經緊繃
neuron [`njʊrɑn]	(n.) 神經元；神經細胞
cerebrum [`sɛrəbrəm]	(n.) 大腦
cerebellum [͵sɛrə`bɛləm]	(n.) 小腦
vertebral column [`vɝtəbrəl `kɑləm]	(n.) 脊柱 (= spinal column)

★**stimulus** [ˋstɪmjələs]	(n.) 刺激 ❗複數形爲 stimuli。
★**respiration** [ˌrɛspəˋreʃən]	(n.) 呼吸
respiratory system [ˋrɛspərəˌtɔrɪ ˋsɪstəm]	(n.) 呼吸系統
inhale [ɪnˋhel]	(v.) 吸入（氣體等）
exhale [ɛksˋhel]	(v.) 呼出
lung [lʌŋ]	(n.) 肺 ● lung capacity 肺活量
nasal cavity [ˋnezḷ ˋkævətɪ]	(n.) 鼻腔
oral cavity [ˋorəl ˋkævətɪ]	(n.) 口腔
larynx [ˋlærɪŋks]	(n.) 喉頭
pharynx [ˋfærɪŋks]	(n.) 咽頭
★**vocal cord** [ˋvokḷ kɔrd]	(n.) 聲帶
trachea [ˋtrekɪə]	(n.) 氣管
pulmonary artery [ˋpʌlməˌnɛrɪ ˋɑrtərɪ]	(n.) 肺動脈
diaphragm [ˋdaɪəˌfræm]	(n.) 橫隔膜
aorta [eˋɔrtə]	(n.) 主動脈，大動脈
★**digest** [daɪˋdʒɛst]	(v.) 消化；融會貫通 ㊜ digestive system 消化系統

esophagus [i`sɑfəgəs]	(n.) 食道 (= gullet)
stomach [`stʌmək]	(n.) 胃 ● a sour stomach 腸胃不適
duodenum [ˌdjuə`dinəm]	(n.) 十二指腸 參 duodenal (adj.) 十二指腸的 ● a duodenal ulcer 十二指腸潰瘍
small intestine [smɔl ɪn`tɛstɪn]	(n.) 小腸
large intestine [lɑrdʒ ɪn`tɛstɪn]	(n.) 大腸
rectum [`rɛktəm]	(n.) 直腸
pancreas [`pæŋkrɪəs]	(n.) 胰臟
vermiform appendix [`vɝməˌfɔrm ə`pɛndɪks]	(n.) 闌尾，盲腸
appendicitis [əˌpɛndə`saɪtɪs]	(n.) 闌尾炎，盲腸炎 ● He was operated on for appendicitis. 他因為盲腸炎而動手術。
liver [`lɪvɚ]	(n.) 肝臟
gall bladder [gɔl `blædɚ]	(n.) 膽囊
bladder [`blædɚ]	(n.) 囊狀物；膀胱
uremia [jʊ`rimɪə]	(n.) 尿毒症
urethra [jʊ`riθrə]	(n.) 尿道
***kidney** [`kɪdnɪ]	(n.) 腎臟

skull [skʌl]	(n.) 頭蓋骨
forehead [ˋfɔr,hɛd]	(n.) 前額 (= brow)
temple [ˋtɛmpḷ]	(n.) 太陽穴
navel [ˋnevḷ]	(n.) 肚臍
knee [ni]	(n.) 膝，膝部 ● draw up one's knees 屈膝上提（屈起膝蓋後上提至胸部的動作）
***ankle** [ˋæŋkḷ]	(n.) 足踝；踝關節 ● sprain one's ankle 扭傷腳踝
toe [to]	(n.) 腳趾
trunk [trʌŋk]	(n.) 軀幹，身軀
hip [hɪp]	(n.) 屁股，臀部
waist [west]	(n.) 腰部
buttock [ˋbʌtək]	(n.) 屁股
***thigh** [θaɪ]	(n.) 大腿
heel [hil]	(n.) 腳後跟
elbow [ˋɛlbo]	(n.) 手肘 (v.) 用肘推擠前進 ● elbow someone aside 用手肘將人擠開
wrist [rɪst]	(n.) 腕；腕關節
palm [pɑm]	(n.) 手掌，手心

auditory [ˋɔdəˏtorɪ]	(adj.) 耳朵的；聽覺的 ● auditory difficulties 聽覺障礙
★**impulse** [ˋɪmpʌls]	(n.) 神經衝動；衝動 ● on impulse 衝動地，不加思索地
★**retina** [ˋrɛtɪnə]	(n.) 視網膜
pupil [ˋpjupḷ]	(n.) 瞳孔
pore [por]	(n.) 毛孔；氣孔
platelet [ˋpletlɪt]	(n.) 血小板
★**clot** [klɑt]	(n.)（血等的）凝塊 (v.) 凝結成塊 ● a clot of blood in the cut 傷口的血塊
white blood cell [hwaɪt blʌd sɛl]	(n.) 白血球
★**hormone** [ˋhɔrmon]	(n.) 荷爾蒙
saliva [səˋlaɪvə]	(n.) 唾液，涎 (= spittle)
★**physician** [fɪˋzɪʃən]	(n.) 醫師；內科醫生
★**surgeon** [ˋsɝʤən]	(n.) 外科醫生
pediatrician [ˏpidɪəˋtrɪʃən]	(n.) 小兒科醫師 參 pediatrics (n.) 小兒科
★**infection** [ɪnˋfɛkʃən]	(n.) 傳染；傳染病
★**vaccine** [ˋvæksin]	(n.) 牛痘苗；疫苗
vaccinate [ˋvæksṇˏet]	(v.) 接種牛痘，接種疫苗 ● Tourists from foreign countries must be vaccinated against yellow fever. 外國觀光客必須接種黃熱病疫苗。

醫學

★**smallpox** [ˋsmɔl͵pɑks]	(n.) 天花
diphtheria [dɪfˋθɪrɪə]	(n.) 白喉
typhoid [ˋtaɪfɔɪd]	(n.) 傷寒
★**polio** [ˋpolɪo]	(n.) 小兒麻痺症
tumor [ˋtjumɚ]	(n.) 腫瘤；腫塊
★**cancer** [ˋkænsɚ]	(n.) 癌症；惡性腫瘤 ● terminal cancer patients 癌症末期病患
★**correlation** [͵kɔrəˋleʃən]	(n.) 相互關係；相關性 ● There is a correlation between smoking and lung cancer. 抽菸和肺癌之間有關聯性。
AIDS [edz]	(n.) 愛滋病；後天免疫不全症候群 (Acquired Immunodeficiency Syndrome/Acquired Immune Deficiency Syndrome)
HIV	(n.) 愛滋病病毒；人體免疫缺損病毒 (the human immunodeficiency virus)
★**deficiency** [dɪˋfɪʃənsɪ]	(n.) 不足；缺陷 ● a vitamin deficiency 維他命不足
★**syndrome** [ˋsɪn͵drom]	(n.) 症候群，綜合症狀
★**anesthetize** [əˋnɛsθə͵taɪz]	(v.) 使麻醉，使麻痺
★**anesthesia** [͵ænəsˋθiʒə]	(n.) 麻醉 參 anesthetic (adj.) 麻醉的
★**transplant** [trænsˋplænt]	(v.) 移植 ● transplant a heart 移植心臟
arthritis [ɑrˋθraɪtɪs]	(n.) 關節炎

★**diabetes** [ˌdaɪəˋbitiz]	(n.) 糖尿病 ! 聽力測驗時注意發音。
diabetic [ˌdaɪəˋbɛtɪk]	(n.) 糖尿病患者 (adj.) 糖尿病的；罹患糖尿病的
★**obesity** [oˋbisətɪ]	(n.) 肥胖症，過胖 參 obese (adj.) 肥胖的
nausea [ˋnɔʃɪə]	(n.) 噁心，作嘔
dizziness [ˋdɪzənɪs]	(n.) 暈眩，頭昏眼花 參 dizzy (adj.) 暈眩的
★**coma** [ˋkomə]	(n.) 昏睡狀態，昏迷 (= lethargy) ● go into a coma 陷入昏迷
★**bleed** [blid]	(v.) 流血；給…抽血 ● bleed to death 流血過多而死
sprain [spren]	(v.) (n.) 扭傷 (= twist) ● sprain one's ankle 扭傷腳踝
★**fracture** [ˋfræktʃɚ]	(n.) 骨折；斷裂 ● suffer a fracture 骨折
dislocation [ˌdɪsloˋkeʃən]	(n.) 脫臼
★**bandage** [ˋbændɪdʒ]	(n.) 繃帶 (v.) 用繃帶包紮 ● put a bandage on a wound 用繃帶包紮傷口
adhesive-plaster [ədˋhisɪv ˋplæstɚ]	(n.) OK 繃
★**ointment** [ˋɔɪntmənt]	(n.) 軟膏；藥膏 ● rub ointment into one's arms 在手臂上塗抹藥膏
★**x-ray** [ˋɛks ˋre]	(n.) X 光；X 光檢查
forceps [ˋfɔrsəps]	(n.)〔用複數形〕（醫療用的）鑷子
scalpel [ˋskælpəl]	(n.)（手術用的）解剖刀

★**stretcher** [`strɛtʃɚ]	(n.) 擔架
★**throat** [θrot]	(n.) 喉嚨，咽喉 ● I have a sore throat. 我喉嚨痛。
★**chest** [tʃɛst]	(n.) 胸部
★**abdomen** [`æbdəmən]	(n.) 腹部 (= belly)
★**rib** [rɪb]	(n.) 肋骨
★**joint** [dʒɔɪnt]	(n.) 關節 ● set the arm in joint 把（脫臼的）手關節接回去
gullet [`gʌlɪt]	(n.) 食道
spleen [splin]	(n.) 脾臟
anus [`enəs]	(n.) 肛門
★**womb** [wum]	(n.) 子宮；孕育處 ● from womb to tomb (= from cradle to grave) 從生到死，一生
jaw [dʒɔ]	(n.) 顎，下巴
chin [tʃɪn]	(n.) 下巴
gum [gʌm]	(n.) 齒齦
encephalomyelitis [ɛn,sɛfəlo,maɪə`laɪtɪs]	(n.) 腦脊髓炎
aneurysm [`ænjə,rɪzəm]	(n.) 動脈瘤 參 varicose veins 靜脈瘤，靜脈曲張
arachnoid [ə`ræknɔɪd]	(n.) 蛛網膜 (adj.) 蛛網膜的 參 subarachnoid hemorrhage 蛛網膜下腔出血

★**spine** [spaɪn]	(n.) 脊柱；脊椎骨
spinal [ˋspaɪnḷ]	(adj.) 脊髓的；脊柱的 ● spinal anesthesia 脊髓麻醉
spinal cord [ˋspaɪnḷ kɔrd]	(n.) 脊髓
★**spinal injury** [ˋspaɪnḷ ˋɪndʒərɪ]	(n.) 脊髓損傷
hernia [ˋhɝnɪə]	(n.) 疝氣；脫腸 (= rupture)
metastases [məˋtæstəsɪs]	(n.) 轉移；新陳代謝
amnesia [æmˋniʒɪə]	(n.) 記憶喪失；健忘症
brain tumor calcification [bren ˋtjumɚ ˏkælsəfɪˋkeʃən]	(n.) 腦瘤鈣化
★**artery** [ˋɑrtərɪ]	(n.) 動脈 參 vein (n.) 靜脈
encephalitis [ˏɛnsɛfəˋlaɪtɪs]	(n.) 腦炎
nodule [ˋnɑdʒul]	(n.) 小瘤；小結
pituitary [pɪˋtjuəˏtɛrɪ]	(adj.) 腦下垂體的
ovule [ˋovjul]	(n.)（植物）胚珠；（動物）卵細胞
jugular [ˋdʒʌgjəlɚ]	(adj.) 頸部的；頸靜脈的 (n.) 頸靜脈
hydrocephalus [ˏhaɪdrəˋsɛfələs]	(n.) 腦水腫
hemorrhage [ˋhɛmərɪdʒ]	(n.) 出血 ● suppress a hemorrhage 止血

Parkinsonism [`parkɪnsə,nɪzm̩]	(n.) 帕金森氏症
★**stroke** [strok]	(n.) 中風
thyroid [`θaɪrɔɪd]	(n.) 甲狀腺
goiter [`gɔɪtɚ]	(n.) 甲狀腺腫
iodine [`aɪə,daɪn]	(n.) 碘
thyroid calcification [`θaɪrɔɪd ,kælsəfɪ`keʃən]	(n.) 甲狀軟骨鈣化
thyroid carcinoma [`θaɪrɔɪd ,karsɪ`nomə]	(n.) 甲狀腺癌
abdominal muscle [æb`damənl̩ `mʌsl̩]	(n.) 腹部肌肉
Achilles tendon [ə`kɪliz `tɛndən]	(n.) 阿基里斯腱；跟腱（腳跟與小腿間的大塊肌腱）
airborne irritant [`ɛr,born `ɪrətənt]	(n.) 空氣中的刺激物（如花粉等）
amniocentesis [,æmnɪosɛn`tisəs]	(n.) 羊膜穿刺術
amniotic fluid [,æmnɪ`atɪk `fluɪd]	(n.) 羊水
★**anemic** [ə`nimɪk]	(adj.) 貧血（症）的 參 anemia (n.) 貧血（症）
anticoagulant [,æntɪko`ægjələnt]	(n.) 抗凝血劑
★**antibiotic** [,æntɪbaɪ`atɪk]	(n.)〔常用複數〕抗生素 • administer antibiotics to the patient 開抗生素給患者
antibody [`æntɪ,badɪ]	(n.) 抗體

blood clotting [blʌd `klatɪŋ]	(n.) 凝血
★**blood pressure** [blʌd `prɛʃɚ]	(n.) 血壓 參 manometer (n.) 血壓計
★**blood vessel** [blʌd `vɛsḷ]	(n.) 血管
Caesarean birth [sɪ`zɛrɪən bɝθ]	(n.) 剖腹生產
chemotherapy [ˏkimo`θɛrəpɪ]	(n.) 化學療法
★**chronic illness** [`kranɪk `ɪlnɪs]	(n.) 慢性病 參 an acute illness 急症
circumcision [ˏsɝkəm`sɪʒən]	(n.) 割包皮，割禮
colostrum [kə`lastrəm]	(n.)（產婦的）初乳
compress [`kamprɛs]	(n.)（止血用的）壓布；濕敷布
★**constipation** [ˏkanstə`peʃən]	(n.) 便秘
★**contraction** [kən`trækʃən]	(n.)（疾病等）感染；收縮 ● the contraction of a disease 罹患某種疾病
cough [kɔf]	(n.) 咳嗽；咳嗽聲 (v.) 咳嗽；咳出 ● cough suppressant 止咳劑 ● whooping cough 百日咳
decongestant [ˏdikən`dʒɛstənt]	(n.)（尤指鼻子的）充血緩和劑；鼻塞藥
★**dehydration** [ˏdihaɪ`dreʃən]	(n.) 脫水
diuretic [ˏdaɪjʊ`rɛtɪk]	(adj.) 利尿的 (n.) 利尿劑
Down's syndrome [daʊnz `sɪnˏdrom]	(n.) 唐氏症；蒙古症（因專攻此症的 J.L.H. Down 醫師而得名）

eczema [ˋɛksɪmə]	(n.) 濕疹
emphysema [ˌɛmfɪˋsimə]	(n.) 氣腫；肺氣腫
glucose [ˋglukos]	(n.) 葡萄糖
fetal [ˋfitḷ]	(adj.) 胎兒的；胚胎的
★**fetus** [ˋfitəs]	(n.) 胎兒
★**embryo** [ˋɛmbrɪˌo]	(n.) 胚胎（尤指受孕至第八週）；胚芽
swaddle [ˋswɑdḷ]	(n.) 襁褓
genital [ˋdʒɛnətḷ]	(adj.) 生殖的；生殖器的 (n.)〔常用複數〕生殖器官
gestation [dʒɛsˋteʃən]	(n.) 懷孕 (= pregnancy/conception)；懷孕期
★**pregnant** [ˋprɛgnənt]	(adj.) 懷孕的 ● She is pregnant. (= She is expecting a baby.) 她懷孕了。
frostbite [ˋfrɔstˌbaɪt]	(n.) 凍傷，凍瘡 ● suffer from frostbite 凍傷
glaucoma [glɔˋkomə]	(n.) 青光眼
gonorrhea [ˌgɑnəˋriə]	(n.) 淋病
heartburn [ˋhɑrtˌbɝn]	(n.) 胃灼熱 (= upset stomach)
★**hepatitis** [ˌhɛpəˋtaɪtɪs]	(n.) 肝炎

hepatitis B
[ˌhɛpəˋtaɪtɪs bi]

(n.) B 型肝炎
• provide proof of full immunization against the hepatitis B virus 提出 B 型肝炎免疫證明

hepatitis B vaccine
[ˌhɛpəˋtaɪtɪs bi ˋvæksin]

(n.) B 型肝炎疫苗

herpes
[ˋhɝpiz]

(n.) 皰疹

histamine
[ˋhɪstəˌmɪn]

(n.) 組織胺

humidifier
[hjuˋmɪdəˌfaɪɚ]

(n.) 增濕器

★**hypersensitivity**
[ˌhaɪpɚˌsɛnsəˋtɪvɪtɪ]

(n.) 過敏症

★**hypertension**
[ˌhaɪpɚˋtɛnʃən]

(n.) 高血壓 (= high blood pressure)
參 hypotension (n.) 低血壓

hypothermia
[ˌhaɪpəˋθɝmɪə]

(n.) 低體溫症

hysterectomy
[ˌhɪstəˋrɛktəmɪ]

(n.) 子宮切除術

insulin
[ˋɪnsəlɪn]

(n.) 胰島素

intravenous
[ˌɪntrəˋvinəs]

(adj.) 靜脈內的；靜脈注射（用）的

jaundice
[ˋdʒɔndɪs]

(n.) 黃疸，黃疸病

laryngitis
[ˌlærɪnˋdʒaɪtɪs]

(n.) 喉頭炎

lesion
[ˋliʒən]

(n.) 機能障礙；器官損害

letdown
[ˋlɛtˌdaʊn]

(n.) 減低；減退 (= decline)

ligament
[ˋlɪgəmənt]

(n.) 韌帶

★**membrane** [ˋmɛmbren]	(n.) 膜，薄膜
menopause [ˋmɛnə͵pɔz]	(n.) 更年期
★**miscarriage** [mɪsˋkærɪʤ]	(n.)（自然）流產 參 abortion (n.) 墮胎
ovary [ˋovərɪ]	(n.) 卵巢
★**pelvis** [ˋpɛlvɪs]	(n.) 骨盆 ● the pelvis major/minor 大 / 小骨盆
placenta [pləˋsɛntə]	(n.) 胎盤
postpartum [͵postˋpɑrtəm]	(adj.) 產後的 ● postpartum depression 產後憂鬱症
prostate gland [ˋprɑs͵tet glænd]	(n.) 前列腺
rash [ræʃ]	(n.) 起疹子 (= eruption)
rubella [ruˋbɛlə]	(n.) 德國麻疹
★**secrete** [sɪˋkrit]	(v.) 分泌；隱藏 參 secretion (n.) 分泌（物）
spasm [ˋspæzm]	(n.) 痙攣，抽搐
★**sterilization** [͵stɛrələˋzeʃən]	(n.) 絕育（手術）；殺菌；消毒 參 sterile (adj.) 不孕的；殺菌的
syphilis [ˋsɪfəlɪs]	(n.) 梅毒
testis [ˋtɛstɪs]	(n.) 睪丸
tetanus [ˋtɛtənəs]	(n.) 破傷風 (= lockjaw)

toxemia
[tɑks`imɪə]
(n.) 毒血症

tranquilizer
[`træŋkwɪˌlaɪzɚ]
(n.) 鎮定劑

tuberculin skin test
[tju`bɝkjəlɪn skɪn tɛst]
(n.) 結核菌素皮膚試驗（反應）(= tuberculin reaction)

umbilical cord
[ʌm`bɪlɪkḷ kɔrd]
(n.) 臍帶

uterus
[`jutərəs]
(n.) 子宮 (= womb)

★**viral infection**
[`vaɪrəl ɪn`fɛkʃən]
(n.) 病毒感染

wheeze
[hwiz]
(n.) 氣喘所發出的聲音

★**breakdown**
[`brekˌdaʊn]
(n.)（精神、體力等）衰弱；崩潰
- a nervous breakdown 精神崩潰

cholesterol level
[kə`lɛstəˌrol `lɛvḷ]
(n.) 膽固醇指數

★**malady**
[`mælədɪ]
(n.) 病 (= disease)

★**curtail**
[kɜ`tel]
(v.) 縮減，削減
- curtail medical spending 削減醫療經費

★**pulse**
[pʌls]
(n.) 脈搏
- The doctor felt/took her pulse.
  醫生測量她的脈搏。

★**coronary**
[`kɔrəˌnɛrɪ]
(n.) 冠狀動脈 (adj.) 冠狀的；冠狀動脈的
- a coronary occlusion 冠狀動脈閉塞
- coronary thrombosis 冠狀動脈血栓

★**epidemic**
[ˌɛpɪ`dɛmɪk]
(n.) 流行病；（流行病的）傳播

★**incubation**
[ˌɪnkjə`beʃən]
(n.) 潛伏期 (= incubation period)

★**plague** [pleg]	(n.) 瘟疫 (v.) 使苦惱
★**intoxication** [ɪn͵tɑksə`keʃən]	(n.) 中毒；醉
★**poisoning** [`pɔɪzənɪŋ]	(n.) 中毒 ● lead poisoning 鉛中毒
★**addiction** [ə`dɪkʃən]	(n.) 成癮；沉溺 參 addict (v.) 使上癮 (n.) 上癮者
distend [dɪ`stɛnd]	(v.) 膨脹；擴張 ● Rapid ascent in water distends a lung. 在水中急速上升會使肺膨脹。
★**rupture** [`rʌptʃɚ]	(n.) 破裂；疝氣 (v.) 破裂

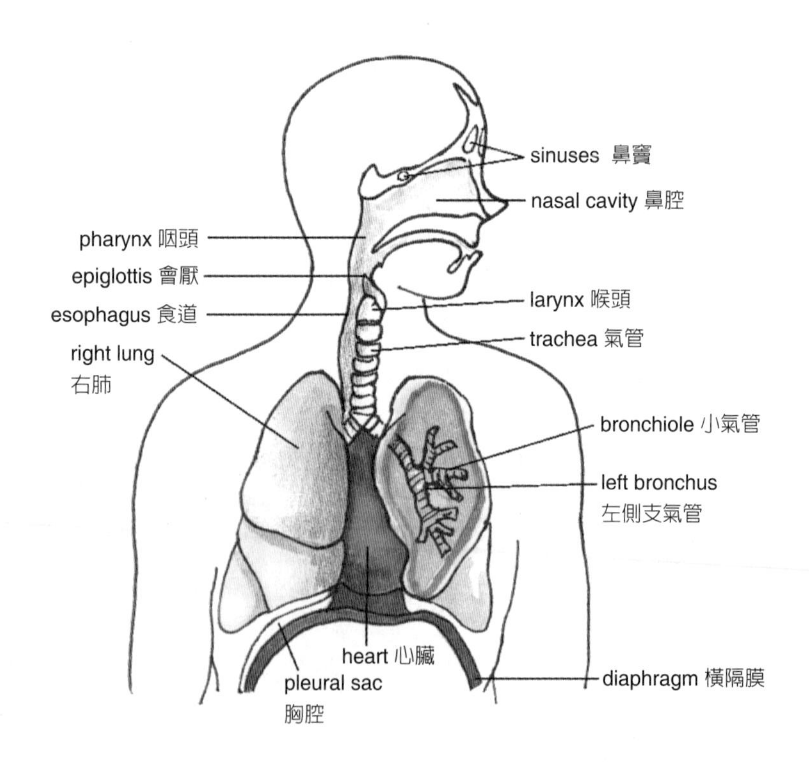

Meteorology

氣象學

MP3 167

parch [partʃ]	(v.) 使乾透；使燥熱
★**arid** [ˋærɪd]	(adj.) 乾旱的；乾燥的
icicle [ˋaɪsɪkḷ]	(n.) 冰柱，垂冰
★**fallout** [ˋfɔl͵aʊt]	(n.) 原子塵，輻射性落塵 (= radioactive fallout)
★**melt** [mɛlt]	(v.) 融化；熔化；溶解
★**devastating** [ˋdɛvəs͵tetɪŋ]	(adj.) 破壞性極大的，毀滅性的 ● a devastating flood 毀滅性的洪水
mist [mɪst]	(n.) 薄霧，靄 ● a thick mist 濃霧
fog [fag]	(n.) 霧，霧氣 ● A heavy/thick/dense fog hinders planes from landing. 濃霧阻礙了飛機的降落。
dew [dju]	(n.) 露 ● drops of dew 露珠
sleet [slit]	(n.) 霙；雨夾雪
hail [hel]	(n.) 冰雹
drizzle [ˋdrɪzḷ]	(n.) 毛毛雨 (v.) 下毛毛雨
squall [skwɔl]	(n.) 暴風
hurricane [ˋhɝɪ͵ken]	(n.) 颶風；暴風雨

snowstorm [ˋsno͵stɔrm]	(n.) 暴風雪
★**myriad** [ˋmɪrɪəd]	(n.) 無數，大量 ● myriads of particles 無數的粒子
★**minute** [maɪˋnjut]	(adj.) 微小的 ● minute dust 微小的灰塵
minuscule [mɪˋnʌskjul]	(adj.) 極小的
crystal [ˋkrɪstl̩]	(n.) 水晶；結晶體 ● crystals of snow 雪的結晶
★**stratum** [ˋstretəm]	(n.) 層 (= layer) ! 複數形是 strata。
★**cluster** [ˋklʌstɚ]	(n.) 簇；群
★**terrain** [ˋtɛren]	(n.) 地域；地形 ● hilly terrain 丘陵地帶
weather map [ˋwɛðɚ mæp]	(n.) 天氣圖，氣象圖 (= weather chart)
barometric pressure [͵bærəˋmɛtrɪk ˋprɛʃɚ]	(n.)（以水銀柱高度標示的）大氣壓力；氣壓 (= atmospheric/air pressure)
trough [trɔf]	(n.) 低壓槽；低谷
isobar [ˋaɪsə͵bɑr]	(n.) 等壓線
vapor [ˋvepɚ]	(n.) 水汽，蒸汽
★**centigrade** [ˋsɛntə͵gred]	(n.) (adj.) 攝氏（的）(= Celsius) ● 30°C (thirty degrees centigrade) 攝氏 30 度
★**Celsius** [ˋsɛlsɪəs]	(n.) (adj.) 攝氏（的）(= centigrade)
★**Fahrenheit** [ˋfærən͵haɪt]	(n.) (adj.) 華氏（的） ● 90°F (ninety degrees Fahrenheit) 華氏 90 度

gas composition [gæs ˌkampəˋzɪʃən]	(n.) 氣體組成
troposphere [ˋtrapəˌsfɪr]	(n.) 對流層
★**phenomenon** [fəˋnaməˌnan]	(n.) 現象 ! 複數形是 phenomena。
stratosphere [ˋstrætəˌsfɪr]	(n.) 同溫層，平流層
mesosphere [ˋmɛzəˌsfɪr]	(n.) 中氣層，中間層
thermosphere [ˋθɝməˌsfɪr]	(n.) 熱大氣層；熱電離層
ionosphere [aɪˋanəˌsfɪr]	(n.) 電離層
radio signal [ˋredɪˌo ˋsɪgnl̩]	(n.) 無線電訊號
ionized particle [ˋaɪənˌaɪzd ˋpartɪkl̩]	(n.) 離子化粒子
turbulence [ˋtɝbjələns]	(n.)（大氣的）亂流
northern hemisphere [ˋnɔrðɚn ˋhɛməsˌfɪr]	(n.) 北半球
southern hemisphere [ˋsʌðɚn ˋhɛməsˌfɪr]	(n.) 南半球
albedo [ælˋbido]	(n.) 反照率
★**transparent** [trænsˋpɛrənt]	(adj.) 透明的 ● transparent substance 透明物質
cirrus cloud [ˋsɪrəs klaud]	(n.) 卷雲
cumulonimbus [ˌkjumjəloˋnɪmbəs]	(n.) 積雨雲

★**lightning** [ˋlaɪtnɪŋ]	(n.) 閃電，閃光
tornado [tɔrˋnedo]	(n.) 龍捲風 (= twister)
moisture [ˋmɔɪstʃɚ]	(n.) 濕氣，潮濕
★**humidity** [hjuˋmɪdətɪ]	(n.) 濕氣，濕度
★**cold front** [kold frʌnt]	(n.) 冷鋒
★**warm front** [wɔrm frʌnt]	(n.) 暖鋒
stationary front [ˋsteʃənˏɛrɪ frʌnt]	(n.) 滯留鋒
★**probe** [prob]	(n.) (v.) 探查 ● a space probe 太空探測器
doldrums [ˋdaldrəmz]	(n.) 赤道無風帶
El Niño [ɛl ˋninjo]	(n.) 聖嬰現象（西班牙文。指赤道太平洋地區東部和中部海水溫度異常變暖的現象）
★**maritime** [ˋmærəˏtaɪm]	(adj.) 海的；沿海的
cyclone [ˋsaɪklon]	(n.) 氣旋；（熱帶性）低氣壓
thunderstorm [ˋθʌndɚˏstɔrm]	(n.) 大雷雨
breeze [briz]	(n.) 微風
gale [gel]	(n.) 強風（時速 32 至 63 英里）
★**swirl** [swɝl]	(v.) 打轉 (n.) 漩渦

congregate [`kaŋgrɪˏget]	(v.) 聚集；集合
★**mirage** [mə`raʒ]	(n.) 海市蜃樓
sighting [`saɪtɪŋ]	(n.) 觀測

27 Music & Theater
音樂與戲劇

MP3 168

lyre [laɪr]	(n.) 古希臘的七弦豎琴
overture [\`ovɚtʃɚ]	(n.)（歌劇的）序曲，前奏曲
***theatrical** [θɪ\`ætrɪkl]	(adj.) 劇場的，戲劇的；戲劇性的
***routine** [ru\`tin]	(n.) 固定劇目；一套固定舞步或動作
fugal [\`fjugəl]	(adj.) 賦格曲的 參 fugue (n.) 賦格曲
***compose** [kəm\`poz]	(v.) 作曲 (= write) • compose a symphony 作一首交響曲
symphony [\`sɪmfənɪ]	(n.) 交響曲，交響樂；和聲 參 concerto (n.) 協奏曲
choreography [ˌkorɪ\`agrəfɪ]	(n.)（芭蕾舞）編舞
sonata [sə\`natə]	(n.) 奏鳴曲
***piece** [pis]	(n.) 作品，曲，篇 • play a few pieces by Bach 彈奏幾首巴哈的作品
***improvisation** [ˌɪmprəvaɪ\`zeʃən]	(n.) 即興演出，即興創作 參 improvise (v.) 即興表演
nocturne [\`naktɜn]	(n.) 夜曲
suite [swit]	(n.) 組曲
woodwind [\`wudˌwɪnd]	(n.) 木管樂器 參 brass (n.) 銅管樂器 strings (n.) 絃樂器 percussion (n.) 打擊樂器

28 Philosophy

哲學

MP3 169

★**momentum** [mo`mɛntəm]	(n.) 動力；氣勢
Confucianism [kən`fjuʃə,nɪzm̩]	(n.) 孔子學說；儒學
★**ethics** [`ɛθɪks]	(n.) 倫理學；倫理，道德
expound [ɪk`spaʊnd]	(v.) 解釋，詳細述說 ● expound a hypothesis to someone 向某人詳細解釋一項假設
★**premise** [`prɛmɪs]	(n.) 假定，假設 ● the major premise （三段論法的）大前提
★**presume** [prɪ`zum]	(v.) 假定，推測 參 presumably (adv.) 也許，大概
★**attest** [ə`tɛst]	(v.) 證實，證明 ● He attested the truth of her statement. 他證實她的陳述屬實。
★**brood** [brud]	(v.) 沉思 ● brood over/on... 沉思…；憂慮…
fallibility [,fælə`bɪlətɪ]	(n.) 容易犯錯；出錯性
inexorable [ɪn`ɛksərəbl̩]	(adj.) 無法改變的；無情的 ● inexorable doom 無法改變的命運
★**reason** [`rizn̩]	(n.) 理性；理由；道理
★**paradigm** [`pærə,daɪm]	(n.) 範式，範例
determinism [dɪ`tɝmɪn,ɪzm̩]	(n.) 決定論

dualism [ˋdjuəlˏɪzm̩]	(n.) 二元論；雙重性
empiricism [ɛmˋpɪrəˏsɪzm̩]	(n.) 經驗主義；經驗論
exemplar [ɪgˋzɛmplɚ]	(n.) 模範；範例
★**introspection** [ˏɪntrəˋspɛkʃən]	(n.) 內省，反思 參 introspect (v.) 內省，反省
monism [ˋmɑnɪzm̩]	(n.) 一元論
normative [ˋnɔrmətɪv]	(adj.) 基準的；規範的 ● normative grammar 規範文法
paranormal [ˏpærəˋnɔrməl]	(adj.) 超過正常範圍的；超自然的
★**pragmatism** [ˋprægməˏtɪzm̩]	(n.) 實用主義
rationalism [ˋræʃənl̩ˏɪzm̩]	(n.) 理性主義
★**syllogism** [ˋsɪləˏʤɪzm̩]	(n.) 演繹推理；推斷
dogma [ˋdɔgmə]	(n.) 教條，教義；武斷
utilitarianism [ˏjutɪləˋtɛrɪənɪzm̩]	(n.) 功利主義
libertarianism [ˏlɪbɚˋtɛrɪənɪzm̩]	(n.) 自由意志論
communitarianism [kəˏmjunəˋtærɪənɪzm̩]	(n.) 社群主義（1993 年興起的一種政治理論，兼重公民個人權益與個人對社會的義務） 參 libertarianism (n.) 自由意志主義
altruism [ˋæltruˏɪzm̩]	(n.) 利他主義 參 egoism (n.) 利己主義

29 Physics
物理學

MP3 170

constrict
[kən`strɪkt]
(v.) 壓縮；束緊
● The instrument is constricted in the middle.
這種器具的中間部位束緊（例如沙漏）。

★**demolish**
[dɪ`malɪʃ]
(v.) 推翻；破壞；拆除
● That physicist demolished the homing theory.
那位物理學家推翻了歸巢理論。

★**magnify**
[`mægnə͵faɪ]
(v.) 放大；誇大
● This lens magnifies objects 1,000 times.
這個透鏡將物體放大一千倍。

★**static**
[`stætɪk]
(adj.) 靜電的；靜的 (n.)〔複數〕靜力學
● static electricity 靜電
反 dynamic (adj.) 動的

coil
[kɔɪl]
(v.) 捲，盤繞

★**conduction**
[kən`dʌkʃən]
(n.)（熱、電流等的）傳導

congeal
[kən`dʒil]
(v.) 凍結；凝結
● The fat congealed on the cold plates.
脂肪在冰冷的盤子上凝固了。

★**elastic**
[ɪ`læstɪk]
(adj.) 有彈性的，有彈力的
● an elastic bandage 彈性繃帶

★**friction**
[`frɪkʃən]
(n.) 摩擦；摩擦力
● the coefficient of friction 摩擦係數

★**gear**
[gɪr]
(n.) 齒輪；傳動裝置；（汽車）排檔
● the landing gear of an airplane 飛機的起落架

gleam
[glim]
(v.) 發微光；閃爍

plumb [plʌm]	(n.) 鉛錘，測鉛
★**reflex** [`riflɛks]	(n.) 反射；反射作用 (adj.) 反射的；反射作用的
★**simulation** [ˌsɪmjə`leʃən]	(n.) 模擬
★**vibrate** [`vaɪbret]	(v.) 顫動，震動
★**inversion** [ɪn`vɜʃən]	(n.) 反向，倒轉
★**slant** [slænt]	(v.) 傾斜，歪斜
★**upright** [`ʌpˌraɪt]	(adj.) 筆直的；垂直的 ● stand in an upright position 直挺挺地站著
★**relativity** [ˌrɛlə`tɪvətɪ]	(n.) 相對性；相關性，關聯性 ● Relativity 相對論
acoustics [ə`kustɪks]	(n.)〔作單數〕音響學；〔常作複數〕音響效果，音質
resonance [`rɛzənəns]	(n.) 共鳴；反響；共振
retention [rɪ`tɛnʃən]	(n.) 保留，保持；記憶力
★**optics** [`ɑptɪks]	(n.)〔作單數〕光學
quantum mechanics [`kwɑntəm mə`kænɪks]	(n.) 量子力學
vacuum [`vækjʊəm]	(n.) 真空
★**reflect** [rɪ`flɛkt]	(v.) 反射
★**reflection** [rɪ`flɛkʃən]	(n.) 反射；反射作用

refract [rɪˋfrækt]	(v.) 折射 ● refracting telescope 折射望遠鏡
★**refraction** [rɪˋfrækʃən]	(n.) 折射
convex lens [ˋkɑnvɛks lɛnz]	(n.) 凸透鏡
concave lens [ˋkɑnkev lɛnz]	(n.) 凹透鏡
objective [əbˋdʒɛktɪv]	(n.) 顯微鏡的接物鏡
eyepiece [ˋaɪˏpis]	(n.) 接目鏡
★**conduct** [kənˋdʌkt]	(v.) 傳導（熱、電等） ● conduct electricity 傳導電流
dynamo [ˋdaɪnəˏmo]	(n.) 發電機
resistance [rɪˋzɪstəns]	(n.) 阻力；電阻 ● overcome air resistance 克服空氣的阻力
IC	(n.) 積體電路 (= integrated circuit)
★**fission** [ˋfɪʃən]	(n.) 分裂 ● nuclear fission 核分裂
★**radio-** [ˋredɪˏo]	表示「無線電」、「輻射」、「放射」、「鐳」、「X 射線」的字根
kinematics [ˏkɪnəˋmætɪks]	(n.) 動力學，運動學
★**velocity** [vəˋlɑsətɪ]	(n.) 速度
★**frequency** [ˋfrikwənsɪ]	(n.) 頻率 ● frequency modulation 調頻；調頻廣播（簡稱 FM）
neural [ˋnjʊrəl]	(adj.) 神經的

prism [`prɪzm]	(n.) 稜鏡
vector [`vɛktɚ]	(n.) 向量；矢量
*__coordinate__ [ko`ɔrdnɪt]	(n.) (adj.) 座標（的）
viscosity [vɪs`kɑsətɪ]	(n.) 黏度，黏性
hydrostatic pressure [ˌhaɪdrə`stætɪk `prɛʃɚ]	(n.) 流體靜力壓力
streamline [`strimˌlaɪn]	(n.) (adj.) 流線型（的）
laminar flow [`læmɪnɚ flo]	(n.) 層流
turbulent flow [`tɝbjələnt flo]	(n.) 亂流；紊流
phase velocity [fez və`lɑsətɪ]	(n.) 相速度，相速
convection [kən`vɛkʃən]	(n.)（熱、電的）對流
thermodynamics [ˌθɝmodaɪ`næmɪks]	(n.)〔作單數〕熱力學
kinetic energy [kɪ`nɛtɪk `ɛnɚdʒɪ]	(n.) 動能
potential energy [pə`tɛnʃəl `ɛnɚdʒɪ]	(n.) 位能
*__inertia__ [ɪn`ɝʃə]	(n.) 慣性，惰性 ● roll under its own inertia 在慣性下滾動
torque [tɔrk]	(n.) 力矩；轉矩

30 Political Science

政治學

MP3 171

★**nationality** [ˌnæʃə`nælətɪ]	(n.) 國籍；民族
outcry [`aʊtˌkraɪ]	(n.) 吶喊；強烈的抗議
uphold [ʌp`hold]	(v.) 支持；舉起 ● uphold a district court's decision 支持地方法院的判決
★**ally** [ə`laɪ]	(v.) 結盟；聯合 ● The country has been allied with the US for more than half a century. 該國和美國結盟已逾半世紀。
★**deterrent** [dɪ`tɜrənt]	(n.) 抑制；抑制力 (adj.) 抑制的 ● the nuclear deterrent 核防禦力
★**autonomy** [ɔ`tɑnəmɪ]	(n.) 自治；自治團體
★**censor** [`sɛnsɚ]	(n.)（出版品、電影等的）審查員 (v.) 審查（出版品、電影等）
council [`kaʊnsḷ]	(n.) 會議；協調會；地方議會
despotism [`dɛspətˌɪzṃ]	(n.) 專制政治 (= autocracy/tyranny)
dispatch [dɪ`spætʃ]	(v.) 派遣；快遞 ● dispatch the Foreign Minister to the U.N. General Assembly 派遣外交部長參加聯合國大會
★**doctrine** [`dɑktrɪn]	(n.) 主義；信條；政策；學說 ● the Monroe Doctrine 門羅主義（1823 年由門羅總統在國會咨文中宣布的外交政策，內容為美歐兩洲互不干涉彼此的政治）
domineer [ˌdɑmə`nɪr]	(v.) 跋扈，作威作福

enactment [ɪn`æktmənt]	(n.)（法律的）制定
***enact** [ɪn`ækt]	(v.) 制定（法律） ● The bill is expected to be enacted during the present session. 該法案可望在這個會期中通過。
espouse [ɪs`paʊz]	(v.) 擁護，支持；信奉（主義、學說等） ● He enthusiastically espoused the Monroe Doctrine. 他熱烈支持門羅主義。
***expel** [ɪk`spɛl]	(v.) 驅逐；開除，把…除名 ● be expelled from... 從…驅逐；被逐出…
***federal** [`fɛdərəl]	(adj.) 聯邦（制）的；聯邦政府的 ● the federal government of the U.S. 美國聯邦政府 參 state government 州政府
forfeit [`fɔrfɪt]	(n.)（權利、名譽等的）喪失；沒收物；罰金 ● the forfeit of one's civil rights 公民權的喪失
***imprison** [ɪm`prɪzn̩]	(v.) 監禁；束縛
***inaugurate** [ɪn`ɔgjə,ret]	(v.) 為…舉行就職典禮；使正式就任；開始
***jurisdiction** [,dʒʊrɪs`dɪkʃən]	(n.) 司法；司法權
***ministry** [`mɪnɪstrɪ]	(n.)〔字首常大寫〕政府的部，內閣 ● The Ministry has resigned. 內閣已總辭。
***nominate** [`nɑmə,net]	(v.) 提名；任命，指派
***oversee** [`ovɚ`si]	(v.) 監督，監視
postal [`postl̩]	(adj.) 郵政的；郵局的 ● In the early days of the United States, postal charges were paid by the recipient. 在美國早期，郵資是由收件人支付的。
***premier** [`primɪɚ]	(n.) 首相，總理

★**regime** [rɪ`ʒim]	(n.) 政體；政權 ● a socialist regime 社會主義政體
★**regulation** [ˌrɛgjə`leʃən]	(n.) 規定；規章 ● traffic regulations 交通法規
reinstate [ˌriɪn`stet]	(v.) 使復職；使復原，使恢復 (= restore)
★**resign** [rɪ`zaɪn]	(v.) 辭去，辭職 (= step down) ● resign one's position as the Secretary of State 辭去國務卿的職務
★**resignation** [ˌrɛzɪg`neʃən]	(n.) 辭職；辭呈
restitution [ˌrɛstə`tjuʃən]	(n.) 復職；歸還；賠償
★**scapegoat** [`skepˌgot]	(n.) 代罪羔羊
★**sovereign** [`sɑvrɪn]	(n.) 君主，元首，最高統治者 參 sovereignty (n.) 主權
stipulate [`stɪpjəˌlet]	(v.)（契約、條款等）規定；約定
subordinate [sə`bɔrdnɪt]	(adj.) 下級的；次要的；隸屬的 (n.) 部屬
subversion [səb`vɜʃən]	(n.) 顛覆，打倒
★**superintend** [ˌsupərɪn`tɛnd]	(v.) 監督，管理，指揮
★**treason** [`trizn̩]	(n.) 叛國罪；通敵 ● high treason（對國家、元首等的）叛逆罪
denigrate [`dɛnəˌgret]	(v.) 詆毀，中傷
★**denounce** [dɪ`naʊns]	(v.) 公開譴責，指控 ● He was denounced by the press as a coward. 他被媒體公開指責為懦夫。

***forum** [`forəm]	(n.) 論壇，公開討論的場所；討論會
***ideology** [ˌaɪdɪ`ɑlədʒɪ]	(n.) 意識型態；思想體系
***intrigue** [ɪn`trig]	(n.) 陰謀，策劃，密謀 (v.) 耍陰謀；激起好奇心或興趣
leak [lik]	(v.) 滲，漏；洩漏（祕密等）
notify [`notəˌfaɪ]	(v.) 通知，公告
precept [`prisɛpt]	(n.) 訓誡，告誡
***proclaim** [prə`klem]	(v.) 宣告，公布，聲明 ● proclaim the country a republic 宣告該國為共和國
retort [rɪ`tɔrt]	(v.) 反擊；反駁
stenographer [stə`nɑgrəfɚ]	(n.) 速記員
stricture [`strɪktʃɚ]	(n.) 苛評，非難
***tacit** [`tæsɪt]	(adj.) 緘默的，不說話的
underscore [ˌʌndɚ`skor]	(v.) 強調；在…下方畫線 (= underline)
***alternative** [ɔl`tɝnətɪv]	(n.) 二擇一 (adj.) 兩者（或若干）擇一的；替代的 ● The only alternative to surrender is fighting. 投降以外的唯一選擇就是戰鬥。
antipode [`æntɪˌpod]	(n.) 正相反的事物
appraise [ə`prez]	(v.) 評價，鑑定 ● appraise a house for taxation 估算房子的價值以作為課稅依據

★**appropriate** [ə`proprɪɪt]	(adj.) 適當的；相稱的 參 appropriateness (n.) 適當
★**blunder** [`blʌndɚ]	(n.) 大錯 (v.) 犯大錯；跌跌撞撞地走或做事
boycott [`bɔɪˏkat]	(v.) 聯合抵制，拒絕參加（或購買等） ● boycott foreign products 抵制外國貨
★**coercion** [ko`ɝʃən]	(n.) 高壓政治；強制，強迫 參 coerce (v.) 強制，強迫
★**coherence** [ko`hɪrəns]	(n.) 一致性 參 cohesion (n.) 凝結（力）
constrain [kən`stren]	(v.) 強迫；限制 ● He was constrained to agree. 他被迫同意。
crass [kræs]	(adj.) 非常的；全然的；愚鈍的 ● crass ignorance 全然的無知
creditably [`krɛdɪtəblɪ]	(adv.) 值得稱讚地；有好名聲地
★**discrepancy** [dɪ`skrɛpənsɪ]	(n.) 不一致，不符；矛盾 (= contradiction)
fatuous [`fætʃʊəs]	(adj.) 愚昧的，昏庸的
frantic [`fræntɪk]	(adj.)（因喜悅、憤怒）發狂似的；狂亂的
hospitable [`haspɪtəbl̩]	(adj.) 好客的，招待周到的；（氣候環境等）宜人的
★**hospitality** [ˏhaspɪ`tælətɪ]	(n.) 好客，殷勤招待
★**impartial** [ɪm`parʃəl]	(adj.) 不偏不倚的，公正的 (= fair/equitable/even)
impotent [`ɪmpətənt]	(adj.) 無力的，虛弱的
injunction [ɪn`dʒʌŋkʃən]	(n.) 命令，指令；（法院的）禁止令，強制令

★**legitimate** [lɪˋdʒɪtəmɪt]	(adj.) 合法的；正當的 (v.) 使合法；使正當化 (= legitimize/legitimatize)
★**manifest** [ˋmænə͵fɛst]	(adj.) 顯然的，清楚的
militant [ˋmɪlətənt]	(adj.) 好戰的；激進的
★**neutral** [ˋnjutrəl]	(adj.) 中立的 ● neutral parties 中立的黨派 參 neutralize (v.) 使中立
piquant [ˋpikənt]	(adj.) 辛辣的；夠刺激的
★**priority** [praɪˋɔrətɪ]	(n.) 優先；優先權；優先考慮的事 ● give priority to... 給予…優先權
★**promising** [ˋpramɪsɪŋ]	(adj.) 有希望的，有前途的 ● a promising young politician 大有前途的年輕政治家
★**reconcile** [ˋrɛkən͵saɪl]	(v.) 使和解，調停
stricken [ˋstrɪkən]	(adj.) 被擊中的
tangible [ˋtændʒəbl̩]	(adj.) 明確的；實體的
vehement [ˋviəmənt]	(adj.) 熱烈的；猛烈的 ● vehement argument 激烈的爭論
★**wholesome** [ˋholsəm]	(adj.) 有益健康的；有益的 ● wholesome advice 有益的忠告
★**allotment** [əˋlatmənt]	(n.) 分派；分配
alteration [͵ɔltəˋreʃən]	(n.) 變更，修改
alternation [͵ɔltɚˋneʃən]	(n.) 交替，輪流 ● alternation of generations 世代交替

centralize [ˋsɛntrəˌlaɪz]	(v.) 集中
clarify [ˋklærəˌfaɪ]	(v.) 澄清，闡明
★**clash** [klæʃ]	(n.) 衝突；(意見等) 不合 (v.) 衝突 ● a clash of opinions 意見不一致
convene [kənˋvin]	(v.) 聚集；集會；召集 (會議等)
★**discard** [dɪsˋkard]	(v.) 拋棄，摒棄
disqualify [dɪsˋkwaləˌfaɪ]	(v.) 使喪失資格 ● He was disqualified by his age. 他因為年齡而喪失資格。
★**distort** [dɪsˋtɔrt]	(v.) 扭曲；曲解 ● distort the truth 扭曲事實
★**entitle** [ɪnˋtaɪtl̩]	(v.) 給…權力、資格；給…稱號 ● He is not entitled to choose his own successor. 他無權選擇自己的繼承人。
escalate [ˋɛskəˌlet]	(v.) 逐步上升、增強或擴大
★**evade** [ɪˋved]	(v.) 逃避，迴避
★**facilitate** [fəˋsɪləˌtet]	(v.) 使 (事情) 容易；促進
outburst [ˋaʊtˌbɝst]	(n.) (情感、力量等) 爆發
pacify [ˋpæsəˌfaɪ]	(v.) 使平靜，撫慰
★**partake** [parˋtek]	(v.) 參加 (= take part/participate)；分享
★**suppress** [səˋprɛs]	(v.) 鎮壓，平定

terminate [ˋtɜmə͵net]	(v.) 結束，終止 ● terminate the meeting by 5 五點前結束會議
★**exponent** [ɪkˋsponənt]	(n.)（原理、學說等的）闡述者；倡導者；典型 ● He was one of the early exponents of free trade. 他是最早倡導自由貿易的人士之一。
coordination [ko͵ɔrdn̩ˋeʃən]	(n.) 協調，調和
★**defer** [dɪˋfɜ]	(v.) 推遲；延期 (= delay/postpone/put off)
deflect [dɪˋflɛkt]	(v.)（使）偏斜；（使）轉向
detract [dɪˋtrækt]	(v.) 轉移，使分心 (= distract)；減損（價值、名聲等）
★**divert** [dəˋvɜt]	(v.) 使轉向；轉移（注意力），使分心 ● divert the course of a stream 使河流改道
★**drastic** [ˋdræstɪk]	(adj.) 猛烈的；嚴厲的；極端的 ● take drastic measures 採取激烈的手段
duration [djʊˋreʃən]	(n.)（時間的）持續；持久；持續期間 ● filing period duration 接受申請期間
entangle [ɪnˋtæŋgl̩]	(v.) 纏住；使捲入，連累
★**menace** [ˋmɛnɪs]	(n.) 威脅，恐嚇
neighboring [ˋnebərɪŋ]	(adj.) 鄰近的 (= adjacent)
perpetuate [pɚˋpɛtʃʊ͵et]	(v.) 使永久存在，使不朽
★**plight** [plaɪt]	(n.) 困境，苦境
★**predecessor** [ˋprɛdɪ͵sɛsɚ]	(n.) 前任，前輩；（被取代的）原有事物
★**premature** [͵priməˋtjʊr]	(adj.) 過早的；不成熟的 ● premature decision 倉促的決定

★**quantum** [ˋkwantəm]	(n.) 定量；總量
★**reciprocal** [rɪˋsɪprəkḷ]	(adj.) 相互的；互惠的 參 reciprocity (n.) 相互利益
★**versus** [ˋvɜsəs]	(prep.) 對抗；與…相對 ! 常簡寫為 v.s.。
★**dissolve** [dɪˋzalv]	(v.) 解散；分解；溶解 • dissolve Congress 解散國會
parliamentary politics [ˌparləˋmɛntərɪ ˋpalətɪks]	(n.) 議會政治
★**deregulation** [dɪˌrɛgjʊˋleʃən]	(n.) 撤銷管制規定
administrative reform [ədˋmɪnəˌstretɪv rɪˋfɔrm]	(n.) 行政改革
★**move** [muv]	(v.) 提出（動議），提案 • I move that we should adjourn. 我提議休會。
introduce a motion [ˌɪntrəˋdjus] [ˋmoʃən]	(v.) 提出動議
★**second** [ˋsɛkənd]	(v.) 支持，贊成（動議、提案等） • Committeemen seconded his motion. 委員支持他的動議。
urgent motion [ˋɜdʒənt ˋmoʃən]	(n.) 緊急動議
★**censorship** [ˋsɛnsɚˌʃɪp]	(n.)（出版品等的）審查制度
★**consensus** [kənˋsɛnsəs]	(n.)（意見等的）一致；共識 • reach a consensus on the matter 在那個問題上達成共識
public interest [ˋpʌblɪk ˋɪntərɪst]	(n.) 公眾利益
★**Parliament** [ˋparləmənt]	(n.) 議會；（加拿大、英國的）國會 參 parliamentarian (n.) 國會議員 (= parliamentary member)

★**senator** [`sɛnətɚ]	(n.)〔字首常大寫〕參議員；(古羅馬）元老院議員
representative [ˌrɛprɪ`zɛntətɪv]	(n.)〔字首常大寫〕眾議院議員
★**congressman** [`kaŋgrəsmən]	(n.)〔字首常大寫〕國會議員（尤指美國眾議院議員）
the Diet [`daɪət]	(n.)（丹麥、日本等國的）國會，議會
★**caucus** [`kɔkəs]	(n.) 幹部會議；(政黨等的）核心小組
★**statutory** [`stætʃʊˌtorɪ]	(adj.) 法令的，法定的
committee [kə`mɪtɪ]	(n.) 委員會；監護人 ● He is on the finance committee. 他是財政委員會委員。
★**amend** [ə`mɛnd]	(v.) 修正（規則、提案等） ● amend the Constitution 修憲
political turmoil [pə`lɪtɪkḷ `tɝmɔɪl]	(n.) 政治騷動，政治不安
corruption [kə`rʌpʃən]	(n.)（道德的）墮落；敗壞；貪汙 ● corruption of political ethics 政治倫理敗壞
★**budget** [`bʌdʒɪt]	(n.) 預算 ● Congress approved the budget. 國會通過預算案。
★**tax revenue** [tæks `rɛvəˌnju]	(n.) 稅收
★**voter** [`votɚ]	(n.) 選舉人；投票人 參 voting (n.) 投票
★**election campaign** [ɪ`lɛkʃən kæm`pen]	(n.) 競選活動
hard money [hard `mʌnɪ]	(n.) 在競選募款中，直接捐給候選人的競選經費
soft money [sɔft `mʌnɪ]	(n.) 在競選募款中，不是直接捐給候選人，而是捐給政黨的競選經費

local assembly
[ˋlokḷ əˋsɛmblɪ]
(n.) 地方議會

exit poll
[ˋɛksɪt pol]
(n.)（對投票結果的）民意調查，出口民調

*__local authority__
[ˋlokḷ əˋθɔrətɪ]
(n.) 地方當局；地方政權

*__faction__
[ˋfækʃən]
(n.)（政黨等組織內部的）派別；小集團
● a political faction 政治派系

*__independent__
[ˌɪndɪˋpɛndənt]
(n.) 無黨派者

*__opposition party__
[ˌapəˋzɪʃən ˋpartɪ]
(n.) 反對黨，在野黨

*__ruling party__
[ˋrulɪŋ ˋpartɪ]
(n.) 執政黨

*__coalition__
[ˌkoəˋlɪʃən]
(n.)（政黨、國家等臨時結成的）聯盟；聯合
● a coalition cabinet 聯合內閣

pledge
[plɛʤ]
(n.) 保證，誓言
● a formal pledge to support the coalition cabinet 正式宣誓支持聯合內閣

*__civil war__
[ˋsɪvḷ wɔr]
(n.) 內戰
● the Civil War（美國）南北戰爭；（英國）清教徒革命戰爭

lobbyist
[ˋlabɪɪst]
(n.) 遊說通過議案者

*__run__
[rʌn]
(v.) 競選
● run for President 競選總統

*__candidate__
[ˋkændədet]
(n.) 候選人
● a presidential candidate 總統候選人

elector
[ɪˋlɛktɚ]
(n.) 選舉人

*__electoral__
[ɪˋlɛktərəl]
(adj.) 選舉的；選舉人的
● an electoral system 選舉制度

bill [bɪl]	(n.)（向國會提出的）法案，議案（bill 通過後即成為 act）；鈔票
★**constitution** [ˌkɑnstə`tjuʃən]	(n.) 憲法；制定 ● the Constitution 憲法 參 unconstitutional (adj.) 違憲的
judicial [dʒu`dɪʃəl]	(adj.) 司法的；審判的；法官的
house [haʊs]	(n.)〔字首大寫〕議院 ● the House of Representatives 美國眾議院
★**executive** [ɪg`zɛkjʊtɪv]	(adj.) 行政上的 ● executive powers 行政權 ● executive authority 行政當局
hearing [`hɪrɪŋ]	(n.) 公聽會 (= a public hearing)；審訊；聽取
impeach [ɪm`pitʃ]	(v.) 彈劾；檢舉 參 impeachment (n.) 彈劾；檢舉
secretary [`sɛkrəˌtɛrɪ]	(n.)〔字首大寫〕政府部門的首長 ● the Secretary of State（美國）國務卿
★**cabinet** [`kæbənɪt]	(n.) 內閣 ● cabinet reshuffle 內閣改組
★**administration** [ədˌmɪnə`streʃən]	(n.) 行政機構；政府 ● the new administration starting next month 新政府下個月上任
cabinet meeting [`kæbənɪt `mitɪŋ]	(n.) 內閣會議
★**monarch** [`mɑnɚk]	(n.) 君主；最高統治者
★**monarchy** [`mɑnɚkɪ]	(n.) 君主政治；君主政體
★**aristocracy** [ˌærəs`tɑkrəsɪ]	(n.)〔總稱〕貴族；特權階級；貴族統治
★**aristocrat** [æ`rɪstəˌkræt]	(n.)〔指個人〕貴族；主張貴族統治者

*check [tʃɛk]	(v.) 阻止；抑制 (n.) 阻止；制止 ● check one's anger 抑制怒氣
*appropriation [əˌproprɪˋeʃən]	(n.) 撥款；挪用，盜用 ● the Senate Appropriations Committee 美國參議院預算委員會
*treaty [ˋtritɪ]	(n.) 條約，協定；協議
*ratify [ˋrætəˌfaɪ]	(v.)（正式）批准，認可
*veto [ˋvito]	(n.) 否決；否決權 ● exercise the veto over the bill 對法案行使否決權
deputy [ˋdɛpjətɪ]	(n.) 代理人，代表；副手
camp [kæmp]	(n.) 陣營；擁護某一主義（或黨派）的人
deploy [dɪˋplɔɪ]	(v.) 展開；部署
defection [dɪˋfɛkʃən]	(n.) 背叛，變節
*census [ˋsɛnsəs]	(n.) 人口普查 ● a census taker 人口普查員
*constituency [kənˋstɪtʃuənsɪ]	(n.) 選舉區的全體選民；選舉區 ● strengthen one's constituency 鞏固地方選票
constituent [kənˋstɪtʃuənt]	(adj.) 有選舉權的；有憲法制訂（或修改）權的 (n.) 選民；委託人
hierarchy [ˋhaɪəˌrarkɪ]	(n.) 階級制度
municipal [mjuˋnɪsəpḷ]	(adj.) 市政的；地方自治的 ● municipal government 市政府
petition [pəˋtɪʃən]	(n.) 請願；請願書 ● sign a petition 簽署請願書

poll [pol]	(n.) 民意調查；投票；選舉 ● a telephone poll 電話投票
***preliminary** [prɪˋlɪməˏnɛrɪ]	(adj.) 預備的；初步的 ● preliminary elections 初選，預備選舉
***rally** [ˋrælɪ]	(n.)（政治上的）集會 ● a political rally 政治集會

31 Psychology

心理學

MP3 174

behaviorism [bɪˋhevjəˏɪzm̩]	(n.) 行為主義（即從純粹客觀立場觀之，人類或動物的一切行為，均可分析為刺激與反應）
egoist [ˋigoɪst]	(n.) 利己主義者；自我中心者
egotistical [ˏigəˋtɪstɪkl̩]	(adj.) 自我本位的；自負的
★**association** [əˏsosɪˋeʃən]	(n.) 聯想 ● There is an association between Lincoln and antislavery. 林肯和反奴隸制度常被聯想在一起。
★**hypocrisy** [hɪˋpɑkrəsɪ]	(n.) 偽善，虛偽
hysterics [hɪsˋtɛrɪks]	(n.) 歇斯底里
★**trauma** [ˋtrɔmə]	(n.)（精神方面的）創傷
affectation [ˏæfɪkˋteʃən]	(n.) 做作，裝模作樣；假裝
cognitive development [ˋkɑgnətɪv dɪˋvɛləpmənt]	(n.) 認知發展
ESP	(n.) 第六感 (= extrasensory perception)
clinical [ˋklɪnɪkl̩]	(adj.) 臨床的 ● clinical psychology 臨床心理學
functionalism [ˋfʌŋkʃənl̩ɪzm̩]	(n.) 功能主義；機能心理學
ganglion cell [ˋgæŋglɪən sɛl]	(n.) 神經節細胞
hypnosis [hɪpˋnosɪs]	(n.) 催眠狀態 ● under hypnosis 在催眠狀態中

*agony [`ægənɪ]	(n.) 極度痛苦；苦惱
*apprehension [ˌæprɪ`hɛnʃən]	(n.) 恐懼；憂心 (= anxiety/fear/concern)
*disdain [dɪs`den]	(v.) 蔑視，不屑 (= scorn) ● disdain a man for his vulgarity 輕視某人的粗俗
envision [ɪn`vɪʒən]	(v.) 想像 (= envisage)，展望
extrovert [`ɛkstroˌvɜt]	(adj.) 外向的 反 introvert (adj.) 內向的
indulgent [ɪn`dʌldʒənt]	(adj.) 縱容的，放縱的 參 indulge (v.) 放縱；沉溺
marked [mɑrkt]	(adj.)有記號的；顯著的 (= remarkable/striking/ noticeable/outstanding)
masochism [`mæzəˌkɪzm̩]	(n.) 性受虐狂；被虐待狂 反 sadism (n.) 虐待狂
mnemonic [nɪ`mɑnɪk]	(adj.) 記憶的；有助於記憶的 參 mnemonics (n.) 記憶術
*obsession [əb`sɛʃən]	(n.) 執念，擺脫不了的念頭或情感 參 obsessional (adj.) (n.) 患強迫症的（患者）
smug [smʌg]	(adj.) 沾沾自喜的
transcend [træn`sɛnd]	(v.) 超越，優於 參 transcendentalism (n.)（康德的）先驗論；（愛默生的）超越主義
*evoke [ɪ`vok]	(v.) 喚起（記憶等） ● His sermon evoked the past. 他的講道喚起過去的回憶。
*induce [ɪn`djus]	(v.) 誘發；導致 參 inducement (n.) 誘導；誘因
interwoven [ˌɪntɚ`wovən]	(adj.) 交織的；混雜的

★inferiority complex [ɪn,fɪrɪ`arətɪ `kamplɛks]	(n.) 自卑感 反 superiority complex 優越感
★hallucination [hə,lusn̩`eʃən]	(n.) 幻覺，妄想
neurosis [njʊ`rosɪs]	(n.) 神經官能症；神經病 參 neuro- 表「神經」之意的字根
★illusion [ɪ`ljuʒən]	(n.) 錯覺，幻覺
★anxiety [æŋ`zaɪətɪ]	(n.) 焦慮，掛念；渴望 參 anxious (adj.) 焦慮不安的；渴望的
★psychiatric [,saɪkɪ`ætrɪk]	(adj.) 精神病學的
psychiatric examination [,saɪkɪ`ætrɪk ɪg,zæmə`neʃən]	(n.) 精神檢查 (= mental examination)
psychoanalysis [,saɪkoə`næləsɪs]	(n.) 精神分析（學）；心理分析（學）
couch [kaʊtʃ]	(n.)（病人接受心理治療時躺的）沙發 ● a couch doctor 精神科醫生 (= psychiatrist)
★therapy [`θɛrəpɪ]	(n.) 治療，療法 ● speech therapy 語言障礙治療
psychotherapy [,saɪko`θɛrəpɪ]	(n.) 精神療法；心理療法
client [`klaɪənt]	(n.) 顧客，委託人
★conditioned response [kən`dɪʃənd rɪ`spans]	(n.) 條件反射 (= conditioned reflex)
★reinforce [,riɪn`fɔrs]	(v.) 強化（對刺激的反應），加強
reinforcement [,riɪn`forsmənt]	(n.) 強化，增強
peripheral [pə`rɪfərəl]	(adj.)（神經）末稍的；周圍的 ● peripheral nerves 末梢神經

somatic [so`mætɪk]	(adj.) 細胞體的；身體的；軀體的
parasympathetic [ˌpærəˌsɪmpə`θɛtɪk]	(adj.) 副交感神經的
sympathetic [ˌsɪmpə`θɛtɪk]	(adj.) 交感神經的
★**sensation** [sɛn`seʃən]	(n.) 感覺，知覺
★**phobia** [`fobɪə]	(n.) 恐懼症 參 acrophobia (n.) 懼高症
paranoid [`pærəˌnɔɪd]	(adj.) (n.) 偏執狂的（患者）
narcissistic [ˌnɑrsɪ`sɪstɪk]	(adj.) 自戀的，自我陶醉的 參 narcissism (n.) 自戀，自我陶醉
antisocial [ˌæntɪ`soʃəl]	(adj.) 反社會的
dissociative [dɪ`soʃɪˌetɪv]	(adj.)（心理）分裂的；反社會的
dissociate [dɪ`soʃɪˌet]	(v.)（意識）分裂；使分離 ● a dissociated personality 分裂人格
psychotic [saɪ`kɑtɪk]	(adj.) (n.) 精神病的（患者）
schizophrenia [ˌskɪtsə`frinɪə]	(n.) 精神分裂症
bias [`baɪəs]	(n.) 偏見；偏心 ● bias errors（統計學）誤差（推測值和正確值之間的差異）
phrenology [frɛ`nɑlədʒɪ]	(n.) 骨相學

32 Religious Studies
宗教學

MP3 175

cardinal
[ˋkɑrdnəl]
(n.)（羅馬天主教的）紅衣主教；樞機主教

deity
[ˋdiətɪ]
(n.) 神；神性
- the deities of ancient Greece 古希臘神祇

demon
[ˋdimən]
(n.) 惡魔，惡靈

★**mundane**
[ˋmʌnden]
(adj.) 世俗的；日常的

★**secular**
[ˋsɛkjələ˞]
(adj.) 世俗的 (= worldly)

parochial
[pəˋrokiəl]
(adj.) 教區的；地方性的

Pope
[pop]
(n.) (the~)（羅馬天主教）教宗
參 papal (adj.) 羅馬教宗的；天主教的

resurrection
[͵rɛzəˋrɛkʃən]
(n.)〔字首大寫〕耶穌復活；復活；復甦

★**sacred**
[ˋsekrɪd]
(adj.) 神的；神聖的
- sacred writings 宗教經典；聖書

salvation
[sælˋveʃən]
(n.) 拯救，救世

sanctify
[ˋsæŋktə͵faɪ]
(v.) 使神聖化

savior
[ˋsevjə˞]
(n.)〔字首大寫〕救世主，上帝

★**terminology**
[͵tɝməˋnɑlədʒɪ]
(n.) 術語，專門用語

★**theological**
[͵θiəˋlɑdʒɪkḷ]
(adj.) 神學上的
參 theology (n.) 神學

auspicious [ɔ`spɪʃəs]	(adj.) 吉利的，吉兆的；幸運的
chaste [tʃest]	(adj.) 貞潔的，純潔的 (= pure)
justice [`dʒʌstɪs]	(n.) 正義；公平 參 justification (n.) 正當化
mystify [`mɪstə,faɪ]	(v.) 使神祕化；欺騙，蒙蔽
★**inflict** [ɪn`flɪkt]	(v.) 給予（打擊），施以（處罰等）
purify [`pjʊrə,faɪ]	(v.) 純淨，淨化
revelation [,rɛvḷ`eʃən]	(n.) 天啓；揭示；暴露 ● the Revelation 啓示錄（《新約聖經》的末卷）
★**revive** [rɪ`vaɪv]	(v.) 復甦；復興 參 revival (n.) 復活，再生
★**missionary** [`mɪʃən,ɛrɪ]	(n.) 傳教士；倡導者
Christianity [,krɪstʃɪ`ænətɪ]	(n.) 基督教
Christian Fundamentalism [`krɪstʃən ,fʌndə`mɛntḷ,ɪzṃ]	(n.) 基督教基本要義派
Islam [`ɪsləm]	(n.) 回教，伊斯蘭教
Judaism [`dʒudɪ,ɪzṃ]	(n.) 猶太教
Buddhism [`bʊdɪzṃ]	(n.) 佛教
Confucius [kən`fjuʃəs]	(n.) 孔子

★**sin** [sɪn]	(n.)（宗教或道德上的）原罪；罪惡 ● the seven deadly sins 使人墮入地獄的七大罪（pride 傲慢，greed 貪婪，lust 邪淫，wrath 憤怒，gluttony 貪吃，envy 忌妒，sloth 怠惰）
★**redemption** [rɪ`dɛmpʃən]	(n.) 贖罪，救贖
serpent [`sɝpənt]	(n.) 蛇（尤指大蛇、毒蛇）(= snake)
★**atonement** [ə`tonmənt]	(n.)（耶穌的苦難和死促成的）上帝與人的和解；補償
★**service** [`sɝvɪs]	(n.) 宗教儀式；禮拜 ● The church holds 2 services on Sundays. 該教會每逢週日舉行兩次禮拜。
cathedral [kə`θidrəl]	(n.) 大教堂；主座教堂
mosque [mɑsk]	(n.) 清真寺
crusade [kru`sed]	(n.)〔字首常大寫〕十字軍東征；聖戰
Catholicism [kə`θɑlə͵sɪzm̩]	(n.) 天主教；天主教義、信仰及組織
Protestantism [`prɑtɪstənt͵ɪzm̩]	(n.) 新教；新教教義
theism [`θiɪzm̩]	(n.)（基督教的）一神論；有神論
atheism [`eθɪ͵ɪzm̩]	(n.) 無神論 參 atheist (n.) 無神論者
deism [`diɪzm̩]	(n.) 自然神論
monotheism [`mɑnoθi͵ɪzm̩]	(n.) 一神論；一神教 參 polytheism (n.) 多神論；多神教
★**sect** [sɛkt]	(n.) 分裂出來的教派（尤指異端）；派別

★**cult** [kʌlt]	(n.) 異教；教派；（一時的）狂熱，流行 ● He belonged to a strange religious cult. 他隸屬於一個奇特的教派。
★**adherent** [əd`hɪrənt]	(n.) 追隨者，擁護者 (= follower)
heathen [`hiðən]	(n.) 異教徒 (= pagan)
★**convert** [kən`vɝt]	(v.) 皈依，改變信仰 ● He was converted to Islam. 他改信回教。
★**faith** [feθ]	(n.) 信仰；信條
congregation [ˌkaŋgrɪ`geʃən]	(n.)（宗教的）集會；（教堂的）會衆
Anglican Church [`æŋglɪkən tʃɝtʃ]	(n.) 英國國教，聖公會
dissent [dɪ`sɛnt]	(v.) 不信奉國教
★**separate** [`sɛpəˌret]	(v.) 分開；脫離 ● Pilgrim Fathers separated from Anglican Church. 清教徒先驅脫離英國國教而獨立。
monastery [`manəsˌtɛrɪ]	(n.)（男子）修道院
denomination [dɪˌnamə`neʃən]	(n.) 宗派；教派 ● Protestant denominations 新教的各教派 參 sect (n.) 教派；分派
Presbyterianism [ˌprɛzbə`tɪrɪənˌɪzm̩]	(n.) 長老會；長老會教義
Methodist [`mɛθədɪst]	(n.) 衛理公會派教徒
Baptist [`bæptɪst]	(n.) 浸禮會教友 參 baptize (v.) 為…施洗或行浸禮
nonconformist [ˌnankən`fɔrmɪst]	(n.)〔字首大寫〕不屬於聖公會的英國基督教徒； 不順從一般公認信念習慣的人

Ecumenical Movement [ˌɛkjʊˋmɛnɪkḷ ˋmuvmənt]	(n.) 普世教會合一運動（指 19 世紀中葉以來教會合一的趨勢）
Gospel [ˋgɑspḷ]	(n.) 福音；福音書 參 evangelist (n.) 福音傳道者
christen [ˋkrɪsn̩]	(v.) 為…施洗；（施洗時）給…命名 ● They christened him John. 他們為他施洗並命名為約翰。
* **pious** [ˋpaɪəs]	(adj.) 虔誠的，篤信神的 (= devout/religious)
* **devout** [dɪˋvaʊt]	(adj.) 虔誠的，虔敬的 ● a devout Christian 虔誠的基督徒
* **worship** [ˋwɝʃɪp]	(v.) 崇拜 (= consecrate)
* **sermon** [ˋsɝmən]	(n.) 布道；說教
* **clergyman** [ˋklɝdʒɪmən]	(n.) 神職人員；牧師，教士 (= priest/pastor/parson/minister/reverend/rector)
* **preach** [pritʃ]	(v.) 布道，講道 ● preach on grace to people 對眾人布道，頌揚神的恩典
hymn [hɪm]	(n.) 讚美詩，聖歌
Fundamentalism [ˌfʌndəˋmɛntḷˌɪzm̩]	(n.) 基要主義
* **puritanical** [ˌpjʊrəˋtænɪkḷ]	(adj.) 道德上嚴格的；禁慾的
occult [əˋkʌlt]	(n.) 神祕學；神祕儀式 (adj.) 難以理解的；超自然的

33 Sociology
社會學

MP3 176

★**anonymous** [ə`nanəməs]	(adj.) 匿名的；來源不明的 ● an anonymous letter 匿名信
cater [`ketɚ]	(v.) 滿足需要（或慾望）(= supply)；提供飲食；承辦宴席 ● We cater to the needs of the disabled. 我們滿足殘障人士的需要。
★**celebrity** [sə`lɛbrətɪ]	(n.) 名人；名聲
civility [sɪ`vɪlətɪ]	(n.) 禮貌，客氣
★**inherent** [ɪn`hɪrənt]	(adj.) 內在的；與生俱來的 (= innate/inborn/natural) ● inherent rights 與生俱來的權利
onlooker [`an,lʊkɚ]	(n.) 觀衆；旁觀者
★**pedestrian** [pə`dɛstrɪən]	(n.) 步行者 (adj.) 行人的 ● Right of Way for Pedestrians 行人優先
populate [`papjə,let]	(v.) 居住於 ● a densely populated area 人口稠密地區
premarital [pri`mærətḷ]	(adj.) 婚前的
reception [rɪ`sɛpʃən]	(n.) 接待，接見；招待會 ● a wedding reception 婚宴
★**discrimination** [dɪ,skrɪmə`neʃən]	(n.) 歧視，不公平待遇 ● racial discrimination 種族歧視
discriminate [dɪ`skrɪmə,net]	(v.) 歧視 ● discriminate against a minority group 歧視少數團體
sexism [`sɛks,ɪzṃ]	(n.) 性別歧視 (= sex discrimination)

taboo [tə`bu]	(n.) 禁忌
★**sociable** [`soʃəbl̩]	(adj.) 好交際的；善交際的
socialize [`soʃə͵laɪz]	(v.) 使適應社會生活；社會化
stepmother [`stɛp͵mʌðɚ]	(n.) 繼母 參 stepfather (n.) 繼父
widower [`wɪdoɚ]	(n.) 鰥夫
boulevard [`bulə͵vard]	(n.) 林蔭大道；大馬路
bourgeois [bʊr`ʒwa]	(n.) 中產階級的人；資本家；庸俗的人 (adj.) 中產階級的；資產階級的；庸俗的
caste [kæst]	(n.)（印度社會的）種姓制度；（世襲的）社會等級
chaperon [`ʃæpə͵ron]	(n.)（陪伴未婚少女去社交場所的）年長女伴；（青少年社交聚會時在場的）監護人
civic [`sɪvɪk]	(adj.) 城市的；市民的 ● a civic duty 市民的義務
communal [`kamjʊnl̩]	(adj.) 自治體的；共同的；共有的
compartment [kəm`partmənt]	(n.) 隔間；（火車上的）小房間
★**compensation** [͵kampən`seʃən]	(n.) 補償；賠償；賠償金
★**corps** [kɔr]	(n.) 兵團；軍；部隊；團體 ● the Marine Corps （美國）海軍陸戰隊 ● the press corps 記者團 ! 注意發音。單複數同形，複數發音爲 [kɔrz]。

★**affect** [ə`fɛkt]	(v.) 影響；對…發生作用 (= have an effect on) ● The expansion of industries affected interior cities like Denver, Phoenix, and Salt Lake City. 各種產業的發展，對於丹佛、鳳凰城和鹽湖城等內陸城市產生影響。
depopulate [di`papjə͵let]	(v.)（戰爭、疾病等）使人口減少；滅絕（某地）人口 參 depopulation (n.) 人口減少
destitution [͵dɛstə`tjuʃən]	(n.) 窮困；缺乏
detour [`ditʊr]	(n.) 繞道，迂迴 ● make/take a detour 繞道
★**donate** [`donet]	(v.) 捐獻，捐贈 ● donate $10,000 to a charity 捐一萬美元給慈善團體
gangway [`gæŋ͵we]	(n.) 舷梯；（劇場等）座位間的通道
impoverish [ɪm`pavərɪʃ]	(v.) 使赤貧；耗盡（精力等）
industrialized [ɪn`dʌstrɪəl͵aɪzd]	(adj.) 工業化的 ● industrialized nations 工業國
instigate [`ɪnstə͵get]	(v.) 唆使，慫恿 ● instigate the students to resort to violence 煽動學生訴諸暴力
insurgent [ɪn`sɝdʒənt]	(adj.) 暴動的
lighthouse [`laɪt͵haʊs]	(n.) 燈塔 (= beacon)
locomotive [͵lokə`motɪv]	(n.) 火車頭
★**lottery** [`latərɪ]	(n.) 彩券
metropolitan [͵mɛtrə`palətn]	(adj.) 首都的；大都市的

parlor [ˋparlɚ]	(n.) 商店；客廳，起居室 ● a beauty parlor 美容院
paternity [pəˋtɝnətɪ]	(n.) 父權；父子關係
patriarchy [ˋpetrɪˌarkɪ]	(n.) 父權制；家長（或族長）統治；父系社會 反 matriarchy (n.) 母系社會
***paucity** [ˋpɔsətɪ]	(n.) 少量；缺乏 ● a paucity of information 資訊的缺乏
proprietor [prəˋpraɪətɚ]	(n.)（企業）所有人，經營者
***riot** [ˋraɪət]	(n.) 暴亂，騷亂 (= disturbance/uprising) ● Riots broke out in Los Angeles. 洛杉磯發生暴動。
***shipment** [ˋʃɪpmənt]	(n.) 裝運；裝載的貨物（量）
strand [strænd]	(v.) 處於困境；擱淺 ● be stranded at the airport 被困在機場
***thrifty** [ˋθrɪftɪ]	(adj.) 節儉的；茂盛的；繁榮的
tourism [ˋturɪzm̩]	(n.) 旅遊；觀光業
WASP [wasp]	(n.) 白盎格魯薩克遜新教徒 (= White Anglo-Saxon Protestant)（美國社會的北歐後裔，通常被當作有權勢、有影響力的代表）
***colloquial** [kəˋlokwɪəl]	(adj.) 口語的 (= spoken)
compliment [ˋkampləmənt]	(n.) 讚美，恭維 (= praise/tribute)
***materialism** [məˋtɪrɪəlˌɪzm̩]	(n.) 唯物主義；唯物論 參 materialist (n.) 唯物論者
questionnaire [ˌkwɛstʃənˋɛr]	(n.) 問卷，意見調查表

★**adverse** [æd`vɜs]	(adj.) 不利的，有害的；相反的 ● adverse criticism 不利的批評
★**aloofness** [ə`lufnɪs]	(n.) 冷漠，不關心
★**apathy** [`æpəθɪ]	(n.) 冷淡，漠不關心 參 apathetic (adj.) 漠不關心的
appall [ə`pɔl]	(v.) 使驚恐 ● be appalled at... 對…感到驚恐
appease [ə`piz]	(v.) 平息，緩和；撫慰 ● Management tried to appease labor by offering them a bonus. 資方試圖以提供紅利來安撫勞方。
bland [blænd]	(adj.) 和藹的；溫和的；枯燥乏味的 ● a bland story 枯燥乏味的故事
★**conform** [kən`fɔrm]	(v.) 遵守；適應；符合 ● Students were supposed to conform to the school dress code. 學生應該遵守學校的服裝規定。
confound [kən`faʊnd]	(v.) 使混亂；使不知所措；混淆 ● His strange behavior confounded us. 他怪異的舉止使我們感到困惑。
detrimental [ˏdɛtrə`mɛntḷ]	(adj.) 有害的 (= injurious)
★**discern** [dɪ`zɜn]	(v.) 分辨，看出 ● We could discern from his appearance that he was upset. 從他的樣子可以看出他很沮喪。
disconcerting [ˏdɪskən`sɜtɪŋ]	(adj.) 使人窘迫的，使人倉皇失措的
discredit [dɪs`krɛdɪt]	(n.) 不信任；名聲敗壞 (v.) 使丟臉；敗壞…的名聲；不信任 ● cast discredit on a theory 質疑一項理論
★**dismay** [dɪs`me]	(v.) 驚慌；沮喪 ● We were dismayed at the news of his death. 我們對他的死訊感到相當震驚。

exasperate [ɪgˋzæspəˏret]	(v.) 使惱怒；激怒 ● be exasperated at/by someone's behavior 被某人的行為激怒
★**exotic** [ɛgˋzɑtɪk]	(adj.) 異國情調的；外來的
fake [fek]	(n.) 冒牌貨；仿造品 (= counterfeit/imitation)
fervor [ˋfɝvɚ]	(n.) 熱烈，熱情 ● religious fervor 宗教的熱情
frenzy [ˋfrɛnzɪ]	(n.)（暫時的）狂熱；狂怒
★**folly** [ˋfɑlɪ]	(n.) 愚蠢，愚笨 ● the folly of speaking without notes 不看稿演講的蠢事
haphazard [ˏhæpˋhæzɚd]	(adj.) 無計畫的，隨意的
★**heed** [hid]	(n.) (v.) 留心，注意
inconsequential [ɪnˏkɑnsəˋkwɛnʃəl]	(adj.) 不合理的；不重要的
ingenuous [ɪnˋdʒɛnjʊəs]	(adj.) 率直的；無邪的
★**invaluable** [ɪnˋvæljəbḷ]	(adj.) 非常貴重的，無價的
invidious [ɪnˋvɪdɪəs]	(adj.) 誹謗的 (= insulting)；惹人不快的 (= offensive)
irritate [ˋɪrəˏtet]	(v.) 使惱怒；使煩躁 ㊜ irritability (n.) 暴躁，易怒 irritation (n.) 激怒
junk [dʒʌŋk]	(n.) 垃圾；廢話
mortify [ˋmɔrtəˏfaɪ]	(v.) 使羞愧；使悔恨 (= chagrin/frustrate)
★**nuisance** [ˋnjusṇs]	(n.) 討厭的人或事物；（非法）妨害；騷擾行為 ● a public nuisance 妨害公眾利益的人或物

obnoxious [əb`nɑkʃəs]	(adj.) 討厭的，可憎的
★**orderly** [`ɔrdəlɪ]	(adj.) 整齊的；有條理的；守秩序的 ! -ly 在此是形容詞字尾。
ostensibly [ɑs`tɛnsəblɪ]	(adv.) 表面上；明顯地
★**overwhelm** [ˌovə`hwɛlm]	(v.) 戰勝，征服；使不知所措
palpable [`pælpəbḷ]	(adj.) 可觸知的；可摸到的
pernicious [pə`nɪʃəs]	(adj.) 有害的 • an ideology pernicious to society 有害社會的思想
precarious [prɪ`kɛrɪəs]	(adj.) 不穩定的 (= unstable/unsteady/unsettled)
preclude [prɪ`klud]	(v.) 排除；防止，杜絕
★**prone** [pron]	(adj.) 有⋯傾向的；易於⋯的 (= liable) • She is prone to colds/catching colds. 她很容易感冒。
pungent [`pʌndʒənt]	(adj.)（氣味等）有刺激性的 (= sharp/strong) • a pungent smell of riot gas 催淚瓦斯的刺鼻味
remonstrate [rɪ`mɑnˌstret]	(v.) 抗議 (= protest)；反對；告誡 • Many consumer groups remonstrated with the government against high prices. 許多消費者團體因為高物價對政府提出抗議。
repel [rɪ`pɛl]	(v.) 擊退；排斥；抵制
repress [rɪ`prɛs]	(v.) 抑制 (= control)，壓抑；鎮壓 參 repressive (adj.) 抑制的；鎮壓的
righteousness [`raɪtʃəsnɪs]	(n.) 公正；正直；正當
★**ruthless** [`ruθlɪs]	(adj.) 無情的，殘忍的 (= cruel/merciless)

*salient [ˋselɪənt]	(adj.) 顯著的，突出的 (= prominent)
sanity [ˋsænətɪ]	(n.) 心智正常；神智清楚 參 sane (adj.) 神智清楚的；(思想) 健全的
*satiation [ˏseʃɪˋeʃən]	(n.) 滿足，滿意 參 satiate (v.) 使滿足
scrutinize [ˋskrutn̩ˏaɪz]	(v.) 詳細檢查 (= examine)
shrewd [ʃrud]	(adj.) 精明的；狡猾的；機靈的 ● He is shrewd in business. 他做生意很精明。
shun [ʃʌn]	(v.) 躲開，避開，迴避 (= avoid)
snobbery [ˋsnɑbərɪ]	(n.) 講究派頭；勢利眼 參 snob (n.) 勢利眼的人
stifling [ˋstaɪflɪŋ]	(adj.) 令人發悶的；令人窒息的 ● a stifling room 令人窒息的房間
tedious [ˋtidɪəs]	(adj.) 冗長乏味的；使人厭煩的 (= boring/dull/weary)
tenacious [tɪˋneʃəs]	(adj.) 堅韌的 (= tough)；堅持的
*trifle [ˋtraɪfl̩]	(v.) 輕視，疏忽 (n.) 瑣事；沒有價值的東西 ● This matter should not be trifled with. 這件事不可輕忽。
vigilance [ˋvɪdʒələns]	(n.) 警戒；警覺 (性) (= watch/caution/precaution)
abate [əˋbet]	(v.) 減少，減弱，減輕 ● abate someone's pain 減輕某人的痛苦
*arouse [əˋraʊz]	(v.) 喚起，激起
*crash [kræʃ]	(v.) (猛烈) 碰撞；(飛機等) 墜毀；失敗；破產 ● Two cars crashed (= collided) head on. 兩輛車迎面撞上。

dispense [dɪ`spɛns]	(v.) 免除；分配；分發 ● The linotype dispensed with hand-setting of type. 鑄排機省去了人工排字的麻煩。
dispersion [dɪ`spɝʃən]	(n.) 分散；散布
falsify [`fɔlsə,faɪ]	(v.) 竄改，偽造
*****fetch** [fɛtʃ]	(v.) 去拿來 (= go, get, and bring something)
huddle [`hʌdḷ]	(v.) 縮成一團；聚在一起
intensify [ɪn`tɛnsə,faɪ]	(v.) 加強，強化 ● The incident intensified his feeling of inferiority. 那個事故更加深了他的自卑感。
*****intrude** [ɪn`trud]	(v.) 侵入，闖入；打擾
*****jostle** [`dʒasḷ]	(v.) 推，擠 ● jostle someone away 把某人擠開
mingle [`mɪŋgḷ]	(v.) 混合；往來
*****obstruction** [əb`strʌkʃən]	(n.) 阻礙，障礙 (= obstacle/hindrance/bar/block/barrier)
pry [praɪ]	(v.) 窺探，窺視
*****publicity** [pʌb`lɪsətɪ]	(n.)（公眾的）注意，名聲；宣傳 ● gain publicity 出名
publicize [`pʌblɪ,saɪz]	(v.) 宣傳，公布
relinquish [rɪ`lɪŋkwɪʃ]	(v.) 放棄；讓與
stride [straɪd]	(v.) 跨大步走；跨越 (n.) 闊步；一大步的距離 ● stride off/away 邁大步走開

★tamper
[ˋtæmpɚ]
(v.) 竄改，偽造
- The document has been tampered with.
這份文件已被竄改過。

★thrust
[θrʌst]
(n.) 推進力，驅動力 (v.) 猛推
- The basic thrust of Western civilization is the pursuit of individual freedom.
促成西方文明的基本推動力是對於個人自由的追求。

★transmit
[trænsˋmɪt]
(v.) 傳送；傳遞 (= pass on)；傳播

travail
[ˋtrævel]
(n.) 辛苦勞動 (= pains/trouble/hardship)

utilize
[ˋjutḷˏaɪz]
(v.) 利用

estate
[ɪsˋtet]
(n.) 地產；財產

★access
[ˋæksɛs]
(n.) 接近；進入（的機會或權利）
- have access to something 能接近或使用某物

accessible
[ækˋsɛsəbḷ]
(adj.) 可接近的；可進入的；可使用的

beep
[bip]
(v.) 發嗶嗶聲；吹警笛
參 beeper (n.) 攜帶型的傳呼器 (= pager)

congest
[kənˋdʒɛst]
(v.) 充塞，擁擠
參 congestion (n.) 充塞，擁擠
- urban congestion 都會區的擁擠

★detergent
[dɪˋtɝdʒənt]
(n.) 洗潔劑

highbrow
[ˋhaɪˏbraʊ]
(n.) 知識份子

hinge
[hɪndʒ]
(v.) 給…裝鉸鏈；決定於 (n.) 鉸鏈；樞紐；關鍵
- Everything hinges on what we do next.
一切要看我們接下來的行動而決定。

hoop
[hup]
(n.) 箍；箍狀物；鐵環

★**impetus** [ˋɪmpətəs]	(n.) 推動，促進；推動力 ● The flow of people into these areas provided an enormous impetus to the expansion of the service industries. 這些地區因人口湧入，大幅刺激了服務業的發展。
★**outfit** [ˋaʊtˏfɪt]	(n.) 全套裝備；（尤指在特殊場合穿的）全套服裝 ● a complete cowboy outfit 一整套牛仔服裝
deviate [ˋdivɪˏet]	(v.) 偏離，出軌 ● deviate from social norms 不符合社會規範
★**devoid** [dɪˋvɔɪd]	(adj.) 缺乏的，沒有的 ● the world devoid of humor 缺乏幽默的世界
dislocate [ˋdɪsləˏket]	(v.) 使移動位置；使混亂 ● dislocate the operations of a factory 打亂了工廠的作業
displace [dɪsˋples]	(v.) 取代 (= substitute/replace)；移動，挪開；迫使…離開原來的位置 ● Oil has displaced (= replaced) coal. 石油已經取代了煤。
enormous [ɪˋnɔrməs]	(adj.) 巨大的，龐大的
formidable [ˋfɔrmɪdəbl̩]	(adj.) 可怕的，令人畏懼的；難以克服的 ● a formidable barrier between peoples 種族間難以跨越的障礙
haven [ˋhevən]	(n.) 避風港；避難所 (= shelter)
in-depth [ˋɪnˋdɛpθ]	(adj.) 深入的，徹底的 ● an in-depth analysis of an American city 對美國城市的深入分析
mockery [ˋmɑkərɪ]	(n.) 嘲笑，嘲弄 (= scorn/ridicule/taunt/jeer)
molestation [ˏmoləsˋteʃən]	(n.) 干擾；妨害
objectify [əbˋdʒɛktəˏfaɪ]	(v.) 使具客觀性；使具體化

outright [ˋaʊtˋraɪt]	(adj.) 徹底的，完全的 (= thorough/total)
overall [ˋovɚˏɔl]	(adj.) 全部的，全面的 ● an overall abolition 全面的廢止
queue [kju]	(v.) 排隊 (n.)（人或車輛為等候而排的）長列
★**realm** [rɛlm]	(n.) 領域；範圍 ● the realm of socially acceptable behavior 社會可接受的行為範圍
recipient [rɪˋsɪpɪənt]	(n.) 接受者 ● a heart transplant recipient 接受心臟移植手術的人
residue [ˋrɛzəˏdju]	(n.) 剩餘，殘餘 (= remainder)
★**revert** [rɪˋvɝt]	(v.) 回復；重提 參 revertible (adj.)（地產等）可歸還的
seclusion [sɪˋkluʒən]	(n.) 隔絕；隱居；孤立 (= isolation)
★**stale** [stel]	(adj.) 不新鮮的，腐壞的 ● stale bread 乾硬的麵包
★**national pension system** [ˋnæʃənl̩ ˋpɛnʃən ˋsɪstəm]	(n.) 國民年金制度 參 pension (n.) 退休金
old age pension [old edʒ ˋpɛnʃən]	(n.) 老人年金 ● Inflation has eroded an old age pension. 通貨膨脹使得老人年金減少。
★**segregation** [ˏsɛgrɪˋgeʃən]	(n.) 種族隔離 反 desegregation (n.) 廢止種族隔離
★**assimilate** [əˋsɪml̩ˏet]	(v.) 使（民族、語音等）同化；消化 ● The immigrants were assimilated with the natives. 移民和原住民同化了。
★**exile** [ˋɛksaɪl]	(n.) 放逐；流亡；被放逐者 (v.) 流放，放逐 ● He has been an exile from his native land for many years. 他離鄉背井許多年。

★**deportation** [ˌdiporˋteʃən]	(n.) 驅逐出境，放逐 ● a deportation order 驅逐令
★**convention** [kənˋvɛnʃən]	(n.) 慣例，習俗；會議；協定 ● break social conventions 打破社會習俗
★**custom** [ˋkʌstəm]	(n.)（社會團體的）習俗；慣例；〔字首常大寫，用複數〕海關；關稅 ● Bathing in River Ganges is a religious custom among Hindus. 在恆河中沐浴是印度教徒的一種宗教習俗。
★**coin** [kɔɪn]	(v.) 創造；鑄造（貨幣） ● Do you know who coined the New Deal? 你知道是誰創造了「新政」一詞嗎？
homosexuality [ˌhoməsɛkʃʊˋælətɪ]	(n.) 同性戀
heterosexuality [ˌhɛtərəˌsɛkʃʊˋælətɪ]	(n.) 異性戀
spouse [spaʊz]	(n.) 配偶 ● apply for a spouse visa 申請配偶的簽證
nuclear family [ˋnjuklɪɚ ˋfæməlɪ]	(n.) 核心家庭，小家庭（僅由父母及子女組成）
★**generation gap** [ˌdʒɛnəˋreʃən gæp]	(n.) 代溝
★**divorce** [dəˋvors]	(v.) (n.) 離婚 ● The couple asked to be divorced. 這對夫妻訴請離婚。
★**norm** [nɔrm]	(n.) 基準，規範 (= standard)
suicide [ˋsuəˌsaɪd]	(n.) 自殺
★**bias** [ˋbaɪəs]	(n.) 偏見 (= prejudice) ● political bias 政治偏見
★**population density** [ˌpapjəˋleʃən ˋdɛnsətɪ]	(n.) 人口密度

★**prejudice** [`prɛdʒədɪs]	(n.) 偏見；偏袒 (v.) 使抱偏見
★**distribution** [ˌdɪstrə`bjuʃən]	(n.) 分發；分配 ● population distribution 人口分布
★**population explosion** [ˌpɑpjə`leʃən ɪk`sploʒən]	(n.) 人口爆炸 (= population boom)
boom [bum]	(n.) 景氣繁榮；激增 (v.) 使迅速發展；使興旺 參 a baby boomer 美國出生於嬰兒潮時期的人
expansion [ɪk`spænʃən]	(n.) 擴展，擴張 ● a rapid expansion of population 人口的激增
★**surge** [sɝdʒ]	(v.)（海浪）洶湧；（人）蜂擁而至；激增 (n.) 波濤；激增
sparse [spɑrs]	(adj.) 稀疏的，稀少的 ● a sparse population 人口稀少 反 dense (adj.) 密集的
★**burgeon** [`bɝdʒən]	(v.) 萌芽；急速成長 ● the burgeoning suburbs 快速成長的郊區
influx [`ɪnflʌks]	(n.) 湧進，匯集；流入 ● the influx of immigrants 移民的湧入
mores [`mɔriz]	(n.)（一個社會共同的）習慣，習俗；道德觀
subculture [`sʌbˌkʌltʃɚ]	(n.) 次文化；亞文化群
counterculture [`kaʊntɚ`kʌltʃɚ]	(n.) 反文化（年輕一代對當今文化的反動）
★**fertility rate** [fɝ`tɪlətɪ ret]	(n.) 生育率，出生率
★**mortality rate** [mɔr`tælətɪ ret]	(n.) 死亡率 (= mortality/death rate)
acculturation [əˌkʌltʃə`reʃən]	(n.) 文化適應；同化過程

expulsion [ɪk`spʌlʃən]	(n.) 驅逐；開除；排除 ● an expulsion order（對外國人的）驅逐令
★**gender** [`ʤɛndɚ]	(n.) 性別 ● the feminine gender 女性
socialism [`soʃəl,ɪzṃ]	(n.) 社會主義 參 socialist party 社會主義黨
★**capitalism** [`kæpətḷ,ɪzṃ]	(n.) 資本主義（制度）
★**latent** [`letnt]	(adj.) 潛伏的；潛在的 (= potential) ● latent ability 潛在的能力
upward mobility [`ʌpwɚd mo`bɪlətɪ]	(n.) 向上流動；提升自己的政經地位
extended family [ɪk`stɛndɪd `fæməlɪ]	(n.) 大家庭（尤指三代以上同堂者） 參 nuclear family 小家庭
single-parent household [`sɪŋgḷ `pɛrənt `haus,hold]	(n.) 單親家庭
monogamy [mə`nɑgəmɪ]	(n.) 一夫一妻制
polygamy [pə`lɪgəmɪ]	(n.) 一夫多妻（制）；一妻多夫（制）
exogamy [ɛks`ɑgəmɪ]	(n.) 異族通婚
endogamy [ɛn`dɑgəmɪ]	(n.) 同族結婚
egalitarianism [ɪ,gælɪ`tɛrɪənɪzṃ]	(n.) 平等主義
★**fad** [fæd]	(n.) 一時的流行
★**vogue** [vog]	(n.) 流行；流行物 ● come into vogue 開始流行

comprehensive [ˌkamprɪˋhɛnsɪv]	(adj.) 廣泛的；無所不包的 ● CTBT (Comprehensive Test Ban Treaty) 全面禁止核試驗條約
widow [ˋwɪdo]	(n.) 寡婦
orphan [ˋɔrfən]	(n.) 孤兒
allowance [əˋlaʊəns]	(n.) 零用錢；津貼
***elderly** [ˋɛldəlɪ]	(adj.) 年老的 ● the elderly 老人
***the disabled** [dɪsˋebḷd]	(n.) 殘障者
charity [ˋtʃærətɪ]	(n.) 施捨；慈善事業 ● live on charity 靠救濟維生
***welfare** [ˋwɛlˌfɛr]	(n.) 福利；福利事業 ● social welfare 社會福利
***scheme** [skim]	(n.) 計畫；方案
***day-care** [ˋde ˌkɛr]	(adj.) 日間托兒的 ● a day-care center 托兒所
***leave** [liv]	(n.) 許可；休假 ● sick leave 病假
feminist [ˋfɛmənɪst]	(n.) 男女平等主義者；女性主義者
harass [ˋhærəs]	(v.) 騷擾；使煩惱
harassment [ˋhærəsmənt]	(n.) 騷擾；煩擾 ● sexual harassment 性騷擾
Women's Lib [ˋwɪmɪnz lɪb]	(n.) 婦女解放運動 (= Women's Liberation)

crusade [kru`sed]	(n.)〔字首常大寫〕十字軍東征；聖戰 ● a crusade against crime 打擊犯罪運動
workforce [`wɜk,fors]	(n.) 勞動力 (= labor force)
contraception [,kantrə`sɛpʃən]	(n.) 避孕（法）
***birth control** [bɜθ kən`trol]	(n.) 節育；避孕
***abortion** [ə`bɔrʃən]	(n.) 墮胎；流產
***incorporate** [ɪn`kɔrpə,ret]	(v.) 包含；吸收；合併 ● incorporate changes into the plan 將改變納入計畫中
profile [`profaɪl]	(n.) 人物簡介；概況；側面（像）
***inhabitant** [ɪn`hæbətənt]	(n.)（某地區的）居民 (= resident/dweller/citizen)
adjacent [ə`dʒesənt]	(adj.) 毗鄰的，鄰近的 ● The hotel is adjacent to the stadium. 那家旅館鄰近體育場。
***ration** [`ræʃən]	(n.) 糧食 (= provision/food)；定量
sustenance [`sʌstənəns]	(n.) 食物，糧食；生計
thaw [θɔ]	(v.)（冰、雪等）融化；溶解 ● thaw frozen food 把冷凍食品解凍
donor [`donɚ]	(n.) 贈送人；（器官等）捐贈者 ● a kidney donor 腎臟捐贈者
accommodation [ə,kamə`deʃən]	(n.) 住宿；適應；調節 ● The hotel has accommodations for 500 guests. 那家旅館可容納 500 名客人住宿。
trickle [`trɪkl̩]	(v.) 滴；細細地流

Appendix
附錄

附錄
Appendix

留學小辭典

以下整理出留學生到國外求學生活時常遇到的詞彙。

academic advisor	**輔導老師，指導教授**。就選科、選課、修習學分數等課業問題為學生提供建議者。
academic calendar	**學校行事曆** (= college calendar)。
academic year	**學年**，從九月至翌年五月，通常分為兩個學期 (semester) 或四個學季 (quarter)。
acceptance	**入學許可**。acceptance letter 即「入學許可書，錄取通知書」。
accreditation	**認可，認定**。美國沒有相當於台灣的教育部等負責認可大學機構的機關，大學機構的認可與管理由各地方政府負責執行。
add	**加選（課程）**。
admission	**入學許可**。admission with advanced standing 指「抵免學分入學」，admission as freshman 則是「入學成為大一生」。
admission office	**入學許可辦公室，招生處**。提供入學相關資料和申請書的窗口。
admissions committee	**入學審核委員會，招生委員會**。
adult education	**成人教育，進修教育**。以社會人士為對象的大學公開課程。也稱為 continuing education。
adult school	**成人學校，成人教育中心**。專為社會人士提供教育訓練課程的機構，有些地方政府機構或教會也會開設成人教育課程，例如為新移民開設英語課程。
advance deposit	**入學預訂金**。為了確認學生的就讀意願，有些學校會要求學生於正式入學前繳交訂金。
advanced standing	**學分承認，抵免學分**。學生轉學時，若在其他大學所修的學分被認定為有效，可以直接插入大二或大三就讀。

affidavit	**宣誓書**。申請外國學校時，有些學校會要求學生繳交 Affidavit of Financial Support，也就是「費用資助同意書」，以此證明學生有經費支援來源。
Alien Registration Card	**綠卡，永久居留證**。持有綠卡者沒有美國國籍，不算美國公民。
alumna/alumnae	**女校友〔單〕/〔複〕**。
alumnus/alumni	**男校友〔單〕/〔複〕**。
assignment	**作業，研究課題**。
assistantship	**助教、研究助理獎學金**。研究生若取得 assistantship，透過當助教或研究助理，每週工作 10-20 小時，即可取得學費全免或部分減免。
associate degree (AA/AS)	**準學士，副學士**。修畢二年制公立大學課程所取得的學位。(Associate of Arts：文科準學士 / Associate of Science：理科準學士)
attendance	**出席**。學生的學期成績會由出席率、上課發言情形 (class participation)、報告 (paper) 以及考試成績整合計算。
audit	**旁聽**。以旁聽生的身分在課堂中聽講，無法取得學分。
BA	**文科學士**，Bachelor of Arts 的簡稱。
BS	**理科學士**，Bachelor of Science 的簡稱。
blue book	**筆試作答簿**。在某些大學，筆試的作答簿為一本藍色封面的本子，考試前須自行至學校書局購買。
brainstorming	**集體研討，腦力激盪**。在小組討論中，大家各自提出點子以激發更多可能性，藉此取得討論結果。
bulletin	**大學發行的刊物**，介紹學校概況、規定及課程等。也可稱作 catalog。
cafeteria	**自助式餐廳**。
case study	**個案研究**。提出實際的例子加以分析，繼而整理出一套理論的研究方法。MBA 課程經常使用的方法。

cashier's office	**會計室，出納組** (= bursar's office)。
catalog	**大學發行的刊物**，介紹大學概況、規定、課程等。也可稱作 bulletin。
certificate program	**證照課程，證書課程**。通常是指社區大學的職業訓練課程，修畢一年課程即可取得結業證書。
check	**個人支票** (= personal check)。在美國的銀行開戶時，會同時開設一個支票帳戶 (checking account)。
citation	**引用**。寫論文時，必須明確標示所引用文句的出處。引用標註方式依論文格式而異。要特別注意避免產生抄襲 (plagiarism) 的情形。
class	**年級**。從第一年開始，大學四年分別稱為 freshman year, sophomore year, junior year, senior year。class 也可用於畢業班，例如 class of 2012（2012 年的畢業班級）。
class participation	**在課堂上踴躍發言或討論**。
class performance	**課堂表現**。例如出席情況，這對學期成績會有很大的影響。
coed	**男女合校**，co-education 的簡稱。也常用於表示男女混合的宿舍。
commencement	**畢業典禮** (= graduation ceremony)。在 5-6 月時舉行的學位授與儀式，畢業生通常會穿著學士服。
community college	**二年制公立大學，社區大學**。除了提供職業訓練課程，另有為了插班進入四年制大學而設的課程。對留學生來說，比較容易申請進入就讀。
comprehensive exam	**博士綜合測驗，資格考**。博士生在修習一定的學分之後，必須通過博士綜合測驗，才能成為博士候選人。與 qualifying exam 性質相近。
conditional acceptance	**條件式入學**。有些學校開放條件式入學，亦即申請學生若語言能力測驗成績未達標準，可先至學校修習語言課程以取得入學資格。

consortium	**由多所大學組成的大學聯盟**。學生可以使用聯盟中任何一所大學的資源設施，甚至可以至任何一所大學修課。
continuing education	**進修課程**。主要為提供給社會人士的公開課程，不過這些課程沒有給予學分。等於 adult education。
core curriculum	**必修通識課程**。等於 core requirements。
correspondence course	**函授課程**。透過信件指導的課程，目前已被線上課程 (online course) 取代。
course description	**課程概要**。詳列課程的授課教授、內容、授課時間、學分數、課程代碼等。
course load	**一學期 (semester) 所修的所有學分**。各科系每學期的必修學分通常介於 12-18 學分。
course number	**課程代碼**。為了方便選課並區別課程內容，所有課程都會編上一組號碼。通常編號愈大，課程難度就愈高。
course work	**修習科目**。指在大學或研究所修的科目。
cram	**考試前臨時抱佛腳**。cram school 指的是「補習班」。
credit	**學分 (= unit)**。大學的修課單位。學生能否畢業，不是看學生在大學上了幾年課，而是取決於是否取得足夠的學分。
curriculum vitae	**履歷表，工作經歷表 (= resume)**。
cut	**缺席，蹺課**，也可以用 skip。
deadline	**截止日期 (= the due date)**。
dean	**學院院長**。
dean's list	每學期公布的「**成績優秀者名單**」。
deferred admission	**延遲入學**。有些學校提供延遲入學制度，給學生多一點時間考慮跟準備，例如延遲一年入學。
degree	**學位**。
department	**科系，學系**。

diploma	**學位證書**，為證明取得足夠學分以及學位的證書。與畢業證書同義。
dismissal	**退學** (= kick out)。Class dismissed! 則是指「下課！」。
dissertation	**學術論文（主要是指博士論文）**。為 thesis 的同義字。
dorm	**宿舍**，dormitory 的簡稱，也可稱作 residence hall。
double major	**雙主修**，同時修兩個主修，畢業時可取得兩個學位，即雙學位，也稱作 dual major。
draft	**報告或論文的草稿**。加上 first, second, final 等字，可用來表示稿子完成的階段，例如 first draft（初稿）。
drop	**退選**。在學期中取消原本登記要修的課程。取消的時間愈早，愈有可能退回該課程學分費。
dropout	**中途退學（者）**。
due	**期限到了，要截止的**。例如：My history paper is due next Monday.（歷史報告的繳交期限是下週一。）
elective	**選修科目**。指必修科目之外，可以自由選修的科目。
ELP/ESL	English Language Program/English as a Second Language 的簡稱。指的是為非以英語為母語的學生舉辦的「**英語密集課程**」。
enroll	**註冊，入學**。
EPT	「**英語能力檢定測驗**」，為 English Proficiency Test 的簡稱。proficiency 意指「熟練」。
escort services	**校園護送服務**。基於安全考量，在學生有正當理由下，可聯絡學校的護送服務單位，護送學生至指定地點。例如深夜時護送學生從圖書館回到宿舍。
evaluation	**評價，調查報告**。
extension course	**為正規生之外的人開設的課程**，無法取得正式的學分。
extension of stay	**延長居留**。另外，要求延長論文的繳交期限也可以使用 extension 這個字，例如 ask for an extension（請求延長期限）。

extracurricular-activity	**課外活動**。
F/fail	**不及格**。在成績單上以 F 表示。
F-1	**學生簽證**。要赴美唸書的學生，在取得學校所發的 I-20（入學許可）之後，就可以去申請學生簽證。
faculty	**教授，全體教職員**。如果要單指一名教職員，則要用 a faculty member。faculty 也可以用來表示「學院」，例如 the Faculty of Theology（神學院）。
fee	**學費**。一般用 tuition and fees。
fellowship	特別指「**以研究生、研究員為對象的獎學金**」。另外，scholarship 泛指「獎學金」，grant 通常是指非營利機構（例如政府）提供的「補助金，助學金」，而 loan 則是「貸款」。
field of study	**研究領域**。
field work	**田野調查，實地考察** (= field trip)。運用觀察、訪問、問卷調查等方式進行的調查研究。
final/final exam	**期末測驗，期末考**。
financial aid	**獎學金、助學貸款等經濟援助**。
financial statement	**財務證明**。為申請外國學校或簽證時的必備文件，通常是指 bank/account statement（帳戶明細）。
fraternity	**兄弟會**。大學中由男學生組成的社交組織，有嚴格的入會標準。女學生的社交組織為 sorority。
freshman	**大學新生，大學一年級學生**。
FSA	**留學生顧問**，foreign student advisor 的簡稱。學生在申請入學許可 (I-20) 或學生簽證時，可以透過 FSA 取得協助。
full load	**每學期正規生必須修習的學分**。
full-time student	**正規生**。每學期的學分不得低於規定，大學一般規定必須修習 12 個學分以上，研究所則是 9 個學分以上。持學生簽證的留學生，一般都必須是 full-time 的正規生。

furnished studio	**附家具的公寓**。
GED	**高中同等學力測驗**，General Educational Development test 的簡稱。如果通過了，就會給予與高中畢業同等學歷的證明。
general education	**通識教育**。大學一、二年級學生所修的基礎科目，等於 general studies/liberal arts。
GMAT	申請 MBA（企業管理研究所）課程的入學適性測驗，Graduate Management Admission Test 的簡稱。測驗內容涵蓋英語、數學、分析能力。
go over	**複習** (= review)。
GPA	**平均分數**，Grade Point Average 的簡稱。這是入學審查的評定項目之一。
grading system	**成績評定法**。在美國，學生的成績是以 A, B, C, D, F 五個等級評判。而在計算 GPA 時，就可以依照 A = 4 分、B = 3 分、C = 2 分、D = 1 分、F = 0 分的方法計算。
graduate assistant	**研究生助理**。協助教授授課或研究的研究生。
graduate school	**研究所**。
grant	**提供給清貧學生或研究計畫的助學金**。
GRE	要申請美國各大學研究所（企管、醫學、法學以外）所必須參加的測驗，Graduate Record Examinations 的簡稱。有一般測驗（英語、數學）和專業科目測驗。
handicapped sticker	**身障者專用停車格貼紙**。
handout	**講義**。
health center	**健康中心**。大學裡的健康中心，學生在這裡可以得到醫療上的照護。
health insurance	**健康保險**。
higher education	主要指「**大學教育**」。
honor society	**榮譽學會**。只邀請成績優秀的學生加入，有特別課程、獎學金等諸多特別待遇，相當有助於學生日後的發展。

honors program	**資優生計畫**。以資優學生為對象，使其能充分發揮才能的計畫。
housing office	**協助辦理學生住宿等相關事宜的事務所**。例如申請學校宿舍，通常透過這裡辦理。
(the) humanities	**人文科學**。
I.D.	**身分證**，identity card 或 identification card 的簡稱。student ID 指「學生證」。
I-20	**入學許可**。學生取得學校所發的 I-20 後，才能辦理學生簽證。
I-94	**出入境表格**。入境美國的外籍旅客所必須填寫的表格。
immunization requirement	**免疫接種要求**。依據各州的規定，學生於入學前必須提供已接種德國麻疹等預防注射的證明。
independent study	**獨立研究**。在教授的指導之下，研究生獨立進行研究以取得學分的課程。
instructor evaluation sheet	**授課評分表**。由學生針對教授的授課填寫的評分表，最後繳交至教務處。
interdisciplinary major	**跨學科主修**。學生透過選修跨科系或領域的科目，組合出自己有興趣、但該大學科系沒有提供的主修。例如環境資訊、綜合政策等。
internship	**實習**。實際參與和主修領域相關的工作，並進行研究報告以取得學分的修習計畫。
interview	**面試**。申請 MBA 或 LLM 時，大多會有這一項入學審查項目。
JD	**法律士**，Juris Doctor 的簡稱。指的是在 law school 完成 3-4 年課程而取得的學位。
joint degree	**雙聯學位**。某些大學提供學生至其他大學選修不同課程，畢業時可取得兩個學位，例如 MBA & International Relations 等。
junior	**四年制大學的三年級生**。
junior college	**二年制大學**，可以取得準學士學位。

kick-out	**退學** (= dismissal)。
laboratory/lab	**實驗室**。
late registration	**延遲選課登記**。
leave of absence	**休學**。由於生病等因素，學生可以申請休學一段時間。
lecture	**授課**。
liberal arts	**人文教育，文科教育**。有人文科學、社會科學、自然科學等領域。
liberal arts college	**文理學院**。比起專業科目，其重點大多放在人文教育方面的科目上。大多是學生人數少的私立大學。
LLM	**法學碩士**，Master of Laws 的簡稱。修畢 law school 的研究所課程而取得的學位。
loan	**助學貸款**。提供給學生的貸款，一般規定於畢業後幾年要開始還款。
lower-division course	**基礎課程**，通常課程代碼落在 100-200 間。
LSAT	**法學院入學測試**，Law School Admission Test 的簡稱。為美國法學院申請入學的審核項目之一。
major	**主修**。留學生申請學校時就必須決定主修，不過在美國大學要更改主修並不會太困難。
make-up exam	**補考**。針對有正當理由無法參加考試的學生而增設的考試。
mandatory	**必修的**。也可以用 required。
Master's degree	**碩士**。通常完成兩年研究所課程就可以取得碩士學位，依據主修，有 MA（文學碩士）、MS（理學碩士）、MBA（企業管理碩士）、LLM（法學碩士）等。
matriculation	**註冊，大學入學許可**。matriculation student 為「取得正式入學許可的學生」。
MD	**醫學博士**，Doctor of Medicine 的簡稱。完成 medical school 研究所課程的學生所取得的學位。

meal plan/meal card	有些學校的學生餐廳，會推出有優惠折扣的方案及預付卡，學生持預付卡至餐廳用餐，就可以享有不同折扣。
medical insurance	**醫療保險**。
midterm/midterm exam	**期中測驗，期中考**。
minor	**副修**。
natural sciences	**自然科學**。
non-resident	**非當地居民的外籍居住者**，例如留學生。由於不用繳納稅金，所以就算是就讀州立大學，學費也很高。
notary public	**公證人**。於申請人提出文件時證明其身分或為其作保。
notification	**錄取與否的通知**。
office hours	教授待在研究室、開放給學生的時間，以回應學生的提問或討論。
on-campus work	**校園內的工讀**，例如助教 (TA)、處理宿舍事宜的宿舍諮詢員 (RA) 等，工作內容多元。
online application	有些學校提供「**線上入學申請**」。不過，大部分仍必須寄送財力證明、成績單等文件。
open admission	不用入學審查，當申請者提出申請即可入學。社區大學一般採用這個方式。
open-book exam	**可以帶參考書、字典等的測驗**。
oral exam	**口試**。
orientation	**新生訓練**。在新學期時針對新生舉辦的說明會，介紹選課、校園生活等事宜。
overload	選修學分已達每學期的上限，但仍可加選。這是對上一學期成績優異的人所特別開放的。
paper	**報告**。一般會用 term paper 來表達。
parking sticker	**停車證**。
part-time student	**兼職生**。所修的學分數低於正規生。通常不開放給留學生。

pass-fail grading system	不以 A, B, C 等級數評分，而是以及格或不及格來評分的方式。
PE	**體育**，physical education 的簡稱。
personal check	**個人支票**。與 check 同義。
PhD	**博士**，Doctor of Philosophy 的簡稱。完成研究所的博士課程後取得的最高學位。
physical sciences	**（生物以外的）自然科學**。
placement test	**能力分級測驗**。有些科系要求能力分級測驗，學生可依據測驗結果選擇適合的課程。
plagiarism	**抄襲**。寫論文時，任意引用或盜用文獻的行為。這是非常嚴重的情形，可能會遭學校處罰、甚至退學處分。
pop quiz	**小考，臨時測驗**。
portfolio	**作品集**。申請藝術或建築等系所的學生，在入學審查時，大多需要附上相關作品集。
postgraduate	**研究所** (= graduate)。
practical training	**實習**。在大學、研究所畢業後一年內，可以利用學生簽證於專業領域內進行實習的制度。
prerequisite	**先修課程**。在選修某課程之前必須先修過的課程，有時若教授許可，可以免修。例如基礎會計即為高等會計的先修課程。
presentation	**口頭報告，簡報** (= oral report)。
probation	**留校察看**，也稱作 academic probation。大部分學校都會要求學生的 GPA 成績，對於 GPA 成績過低的學生，會給予 probation 警告，若成績依舊沒有起色，可能會遭退學處分。
professional school	**專業研究所**。與學術系統有別，分為 business school, medical school, law school 等。
professor emeritus	**名譽教授**。
prospective student	**預備學生**。尚未正式錄取，將來有機會被錄取的學生。

qualifying exam	**博士資格考**。博士生在修習一定的學分後，必須通過資格考，才能成為博士候選人 (candidate)。
quarter	**學季**。一個學年分為四個學季，一學季約為 11 個星期。通常是九月、一月、四月和六月時開學。
questionnaire	**問卷調查表**。
quiz	**在課堂中舉行的小測驗**。
RA	**宿舍諮詢員**，resident assistant 的簡稱。通常是由住在宿舍中的學生擔任。另外，research assistant 則是「研究助理」。
readmission	以前曾入學的學生「**再次申請入學**」。
reapply	**再次提出申請**。曾經提出申請，但是沒有通過，再次提出申請。
recess	**休假，休息** (= break)。例如 Christmas recess（聖誕假期）。
recommendation	**推薦信**。申請學校時必須附上的文件之一，主管、教授或具社會地位的人皆可為推薦人。
reference	**參考文獻**。也常用來表示申請者的保證人或推薦函。reference book 是「參考書」。
refund	**退還；退還金**。
register for	**登記** (= sign up for)。經常使用在登記選課上。
registration	**選課登記，課程登記**。在學期剛開始時，要登記自己要選修的課程，並繳納學分費用，現在則以線上登記為主流。
remedial course	對於程度不足的學生進行的「**補強課程**」，通常是某些學科的基礎課程。但這不能算入畢業學分。
required course	**必修課**。取得學位的必修課程。
research paper	**研究論文**。
residence hall	**大學宿舍**，也可稱作 dormitory, dorm。

residency requirement	**最低居住期間**。有些州立大學規定入學學生必須在當地居住超過一定時間，才能享有州立大學提供給該州居民的學費待遇。
resume	**履歷表，工作經歷表**。申請某些研究所時，必須附上履歷表。
retake	**補考，補修**。
rolling admission	**先到先審制**。在申請入學期限截止前，學校只要收到完整申請文件，就會進行審核並隨即通知學生申請的結果。
room and board rates	**住宿費和餐費**。
sabbatical leave	教授通常每七年就會有一年的「**給薪假**」。
SAT	Scholarship Assessment Test 的簡稱。美國的高中生升大學前所做的學能傾向測驗。
savings account	**儲蓄帳戶**。支票帳戶為 checking account。
scholarship	**獎學金**。
second-hand bookstore	**二手書店**。
security deposit	**保證金**。在簽訂宿舍或公寓等契約時所支付的金額，於契約終止時歸還。
semester	**學期**。一學期約有 17 週。
seminar	**研討班，研究班**。由教授指導的小型研討課程，人數不多，針對某領域或主題做獨立研究和課堂討論。
senior	四年制大學的四年級生，二年制大學的二年級生，高中的三年級生。
sign up for	**登記**。
skip	**缺席**，與 cut 同義。
social science	**社會科學**。
social security number	**社會保險號碼**。每個美國公民都有一個九位數的號碼，這是證明身分的一個重要機制。

sophomore	**四年制大學或高中的二年級生。**
sorority	**姊妹會**。大學女學生的社交組織，有些姊妹會的入會規定非常嚴格。
state university	**州立大學**。
statement of purpose	**讀書計畫**。申請學校的必備文件，包含了申請動機、申請計畫、未來目標等說明申請該學校的原因。
stipend	**助學金**。
student union	**學生活動中心** (student center)。
summer school/ summer session	暑假期間所開設的「**暑期課程**」。課程項目少，但是可以較快取得較多的學分。
syllabus	**教學計畫，課程大綱**。記載整學期的課程概要、進度，有時也會註明教科書、參考文獻、測驗日期、成績查詢方式等內容。
TA	**助教**，Teaching Assistant 的簡稱。成績優秀的研究生，於指導教授的指導之下，對大學生進行部分授課或全程授課。
take-home exam	將試題帶回家中，於期限之前完成並繳交的測驗方式。
tenure	**終身職位**。
term	**學期**。
term paper	**期末報告**。
theme	**論文主題，主題**。
thesaurus	**同義詞詞典**。
thesis	**畢業論文，學位論文**。於所有課程修習結束時，將研究成果加以整理並書寫而成的論文。
transcript	**成績單**。
transfer	**轉校，插班**。

trimester	**三學期制**。採用此學制的大學不多，通常一學期有15週，大多是在九月、一月、五月時開學。
tuition	**學費，課程費用**。也可以用 tuition (and) fees 這個說法涵蓋課程費用、登記費用、設施使用費用等。
tutor	**個別指導員**。有些學校會請成績優秀的學生或研究所學生，撥出時間對課業可能落後的學生進行個別指導。
undeclared major	**尚未決定主修**。大學入學時或一般通識課程期間，可以先不決定主修也沒關係。
undergraduate	**大學生，大學肄業生**。
unit	**課程學分** (= credit)。
upper-division course	**大學三、四年級生的進階課程**，課程代碼通常落在 300-400 之間。
used books	**二手書，二手教科書**。有時候可以在大學裡的書店買到二手教科書。
visa	**簽證**。入境他國所必備的證明文件，依據目的而有不同種類，學生簽證 (F-1) 也是其中一種。
vocational school	**職業學校**。可學習到美容、音樂、寶石鑑定等特定的專業知識或技能，並取得從事這類行業的資格。
waive	**放棄（權利），免除（規則）**。常用於指免除修課（例如在大學修過某門課程，研究所就可申請免修那門課）。
withdrawal	**中途退學**，或是在課程加退選期限之後，「**退選**」某課程。
work study	**工讀**。有些學校提供學生工讀機會，例如聯邦工讀計畫 (Federal Work-Study Program，簡稱 FWS)，申請者需要通過審核，工讀期間通常為一個學期。
workshop	**研究研討會**。通常由學校舉辦或教授發起，提供某個特定主題的研討或某種特定技能的訓練或進修。
yield	**入學率**，指申請入學與實際入學的比例。

Index

A

B

C

D

E

F

G

H

I

J

N

O

P

S

T

U

V

W

X-Z

附錄
Appendix

參考書目

印刷品 / CD-ROM

Microsoft, Encarta Premium 2008 Encyclopedia. Microsoft Corporation, 2008

Compton's Interactive Encyclopedia Deluxe. SoftKey Multimedia Inc., 2001

Encyclopedia Britannica. britannica.com 2001

M. J. Clugston, Dictionary of Science. Penguin Books 1998

Guide to American Literature from Emily Dickinson to the Present. Barnes & Noble Books, 1990

Siever, Raymond. Understanding Earth. W. H. Freeman and Company, 1998

Asimov, Isaac. Words from History II. Yumi Press, 1994

The Official Guide to the TOEFL iBT with CD-ROM, Third Edition. Educational Testing Service, 2009

小西友七編，Genius 英日大辭典，大修館書店，2001

新村出編，廣辭苑第 6 版，岩波書店，2008

崎川範行，英日科學用語辭典，講談社，1996

大石不二夫，理工英語小辭典，三共出版股份有限公司，1997

林功，TOEFL iBT 常考英文單字 1700，Beret 出版，2006

林功（日文版審定），托福官方考試指南 CD-ROM 版，美國教育測驗服務社 (ETS)，2009

網路

Susan Braun, eHow.com
http://www.ehow.com/list 5943872 parts-arch-roman-architecture.html

Infoplease.com
http://www.infoplease.com/ce6/ent/A0859011.html

Office of Naval Research, Science & Technology Focus
http://www.onr.navy.mil/focus/ocean/water/salinity1.htm

University of California Museum of Paleontology, UCMP
http://www.ucmp.berkeley.edu/exhibits/biomes/tundra.php

國家圖書館出版品預行編目 (CIP) 資料

TOEFL® iBT 托福分類字彙［增訂版］/ 林功作；林錦慧譯.
-- 初版 . -- 臺北市：眾文圖書，民 102.08　面；公分
ISBN 978-957-532-437-7（平裝附光碟片）1. 托福考試　2. 詞彙
805.1894　102012741

TT012

TOEFL® iBT 托福分類字彙［增訂版］

定價 550 元
2016 年 3 月　初版 6 刷

作者　林功
譯者　林錦慧
責任編輯　黃炯睿

主編　陳瑠琍
副主編　黃炯睿
資深編輯　黃琬婷・蔡易伶
美術設計　嚴國綸
行銷企劃　李皖萍・莊佳樺
發行人　黃建和
發行所　眾文圖書股份有限公司
台北市 10088 羅斯福路三段 100 號
12 樓之 2
網路書店　www.jwbooks.com.tw
電話　02-2311-8168
傳真　02-2311-9683
郵撥帳號　01048805

ISBN 978-957-532-437-7
Printed in Taiwan